PULSE

PULSE

MEDICAL KIDNAP FILES
7

P.D WORKMAN

ISBN: 9781774686409 (KDP Paperback)
ISBN: 9781774686416 (KDP Hardcover)
ISBN: 9781774686423 (Large Print)
ISBN: 9781774686430 (Lulu Paperback)
ISBN: 9781774686447 (ePub)
ISBN: 9781774686454 (Accessible Audio)

ALSO BY P.D WORKMAN

Medical Kidnap Files:

YA Suspense

Mito

EDS

Proxy

Toxo

Pain

Fail

Pulse

Between the Cracks:

Gritty Contemporary YA Family Saga

Ruby

June and Justin

Michelle

Chloe

Ronnie

June, Into the Light

Tamara's Teardrops:

Gritty Contemporary YA

Tattooed Teardrops

Two Teardrops

Tortured Teardrops

Vanishing Teardrops

AND MORE AT PDWORKMAN.COM

To all of those with broken hearts

———

CHAPTER ONE

J oseph's phone alarm went off, jolting him rudely out of sleep, as it did every morning. But this wasn't just any morning.

He sat bolt upright, feeling for his phone, trying to shut off the klaxon, his heart beating rapidly in his chest.

Not just rapidly. He wasn't sure what the word was for the racing train engine in his chest. He couldn't even discern each individual beat; it was going so fast that he thought he was going to have a heart attack.

After finally putting his hands on his phone, blindly jabbing at the screen and pushing the volume buttons, he finally got it silenced. He took deep gulps of air, trying to get the oxygen that his racing heart was demanding, knowing that if he waited for a minute or two, his heart rate would return to normal and he could relax and start his day as usual.

Well, not as usual, because there would be no lying around lazily in bed today. With his startled awakening and near heart attack, there was no way he would be drowsy enough to curl up and go back to sleep. And he couldn't even think about the five or six follow-up alarms going off. Normally, it took a few times before he was awake enough—or worried enough about being late for school or practice—

that he finally hauled his butt out of bed to get showered and dressed. And maybe eat something before racing out the door.

His heart kept pounding at its racing, frenetic pace, even as he squinted at his phone screen and thumbed through a few messages he had received during the night, thinking that if he just proceeded with his usual activities and distracted his brain, his heart would slow down again and he would be fine.

It kept beating uncomfortably fast, giving him a dull ache in his chest that was probably just from holding his muscles so tense.

Joseph took another deep breath and let it out slowly. He plugged in his phone so that it would charge while he was in the shower and shuffled to the bathroom to take care of business.

"Are you up?" Mira Demain called from the kitchen.

Since there was no one else in the house, it wasn't like she didn't know who was wandering around.

"Yeah, Mom," Joseph growled, irritated at having to speak first thing in the morning. He didn't like the way that she talked to him as soon as she heard him up, quickly going from asking him how his sleep was to peppering him with other questions about his plans for the day. He needed space and quiet when he woke up, time to get his brain functioning without having to speak or compose answers to questions.

And this morning, even more so, trying to calm his heart down and go about his routine, pretending everything was normal.

He stepped into the bathroom and shut the door very firmly to signal that he didn't want to be disturbed. He was in the bathroom, a private space, which should be protected by a cone of silence. He caught a glimpse of himself in the mirror, skin pale and clammy, and attempted to smooth down the blond hair sticking up all over his head without success.

He could hear Mira walking down the hall from the kitchen.

"How did you sleep?" she shouted through the door.

Joseph growled, not answering.

"Did you have a good sleep?" Mira persisted.

"I can't talk right now," Joseph told her. "Leave me alone."

"Are you okay? You sound funny."

"Mo-om!" Joseph complained, drawing the word out into two syllables in protest.

Mira sighed loudly at his refusal to hold an early-morning conversation through the bathroom door. "Fine. Come and talk to me when you're out."

Joseph grunted at her.

He sat on the toilet for a while, both too tired to move and rooted to the spot by the pain in his chest and the insistent racing of his heart.

But it gradually slowed down, returning to his cardio target zone, and finally to a more normal resting rate. Joseph thought it might still be a little fast but, at least, nothing like it had been. He continued to take deep breaths, trying to calm his body and convince his brain that there was nothing to panic about.

Eventually, he shed the shorts and muscle shirt he wore for bed and climbed into the shower.

———

"Are you okay?" Mira asked as soon as he showed his face, even though he hadn't yet sought her out. "Feeling all right this morning?"

"Yeah, Mom, I'm fine," he growled, trying to pass her in the hallway to get to his room to finish dressing and getting ready for the day.

"You aren't usually up this early. And you look… pale or sick. Are you sure you're okay?"

"I just woke up earlier than I wanted to." He rubbed his eyes. "I thought you would be happy about that. You're always telling me that I need to get up earlier so that I don't have to rush getting ready for school."

Mira pushed a hank of dirty blond hair behind her ear. "I am happy about it," she told him immediately. "I was just worried that you might not be feeling well. You're not usually up so early, and you look… drawn. I don't know. It's just the morning light," she laughed, but it sounded forced. "I never see you by this light anymore. You're

3

like a vampire. Up all night and then sleeping when the day actually starts. Until the last minute before school."

She didn't look that great herself. She was working too much and her face was tired and lined.

"I know. But this morning, I'm up, so don't get on my case about it."

"I'm not." She patted his arm soothingly. "What do you want for breakfast? Do you want me to get you something?"

"No. I'll get my own breakfast. After I get dressed."

He didn't feel much like eating. He was a bit nauseated. Probably just from getting up too early. He knew he was supposed to eat something before school, but he didn't feel much like it most mornings. His stomach wasn't really awake until halfway through the day. But he had to eat before taking his meds, which meant he had to force himself to have something. Maybe just a Pop-Tart or something. Not something that his mother would approve of as an appropriate breakfast for a growing boy.

Luckily, he usually didn't have breakfast until after she had left for work.

And who was it that bought the Pop-Tarts anyway?

CHAPTER TWO

By the time he got to school, Joseph was feeling back to normal. He still had some tightness in his chest, which he thought was just from holding himself tense. He was distracted monitoring his heart rate, but other than that, everything was fine.

He'd had breakfast and his meds, which should prevent him from having any more panic attacks. Dr. Shapiro would tell him that he needed to practice anxiety-calming techniques, stress reduction, and all of that emotional resilience stuff—which sounded good when he lectured Joseph but, later, when Joseph needed real help, he found they were just empty words.

Soccer was the way to burn off his anxiety. The meds helped, of course, but the only thing he could do to send the anxiety packing when he was having a hard day was to run like crazy, preferably in a soccer game where it was constructive and would benefit the team. Soccer was his life preserver. That one thing he could grab on to when everything else failed.

"Hey, Demain!" greeted an awkward-looking, too-tall girl with a blond ponytail, as he slammed his locker door and twisted the dial on the lock. "How goes it?"

"Hey, Lora."

"How was your weekend?"

"Okay, I guess. Not like I did anything. How was yours?"

She shrugged. "Nothing big. But hey, here we are, together again!" She made an all-embracing gesture.

"At school," Joseph intoned.

"I know. But it could be worse."

He opened his mouth to answer.

"It could be prison," Lora pointed out.

Joseph laughed. "It kind of is."

"Yeah, well…" She shrugged again. "Were you at Mom's or Dad's?"

Joseph resisted answering questions about his family situation, looking for a way to change the subject. "Are you coming to the game this week?"

"Uh-huh. As long as I don't have to babysit. I'm not supposed to, but… you know that can change at the last minute."

Joseph nodded. "Yeah, sure. I just meant were you planning to."

"Yeah, sure. Of course. I'm the team trainer, aren't I?"

"Well… not exactly. You took some courses and kind of… bullied coach into letting you hang out on the sidelines."

"I'm the team trainer," she said firmly. "That's why I'm there."

Joseph shrugged and let it go. Lora would go where she wanted to go and be what she wanted to be. She was that kind of a girl. When she set her mind to something, there was no talking her out of it with logic or reasoning. It didn't matter what obstacles were in her way or what the various personalities involved had to say about it; she was going to get her way. Joseph wasn't quite sure how she did it, other than just by being hardheaded. She seemed to always find a way.

―――――

At the end of the school day, Joseph was feeling tired and worn out. He assumed it was because he hadn't gotten as much sleep as usual, and the panic attack had drained a significant amount of his energy. He stopped at the convenience store across the street from the school to grab an energy bar before practice. Beside the till, they had one-shot caffeine energy drinks that promised five hours of energy. Joseph usually avoided those, trying to stick to more nutritious foods to keep in shape, but decided that today would be an exception. He could have caffeine now and then. And on a day he was short on sleep, feeling out of sorts, and needed to get through a couple of hours of practice, he figured that he deserved it. It wasn't like he was taking steroids.

He paid for his snack and slammed the fruity energy drink, throwing the can in the garbage in front of the convenience store rather than carrying it back to the school and letting anyone there see him with it.

Joseph rushed back to the school, determined to make it to practice on time. Most of the other players were ahead of him, some already out on the field. As he changed, he bantered with his remaining teammates, using their energy and enthusiasm to fuel his own. He mentally prepared himself for the intense practice ahead. Maintaining focus and giving his all was crucial, and the coach would notice immediately if he were off his game.

"See you out there," Marcus told Joseph as he left.

"Yeah, see you in a minute."

As Joseph shut his locker door, he was hit with a sudden wave of dizziness.

"Whoa…" He leaned on the door, waiting for the head rush to pass so that he could go on.

"You okay, Demain?" William asked.

"Uh… yeah, in a minute…" The dizziness didn't immediately pass as he expected it to. He started to sweat. Did he have a fever? Maybe he was sick? That might explain the early-morning racing heart, how he had dragged around all day, and the dizziness. He was coming down with something—the flu.

He tried to push back the other feeling that was threatening to overwhelm him. A sense of doom and dread. Something terrible was about to happen. He didn't know what it was, but it was serious. He felt like someone was going to die. One of his parents? Was it a premonition of something that was really going to happen?

7

The sweat was coming on stronger now. Gathering at his temples and also running down his back in a cold stream.

"Demain?" William approached him. "You're not looking so good, man. You're as white as a sheet."

William grabbed Joseph by the shoulders, maneuvering him to one of the benches. "Sit down. Are you feeling faint? Nauseous?"

Joseph laced his hands behind his neck and leaned forward. "Just... dizzy for a minute. Maybe a fever, I don't know."

William touched his forehead with the back of his hand. "Maybe. It's probably the flu. Something is going around. You want me to tell Coach?"

"I'll be okay," Joseph said, pressing a knuckle to his head. "If I just wait for a minute, I think it will pass."

"I don't think so," William disagreed. "I'm going to go get Coach."

There wasn't any point in arguing; William was going to whether Joseph liked it or not. Joseph sat there on the bench with his head bowed. He put his elbows on his knees and cradled his head in his hands, waiting for the dizziness to pass.

Even though he said that he was sure it would pass, he didn't think it would. He had a foreboding this was the beginning of something new in his life, something that was going to doom him and keep him from soccer forever. It felt like the ceiling was pressing down on him. Like the sky was pressing down on the building outside and everything was being compressed. How did the story about the little chicken go? The sky is falling?

CHAPTER THREE

Demain?" Joseph startled at the voice. He hadn't heard anyone coming, and the locker room had been cavernously silent. He jerked up and looked at Lora, heart pounding.

"What are you doing here?" he growled, "You're not allowed to be in the boys' locker room."

"I'm the trainer," she told him archly. "I can go wherever I want."

He rubbed his face. "I don't need a trainer."

"You need a doctor? What's going on?"

"It's just... just the flu or something. I was fine, and it just hit me all of a sudden. I thought it would go away if I just sat down for a few minutes, but it's not working. It's not going away."

"What? Sick stomach?"

"Dizzy, sweaty, everything is just... wrong. I don't know. I feel terrible."

Lora shook her head. She laid her hand on his forehead for a moment, clicking her tongue. "Well, you can't play if you're sick. I'll tell the coach you can't make it today."

"He can't make it?" Coach Beiderman's voice boomed in the locker room as he approached, coming from down the dim, smelly corridor to the field. "What's going on?"

Joseph tried to straighten up. To get to his feet to show the coach

9

he could play. He wasn't being a wuss. He swayed on his feet and Lora grabbed him, holding him steady.

"He can hardly even stand," she told Beiderman in a cross tone. "He can't practice today. He'll pass out."

She pushed Joseph back down to the bench. Joseph swallowed bile that rose in his throat and tried to breathe through his mouth and not smell the stale, sweaty smell of the locker room.

"We've got a game Thursday," Beiderman said. "You'd better not do this for the game! You'd better be out there to support your team when Thursday comes around. Game day. You can't be sick on game day."

"I'm sure… I'm sure I'll be just fine by Thursday," Joseph assured him, sounding more confident than he felt. "It's probably just a twenty-four-hour bug, right? So this time tomorrow, I'll be feeling better and, when Thursday comes around, I'll be one hundred percent. Right back out there."

"You can't rush recovery," Lora said darkly, scowling.

"I'll be fine," Joseph said again. "There's a bug going around, right? It will be gone by Thursday. I'll be able to play."

"If you can't play…" Beiderman dangled the possibility in front of him, "I'm going to have to reconsider whether you're going to stay on the team."

"You can't kick Joseph off the team because he caught the flu," Lora argued. "He can't help that!"

"He's already missed time because he's been 'sick.' I'm not going to let him slack off while those who work harder and show up for every practice sit on the bench. It's not fair to the rest of the team."

"It's not fair to Joseph if you cut him because he got sick."

"Look, Miss Forrester, this isn't any of your business," Beiderman tried.

Despite feeling so sick, he couldn't help but smile at Lora's persistence. He knew that if it came down to an argument between Lora and Beiderman, it wouldn't be the big, overweight coach who won.

"I'm the trainer," Lora told him. "And I say he is too sick. You put him out there, and you'll get in trouble. His parents will sue and take it to the media, the school board, and the athletic association. You'll end up getting sanctions, maybe even fired. Is it worth your career to cut him from the team because he's missed a few practices due to illness?"

"He didn't miss those other days because he had the flu," Beiderman growled.

"No," Lora said. "He was in the hospital." She stared him down fiercely. "How do you think that will play in the media?"

"It wasn't like he had a broken leg," Beiderman grumbled.

"No," Lora agreed. "And you're comfortable with them finding out you cut him for mental health issues? How's that gonna play?"

He stared at her, but she didn't flinch. Despite the fact that the coach was three times her size and was the highest authority over what happened on the soccer team, he was the one who backed down.

"He'd better be on the field on Thursday," he snapped, and left the locker room to return to his team.

Joseph shook his head. "Don't make trouble for me, Lora. I can look after myself."

"You're sick. And he's not going to cut you because you've missed practices due to your health. I'll see to that."

Joseph just shook his head.

"And you're too sick to be defending yourself right now. I can't believe it—did it just come on all of a sudden?"

"Yeah. Just… I was okay, and I changed, and I was just locking up when it hit me."

"It's like that sometimes with the flu," Lora said authoritatively. "Now, how are you going to get home?"

"I'll walk."

"No, you won't. What time does your mom get off work?"

"Like… four. Five, sometimes…"

And sometimes later. Sometimes quite late.

It wasn't her fault she had to work so hard. Joseph's dad was not sending the child support checks he was supposed to, and someone had to pay the bills. Mira didn't want to move to a smaller, more affordable house or apartment. Joseph didn't want to have to switch schools. He didn't want to start fresh somewhere else, with no friends, no soccer team, no cred. Starting up all over again like a freshman. He had worked hard to get where he was. Really, really hard. He wasn't giving it up.

"You need to call your mom," Lora said. "Tell her you are sick and need to be picked up."

"I can't make her leave work early."

"What, then? Are you going to take a cab or ride share? You got a friend or an auntie who can drive you home?"

His friends with cars were all on the soccer team. They would all be busy until the end of practice. And a family friend or relative that he could call upon? Joseph tried to figure out how to get a ride home without disrupting anyone else's life, but couldn't find a way.

"Give me your phone," Lora ordered.

Joseph looked at her blankly.

"Your phone," Lora repeated.

He handed it to her. His brain was too muddled to figure out why she wanted it. To give him her digits? He already knew her number.

"Call Mom," Lora commanded the phone.

It was too late to stop her. The phone call started to ring through. Joseph rubbed his face, worrying about having to call her. He didn't want to get her in trouble for leaving early. But he didn't know what else to do and, even if he did, it was too late now because the phone was ringing and, even if he hung up the phone before she answered, she would still see that he had called and she would call back.

"Joey?" Mira answered, her voice tentative on the speaker. "I thought you had practice today. Did you forget something?"

Lora held the phone in front of Joseph's face. "Uh, no. I'm not feeling very well," he confessed.

"You still need to get to practice. You don't want to give the coach any reason to cut you from the team."

"He got to practice, Mrs. Demain," Lora told her, "But he's too sick to play. He really needs to go home and go to bed."

"Lora?"

"Yeah."

"Lora, he can't miss practice. He's had enough 'last warnings.'

Coach Beiderman isn't going to let him miss without any consequences."

"I already told Coach you would sue him and go to the school board if he cut Joseph for being sick."

Mira laughed softly. "Lora, you can't do that. You don't have any authority over the team or the coach, and you can't speak for the members of the team or their parents. I know you would like to be in charge, but…"

"He isn't going to cut Joseph for missing today. And if it's just a twenty-four-hour bug, he'll be fine for the game on Thursday."

"I hope so. I'd hate to see him get kicked off of the team." Mira switched to talking to Joseph again. "I'd hate to have you kicked off the team, sweetie. You need to be careful. I understand that you're not feeling very well, but sometimes we have to push through despite our illnesses or injuries."

"He really is sick, Mrs. Demain," Lora inserted.

Mira sighed. "Did he throw up?"

Lora looked at Joseph with her eyebrows up. He shook his head.

"No. But he's really dizzy. He can hardly stand. And he's sweating like a pig. He's not just milking it; he can't play like this. I don't even think he could get out on the field on his own."

"I could," Joseph objected mulishly.

"You couldn't," Lora maintained. "Can you come and pick him up to take him home? Or is there someone else you can call to pick him up? He can't walk home."

"He can't walk?" Mira repeated.

"No."

"Okay." Another deep sigh. Joseph could picture Mira, fingertips pressing into her temples, trying to work out what to do. "It will take me a few minutes to let everyone know what's going on and get out of here. And then time to drive over there. It will be at least half an hour before I'm there."

"Sounds good," Lora said briskly. "I'll make sure he's out at the front waiting for you."

CHAPTER FOUR

By the time Mira got there to pick him up, Joseph was feeling a lot better. Out in the cool air, the sweats and the dizziness gradually dissipated and he felt more grounded. Less panicky.

But it wasn't good that he was feeling better.

If he had a virus, he should still feel bad for the next day or so. He wouldn't be feeling better within half an hour. Viruses didn't work that way. He sat on the cement wall with his head in his hands, trying to figure out how he would explain it to his mother when she got there.

He was anxious. Not as bad as the crushing feeling of doom he'd had when he got out of bed in the morning, but he felt guilty and worried and didn't know how to get rid of it.

He was the only one sitting out there. Everyone else had gone home, or to the mall, or had stayed after for soccer practice or other after-school activities supervised by the school. He could hear voices in the distance, but they only served to emphasize his feeling of being alone and conspicuous. Lora had gone back into the school to help the team. Joseph didn't want her hanging over him while he waited for his mother, feeling like a little kid in the nurse's room in elementary school. He was nearly an adult. Not someone who had to be supervised just because he had to wait for a few minutes.

He saw Mira's car coming and got up, swinging his backpack over one shoulder. He was down to the curb by the time she pulled in. She unlocked the door for him, and looked at him as he slid into the passenger seat.

"I'm doing a bit better now," Joseph growled before she could get after him about how he didn't look sick. "If you don't believe that I was really sick, you can ask Lora or the coach. I just… got to feeling better once I was out in the fresh air for a while."

"Well," Mira spoke in measured tones, "I'm glad you're feeling better than you did; that's good news. Do you want to tell me what happened?"

"I don't know. I guess it was just the same as this morning."

She looked puzzled, frowning at this.

"You thought that I looked bad this morning. I wasn't feeling great, but I figured I was well enough to go to school. It had… come and gone. I guess it's one of those things that comes in waves. It's bad for a little while, and then it's gone again."

"I don't know what to think of this. If you were bad enough that the coach and Lora could both see it, then you shouldn't be feeling better again that quickly."

"But I *was!*" Joseph insisted. "I really was sick."

"Why? What from? If it just keeps showing up randomly, then it isn't a virus. It isn't something going around the school."

"You think that I'm just making it up? That I don't want to go to practice? That I want to miss out and get cut from the team? If I didn't want to be on the team anymore, then I would just quit. Nothing would happen. No one would care. Plenty of other people would be happy to take my place on the team."

"I wouldn't be happy. I don't think Coach Beiderman would be happy."

"But if I didn't want to play anymore, you would let me quit. I'm not saying I want out of soccer," Joseph could see the argument winding up in her eyes before she even said anything. "I'm saying I *don't* want out of soccer. I'm saying this isn't anything to do with soccer."

"You might just be tired and bored of practice. That wouldn't mean you were giving up on soccer, just that you wanted to get away with skipping out of it a bit."

"I was there in the locker room. I was ready to go out on the field. Why would I suddenly decide that I wanted out of it?"

"I don't know." Mira stared straight ahead at the road, not coming up with any other suggestions. But Joseph was afraid that she still had a number of other arguments marshaled in her brain that she was keeping from him because she knew he would lose his crap if she told him all of them.

He felt like such a little kid when she did that. He wasn't a kid. He was a man who knew his mind, and he didn't need to trick anyone to get into or out of soccer. Or whatever other motives she thought that he had. It was crazy. He didn't want to quit, and he didn't want Coach Beiderman thinking that he was a head case, and he didn't want his mother thinking that he was slacking off because he was bored of soccer after all of these years. And Lora... he didn't know what she thought. She was pretty down-to-earth and usually believed what he said, but did she really believe him in her heart of hearts? Or did she still question what had happened in the locker room?

"I want you to lie down when you get home," Mira instructed. "In your bed, not in front of the TV. I want you to get a good rest. You might be feeling better right now but, if you are fighting something, you need to get enough sleep to fight it off. And bed is the best place to be when you are sick."

"Okay, Mom."

"And that doesn't mean you're in bed watching TV on your tablet or phone, either. It means that you close your eyes and sleep."

"I'll try, but I'm not tired right now."

He wasn't about to tell her that he knew he wouldn't be able to sleep because he had taken that caffeine shot earlier in the afternoon. She would freak out. She thought those things were poison. Even caffeinated sodas were enough to get her going, and that stuff barely touched Joseph.

But he could still watch his phone covertly, putting it away when he heard her coming down the hall to check on him. He would go bonkers if all he could do was lie in bed with all that caffeine still coursing through his veins.

They reached the house, and Mira parked her car in front of it as usual. "Do you need anything to eat? Are you hungry?"

"No. My stomach is a bit off."

"Lora said that you didn't throw up."

"I didn't. But my stomach is a bit... rocky."

Mira nodded. "You definitely need to be in bed," she reiterated.

As far as she was concerned, anything that made a teenager say "no" to food had to be pretty serious.

CHAPTER FIVE

Joseph was woken up the next morning, not by his phone, but by Mira. She was gentle and quiet, poking and prodding him a few times until he woke up, groaning and turning over. Not pleased about being woken up before his alarms, but it was nicer to wake up that way than to the insistent clamor of his alarms.

"What is it, Mom?" he groaned. "I don't have to be up yet. You know I can get myself to school on time."

"Yes, I know. We agreed that if you could get yourself to school on time, you could decide what time you get up. And you've been doing really good with that."

He'd only attracted a couple of tardies, and those had been on days when the weather was nasty and everyone else had been late too, the bus kids and the ones who got dropped off, as well as the ones who walked in like Joseph.

Joseph nodded, closing his eyes and snuggling into his pillow. There wasn't any reason for him to have to get up yet.

"You have an appointment with Dr. Shapiro today," Mira told him. "I wanted him to check you out, just to make sure you're not having a reaction to one of your meds."

"Dr Shapiro? But—" Joseph stopped himself from protesting that he wasn't sick. He *had* been sick. And he wanted her to believe he had been sick and wasn't just pretending.

"I know. It's a school day and you don't want to have to miss. But better today than on Thursday, right? We don't want to leave it to the last minute when it could interfere with your game. The sooner we can get this dealt with, the better."

"You really think it's my meds? They weren't making me sick before."

"But you remember Dr. Shapiro said that they have to build up in your bloodstream over time and that some of them take a few weeks or months to reach their full efficacy…"

He could see where she was going with it. If it took time for them to build up in his bloodstream, then he could definitely be feeling different effects after six or eight weeks than after one or two. Most of the early side effects had lessened after he'd been on them for a while or he had grown accustomed to them.

It was better to have a few minor side effects than all of the crap that he'd been dealing with before his stay in the hospital psych ward. He didn't want a repeat of that experience.

"What time?" he grumbled. "I don't want to miss too much school."

"That's why I am waking you up."

Joseph tried to pull the covers over his head, groaning loudly. Mira kept him from covering his face.

"Come on, Joseph. I made it as early as I could so that you wouldn't have to miss more than your first-period class."

"I have to get up now?"

"Yes. You're lucky that the doctor's office opens up nice and early. A lot of them don't open until nine or ten. This way, you can get to school and I can get to the office without missing too much time."

"Now?" he complained again.

But he was starting to laugh. She hated it when he whined and she didn't like his sleeping in until the last possible minute. Mira was an early bird and couldn't understand why anyone would want to sleep after the sun had come up.

She whipped the covers back from him, as he knew she would.

"Do I need to go get the ice cubes?" she threatened.

"I'm up, I'm up," Joseph protested.

"You're not up…"

"I am!" Joseph closed his eyes again.

She jabbed him in the ribs, making him jump and pull away quickly.

"I'm up, I'm up!"

He jumped out of bed and dashed past her for the bathroom. Once inside, he slammed the door and locked it, and turned on the shower before anything else to drown out any noise or requests that she made.

He could stand in the shower for ten minutes under the hot water, which was almost as good as another ten minutes of sleep. He would run the hot water until it ran cold and the walls dripped with condensation. If he didn't turn on the exhaust fan, the steam would set the smoke alarm off. He didn't need *that* alarm shrieking either, so he turned the fan on.

CHAPTER SIX

Joseph didn't really like Dr. Shapiro. The man always seemed busy with something else and never engaged in conversation with Joseph during his appointments. He would breeze in, sounding out of breath and looking over the notes the nurse had left him for about two seconds before asking Mira to explain to him again what Joseph was doing there. He would discuss Joseph's meds and symptoms with Mira without even looking at Joseph.

The two of them would go through things, and it sometimes felt like there wasn't any reason for Joseph to be there other than to provide blood if they wanted to do any tests.

Then Dr. Shapiro would scribble something out on his prescription pad and give them rapid instructions about where to go or what test to have done, how to take the medication, and to contact him if there were any problems.

Of course, if there were any problems, Joseph couldn't just call the guy to ask him what to do or whether to be concerned about something. He would have to get Mira to make an appointment, then go in and pass all of his comments through Mira for Shapiro to listen to them.

He was almost an adult. There was no reason the doctor couldn't talk to him directly. Joseph sometimes considered going to appointments on his own without his mother, or asking her to wait in the waiting room while he talked to Shapiro himself, but he didn't for two reasons.

One was that he was afraid Mira would go off the deep end, thinking he had deep, dark secrets to tell the doctor that he didn't want to reveal to her. Suicidal feelings, sex stuff, or a drug addiction. He knew how she worried and how she would react if he said he didn't want her in the room when he talked to the doctor.

The other reason was that he suspected that even if he were the only one in the room with Dr. Shapiro, the man still wouldn't pay any attention to what Joseph had to say. He would just nod and write out an illegible prescription on his pad and send Joseph away, not having heard anything he had said or enlightening him about what the problem was, if there were a problem.

Joseph sat on the examination table in the tiny waiting room, looking around at the posters and models crowded together on the walls and counter space. Mira was reading something on her phone, not talking to Joseph. She knew that he would get anxious if she peppered him with questions and comments while they waited in the small room. He felt vulnerable there. Even if he was fully clothed, he still felt naked. Small and alone, even though he was there with Mira. He felt like he was under a microscope. Like someone might be watching him from outside the room, on a CCTV video feed he was unaware of.

The door opened with a bang and a whoosh of air, and Dr. Shapiro blew in. He looked at Joseph on the examination table and then back at his notes.

"So, Mr. Demain, you're feeling under the weather, are you?" He looked at Mira. "What's going on with him, Mom?"

"He had to miss practice yesterday because he suddenly felt sick. It just came on really suddenly, and he couldn't play, and by the time I got there, he was feeling better and looked just fine."

"Sometimes it comes in waves," Joseph interposed. "When you are sick, it can come and go."

"It can be intermittent," Mira agreed, speaking to Dr. Shapiro. "I understand some symptoms can come in waves, and you feel relatively good in between."

"Like after you throw up," Joseph pointed out. "And then you feel pretty good afterward."

"But you didn't throw up, right?" Mira asked.

"No. I'm just saying it can be like that."

"What were the symptoms?" Dr. Shapiro asked.

"Mostly dizziness," Mira said. She looked at Joseph. "Right, Joseph, it was mostly dizziness?"

"Yeah. And sweating. I just… didn't feel good all over. I didn't know what was wrong, but I knew everything wasn't okay."

"Any fever?" Shapiro asked.

Mira looked at Joseph. "No."

Joseph shrugged. Lora had said he was warm, but he didn't think he'd actually had a fever. He hadn't had that weak, fever-and-chills feeling that went with a fever. He had been in a cold sweat, but it wasn't exactly like when he had the flu.

"What kind of dizziness?" Shapiro demanded.

They both looked at him. Joseph shook his head. "What?"

"Was the room spinning? Did you just feel unsteady? A head rush from getting up too fast? There are a lot of different sensations that people refer to as 'dizzy.'"

"Oh. Well… more like a head rush, I guess. Only it didn't go away right away."

"But it went away within half an hour."

"Yeah."

"And did it come back? In waves?"

"No, I was pretty good the rest of the night." He looked at Mira. "I stayed in bed. Got lots of rest."

"Headache? Nausea?"

Joseph considered. "Not really. I mean, sort of when I was dizzy, but not later. I was fine when I was in bed."

"Did he eat?" Shapiro went back to talking to Mira.

"Yes, he had supper. It didn't seem to bother his stomach at all."

"Is he a good eater?"

"A good eater?" Mira repeated.

"Does he eat a lot? Does he skip meals? Is he picky? Dieting? Lifting weights?"

"No. Nothing like that. He doesn't always have breakfast; sometimes I get after him for that, but he has a good appetite."

"Any recent weight loss?" Shapiro looked at Joseph speculatively.

"No, not that I'm aware of. He's a growing boy. Sometimes, they get kind of... stretched out. But I don't think he's lost any weight." She looked at him. "Have you? Joseph?"

"No. I'm not dieting or anorexic or anything like that."

"He eats normally?" Shapiro persisted in asking Mira again. "He has a good appetite? Doesn't throw up? Disappear into the bathroom after meals?"

"No."

Shapiro scratched out notes on the paper chart. Why wasn't he using electronic charts by now? He wasn't an old, old guy who refused to adjust to new technology. It would be fairly easy for him to learn to use a tablet or to have a desktop computer in each examining room like the dentist did. Then, everything could be shared across the system, and no one would have to transcribe his notes onto the computer, possibly misinterpreting what he had written.

"This is the first time he's had these symptoms?"

"Yes. As far as I know." Mira looked at Joseph. "You haven't ever had this before?"

"Not... exactly."

They both looked at him, waiting for further explanation.

"I'm sure it wasn't anything," Joseph said. "I just got a bit of the flu or something, but I took care of it right away, so it didn't develop into anything.:"

"You said it came in waves," Shapiro said, showing that he had heard what Joseph had said earlier when talking to Mira, even if he hadn't appeared to have been listening. "That would imply that it happened more than once. Several times, in fact."

"Had you had it before?" Mira demanded. "You were pale in the morning. I thought that maybe you were sick then. You were up early and had to use the bathroom right away."

Joseph cleared his throat uncomfortably. He didn't really want to discuss what had been happening recently. He didn't want to be accused of making things up or looking for attention. Or of trying to get out of playing soccer.

"What happened yesterday morning?" Dr. Shapiro questioned, pen hovering over the clipboard.

"I had… I didn't feel good when I woke up in the morning," Joseph admitted carefully, feeling his way through the topic.

"Nauseated? Dizzy, like later in the day?"

"A little. But I had… I think it was a panic attack."

"What makes you think that?"

"My heart was going really fast. I felt like I was going to have a heart attack or something." Mira looked alarmed at this revelation. "It only lasted for a few minutes," Joseph added hurriedly. "I just had a shower and relaxed, and it was okay, but… I think that's what it was. An anxiety attack."

"Sounds like it. Was that the first one you've had?"

"Well… maybe a couple of others, but not this bad. This one was really bad. It was scary."

"Why didn't you tell me?" Mira demanded. "I asked you what was wrong, and you kept telling me there was nothing."

"I didn't want you to worry," Joseph said lamely. "You always think things are serious, when it's just something little. I didn't want to make a big thing about it. If it was just an anxiety attack… I mean… you already knew that I have anxiety."

"You need to tell me things like this. It could be serious. Couldn't it, doctor?"

"I'm not too alarmed at this point," Shapiro said, making notes on his clipboard. "Joseph is probably correct that it was just an anxiety attack. Not something that we need to panic over. I'll increase the dosage of the anti-anxiety prescription he is on. That will help. Keep track of how often these panic attacks are occurring, and we should see a downward trend."

He pulled out his prescription pad and wrote it down.

"The best way to deal with anxiety is by exposure," he told Joseph.

"You need to face the things that worry you and make you upset. Avoiding them will just set up a positive feedback loop, where you're having more and more anxiety as you try to avoid it."

Joseph nodded, which he knew was the response they expected. But he wasn't sure what he was supposed to be avoiding. It wasn't a particular thought or fear that had given him the panic attack.

"Is it soccer?" Mira asked. "Are you worrying about the game on Thursday? Or you don't want to go to the practices? Are you afraid of getting hurt?"

"Uh… no. Soccer is great. I don't have any worries about it."

"What about your future? Getting into a professional league? Getting scouted out?"

Joseph shifted uncomfortably, making the paper on the examining table crinkle loudly. "Well, if you talk about it that way, I start to get anxious about it, yeah. I mean… my whole life could hinge on how I do this year in soccer, and the coach is threatening to kick me off the team. Why would *that* make me anxious?"

Mira nodded, as if this were the answer to why Joseph was getting anxiety attacks.

"But skipping out on practices would get me kicked off the team," Joseph pointed out. "So having an anxiety attack makes my situation worse, not better. I have to get to all my practices and do what I'm supposed to. I have to show up every time and play my best soccer, even for practices. Having an anxiety attack just makes that worse."

"You don't choose whether to have an anxiety attack or not, though," Mira stated the obvious. "You don't decide whether to have one before practice or a game. They just happen. It is out of your control."

"You can do relaxation exercises," Dr. Shapiro said. "I have some handouts. You can pick them up at the reception desk when you leave. I think that between those and the meds bumped up a bit, you will be just fine."

"Really?" Joseph didn't want to believe it if it weren't true. He didn't want to get his hopes up just to have them knocked down

again. Some people had anxiety attacks for years. They locked themselves in their homes and never came out. He didn't want to end up
like that.

"This will help," Shapiro assured him.

CHAPTER SEVEN

T hey had been sitting for a long time, and Gabriel's muscles were cramping. They were sitting in the mall, where it was warm, but it was spring, and the nights and early mornings were cool, and even when he was warm his joints hurt.

Even if they hadn't spotted any followers, that didn't mean they were safe. Occasionally, their watchers and listeners in the network would report back about people looking for Gabriel and Renata. Judges. Social workers. Doctors, sometimes. People who were unhappy about children in foster care being reunited with the parents they had been taken from, finding their way out of the state or even out of the country to get beyond the reach of DCFS. The fugitive families kept their heads down, working for cash under assumed names, homeschooling their kids, watching out for anyone who might give them a second look. Fearing that moment when someone gave them a look for an instant too long and they knew they had been recognized.

What Gabriel and Renata did was on the edge of the law. They could be arrested and languish in jail awaiting trial to prove that they hadn't actually crossed the line. If all they did was to help teenagers who were old enough to know their minds to find a way away from their foster families and back to their families of origin, they were technically skirting the laws against kidnapping or abetting a runaway.

There was the problem of being homeless, which meant they did end up on the wrong side of laws against begging, vagrancy, and loitering, the typical anti-homeless laws. It meant that Gabriel sometimes ate out of trash bins, but he didn't leave garbage scattered all over the place as others did. He was always careful to leave an area at least as tidy as he had found it and to be clean and tidy himself.

Renata could not eat anything but the special anti-allergen formula she carried with her, and even that she could not take by mouth, but had to pump directly into her stomach. Any other food or method would result in vomiting and possible anaphylaxis. Gabriel could only imagine what it would be like to put his life in danger every time he ate.

"Someone is coming," Renata warned.

Gabriel focused on the scene before him, setting aside thoughts of the law and Renata's health. They had a job to do; he needed to be focused on it. Too many things could go wrong if they didn't.

David Sealy, who was sitting between them, perked up and looked around. His eyes scanned the crowds, but he couldn't spot the person Renata had seen. Gabriel refrained from pointing, as it would attract the attention of nearby shoppers.

"Over there," he nodded very slightly, directing David with his eyes to the woman approaching from their right.

"That's my mom!" David's voice went up excitedly. He moved to get up, and Gabriel and Renata both reached for him at the same time, putting a hand on him to prevent him.

"Stay put," Renata warned him, her voice laced with irritation. They'd given him detailed instructions several times, but nothing they said seemed to sink in. He was too impulsive, too hyperactive. Sitting there with them in the mall, waiting for his mom, had been torture.

"We need to make sure no one is with her or has followed her," Gabriel reminded him. "You can't just go running across the mall to her. If she has Child Services or the cops following her, then you could run straight into a trap. It won't be as easy to get you out a second time."

It hadn't been easy to get him out *this* time. Foster homes were much easier to handle than institutional settings. The Children's Home where David had been staying had pretty good security, and it had taken several long weeks of watching, waiting, and planning before they had a way to get him on his own and away from the building where he'd been "homed" for the previous six months.

If DCFS got their hands on him again, they would put him into a higher security institution. Somewhere, Gabriel and Renata probably would not be able to get him out of again.

David stayed where he was, much to Gabriel's relief. He didn't fight them off or jump up and run to his mother.

They continued to watch her from a distance while she pretended to window shop. They watched for anyone following her or paying too much attention to her. While Child Services could have someone following her, they were not usually trained in covert ops and could be spotted fairly easily. Police, on the other hand, were another story, and they might be hard to spot or work in a team, so that no one person was visible all the time.

Gabriel and Renata had the advantage of having scoped out the mall several times in the last few weeks, which meant that they knew the regulars. They knew the security guards, the caretakers, the bottle pickers, the moms who pushed baby carriages through the mall regularly as part of their exercise routines. All of those people that the cops liked to dress up as because they were anonymous and omnipresent. No one even saw them. That was why Gabriel and Renata had been so diligent about memorizing their faces ahead of time.

"Come on," David whined. "She's going to think that I'm not here and go back home. She won't know why I have to wait so long."

"We've talked to her. She knows the plan," Gabriel assured him. "Just a couple more minutes. Just to be sure."

David sighed and banged his forehead with his fist in frustration, forcing himself to wait. Renata put her hand on his wrist to stop him.

"That attracts attention," she warned. "I'm sorry. I know it's frustrating."

He grabbed a lock of hair and twisted it around his finger, winding it, pulling on it hard, and releasing it, then winding it around again. That was less visible, less likely to attract the attention of other shoppers. Plenty of people fiddled with their hair.

Renata looked at the time on her phone, then finally gave Gabriel a nod. "Okay."

David jumped to his feet. Gabriel stood up much more slowly, grabbing David's arm to stop him from dashing right over to his mother.

"Take your time. You see how slow everyone else is going? No one else is running. No one else is rushing. You don't want to do anything that will set you apart from them." Gabriel let go of David's arm slowly, making sure that he was going to stay and heed Gabriel's warning. Then Gabriel reached back behind the bench to grab a pair of crutches. He didn't need them all the time, but he had found himself tiring more recently, the muscles in his legs just not bearing up against the constant standing and walking that he needed to do. They weren't as bad as they had been when he had been apprehended by DCFS and taken off of all of his meds. But it was troublesome. And it had taken a few weeks of fighting himself before he had finally broken down and admitted to Renata that he needed the crutches.

Of course, she had already known. They did everything—or almost everything—together, and she could see the pain and fatigue that had been taking a toll on him.

"It's about time," she told him. "Don't know why you think you had to be so macho and deny your disabilities."

Gabriel had just sighed and chuckled at himself for thinking he had been keeping anything from her. He shook his head and laughed at himself again as he picked up the crutches to walk with David across the mall to meet his mother.

It might seem like he was making himself more conspicuous by using crutches, but he actually wasn't. People didn't like to look for too long at someone with an obvious disability. They had been taught not to stare. Many of the older generations had been taught it was rude even to notice a disability. Certainly, you didn't say anything to the poor cripple about it. They wouldn't want you drawing attention to their disability and making it obvious that you were judging them or their capabilities.

So people wouldn't look at him. They would notice that there was a young Black man with crutches walking across the mall and then they would look away. They wouldn't look at his face because that would be akin to staring or telling him they noticed his disability.

They wouldn't look at the young man that he was walking with, either. The halo effect of the crutches would extend to his companion, keeping them from looking at him. They would probably not even know he was there if asked about it later.

David was eager to go faster than Gabriel's careful pace. He kept bouncing on his tiptoes, wanting to run ahead to meet his mother. But maybe something they had told him had sunk in after all, and he waited for Gabriel and didn't tell him to move faster. Maybe if it hadn't been for the crutches, he would have told Gabriel to hurry up, but he too had been trained to be polite to those with disabilities.

Gabriel saw the moment at which Mrs. Sealy became aware of her son walking across the mall toward her. There was a current of electricity, an immediate connection between the two of them, and she altered her course slightly so that she would walk directly to him.

They met halfway, and David gave his mother a big hug. Gabriel murmured to them as he watched the reunion.

"Not too big and obvious here," he told them. "Keep it as casual as you can. You'll have plenty of time for the stories and everything else later. Mrs. Sealy, you made all of the necessary arrangements?"

"Yes." She pulled herself out of her son's grasp and tried to look casual. "Everything is set up like you said. We'll leave the city and the state immediately. I have a little place rented. We'll keep our heads down and not let anyone know who we are."

"Good. You got a job lined up?"

"Not yet, but I have a few leads. It won't take me very long."

Gabriel nodded. "Okay. Last thing to do is to walk out of here casually. Just a normal mom and son concluding a normal shopping day. You haven't seen anyone you know or recognize?"

"No."

He held out his hand to shake, and Mrs. Sealy took Gabriel's thin hand in hers and gave it a warm squeeze. "Thank you for everything that you have done. And Renata. Will you tell her thank you, too?"

"Of course. You guys take care."

CHAPTER EIGHT

G ame day!" Marcus shouted as he hustled down the hallway. He banged on a locker door. "Game day, game day!"

There were answering hoots from a number of the other soccer players. Joseph gave a shout-out, but wasn't really feeling it. He was pretty wound up about the game. He had been able to get to his practices the last couple of days, but still had a feeling of doom that permeated everything he did. He was taking the new prescription as directed, but there was no guarantee it would make a difference in just a couple of days. And that was assuming that it would do what it was supposed to in the first place and reduce or eliminate the anxiety attacks.

He was afraid that it wouldn't do anything for him. Or that it would just make the side effects worse and wouldn't even touch the panic attacks or other psychiatric symptoms.

Everybody on the team was depending on him. Everyone in the school was depending on him. His mother and the coach would be watching him carefully for any sign that he couldn't do what he promised. For any indication that what he had was worse than the flu. Worse than the issues that had taken him to the hospital in the first place.

"You all ready?" Lora asked, shutting her locker door so that she could look at him. Her eyes were critical. She looked him up and down, lips pursed, forehead creased. "Well, you look okay. How do you feel?"

"Fine!" Joseph looked around to make sure that no one else was listening. He didn't want anyone to get the idea that he was sick. "I'm great. I'm all ready for the game."

"Good. You were awesome in practice yesterday."

It sounded more like a question than a statement.

"That's right," Joseph agreed. "I was feeling really good. Everything is coming together. And I really think that the team is gelling."

"Yeah," Lora agreed. She had been harping on this for weeks, so Joseph figured if he fed it back to her, she would be really happy about it and not bug him about anything else. "I think it's all starting to come together, and that's great because, when it does, it's magic. You can't stop a team that pulls together and puts one hundred percent into the game. You just can't."

"Yeah," Joseph agreed, trying to sound like he was pumped. "Yeah, yeah. Nothing like it. What a feeling."

She looked at him for a moment with narrowed eyes, as if trying to figure out if he was serious or whether he was mocking her. Then she nodded and gave a reserved smile.

"We're not there yet. But when we hit it… everybody is going to know about it. We are just going to rocket to the front of the line."

Joseph nodded. He glanced at the clock on the wall. "Second bell is going to go; I'd better get going."

She nodded. They split up and headed off in opposite directions. He listened to the squeak of her shoes as she walked off.

+++Joseph was anxious about the game all day. How much good could the anti-anxiety meds be doing if he spent the whole day envisioning the worst possible way things could go wrong at the game? His heart pounded and his stomach hurt so that he couldn't eat.

But would the pills keep him from having another anxiety attack? There was no way to know for sure. So far, he hadn't had any more since the one before practice Monday afternoon. He'd had a couple of episodes where his heart had started racing, but he hadn't gone into full-blown meltdown mode, so maybe it *was* working.

When the final dismissal bell sounded at the end of the day, it was time to go down to the locker room, change, and start getting ready for the game.

The other players were eyeing Joseph as he descended to the locker room and started getting changed, but he tried not to pay any attention to it. Everyone was nervous, that was all. He had been sick earlier in the week and they wanted to make sure that he was up to par and would be able to help them win the game. They didn't know about the panic attacks. Just that he had taken ill suddenly. That could have happened to anyone. Food poisoning, the flu, an allergy, anyone could get sick one day just out of the blue. And then be better the next day.

It could happen to any of them just as well as to him. It wasn't just something that happened to psychos who had to be hospitalized for mental health issues.

He knew that was how everyone thought of him when they saw him walking down the hall at school. Some people felt sorry for him. Some just wanted to make stupid remarks and bully someone because they felt inadequate and threatened by the thought that a person could just lose control one day. But they were all afraid, whether they admitted it or not. Afraid that the same thing could happen to them. Afraid he could blow up one day and hurt himself or someone else. Someone who was mentally ill was unpredictable and a threat. That was how they saw it.

And a couple of years earlier, he would have been in the same boat. He would never have thought that it could happen to him. And then one day, it had.

"You gonna score some goals today, Demain?" asked Tyler Agua. He had that bullying tone in his voice. Not someone who was encouraging a teammate. More like a taunt or a threat. *You get those goals you're supposed to, or you will pay.* He didn't say it out loud, had never voiced any threats, but Joseph was supposed to understand the undertones, and he did.

"More than you," Joseph returned.

Which wasn't a hard bet, since Agua was the goalkeeper. There were a few laughs from others in the locker room.

"You take care of your end and I'll take care of mine," Joseph promised.

He said it with more confidence than he felt. He wanted it to be true. He wanted to be the guy who got all of the goals today. He wanted to be *the man*. And even if he couldn't carry the team, he still wanted to do his part. He really didn't want to disappoint anyone. He could already see them in his head. His mom, Lora, the coach, the rest of the team. All lined up and waiting for him to disappoint them.

His heart started to pound harder. But Joseph wasn't going to let himself have a panic attack now. He was focused on the game. It didn't matter how he felt; he would still play soccer tonight. Nothing was going to stop him. His heart could beat so hard that it burst, and he would just keep going, zombie Joseph, getting all the goals.

The image amused him and, for a minute, he wasn't worried anymore, but just thought about what a great TV show that would make. Agua scowled at Joseph's smile and turned away.

Joseph dressed, not participating in all of the usual locker room smack talk. He kept his mind focused on the goal. He was sweating and his head hurt. His chest was tight and he tasted bile. But he knew it was just a panic attack. The anxiety got worse if he focused on it. If he just ignored it, it would go away.

He should have a ritual. A lot of athletes followed special rituals. They got ready for a game the same way every time, and having that routine in place made it easier and told their brain to be prepared for what was to come. He could listen to a special song on his phone. Or a special playlist. He could wear special underwear on game days. He could make sure that he always did everything the same when he got to the locker room, putting his socks on in a particular order. He could repeat a mantra or say a prayer. There were a lot of things he could do to get ready and keep himself focused on the game and not get distracted by something stupid like anxiety.

Where did anxiety get him? If he were strong enough, he could wipe it off. Just tell his brain that he wasn't putting up with this nonsense.

When he finished dressing, he stood in front of his locker with his eyes closed, saying a prayer. He didn't know how to pray the right way; he didn't know any of the ritual prayers. But that didn't stop him from bargaining with whatever entity might be in charge of the universe and all the outcomes of everyone's lives.

Please, please, please, let me score goals and not have any panic attacks.

CHAPTER NINE

A nd then they were out on the field. The opening ceremonies of the game were all a blur. Joseph was off in his own little world and didn't have any idea what was going on until someone punched him on the arm and told him he was up. Joseph joined the rest of the starting lineup as they ran out onto the field. He focused on the game and nothing else.

He had hardly even started running, but his heart was already pounding like a train engine. Joseph breathed and talked to his body, trying to get it to settle down. It seemed determined to get the blood circulating his body as fast as possible. He could hear a rushing in his ears that pulsed with his heartbeat, uncomfortably rapid.

All he needed to do was to work through the anxiety. He would beat it. He was a disciplined athlete. He could do this.

Joseph took a pass and worked the ball down the field, aware of where everyone was. He could see them in his peripheral vision, and even knew where the ones behind him were from memory and the sounds of their breathing. He kept tight control of the ball, staying away from the members of the opposing team and looking for an opening to pass it. Sweat trickled down his temples and his lips were salty.

Joseph's field of vision narrowed. He focused on the ball and the goal at the end of the field. He could no longer hear the crowd, his teammates calling to him, or the jeers of the other team. He was one with the ball. One with the field.

───────

And then he was flat on his back and had no idea how he had gotten there.

There were voices all around him, asking questions and shouting to each other. Joseph was staring up at the sky. A very pretty shade of blue. Robin's egg blue? China blue? He tried to come up with just the right descriptor in his head. He would tell it to his dad the next time they got together for a visit.

"Demain. Joseph." A nudge on his shoulder and a face getting way too close to him, blocking out the sky and everything else. "Are you okay? Can you talk?"

"Yeah, yeah." Joseph cleared his throat. He tried to sit up and get up, but they pushed him back down.

"Take it easy. Are you okay? What happened?"

Joseph tried again to get up, but someone continued to hold him down, pressing his shoulders into the turf.

"What happened?" Joseph echoed, looking around for someone who could tell him. He spotted Lora's face out of those hovering over him. The team trainer. She would know what had happened. She knew everything that went on on the field. "Lora?"

"Joseph." She pushed other people out of the way, looking grateful to have him talking to her so she had a reason to move closer. They had probably been telling her that she was not a doctor or the coach, that she was just a kid, and to stay out of the way while the grown-ups dealt with the problem. "Hey. What's going on? Are you feeling okay?"

"I… no. I don't know." Joseph shook his head. "I want to get up. This is… everyone is looking at me. The game."

"Don't worry about the game. They can play without you once

you are off the field. We'll take care of you first, and then the game can continue. Do you feel dizzy? Lightheaded?"

"No. Just strange." He rubbed his forehead with the pads of his fingers. Maybe it hurt. He wasn't sure. "What happened?"

"You fainted. One minute, you're taking the ball down the field, and then you're eating dirt. Are you still sick? You know you're not supposed to play if you're sick."

"I... don't know. What happened here?"

"Did you feel sick before you went on? Were you dizzy again? Anything?"

"I don't know. Is my mom here?" Joseph looked for her. He didn't want to talk to anyone about the doctor, the panic attacks, the increased dose of his medication.

"No. I don't think she took the time off to watch the game. She's probably still working, right? Someone is going to call her, let her know what happened."

"No, don't bother her. She has to work." She had already taken time off, first to pick him up from school on Monday, and then to take him to the doctor on Tuesday. He couldn't expect her to take time off from work to deal with his health a third time in a week. She would lose her job. What would they do if she lost her job? They would lose the house. They wouldn't be able to do anything.

"We have to let her know what happened," Lora pointed out. "There would be big trouble if no one told her and she found out another way after the fact. And you're going to have to go to the hospital."

"Why do I have to go to the hospital?"

"Because you fainted in the middle of the field. That's what happens. They have to make sure that it isn't your heart or a seizure or something."

"I just... I think I just didn't have anything to eat. I should have grabbed something to eat, but my stomach wasn't feeling great."

"You didn't have anything to eat?" Coach Beiderman demanded, his pudgy face floating over Joseph's. "How stupid is that? You kids know that you have to take care of yourselves. How could you not eat anything? Since when?"

"I… I had breakfast."

"You didn't have any lunch? Didn't have anything before the game? You know you have to fuel."

"No. I just… I had a granola bar for breakfast." A small fib, since the granola bar was really a Pop-Tart, but the coach didn't need to know that, did he? What was the difference? "Then… I was just nervous later. My stomach wasn't feeling great. I didn't want to throw up."

"Let's get him up," Beiderman suggested. "He just needs something to eat. That's all this is."

"I'm sorry," Joseph apologized. "I just wasn't feeling up to it…"

The hands that had previously been holding him down released and he was allowed to get up, helped to his feet. Lora pushed her way in so that she was taking his arm and putting it around her shoulders, so he had something to lean on as he walked, for support or balance. Joseph was okay to walk. His legs were strong and didn't wobble. He didn't tip over. He was braced for a head rush, a sudden onset of dizziness or pain as he got up, but it didn't come.

He felt a rush of heat, but it wasn't like the sweating from his anxiety attack. It was embarrassment over his situation, being walked off the field like a cripple after fainting. *Fainting! In the middle of a game!*

"I can still play," he told Lora. "Once I have something to eat, I'll be fine, right? I can get back in there." He looked back over his shoulder at the field, wondering who was going to step into his place. How they were going to finish out the play. He really wanted to be the man, the one who would bring the team the win. Now, he was being pulled off over something so stupid.

Beiderman was right. He had been stupid. He never should have played without having had something to eat. He should have eaten anyway. Even if he had to puke in the locker room bathroom before the game. Sometimes, that was something an athlete had to deal with.

There was polite applause from the spectators. Not like at a pro game where they had a standing ovation when an injured player was taken off the field, or managed to stand back up under their own power.

He wasn't that well-liked.

This was high school soccer.

He was taken over to the chairs on the sideline, a cup of Gatorade pushed into his hand.

"Drink it down," Beiderman ordered. "You shouldn't be coming to the game if you haven't had anything to eat. We could get in real trouble for not taking care of you. That's just stupid."

"I know, Coach. I'm sorry."

Beiderman spouted off for a while longer, but then the game resumed and his attention was needed elsewhere.

Lora pulled up the chair next to him. "Don't chug it," she told him. "You'll just throw up. Drink it slowly and let it work."

Joseph took a couple of swallows to show them both that he was doing what he was told and that he would be able to step back into the game after he'd had a few minutes to recover. Lora reached over and sponged his forehead with a damp towel, which felt cool and refreshing.

"You need to take care of yourself," she told him. "If you don't feel well, you need to tell us. I know you don't want to take the game off, but better that than fainting in the middle of the field."

"That wasn't exactly planned."

"I know."

"What an idiot," Marcus told Joseph, punching him in the shoulder as he walked by. "Gotta have all the attention, on and off the field, right?"

Joseph glared at him, unable to come up with the right words to refute this claim.

"Ignore him," Lora said. "He doesn't know what he's talking about."

"I'm not just… trying to get attention," Joseph told her. "You think that this is just an act? Like I want sympathy or something?"

"I know it's not an act. But it was stupid. And you're going to keep hearing that all day long." She shrugged. "Sorry."

Joseph couldn't help chuckling at that. He shook his head. "You can't do something about that?"

"About you being stupid? Hey, man, I do what I can. But I can't fix that."

"I meant about everyone calling me stupid."

"They're right."

"So?"

She blotted his forehead again, more aggressively this time. "Drink your Gatorade."

CHAPTER TEN

Lora was right, of course.

About Joseph's mother and about the need to go to the hospital after his little adventure on the field.

The school had called Mira, and the game wasn't even to half-time before she showed up looking for him, her face white, bags under her eyes like she'd suffered a week of sleepless nights. Joseph felt bad for her. He hadn't wanted her to come to the school, to leave her job for the third time that week to take care of him. He wasn't some five-year-old who needed to be babysat. Even if he was sick, he was perfectly capable of going home and going to bed by himself until she normally got off of work. He didn't need her there, and he didn't need to go to the hospital.

Mira's opinion, however, was somewhat different.

"This is serious, Joey," she told him. "I thought it was just anxiety earlier in the week, but having a seizure in the middle of the game…"

"It wasn't a seizure."

"Then blacking out in the middle of the game. Come on. That's not something to laugh at. We need to go to the hospital, and we need to go now. I'm shocked that they didn't call an ambulance. This could have been really bad. What if you'd had a heart attack? They could be negligent in not getting you to the hospital immediately."

"I told you, it's just because I didn't eat. I know it was stupid," he paused, waiting for her to agree with him, to tell him that yes, he'd been stupid, but she was glad that he was okay, and he didn't need to go to the hospital for that.

Instead, she shook her head, her face grimly set. "Even if that was true, this is the second time this week that you've been having symptoms. And not just minor symptoms, but stuff that has kept you from soccer. I *know* it's serious."

Joseph's heart sped up at the thought that it might not just be fainting from lack of food, or suffering an anxiety attack, but something that was really, truly, life-threateningly serious. Was that why he'd been having such feelings of doom and anxiety that week? Because the machine that was his body was breaking down, no longer reliable, no longer something that he could trust?

He had never thought of himself as being immortal. But he had never really thought about his own mortality, either. About the fact that one day, he was going to die, and that day might be sooner than he expected.

———

So, despite Joseph's insistence that it wasn't anything to be worried about and that he still wanted to support the team and watch the rest of the game, that wasn't going to happen. Mira hovered over Joseph as he finished his Gatorade, wiped his hot face with the damp towel, and said a reluctant goodbye to Lora.

"Can I at least change?"

"I want to get you to the hospital as soon as possible." Mira looked undecided. "You can go get your stuff out of the locker," she said finally. "But don't change, just grab it and let's go."

"I'll go with you," Lora offered.

"No. You stay here," Joseph ordered. "You need to watch the game. Make sure everyone else is okay. I'm perfectly capable of getting the stuff out of my locker."

"But someone should be with you in case you have another... spell."

"I'm just going in and out. You don't need to supervise me."

Lora looked like she would keep arguing, but Mira gave her a quelling look. Apparently, moms had more influence over Lora than coaches and the other school adults that Joseph had seen her deal with, because Lora stopped objecting.

"Go, and be quick," Mira told Joseph. "Or I am going to send her in there after you."

Joseph laughed and headed to the locker room. He was glad that he didn't wobble or sway when he stood up from the chair. He looked and felt just fine. Nothing for Mira to flip out about. It was just as he had said. He hadn't had enough to eat because he'd been so nervous about having an anxiety attack. He'd unintentionally sabotaged himself. He probably would have been just fine if he hadn't spent any time worrying about it.

Once off the field and into the school, Joseph went ahead with his plan, which was *not* to obey his mother by just grabbing his gear. He didn't want to go to the hospital, or anywhere else, wearing his dirty, sweaty soccer gear. He would just attract more looks and he wouldn't be comfortable. He moved quickly, stripping everything off as he walked into the locker room, knowing that Mira and Lora would not give him long before coming to check on him. But there was nothing Mira could do about it if Joseph was changed and back to meet her within five minutes. He didn't have time to shower, but he hadn't been playing for long, and a quick application of deodorant would have to do the job.

———

He had to deal with the silent glares when he got back to the field, and all the way to the hospital, still receiving more nasty looks from Mira as he sat in the emergency room chairs, waiting for what was bound to be hours, and would get them nowhere.

He admittedly did not have a good opinion of doctors. Maybe other people had better luck, but he seemed to draw the short straw every time, coming up with doctor after doctor who was either incompetent or just didn't care. They were more than happy to pat him on the head and send him home, and it took a big push from Mira for them to even consider doing anything proactive. She had been the one who had insisted that he needed to be hospitalized in November. She had been right, of course, but the doctors hadn't believed her and had only complied to shut her up.

Without her pushing, he didn't know if he would even be around anymore to complain about the wait.

"I'm sorry," he tried.

Mira looked at him. "For what?"

It would be a lot easier if she would just accept his apology and not make him go into details. Because he was never sorry about the part she wanted him to be sorry for.

"For… not eating and for getting changed."

She sighed and rubbed her forehead, elbow resting on knees. "You don't have to apologize for being sick… but I wish you would think through your choices. And maybe… consider that I might have a bit more experience in life than you and actually know what I'm talking about now and then."

"I know."

He felt terrible when he worried her but knew he should actually feel bad about not listening to her, which he didn't. While she was an adult with more experience than he had, he didn't see that it made any difference whether he changed his clothes before going to the hospital or not. And if he were to tell the truth, he had eaten several times that day and should not have passed out from low blood sugar. It was just easier to say that was what had happened. Too much exertion after fasting too long, it made sense that he would pass out.

Passing out in the middle of the game for no reason at all did *not* make sense.

Joseph shook his head. He looked back down at his phone, where he had been playing games and messaging with friends while he waited. The truth was, it was just as easy to stay there while playing with his phone as going home and playing with it in bed, aside from the fact that the chairs did not have good back support and he couldn't lounge in them. They forced him to sit up and, of course, playing on the phone, he hunched over, which he knew Mira would

48

get after him for sooner or later. Hopefully, not until much later, because he wasn't going to sit there for hours with nothing to do just because his phone made him hunchbacked.

"Joseph Demain?"

Joseph looked up in surprise at the woman in scrubs who held a clipboard in her hand and looked around at those waiting in the emergency room. He hadn't been expecting to be dealt with so quickly.

Maybe they would just tell him to suck it up and go home, not to bother the emergency room with such little problems. He often heard lectures from doctors on the TV or the internet saying that people should not go to the emergency room with a cold. They couldn't treat the emergency room as if it were their family doctor's office. And, of course, you shouldn't go to the doctor because of a cold anyway. The flu, maybe, but only if you were dehydrated or had pneumonia, or were an old person.

Joseph held up his hand. "That's me."

"Do you want to come with me, Joseph?" She turned around to lead him to the exam area. Joseph stood up and waited for Mira to tuck things into her purse so that they could walk close together instead of her trailing behind him like she wasn't wanted. As much as he wanted to be an adult and treated as one by the doctors and other staff, Joseph was afraid that they wouldn't listen to what he had to say, just like with Dr. Shapiro. And he would need Mira to intervene on his behalf, demanding the answers to questions and keeping his prescriptions straight. He wanted to be an adult, but not to have all of the responsibilities of one.

The nurse led them to an examination area and motioned for Joseph to jump up on the bed to talk to her. He sat there, awkward, with that naked, vulnerable feeling he always got when talking to medical staff.

"So," the nurse read over the notes on her clipboard, though she had probably already read through the description of what he was there for. Someone had triaged him and decided what his place was in the priority order of the patients in the waiting room. "You fainted while playing soccer this afternoon."

"Yeah. I guess so."

"And you think that might be because you hadn't had enough to eat."

"Yeah."

She looked at him for a minute as if waiting for him to tell the truth. Joseph swallowed and tried not to look guilty.

"When was the last time you ate today?"

"I'm not sure." Joseph glanced at Mira and, of course, she was listening closely, as she always did. "I had something in the afternoon. A snack. Umm... I didn't eat very much because my stomach was feeling queasy. Just... pregame nerves, you know?"

"What did you have in the afternoon?"

"A bag of chips or a chocolate bar."

"Which was it? A bag of chips or a chocolate bar?"

"Uh... both, I guess. I shared them with my friend. So I didn't eat all of it. But..."

"Okay. We will want to take some blood samples and see if there is anything strange going on there. And have you had anything since then? Since you fainted?"

"Yeah. Gatorade."

She nodded. "Yes, good. You didn't have any before the game?"

"No."

"Maybe next time you should."

Joseph nodded. "Okay."

"Have you ever fainted before this?"

"No."

Mira gave Joseph a stern look. The nurse caught it and raised her brows. "No?"

"Tell her about Monday," Mira ordered.

"I didn't faint."

The nurse waited, saying nothing.

"I just... I got really dizzy. I had just gotten ready for practice, and I was ready to go out, and then... I didn't feel good. I got really dizzy. But I didn't pass out."

"And how long did that last?"

"Just... I don't know. Ten minutes, maybe."

"And did you go ahead and do your practice?"

"No. Went home to bed."

"What do you think caused that dizzy spell? Had you eaten before practice?"

"I did, yeah. Just, you know, an energy bar and a drink. But I did eat."

"How long before that? Are we talking noon a few hours earlier, or ten minutes before?"

"Ten minutes."

"And is that the only other episode?"

"Yes." Joseph looked at Mira and nodded.

"You need to tell her the rest."

Joseph rolled his eyes. "The rest isn't related."

"It could be."

"I already saw my doctor. He said it was a panic attack. That's all. Just... I have anxiety, and he said it was a panic attack. And he raised my meds. And I haven't had another one since then."

"What meds are you on?" Her pen hovered over the page.

"I don't know." Joseph deferred to Mira.

She knew them off by heart without even looking them up. Joseph was impressed. She didn't know the dosages, though. But the nurse said she would contact Dr. Shapiro's office to get that information.

"How long have you been on these medications?"

"A few months. Since... November."

"And have you had any side effects from them?"

"A few things." Joseph shrugged. "Nothing too bad."

"And have you had other anxiety attacks? Racing heart? Chest pain?"

"Umm. Yeah." Joseph didn't look at Mira.

"Did you talk about them with Dr. Shapiro?"

"No. I didn't think they were anything to worry about. I figured... he would say that was normal. That everybody has that sometimes."

"So it wasn't serious enough for you to be concerned."

"No... not really."

She looked at him briefly before adding some notes to the clipboard. "Mom, is he going to regular follow-up appointments with Dr. Shapiro?"

"Yes. Joseph sees him once a month."

"No concerns raised at those appointments?"

"No."

"Regular bloodwork?"

"Yes."

"No issues?"

"No. He hasn't said anything."

The nurse wrote a few more notes. "Okay. The doctor will be with you shortly. I'm going to bring in an EKG machine for Joseph. We'll get him hooked up so we'll have some data to look at by the time the doctor arrives."

"You think there's something wrong with his heart?" Mira's voice rose in a panicked note.

"Probably not. But it is best to check. Sometimes, the first you know about a kid's heart problems is when he collapses on the field. We are probably not dealing with anything more than low blood sugar here, but we don't want to take any chances. We'll make sure everything is clear."

"Heart problems? You don't think we would have discovered them before this?"

The nurse shrugged and repeated, "Sometimes, it isn't until they collapse that you know there is something wrong. Be thankful that Joseph appears to have just had a fainting episode. Sometimes those kids…" She trailed off and shook her head.

Joseph recalled some news stories he'd heard about athletes collapsing on the field, dead. That was what she was talking about. That was what might have happened to him.

Maybe there were worse things than having to spend an evening in the emergency room to ensure nothing was really wrong with him.

CHAPTER ELEVEN

They had been waiting for the doctor to return with the test results and Joseph's clearance to go home for a couple of hours. It had seemed like everything was moving pretty quickly, and then their progress had ground to a halt. Dr. Hughes, a friendly woman who didn't seem much older than Joseph, had breezed in, looked over his EKG results and clipboard, asked him a few questions, and then was gone. She had promised to return in a few minutes, and it had been nearly two hours. Joseph was getting tired of sitting around, tired of the spotty Wi-Fi coverage in the hospital, and tired of nurses who came to look at him, smiled and promised that the doctor would be there any minute, and then disappeared again.

Joseph knew there was nothing wrong with him. If something were wrong with him, they wouldn't be so casual about it. They would tell him that there was something wrong with his heart. They would give him some drug to settle it down and make sure that he didn't have any more episodes, and they would send him home with a list of rules he had to be sure to follow. It wouldn't be all of this waiting around.

Finally, the young doctor returned to the curtained area Joseph had been imprisoned in for hours. She smiled at him.

"I'll bet you're ready to go home," she sympathized.

"Yeah. Can I go now?"

"Let's go over these test results to start with."

Joseph nodded. Mira opened her phone's notes app, preparing to take notes. Dr. Hughes sat on the edge of Joseph's bed casually.

"So, bloodwork first of all. Everything looks good. All of the levels are where they should be. I don't think that you fainted due to low blood sugar."

"But I had a drink after that," Joseph pointed out. "I've had other food since then. So it wouldn't still be low."

"There isn't any indication that you've had any ongoing blood sugar problems. No diabetes, nothing like that. Which is good news."

She sat there looking at him with a smile, like she was proud of herself. Like this was exactly the news that he had been waiting for and now the party could begin. Joseph forced a smile. "Good."

"What about the EKG?" Mira asked. "Did you find anything out about his heart?"

"I've looked at the EKG and the ultrasound, and I don't see any problems. Everything seems to be operating properly—good, young, athletic heart. No defects. No problems with regulating the beat. No blockages or electrical problems that we could see."

"Then… what do you think happened?"

Dr. Hughes folded her hands. "I think Joseph is probably just fighting a virus. They can cause issues. Or it may be sporadic. Sometimes, someone has a seizure for no obvious reason, and then it never happens again. The majority of teen seizures are like that. Just one and done, and you can never actually tell what happened that one time. Maybe it was a virus or an infection, a flashing light, we don't really know. But it never happens again."

"A seizure?" Joseph asked, feeling suddenly off balance.

"Well, we don't know if it was syncope or a seizure. They can be very hard to tell apart, even if you happened to be hooked up to monitoring equipment at the time. So we consider both. Either way, you only lost consciousness briefly, we're not seeing anything that is of concern or explains it, and probably, this will never happen again. As I said, that's often how it is with teen seizures. Your brain is undergoing a lot of development right now, and sometimes things can happen. Just like… a system reboot. Then you're fine."

"You think my brain just rebooted."

"That's the best explanation we can come up with right now." She gave him a bright smile. "I'm sure that's a big relief for both of you. You can get dressed," Dr. Hughes put her hand on Joseph's knee briefly. "And our social worker will be coming to talk to you briefly before you check out. Then we can let you go and you can enjoy what is left of your evening."

"Okay… thanks."

Dr. Hughes had breezed back out of the room and was gone before Joseph even had a chance to process what she had said. He sat on the bed, frozen for a moment, before turning to Mira with a frown.

"Social worker? Why would a social worker be talking to me?"

She shook her head slowly. "I'm not sure. But sometimes, the hospital has to follow certain procedures, even if it doesn't make much sense to the layperson. I don't know. Maybe because you're a teenager…?"

"So?"

"So, sometimes teenagers need to talk to someone other than their parents. Or the hospital wants to ensure they have someone they can talk to other than the parent."

"Why?"

"I don't know, Joseph," Mira sounded frustrated. She was probably at the end of her rope after sitting in a hard chair all evening. "Because sometimes teenagers have things to talk about that they don't want to discuss in front of their parents."

"Oh. Something to do with me fainting?" He tried to think of how that would make any sense.

"No. Just to check in and make sure there is nothing going on that they should be aware of. Some kids are dealing with abuse, drugs, pregnancy, that kind of thing. Clinics and ERs try to facilitate connections with social programs in case they need them."

Joseph nodded slowly. "Well… at least that's one thing you can be sure you don't have to worry about."

"What is?"

"I promise I'm not pregnant."

Mira laughed, some of the tension leaving her face. "You're such a nut sometimes, Joey."

Joseph chuckled and pulled out his phone to settle in for another gaming session until the social worker arrived. Hopefully, she wouldn't take as long as a doctor.

———

"Knock, knock!"

There was, of course, no door for the woman to knock on, so she just poked her head in through the curtain and called, "knock, knock," as if they couldn't all see each other. Joseph supposed it was intended to be polite, but it was irritating. He didn't know if he were supposed to tell her to come in or if she just would anyway.

"Hi," Mira greeted. "Are you the social worker?"

The woman stepped in through the curtain, nodding. "My name is Mrs. Kelly," she introduced herself. "I'm very glad to meet you, Joseph." She looked at him rather than at Mira.

"Umm, yeah. Great. So… can you tell me why you're here and what I'm supposed to do to get released? I really want to get home."

"I'm sure you do. Well, it isn't anything to be concerned about. I just want to have a little discussion with you on how things are going at home and school, in your life in general, and then you can go home. How does that sound?"

"Okay. It doesn't sound like anything I need, but…"

"If we could have the room, Mrs. Demain?" Mrs. Kelly requested.

Just like Mira had figured. She wanted to talk to Joseph alone so that he could tell her if he needed to report anything he might feel awkward talking about in front of his mother. He let Mira leave without objection and waited for Mrs. Kelly to begin her questions.

"So, how are things?" she asked, leaving it wide open.

"Fine. I'm tired of hanging around the hospital and want to go home now."

"I'm sure. It's not the most pleasant way to spend a day, is it?"

"No."

"Do you want to tell me about what happened that resulted in you seeking help here today?"

It sounded like a survey question. *Rate your satisfaction with our staff today. Tell us how we can serve you better.*

"I had a… an episode during soccer today. Blacked out. And so, of course, my mom brought me here to see what was wrong. Why I fainted. They checked me out and said everything is fine, so I can go home. As soon as I talk to you."

"They didn't find anything?"

"No. They said my heart looked healthy and everything."

"Did they think it was your heart that made you faint?"

"I don't know. It was one of the things that they were looking at. But they said it looked great. Everything was fine."

"I'm sure that was a big relief. Is there anything else that you are supposed to follow up on?"

"No, nothing that they told me."

"So they don't think it was anything to worry about?"

"No."

"Have you had any other recent visits to the hospital?"

Joseph felt uneasy at the question. Of course she knew that he had. It wasn't really a question.

"Well, a few months ago," he told her uncomfortably. "But that isn't anything to do with today." He shrugged, hoping that she would move on and not dwell on it.

"Why don't you tell me about why you were here in November?"

"Well, I guess you know."

She looked at him and didn't offer whether she did or didn't. But of course she did.

"I was here in Psych," Joseph said, rolling his eyes. He didn't think she should have the right to invade his privacy that way. "Because I was having… I was depressed. I needed some help getting back on my feet. That's all."

"You've had problems with depression before?"

"Yeah. A couple of times. And usually, I'm okay. But sometimes, the meds will stop working, or the dosages need to be adjusted because I'm getting bigger. So that's what it was about in November. Just checking in so they could review my meds and get everything stabilized again."

"And how are you feeling now?"

"Fine."

"Not depressed?"

"No."

"Anxious?"

Joseph bit his lip. He couldn't very well say that he hadn't been anxious when he had just seen his doctor about anxiety attacks.

"I had... some issues. I saw my doctor earlier in the week, and he adjusted my meds. So... not anymore."

"You haven't had time to tell whether the updated prescription is working yet, have you?"

"No. But it's fine. I'm sure it will."

"This episode at soccer, it could be related, couldn't it?"

"No. It wasn't anxiety. I just fainted. The doctor said maybe it was a seizure. Sometimes, people have one seizure, and then they never have another one. So it was probably like that."

"Will you be following up with Dr. Shapiro to see if your meds could have caused this seizure?"

"Uh... I guess so. Yeah." He blew out his breath. "My mom will make sure that I see anyone I should for follow-up. She's good at doing all of that stuff."

"That's good. You're lucky to have someone looking after you. I'm glad to hear it."

"Yeah."

"How is your relationship with your mom? What is she like?"

"She's really good. I know she's a good mom. Even though some-times she drives me crazy. Sometimes I wish she wasn't *quite* so involved." He laughed. "You know how it is?"

"You feel that she invades your privacy? Gets involved in things that you would rather handle yourself?"

"Well... not really. But sometimes I wish I could just handle something on my own."

"Like what?"

"Like… I don't know. Appointments with my doctor. Picking out my classes at school. Learning to drive. Some kids my age have their own cars."

"Of course," she laughed. "Parents *can* get in the way sometimes."

"I'm not ten anymore."

"Would you like to be able to handle those things on your own?"

"Yes. But then… I don't want to have all of the responsibility either. So sometimes I don't want that."

She nodded understandingly. Joseph leaned back against the raised section of the bed. He rubbed his eyes. He was tired and just wanted to go home after the extended visit to the hospital. Who knew that waiting around playing games on his phone could be so exhausting?

CHAPTER TWELVE

"hy don't you tell me about your family," Mrs. Kelly suggested. "Is it just you and your mom?"

"No. I have a dad," Joseph said immediately. Then he paused, reconsidering his answer. "I mean... I live with my mom. I see my dad some weekends. They're divorced," he stated the obvious. "So I split time between them. But I live with my mom because she's close to the school. It's the house I grew up in. She kept the house so I could keep going to the same school. It's tough on her. I know the bills are high and it would probably be better if we found somewhere else to live."

"It's hard when your parents divorce, isn't it?"

"Yeah. Sure. But it isn't like I'm the only one going through it. Half the kids at school have divorced parents. Maybe more than that. I don't have a stepdad to worry about. I think that would be harder. Just me and my mom. I can manage that, but I don't know how I would feel if there was another man around trying to make new rules and control me."

"Maybe it would be someone you got along with and enjoyed being with."

"I guess, maybe," Joseph agreed. He did know a few people who had stepparents they got along with. Usually, the stepmoms, not the stepdads, but who knew, his mother could pick someone out Joseph liked and got along with. He didn't think she would ever pick someone who was really strict with Joseph or who was abusive.

"And what about your dad? He hasn't remarried either?"

"No… not yet. He's got a girlfriend. Felicity."

"Oh, that can be difficult. What do you think of her?"

"I guess she's okay. She's too young for him, and I know that…" Joseph cleared his throat, unsure how much he should tell the social worker, "I know he was seeing her before they divorced. Like, they started dating while he and my mom were still together."

"So she already has a strike against her. You're not inclined to like her if you feel like she broke your parents up."

"Yeah. I know it's not *her* fault, it's his. He's the one who decided to go off with someone else. But at some point… she knew he was married and had a kid, and she was breaking up the family."

Mrs. Kelly nodded.

"I guess they probably would have broken up sooner or later anyway. But like I said, it's his fault."

"What about your mom?"

"She doesn't have a boyfriend. She never went with anyone other than my dad."

"But other things can break up marriages and drive couples apart. There were probably other rifts in the marriage that you were unaware of. Other… incompatibilities."

"I guess."

"Did they fight a lot?"

Joseph looked at her and didn't think getting into any more particulars about his parents' relationship was a good idea.

"I don't know. Not around me. Maybe when I wasn't around."

"Sure. Parents try to keep these things from their kids sometimes. It can be quite a shock when you find out that they are breaking up, if you didn't see it coming."

"Yeah."

"How did you feel about them getting divorced?"

"I don't know. Just like you said, shocked. But it wasn't like I could do anything about it. They were getting divorced. I wasn't going to do anything like… you know, in those movies on TV. *Parent Trap* and stuff like that. I didn't try to keep them together or try to get them to fall in love with each other or anything. That's not how it works in the real world."

"Does that make you sad?"

"Yeah. Of course. It's sad to see them breaking up."

"Did it make you depressed?"

Joseph looked at her briefly, thinking of how to handle her question. He didn't think that he should flat-out lie to her, but he didn't want to tell her everything, either. He didn't want her to think that his parents had somehow damaged him by deciding to get a divorce. If that was what they had to do to be happy, then he understood it. Sort of.

"I was sad," he repeated. "But the depression… is something different. It's caused by the chemicals in my brain, not something that happened to me. Or to them."

"Of course. But I don't imagine it was made any better by their separation. You must have felt bad that your family was breaking apart. That you wouldn't be able to see your dad very much anymore."

Her words stirred up the tension that Joseph had felt since they had announced their plan to divorce. The anger, fear, sadness, and guilt over their decision. He could say all he wanted to that it was normal to have divorced parents. That he was happy if they were happy. But he was not. He had felt a horrible bubble of emptiness inside since he'd had to sit down at the kitchen table and they had told him they were getting divorced. He had assured them that he understood.

"It didn't help," he admitted.

"Did you have any counseling?"

Joseph wasn't sure. "Because of my depression or the divorce?"

"I meant because of the divorce. But I don't imagine that you can separate them."

"I saw someone because of the depression. Not because of the divorce," he told her flatly.

They had always been separate in his mind. The depression was bigger than anything that had happened in his life. Bigger than the divorce and his father's affair. Bigger than having to shuttle back and forth between them on weekends and holidays and to get along with both of them. To put up with different rules in different households. Felicity. Those things had not caused his depression.

He could try to inflate them, to make them seem bigger so that the depression made sense, but it never had made sense to him. He had a good life. He still felt like both of them loved him and wanted to be with him. He wasn't abused or neglected. He did okay at school and enjoyed being on the soccer team. He was a star player and loved that part of his life.

There wasn't any trouble in his life that was big enough to have caused his depression. He had known from the start that the depression was not caused by the divorce. He knew that it had been there, in the background, operating at a lower level, before his parents had ever mentioned their intention to divorce. He hadn't understood it as well when he was younger. The depression had been there long before it had gotten bad enough to reveal it to his mother.

"Do you think you might benefit from counseling over the divorce? Maybe have some family therapy, all of you together? Talk things out with a third-party mediating?"

Joseph shuddered at the thought. The last thing he needed was all of them in the same room. Mira, Joe Senior, Felicity, and Joseph.

"No," he said, "I don't think that would be a good idea."

Mrs. Kelly looked at him for a minute, then wrote something down in her notes.

"I'm a little worried about you. I think these episodes you are having... might be helped if you got some more attention. Professional help. What would you say to a more in-depth evaluation, a review of what's going on in your life, your meds, how things are going at school, all of that? I think it could be very beneficial."

Joseph shook his head. "I've done all of that before. I've been in the psych ward a couple of times and... I think it's better for me to be at home. I know some people need to be there, in Psych, to get on the right meds and to make sure they can't hurt themselves or anyone else. But I don't need that right now. And... I don't think you know how hard it is. It's not something you want to do unless you *really* need to."

"Oh, I understand that," she assured him, but he was pretty sure that she did not. "But I think it might be a good idea with everything that is going on right now."

"With everything that is going on?"

"With these… anxiety attacks. I think that is evidence that there is something more we need to look at. We need to dig down deeper to find out what that is and address it."

We?

Joseph shook his head again. He was going to get dizzy shaking it so often. He needed to make her understand that it wasn't going to happen. He wasn't going to be admitted to the psych ward to deal with his anxiety attacks. Not voluntarily. That could be done just as easily as an outpatient. "No! I don't need to be admitted for that."

She raised her eyebrows as if he had just shown her he was emotionally out of control. And he wasn't. He was just trying to make her understand that he did not need to be hospitalized. He was ready to go home. It was time to go home with his mother to his own TV and his own bed and to get back to the school routine tomorrow.

He would show everybody at school that he was just fine and there was no need to be concerned about his mental or physical health. He was the same Joseph Demain he had always been. Star of the soccer team. Good student. Popular. He was *together*, not some damaged, physically or psychologically frail reject.

"I want to go home now."

"I understand that," Mrs. Kelly said calmly. "Just a few more questions…"

"I don't want to answer any more questions. Why do we have to go over this any more?"

"It's my job to ensure everything is okay at home. That you don't need any additional assistance. That your mom is managing things okay and you have all of the supports in place that you need."

"I'm doing fine. And my mom is too."

"She's at home when you get home from school?"

Joseph swallowed. He could see what answer he was supposed to give and knew it was nowhere near what she wanted.

"Sometimes she is. Sometimes she isn't home until later. It depends on how long they need her."

"So she's not at home."

"Sometimes she is. I'm almost an adult. I can take care of myself for a couple of hours. I haven't lit any fires. I do my homework. I don't have parties and drink or do drugs. Most days, I have soccer anyway, so I'm not home from school until later. What's the point in her being home when school lets out if I'm not out yet?"

"We like to know someone is home when kids get home from school. That's why we recommend after-school care."

"For someone my age? Teenagers don't do after-school care. They take care of themselves."

"Teenagers with mental illness?" she asked disapprovingly.

Joseph was caught up short. Depression and anxiety were things that he fought to overcome, to find a way to deal with in his life, but he didn't think that they made him less responsible or unable to take care of himself. He had extra challenges now, but did that mean he needed a babysitter? He stared at Mrs. Kelly.

"I can take care of myself for a few hours. That's crazy. Of course I can."

She raised her brows, nodded slowly, but not in a way that imparted "yes," and added a note to those she had made already.

"I don't need a babysitter," Joseph repeated.

CHAPTER THIRTEEN

The next day, the whole thing seemed like a nightmare. Like it had happened to someone else instead of to Joseph. He woke up as usual in the morning. Better, even, since he woke up before his alarm. And he felt good. He felt relaxed and calm, like he could face the day and put everything that had happened behind him.

Maybe examining his life during the discussion with Mrs. Kelly had been a good thing. Maybe it had made him see things more clearly, so that it made sense and he felt like he had a place in the world. Yes, he had some challenges—his parents' divorce and his father's unwillingness to make himself available when it was his weekend to take Joseph, his struggles with depression and anxiety, and the more recent dizzy or faint spells, whether they were part of the anxiety or something else.

But those were all things he could face and didn't define him. They didn't make him a different person. He was the same Joseph he had always been, with the same abilities and personality and life goals. He was still the son of Mira and Joe Senior, still the best player on his soccer team, still Joseph Demain, the same as ever. None of that had changed.

He felt good going to school. Clean and new. Confident. He was ready to take on his day, whatever it brought. He knew there would be a lot of questions, but he could laugh them off. He didn't have to take them seriously and defend himself and his wacky brain. He could just shrug, joke about it, and continue onward, as he had always done—the undefeatable Joseph Demain.

He even made sure to have something to eat before he left for school. If fainting had suddenly become a problem, he would eat right, at the correct times, good nutritious stuff, and the whole fainting problem would go away. The doctor had said that it would probably go away on its own anyway. A lot of people had one spell, and then that was it. They never recurred.

Mira seemed happy to see Joseph happy. Cheerful when she saw that he was up and happy and getting himself ready for school. He showed her that he was eating, gave her a peck on the cheek, and headed off for school, even though it was early. Maybe he would play a pickup game of basketball while he was waiting for the early bell to ring.

There wasn't anyone else playing basketball, and he hadn't brought a ball with him, so that eliminated the possibility of basketball. He went to his locker, getting everything he would need for his classes and thinking about homework. He hadn't done anything after leaving the field and going to the hospital, so he did have work that needed to be done. He knew that he could blow the teachers off if he wanted to. They couldn't exactly insist that he had to get his work in on time when he had not even been home. He'd been in the hospital, for crying out loud. People in the hospital were exempt from doing homework.

But since he had some time, he took his books to the library, spread them out on an unoccupied table, and started on the homework he was supposed to have done.

Lora found him there before the first bell rang. She looked at the books that he had spread out and raised her brows questioningly. "What's all this?"

"It's called homework," Joseph told her. "You should have learned that by now."

She chuckled. "I don't think I've ever seen you work on homework before."

"I do my homework."

"Yeah, but you do it at home. I always figured that you just had a robot or servant there to do it for you. You take your books home, you bring it back, and everything is all done perfectly. Effortless."

"It isn't effortless. It takes time and energy. And it isn't always perfect. I do make mistakes or teachers mark me down for something." He rolled his eyes. "Some grammar convention that they don't like or something. It's right, but it's not their style." He shrugged. "But anyway… yeah, I do my own homework, as if you didn't know that. I'm not a meathead."

Lora laughed. "I like that word. Meathead. No, you're not one of the stupid jocks who doesn't have any idea what two plus two is."

She sat down at the table with him. Joseph didn't know whether she was going to take out some work of her own, or just sit there and talk and try to distract him from his. It looked like the latter.

"I'm working," he warned.

"I know." She just sat there and looked at him.

"What?" Joseph looked up after a few minutes. "Why are you looking at me?"

"I'm already done my work."

"It's a library. Why don't you find something to read?"

She considered this for a moment, then stood up and browsed the shelves closest to them.

"Hey, it's Demain," William said, crashing into the side of Joseph's table, pushing the books into him and making it wobble. "What are you doing here, superstar?"

"Hey!" Joseph straightened his books and scowled at William. "I'm working. What's your problem?"

"My problem?" William repeated. "My problem is that you're getting all of this attention for doing *nothing*, and those of us who are working hard don't get anything. Does anybody even care if we won the game last night? Care who happened to get the goals? No, it's all, 'But how is Joseph Demain? Do you think he'll be okay?' Do you know how annoying that is?"

Joseph shook his head. "It's not my problem. I'm just minding my own business."

"Yeah, you're just minding your own business," William sneered back.

Joseph turned his attention back to his books and ignored William. Who cared what he thought? It was obvious that he was just jealous of the attention that Joseph was getting. That Joseph always got for carrying the team. Was it Joseph's fault if they didn't practice as much as he did? If they didn't have the same innate talent as he did? He couldn't exactly give it to any of them, could he? A guy had to have his own talent and hard work. He couldn't give it to anyone else, no matter how much he wanted to. And the truth was, he didn't want to. If they didn't want to put in the same hard work as he did, they wouldn't be able to perform at the same level. And the sour grapes told him he was still ahead, even if he had missed one game.

It would be the only game that he would miss. He would get into better shape than ever. No junk food. Plenty of good, healthy, whole fruits and vegetables and lean meats. That was the way to get into top condition.

"You're such a jerk," William mocked. "You used to be fun to be around, but you know what? You're not the guy we thought you were. You were just pretending."

Joseph looked at him, shocked. "What are you talking about?"

"You used to be fun to hang with. Playing pickup games and hanging with the other bros. But you know what? You're pathetic. You're so worried that you're not getting all of the attention that you have to play this 'sick' card. You aren't getting enough attention for your abilities anymore, so you have to get all the attention some other way. What's the matter? No scouts coming out to the games for you anymore? You're past your prime?"

"I am *not*," Joseph growled. "I'm just as good as I ever was. Better. Better than you'll ever be."

"Sure, you just keep telling yourself that. Why do you think the coach wants you off the team, then? If you're the superstar and no one cares about anyone else, then how come he wants to cut you from the team?"

"He doesn't."

"I heard him."

"He's just warning me not to miss any time. That's all. And I can't help what I missed when I was sick. I'm just as good at the game as I ever was and, if you don't see that, you're blind."

"He wants you off. He doesn't want a showboat on the team, someone who hogs the ball and has to get all the goals himself. The rest of us are tired of *The Joseph Demain Show*, you know. So why don't you change the channel? Or turn it off."

"I'm not a showboat. I'm the best goal scorer, that's all. I work hard at it and go to all the practices—all of the practices that I can— just like everybody else. If I'm better at the game, that's not something I'm going to give up just because some… untalented hacks are tired of me being better than them."

William grabbed the edge of the table and flipped it. Joseph's books, pen, and phone went flying everywhere. Lora shrieked. The table knocked over several other chairs and made a massive crash. William stood there with his fists held high, waiting for Joseph to fly up out of his chair and take him on.

"What the hell!" Lora shouted. She shoved William's shoulder and looked from one boy to the other. "What's all this about?"

"Not my fault," Joseph told her, his voice strangled. "He's the one trying to pick a fight."

Despite what had happened and William's eagerness to take him on, Joseph was glued to his seat. He couldn't have gotten out of it if he tried. His heart was going a mile a minute, so fast he couldn't feel the independent beats and it just felt like one searing pain in his chest. His body felt like a rock, so heavy he couldn't pick it up. His breath whistled in his throat, which was so constricted that he couldn't get enough oxygen no matter how hard he pulled.

He lost the few seconds of opportunity to get to his feet and take William on and to show him once and for all who was boss. Teachers and students were rushing over, pulling William away, holding him back. A couple of other teachers stood in front of Joseph, hands up, calming him, preventing him from getting up and retaliating.

CHAPTER FOURTEEN

W hat is this?" demanded the librarian, Mr. Chauvin, with his fussy sweater vests and wire-rimmed spectacles that were too old for his face. "There is no fighting at school. Who started this? What is going on?"

"Joseph was just sitting there, doing his homework," Lora contributed, motioning to him. "He wasn't bothering anyone. William comes over and starts name-calling, and then when Joseph doesn't react, he *throws the table.*"

The table was still rolling back and forth on its side, not yet settled into place. Everyone looked at it and then back at William, disbelief in their eyes.

"Are you gonna believe that?" William demanded. "You know all of the attention-getting behavior from Demain the last couple of weeks. You really think he was just sitting at the table, not doing anything?"

Like spectators at a tennis game, the audience looked from William over to Joseph again, trying to discern who was telling the truth.

Joseph couldn't do anything but breathe, and even that, he wasn't doing very well. He felt like the kids he'd seen on shows on TV, having an allergic reaction to something, their throats swelling shut.

He massaged his throat, trying to tell if it was really swollen or just caused by emotion, like when he was a little kid and would get a big lump in his throat and cry.

He certainly wasn't going to cry in front of all the students and teachers gathered to watch.

"Did he hit you?" Lora asked, shaking her head as if she didn't understand what was happening. "Did the table hit you in the throat or chest?"

Joseph shook his head, but the suggestion was picked up by the other observers, who immediately started repeating to each other that William had thrown the table and it had hit Joseph in the throat.

"You're insane," Lora told William. "What a jerk you are, coming in here and acting like you're such a great athlete and Joseph has taken something away from you. Is it his fault that you're too cool to do drills anymore? That you're so messed up on weed half the time that you don't have a clue what's going on at the other end of the field?"

There were gasps of shock at her accusations. William's face went red and he tried to escape the holds of those who were hanging on to him. Joseph shifted, trying to get to his feet to defend Lora, but the pressure on his chest increased and he still couldn't get up. William saw him shift and jerked back, ready to defend himself. Joseph shook his head and let William's actions speak for themselves.

It wasn't like he really had any choice.

———

There was some confusion getting everything sorted out, even though they were already holding William back and Joseph had never left his chair, and there were witnesses to the fact that Joseph had just been sitting doing his homework when William had come over to goad him into a fight. And the fact that Joseph hadn't taken the bait, but had simply sat where he was while William worked himself into a lather.

Regardless of what had happened, it was apparently requisite for both boys to go to both the principal's office and the nurse's office to follow up on the fight and make sure that everything was properly documented, just as if they had really had a fistfight. Joseph couldn't understand why, but he let Mr. Gerardo, one of the gym teachers, haul him to his feet to escort him to the office. He didn't bother protesting his innocence—Lora was already doing that loudly and with vigor. He just went along, happy that his inertia had been broken and he could walk. He had been worried that if he did get up from the chair, he would collapse.

He tried to hide the fact that his heart was still pounding like a freight engine and he could barely breathe. He just let Mr. Gerardo steer him toward the office so that it didn't matter that everything was swimming in front of his eyes and he couldn't have found his way there on his own if his life had depended on it.

Lora tried to come with him, but was ordered by the teachers to stay in the library so that she wasn't in the way in the office. They knew what a pain she could be, and Joseph had to mentally laugh at that even if he physically couldn't raise a smile. It wouldn't be good for him to smile in front of William or the teachers escorting them anyway. He would be taken as rubbing William's nose in the fact that he was in trouble and had only himself to blame. He hadn't been able to take Joseph down with him.

At least, Joseph assumed that he would not be in trouble once he got into the office. When the story came out, who could blame him for anything? All he had done was to sit there.

Principal Rogers listened to the varying reports of the teachers and supervisors who had seen any part of the fracas, nodding slowly and thoughtfully. But Joseph wondered, studying him from the chair he'd been pushed into, whether he was hearing any of what was being said or thinking of something else, his weekend plans maybe, as the discussion continued.

Eventually, everyone who had anything to contribute to the discussion about the fracas had finished with their stories except for William and Joseph. They were all dismissed, so the two of them were left with Principal Rogers and the coach. Joseph had not seen Beiderman arrive but, apparently, he had at some point during the discussion.

"Well." Principal Rogers folded his hands before him and carefully looked the boys over. "It doesn't sound like there was actually much of a fight. Not much more than an argument."

William folded his arms across his chest, nodding. Things would go much better for him if he were accused of arguing in the library rather than being in a physical fight. Joseph kept his peace and didn't say that William was the instigator. The principal had already heard it all anyway. Or at least all that the available witnesses had been allowed to say, Joseph thought, with a mental head tip toward Lora. It wasn't like her word was needed after everything else that had been said, even if she had been the one closest to the action.

"But, we cannot have any hint of violence, Mr. Kendall," the principal went on. "Throwing around furniture? Someone could have been seriously hurt."

"I just tipped over a table," William argued. "It wasn't that serious."

"I don't think 'tip' is the proper word for what went on, from what I have heard."

William scowled and didn't offer any other words.

"You might have hurt Mr. Demain. In fact, I have not yet heard a report back from Mr. Demain as to whether the table hit or injured him when it was 'tipped' over."

Joseph shook his head.

The principal looked at him for a moment, waiting to see if he had anything else to say, then shrugged and went on.

"You showed a shocking lack of decorum and self-control."

William stared down at the carpet and nodded. He didn't give any excuse for his behavior. Joseph doubted that William's sour grapes would get him anywhere with the principal, and William apparently thought the same.

"A three-day in-school suspension," Principal Rogers declared.

"What?" Coach Beiderman exploded. "You can't put him on suspension! He has soccer games to play."

"He has lost that privilege with his behavior. I'm sorry, Coach, but this kind of activity cannot be tolerated, no matter who it is and what team he plays on."

"Demain is already sidelined. I can't lose William too."

"You'll have to take that up with William." The principal looked at the culprit. "Remind him that playing on the soccer team is a privilege, not a right, and that if he doesn't live up to the expected standards, he will lose those privileges."

"That's not fair," William protested. "Does Demain lose the right to play for three days too?"

"Mr. Demain can play whenever his doctor and coach say he can."

"But he's the one who—"

"I've listened very carefully to all the reports, and he is not the one who started this or deliberately caused you to lose your privileges. You did that all yourself. If it is an offense to sit in the library doing your homework, we will end up with many more suspensions." Rogers gave a little chuckle. He nodded at his joke. "I can't find anything in Mr. Demain's behavior that is an offense."

"He's been showboating in soccer," William insisted. "He's been trying to get everyone to feel sorry for him with these fake medical incidents. You ask the hospital. They didn't find anything wrong with him!"

How could he possibly know anything about what the hospital had found or not found? Joseph shook his head in disbelief. William could only be guessing. Maybe the fact that he was back at school the next morning and that he hadn't given William any reason for his collapse the previous day when William had started accusing him of making it up.

"A three-day suspension," the principal reiterated. "No soccer."

"Demain did this deliberately," Beiderman insisted, pointing at him and shaking his finger. "It is his fault that William was suspended. All of his acting like he is sick or dying. Trying to get everyone's attention. It has brought a lot of negative attention to the team, to the other players. It isn't fair to them, and I want him off the team."

"You have the right to decide who is and isn't qualified to play on the team," Rogers said slowly. "But if I find out you have taken him off for being sick… there will be consequences. I don't want to violate some human rights provisions of the organizations we play under. I think you're a fair man, and you know that such a thing would be a gross miscarriage of justice."

"He's doing it on purpose. Trying to get attention and get other team members angry and in trouble."

Joseph couldn't believe the accusations. How exactly was he trying to get anyone in trouble? He hadn't said a bad word about anyone.

"You purposely got William riled up and sidelined him," Beiderman accused. "You sat there goading him and calling him names until he got so angry that he tipped over the table. And now you have him right where you want him. Sitting on the bench. With you, I might add," Beiderman sneered.

"Suspended players aren't even supposed to be *at* the game," Joseph pointed out. "He can't sit on the bench."

There wasn't any point in trying to tell them that he could still play. Joseph was beginning to wonder whether he was up to playing soccer. The constriction of his throat seemed to have eased and the pressure on his chest had lifted, but he wasn't looking forward to anything that would bring those symptoms back. Maybe a few more days on the revised anti-anxiety prescription would bring him the relief he needed.

CHAPTER FIFTEEN

The other consequence of "getting into a fight" at school was having to go to the nurse's office for evaluation afterward. Joseph did not want to have to follow through with the nurse, but he couldn't very well get away with skipping out. The witnesses said Joseph have been hit by the table. It wasn't true, but the office workers were not about to let Joseph talk his way out of it.

"You've been sick," Rogers insisted, "And now you've sustained an injury. That needs to be fully investigated by the school, or we could be liable. We don't want to be sued." He paused, and added as an afterthought, "Or for anything to happen to you, of course."

Joseph couldn't talk his way out of it, nor could he get around seeing the nurse by just going to his first period class, because they insisted on escorting him. Either they had been fooled too many times by students who appeared to be complying and then didn't, or they didn't trust him specifically because he had already been arguing about not going. It wasn't Principal Rogers, but one of the women who sat behind a desk in the main office, who escorted him there.

He didn't know her name, but he should. The office ladies were well-known to the students, but Joseph had never bothered to learn their names.

There were no patients in the nurse's office ahead of him. Nurse

Vicky was sitting with a fresh cup of steaming coffee on the desk beside her while she wrote something down in a notebook. She looked up as Joseph was escorted in and offered him a reassuring smile.

"Well, what a surprise. It's nice to see you, Mr. Demain."

"Hi, Miss Vicky."

"What is going on?" She looked at his escort, obviously understanding that this was over more than just an upset stomach or need for a bandage.

"Mr. Demain was in a fight with William Kendall. He needs to be checked out to see if he needs any medical attention. He seemed to be having trouble breathing after the incident, according to one witness. And you know that…" the office woman looked at Joseph, "Mr. Demain has had some other… difficulties lately. We don't want there to be any… problems."

"Of course," Nurse Vicky agreed. "Come on in, Joseph. Let's have a look at you."

With Joseph safely in the custody of the nurse, the office worker nodded, satisfied, and left them alone. Nurse Vicky shut the office door and motioned Joseph to a chair. "Have a seat, Joseph. So, tell me about this fight."

"It was only an argument," Joseph said, rolling his eyes. "Nobody hit anybody. They are overreacting."

"Yes, well," she shrugged. "That happens. It's easier to just take the precautions than to try to talk them out of anything."

"I guess." That was, after all, why he was there. He could have kept arguing about it with the principal and just gotten himself into deeper trouble, but there hadn't been any point in that. All he had to do was spend five minutes with Nurse Vicky to get her confirmation that he was not hurt, and then he could go on with his day.

"So this was just an argument?"

She placed her fingers over his wrist to take his pulse. Joseph wanted to pull back, but he didn't. His heart, which hadn't completely returned to normal yet, sped up again. Not to the breakneck pace that it had been, but Joseph was afraid that Nurse Vicky might think that there was something wrong with him, even though he'd had an EKG to clear up any concerns about a heart problem.

She left her warm, dry fingers there for a moment, her touch reassuring, then withdrew. He realized that she was waiting for his response and played the conversation back again in his head.

"Uh… it wasn't anything. Just William bugging me in the library where I was trying to do my homework. I was just ignoring him, trying to get my work done. He got mad that I wasn't responding to him and he tipped over the table that I was working at." Joseph shrugged. "That's all. But you know, there was a big hoopla and now they think that the table hit me, and it didn't. But they have to send me here," Joseph gestured to indicate the office around them, "So that you can confirm that I didn't get beaned in the head so no one can sue the school."

Nurse Vicky laughed softly. "I see. Well, we can certainly help with that, can't we? Did you get hit in the head?"

"No."

She brushed the hair back from Joseph's forehead, and then continued to do a full examination of his head, looking for any bumps or cuts. "I certainly don't see anything. How about the rest of your body. Were you hit in the body at all? Your stomach or your chest?"

"No."

"And how have you been feeling?" She met his eyes.

"What?"

"I hear you've been having some medical issues lately. I was wondering how you are feeling now, and how you were feeling at the time of the fight—the argument."

"I'm fine," he tried to brush her off. "Really. There's nothing wrong with me. I've been all checked out at the hospital, and there isn't anything to be worried about."

"That's good to hear. You collapsed in the middle of a soccer game? That's pretty serious."

"I just hadn't had anything to eat recently," Joseph repeated the falsehood. "It was stupid, I know. I should have been more careful. I've heard all of the lectures."

"I'll bet you have," she agreed. "Well, let's take a look at blood pressure. Your heart rate is pretty quick, but that could just be the excitement."

Joseph couldn't very well stop her. He didn't know whether his blood pressure would be normal or not. He certainly hadn't been feeling normal. But they hadn't said anything about it at the hospital, and they'd had him on one of those fingertip monitors that told them everything they wanted to know.

The nurse took out an old-style blood pressure cuff and strapped it around his upper arm. "This is going to squeeze for a minute. It will be uncomfortable, but then it will relax."

Joseph nodded. He'd had his blood pressure checked enough times before to know what to expect. She pumped up the cuff and then released the valve and listened carefully with her stethoscope. She raised her brows and wrote something in the logbook where she had started to write down the details of their visit.

"I can tell you're an athlete," she told him. "It's nice and low despite all of the excitement. How are you feeling?"

"Fine. First period class has already started, and I should be getting to my class."

"Did you have something to eat this morning?"

"Yes."

"No lightheadedness?"

"No."

She wrote a few more notes.

"You were having trouble breathing after the argument?"

"No."

She looked at him, eyebrows up.

"Well... maybe a little. Not trouble, I was just breathing hard. You know how that works. You get caught up in it, and your heart rate goes up and you breathe harder... It's normal."

"Severe enough that at least one of the witnesses was concerned about it."

"People are just looking for something to be wrong."

"That could be." She checked his pulse again. "I'll tell you what, why don't you have a seat while I check William out and, if your heart rate is back to normal after I am finished with him, we won't worry about it."

Joseph sighed in relief. "Yeah, sure, that sounds good."

She had him sit in the area outside the nurse's office where there were a few chairs for when there were several people waiting for her. She could only take one person in her office at a time. William was sitting in one of the chairs waiting, with Vice Principal Seward keeping an eye on him.

Joseph and William both glared at each other, but didn't say anything. It had all been said already, and they didn't want to talk in front of the nurse and vice principal. The vice principal transferred custody of the second patient to Nurse Vicky, and frowned at Joseph as he sat down in one of the waiting chairs.

"Why are you not going to your class?"

"Nurse Vicky wanted me to wait for a few minutes."

"I want to see if his heart rate goes back down to normal," Nurse Vicky told him, which Joseph thought was personal medical information that she shouldn't be sharing. But maybe, since he had been left in the care of the school, she was allowed to tell Seward what was going on.

Joseph shrugged. "It's fine," he told Seward. "I'm just hyped up."

Nurse Vicky invited William in and then shut the door. Joseph looked up at the vice principal, who was still standing there looking at him thoughtfully.

"Besides, my heart rate always goes up a little around Nurse Vicky," Joseph told him, with a sideways glance.

Seward laughed. He put a hand on Joseph's shoulder briefly.

"Mine too," he said confidentially, and chuckled again. He walked away, leaving Joseph sitting there waiting for the nurse to finish with William.

CHAPTER SIXTEEN

Nurse Vicky frowned as she took Joseph's pulse again. Joseph thought it was doing pretty well. His heart wasn't racing like it had been. It was nearly back to normal again.

"Still higher than I would like," she told him. "It's been quite a while since the argument. I think maybe you should take some time off to rest. Spend another day at home to ensure you're fully recovered after yesterday's incident. It's a Friday—a short day, and you've already missed the first period. You won't miss very much if you go home now."

As nice as it was to be offered the excuse to go home and skip school with permission, Joseph wasn't eager to do as Nurse Vicky suggested. He was already fighting the reputation of acting sick to get more attention, going by William's actions. As if the star soccer player needed to do something *else* to attract attention. As if Joseph would prefer the attention he got for eating dirt in the middle of a soccer game to what he got for scoring points and leading the team to victory. Who would want to be seen as a weak, pathetic, sick person instead of the hero of the field?

If Joseph went home now, that reputation would just be bolstered. *There's Demain again, pretending to be sick and going home to veg in front of the TV, expecting everyone to feel sorry for him.*

He didn't want that kind of attention.

He shook his head at Nurse Vicky. "No, I'm feeling fine. It's just…" He looked for an excuse that would fly with her. "I get anxious about doctors' and nurses' offices. That's all. Especially since I've been having trouble lately. That's why my heart is going."

"Well, that's a possibility, of course, but I would still have expected it to have returned to normal by now. You've been sitting around bored, and it is still higher than I would like."

"The hospital just checked it yesterday," Joseph reminded her. "They did an EKG. If there was anything wrong, they would have found it then. They said my heart is very healthy. Nothing to worry about."

She looked like she was on the edge of agreeing with him. She just needed another gentle nudge to get her over that edge.

"Come on, Nurse Vicky. How is sitting at home any different than sitting at school? I'm not doing anything stressful."

She shook her head. "I know what school is like, Joseph. I know how many different things are going on that could be stressful. Teachers, tests, concepts you don't understand, other students who might be getting on your case. You're obviously having problems with other members of the soccer team. I really don't think this is a non-stressful environment for you."

She sighed and put a comforting hand on his shoulder.

"Why don't you call your mom to come pick you up? You can have a quiet day at home, together with the weekend, and I'm sure that by Monday, you'll either be feeling better or you'll know that this is related to a virus or something like that. I'm just not comfortable with you staying at school when you're still having symptoms. I still think you need to follow up further with your doctor."

"I can't call my mom," Joseph groaned. "Come on, she's already had to leave work early this week to pick me up more than once. She'll get in trouble at work."

"You can't go home on your own. Someone needs to be around to make sure that you're okay. You can't be home alone for hours in this condition."

"Then I guess I'll have to stay at school," he said smartly.

"Your mom will need to get a few hours off. Maybe she can make it up another day. But we need to make sure that you are properly cared for."

"Nurse Vicky, come on. Please. I don't want to get her in trouble."

"Who else can pick you up, then? Do you have an old babysitter, a neighbor, an auntie?"

"I can try my dad… but he works too. And he never leaves early."

"He could make one exception. For a sick child."

Joseph ran his fingers through his hair, frustrated, trying to find one thing to hold on to. "I'll call my mom," he said finally. "But she might not be able to come."

"Make sure she understands that you need to go home and to be supervised. I'm sure she doesn't want you to be sick any more than you want to be sick. It's an inconvenience, but she wants you to be well."

"I'll tell her," Joseph promised.

"Give her a call now." She was watching him, waiting for him to pull his phone out and do what he was told.

Joseph slid his phone out of his pocket and walked toward the door. "Need some privacy," he muttered.

She didn't protest or come after him. Joseph stepped out into the hallway, tapping his screen a few times to make it look like he was calling Mira. He raised his phone to his ear. The door, on a pneumatic closure, clicked softly closed behind him.

Joseph paced up and down the hallway for a few minutes, talking to himself to make it look convincing. He was not going to call Mira home from work again. He didn't want her to lose her job.

And his dad? He couldn't think of any way to tell his dad that he needed to go home early and have someone supervise him because he'd gotten into an argument in the library. Joseph didn't know if Mira had even told him about any of the stuff that had been happening that week with his anxiety. His dad wasn't typically interested in that kind of thing.

Eventually, he ended the fake call and stuck his head back into the nurse's room.

"Okay, she's going to come. I'll see you later!"

"Oh, I'm glad to hear that, Joseph. You can wait in here for her."

"I'm going to go outside. Get some fresh air. I'll just watch for her from out there."

"You should wait here under supervision."

"There will be other people around. I won't be alone."

She had to know how many people hung around the entrance to the school smoking, gossiping, or just avoiding the teachers when they were supposed to be in class. Joseph let the door shut again and went on to his first-period class, even though it was nearly over.

CHAPTER SEVENTEEN

Joseph figured he was in the clear. He had seen the principal. He had seen the nurse. No one needed to know that the nurse had suggested that he should go home. And she would have no idea that he had not gone home with his mother as he had promised.

Everybody was happy and no one had to know that Nurse Vicky had any concerns about his health. She didn't understand that he had already been examined by doctors who were much more knowledge-able and had more data than she did. She was being overly cautious because that was what the school paid her to do. To ensure that there was no possible way that they could be accused of being negligent regarding their students' health.

It would all have been fine if stupid Nestor Smith had not had an asthma attack.

Nurse Vicky stayed in her office during the school day and students came to her if they needed anything. She didn't wander around the school so, as long as Joseph avoided the hallway where her office was located, there was no chance of her seeing him.

Except for Nestor.

Nestor's mother kept an emergency inhaler at the nurse's office because Nestor was prone to leaving his at home, losing it in the chaos of his locker, or running out and not having a replacement when he needed it.

But Nestor couldn't run across the school to get the rescue inhaler when he needed it; it was too much exertion and too dangerous to his health. Instead, Nestor's teacher had called Nurse Vicky, and she had hurried across the school with his inhaler to give it to him and supervise its use. She stayed long enough to ensure that it had worked and Nestor was okay before returning to her office.

And that was when she saw Joseph.

Joseph spotted the nurse and tried to turn away in time, but he was too slow. He saw her look at him with a frown, remembering that he wasn't supposed to be there, but at home resting under his mother's supervision.

"Joseph!" She confronted him, making no effort at being discreet about it. "What are you doing here? Why aren't you at home?"

"Uh... I will be. My mom is picking me up, but she couldn't come right away. So I'm just going to get the work from my teachers so I can do it from home, and then..."

He trailed off, seeing the anger and disbelief on her face. "Where is your mother?"

Joseph looked at the face of his phone as if to check for a message. "She's on her way now. Should be here any minute. I just need to see Mr. Kirkwood, and then she'll be out front."

He waited for Nurse Vicky to nod and return to her office, but she didn't. "You are supposed to be at home relaxing."

"I know, but Mom couldn't come right away. She has to work and they couldn't let her go right off. And I'm okay." He held out his hands to demonstrate that he was there and was in good health. "So everything is good."

"Why couldn't she come?"

"She has an important job. She couldn't just leave it on a moment's notice. She had to finish something first. She'll be here soon." He looked at his phone again, checking the time to telegraph his urgency. "She's going to be here any time. I just need to get that work..."

She looked at him steadily. "Go ahead."

Joseph swallowed. He could see that she wasn't going to be convinced without further action on his part. He gave her a cheerful smile and headed toward Mr. Kirkwood's classroom.

She followed him. Joseph looked back over his shoulder and saw her trailing him. She wasn't going to leave him alone. She didn't believe him and didn't trust him to do what he said he was going to do. He needed to follow through. Demonstrate to her that he was telling the truth.

Only he wasn't.

He didn't have any work to get from Mr. Kirkwood. And Mira was not coming to pick him up. Joseph was stuck. There was no way out of the situation without backing up and trying again.

"I'm feeling just fine," he told the nurse. "I don't need to go home."

"You didn't call your mother."

"She said that she'd come if she could, but she hasn't been able to get away yet…"

"She needs to pick you up."

"I know, but she just can't do it right now. I've already had to be picked up a couple of times this week, and she can't take the chance of leaving at the wrong time and losing her job. She'll leave when she can, but it has to be the right time…"

"I wanted you to be at home relaxing. She should have been here a couple of hours ago."

"I know," Joseph's voice cracked. "But she couldn't make it. And I'm okay."

"Is she going to come today?"

He swallowed. He chewed on his lip, trying to figure out the best approach. "I… I don't think so. There are only two more classes, and then I'll be at home. And I'll spend a lot of time resting over the weekend. I promise. It will be okay."

"I want you to come down to my office. You can stay there until dismissal."

"Uh… but I'm feeling okay."

"I've had enough of you jerking me around, Mr. Demain."

"I'm not… Okay, if you want me to come to your office, I will, but…" He couldn't think of any way to keep the other students from knowing where he was and accusing him of still trying to get attention and sympathy. "I am just fine," he said, raising his voice loudly enough that the students around him could hear him and know that it wasn't his idea. "I don't need anything."

CHAPTER EIGHTEEN

Gabriel woke up alert and on edge. He sat up, leaning on one elbow, listening for any sound that might have woken him up, twitching his head around like a bird, trying to recognize his surroundings and map the walls, doors, and furniture around him.

When he woke up in the middle of the night like that, wide awake, his heart pounding, it wasn't because he had had enough sleep and was ready to get up. Something was wrong. His brain had picked up on something while he was sleeping. Some sound or other sensation that told him they were in danger.

"Renata," he whispered, squirming out of his sleeping bag. He reached out to touch her to wake her up gently.

But she wasn't where she should be. Gabriel crouched, looking around and trying to adjust to the darkness of the room. While they preferred to sleep rough, some nights were too wet or cold for them to be outside. Looking at the weather forecasts, they had decided that they'd better find someone to stay with for a few days, and they had landed with...

Ray Prosper.

Gabriel looked back toward the spot where Renata should be

sleeping beside him, but her sleeping bag was flat and unoccupied. She was very close to Ray—too close, as far as Gabriel was concerned. But Gabriel and Renata were not a couple so, if she had decided to spend some time with Ray, it was none of Gabriel's business.

But Gabriel's heart was still pounding and he didn't know what had woken him up. Maybe just Renata going into Ray's bedroom and shutting the door behind her. Maybe some danger.

"Renata?" he called again, raising his voice slightly this time. "Are you here?"

There was no answer.

Ray's apartment wasn't big. He lived alone, but they could hear the occupants of other apartments talking and moving around. Gabriel didn't like the feeling that other people were living so close and could be aware of their presence there. They couldn't stay in any one area for too long, but cycled through a number of helpful connections in the Underground Railroad and the occasional hotel room when they couldn't sleep rough for one reason or another.

Gabriel crept over to the door to Ray's bedroom and put his ear against the closed door. He couldn't hear any movement or conversation. He was about to tap the door to see if that was where she was when there was a movement in the small kitchen.

"Renata? Is that you?"

"Who do you think it is?"

Gabriel tiptoed across the room to join her in the tiled space. He looked out the window briefly but didn't see anything suspicious.

"Well, Ray might have gotten the munchies."

"He didn't. And I don't have the munchies."

Since she couldn't eat regular food or even ingest her formula the usual way, Renata would not have gotten up for a snack. Not unless something was wrong and she was crashing and needed an emergency boost.

"Are you okay?"

In the dim light from the window, he could see her looking around. Searching for something. Listening. On alert. He was very still, straining to hear what she had heard or to see what she had seen outside. Cold air leaked around the window, raising goosebumps on his arms.

"Someone was out there," Renata said, her head tipping slightly toward the kitchen window.

The hairs on Gabriel's neck stood on end. He looked again out the raindrop-streaked window.

They were on the fourth floor. There was no fire escape and no balcony.

Gabriel didn't see any way someone could have been on the other side of the window unless they were Spider-Man or had wall-climbing equipment. But Renata might have meant that she saw someone on the street below, not necessarily someone staring in the window at them.

"Where? On the street?"

Renata moved beside him and looked out the window. She shook her head. "I don't know. Someone is watching us."

Gabriel stood looking down at the street, searching for any sign of a watcher. Someone in a car with a pair of binoculars, maybe, or a camera with a telephoto lens. Someone walking around trying to look innocent walking a dog or using some other costume or prop to make it seem natural for them to be out there late at night or in the early morning. The street appeared to be deserted. He watched for any movement inside the cars or someone hiding behind one of them.

Nothing.

But that didn't mean that Renata was wrong. Gabriel had gotten good at seeing possibly suspicious watchers or followers himself. Sometimes, the watchers Renata saw were just regular people going about their own business. Her paranoia was a symptom of her mito-chondrial disease, which affected her in a number of ways that Gabriel's mito did not. He was glad that he hadn't ended up with the psychological issues and allergies that she had. Although Renata had been lucky enough to avoid a few of Gabriel's symptoms, too. She was stronger and didn't normally need to resort to crutches or other mobility aids as Gabriel did.

"What do you want to do?" he murmured.

Renata continued to watch out the window, thinking about it. Or ignoring him.

He waited in silence, giving her time. Pushing her would just make her angry and, if she vented her rage, she would quickly burn through her cellular energy stores and bonk. Then they would be stuck there, unable to move on even if they were in danger. Questioning Renata about what she really saw out there would only make her more paranoid, maybe making her suspect him. He lived in fear of the day that she would decide Gabriel was trying to kill her and break with him permanently. Just as she had with her mother.

"There's a back door to the building, but they'll be watching it too," Renata said finally. "If we leave at this time of night, we will be obvious. We have to wait until day and go out when kids are going to school. Camouflage ourselves with them."

"Okay."

They had performed maneuvers like that often enough that it wasn't a shock. And there was nothing they could do until morning. It was doubtful anyone would try to raid them in the early hours of the morning and, even forewarned, there was nothing Gabriel and Renata could do if they did. There was nothing for them to do until morning.

"They're everywhere," Renata complained. "Everywhere I look. I don't know what they want all of a sudden. It isn't like we've been that much more active than usual. Is it because of David? Are they that upset over him getting away?"

Gabriel shook his head. "I haven't heard anything over the network. Have you?"

"No. Maybe he was more important to them than we realized. Do you think?"

Gabriel thought about David Sealy. As far as they knew, he hadn't been connected with anyone rich or powerful. DCFS and the doctors had been trying to get him into a drug trial program that his parents had objected to, but it hadn't seemed like it was a big, well-funded program. Small potatoes compared to Dr. De Klerk's experimental mito protocol Gabriel had been forced into.

But maybe it had still been important to someone to get him into that program. It was impossible to know all of what went on behind the scenes, who all of the people involved were, and who was getting money for the parts they played. Sometimes the payouts, even for a small study, were mind-boggling.

"I didn't think it was a big program," he told Renata, "But I could be wrong. We only did cursory research into it. They might have had big funding coming in later, once they got enough participants."

"Maybe David was the linchpin. The final participant who would finalize the deal."

Gabriel nodded, but wasn't sure if she would be able to see him in the dark. "Maybe so," he agreed. "Do you want to look deeper into the funding?"

"No. Best if we don't know anything about it. No reason to paint a big target on our backs."

"You're probably right."

They stood there in the kitchen, watching and listening, for too long. Gabriel's knees were getting wobbly. He steadied himself on the counter. "I need to sit. You probably do too."

Renata yawned and looked around. "Should probably lie down. Won't help us to get out of here in the morning if we are short on sleep."

"Do you think you can get back to sleep?"

"No. But I can get a bit more rest."

Gabriel walked back to his sleeping bag and crawled inside. His bedding had gotten cold in the time he had been standing in the kitchen. But his body heat would warm it back up again quickly. It was a couple of minutes before Renata joined him, sliding back into her sleeping bag as well.

"I'm not just being paranoid," Renata told him.

"I didn't say you were," Gabriel assured her.

"I don't know," she said after a few more minutes had passed. "I couldn't have heard someone all the way down at street level. And they couldn't have been right outside the window."

"Not very easily," he agreed.

Gabriel could see the outline of Renata's face in the moonlight.

She put her hands over her eyes. "I hate it when I can't trust my own eyes and ears. My stupid brain."

"We'll be careful. We can move on tomorrow either way. Whether there is someone there or not."

"Yeah, but that doesn't fix *me*."

He reached out and touched her in the darkness, putting his hand on her shoulder in comfort. She stiffened at first, then relaxed and put her hand over his.

"Can't fix either one of us," Gabriel agreed. "It's just the way we're made. We'll deal with it, just like always."

"With nanotechnology, maybe someday they'll be able to fix the mitochondria. Gene therapy to repair deletions in the mitochondrial DNA."

"Maybe. But I'm not holding my breath."

"Well, no. That would be pretty stupid." Renata chuckled.

Gabriel relaxed, glad she was able to laugh at their situation. They would get through this, just like every other challenge they had faced so far. Renata had recognized her own paranoia without his saying anything about it. That was a good sign.

If Renata was hallucinating faces outside the window, that was not good. He didn't say anything for a while, waiting to see if Renata would drift off to sleep. She didn't, but moved around restlessly, first pushing his hand away and then later cuddling up to him.

"Do you think you need a med adjustment?" Gabriel asked.

"No." Her tone was sharp and suspicious.

"If you think your paranoia is getting worse, or you're seeing things that aren't—that don't make sense—you might need to have your dosage adjusted. Our needs change over time. Sometimes something stops working or needs to be increased."

"I don't need anything changed. If you think I do..." Her tone was accusing.

"I don't. It's your body, not mine. You know it best. I'm just asking because of what you said. If you're worried that the paranoia is worse, maybe something needs to be changed."

"No one is experimenting on me. No way."

"No. Nothing experimental. Nothing new. No doctors you're not sure of. Nothing like that."

"I don't trust any of them."

"Okay."

"You can't make me go."

"I won't."

"Yeah." There was silence between them for a long time. Then Renata whispered "yeah" again, very softly. Gabriel listened to her breathing until he fell asleep.

CHAPTER NINETEEN

L etty looked at the form before going into the house. She double-checked the house number to ensure she had the right place. It wouldn't do to walk into the wrong house, telling them that they were under investigation when they weren't— no need to give anyone a heart attack unnecessarily.

She was surprised at the house. It was a nice place and, from what she read in the intake, the parent in the home was a single mom with a low-level job. She must be making more than they believed to keep a nice home in a nice area of town.

Letty stepped out of the car, composed her professional-looking suit, and walked up the sidewalk to the door. She rang the doorbell and knocked firmly. A double punch to let them know that this was a serious caller, it also addressed the issue of non-working doorbells. She hated being left on the doorstep wondering whether the bell had rung and they were ignoring her or whether they were just unaware that there was anyone there.

There was no answer. Letty tried again. When there was still no response from the occupants, she walked around the house, looking in windows. It was a fairly neat house, lived-in but not too messy. No immediate red flags for abuse or neglect. The yard was a little unkempt. It was probably low on the list of priorities. Work, kid, house, car, and then the yard. A sign that Mom's plate was full. Whether it was overwhelming, Letty didn't yet know.

Around the side of the house, Letty peered into a study. Maybe once the ex-husband's home office, it now appeared to be the kid's entertainment room—a junior man cave.

The boy in question was hunched over the computer, his attention focused intently on the screen, fingers moving quickly over the keyboard. Gaming, of course. Or maybe chatting with a friend. Unlikely he was doing homework.

Letty banged on the window. With the headphones over his ears blocking out the sound, it took a few times before she got his attention. He turned to look at the window, a frown on his face, and then jumped when he saw someone standing there. He looked at Letty, mouth open in an O.

Letty pointed toward the front door. "Meet me at the front door," she mouthed through the glass.

He stared at her, unsure what to do.

"The door," Letty repeated loudly, motioning toward it again. "Open the door!"

He looked uncertain about this. He had probably been told not to talk to strangers, not to let people he didn't know into the house. But he was old enough and big enough to consider himself equal to an adult, and she was a woman, so he wouldn't feel too threatened by her. Whoever heard of a female kidnapper taking older teenage boys?

He paused his game, took off his headphones, and gestured to indicate that he was going to the door. Letty hurried through the last part of the yard, circling back to the front door.

The boy opened the door. He was taller than she was, blond and skinny, with hair long enough to fall below his ears.

"Yeah?" he asked cautiously.

"Are you Joseph?"

"Yes."

Letty stepped forward, and Joseph took a corresponding step back, letting her into the house.

"Uh—my mom isn't home right now. You should probably come back later, when she's home from work."

"Why don't you give her a call and tell her she needs to come home now?"

He opened his mouth and nothing came out. He opened and closed it a few times, looking flummoxed.

Letty produced her business card and handed it to him, though he could have seen the same information on the badge she wore on a lanyard around her neck.

"I'm Letty Miller from the Department of Family Services."

He shook his head as if he had no idea what that meant.

"I'm a social worker," Letty filled in. "I'm here to follow up on a report filed concerning your safety."

His mouth opened again. This time, he managed to force a few words out.

"What? You're a social worker?"

"Yes."

"Like at the hospital?"

"Some social workers work out of the hospital, yes. I work on reports on endangered children."

"Endangered?"

"Children who are abused, neglected, or at risk in other ways."

"There are no little kids here. There's just… me."

"Yes," Letty agreed evenly, waiting for him to process this. It took time to get the point across sometimes. Some families had been involved with family services a lot and knew what was going on as soon as she showed up. Some had tiny children who knew exactly who she was and had been told what to say to her. Or not say. The Demain family had not had much contact with DCFS in the past, so it took Joseph some time to get used to the idea.

"You think *I'm* in danger?" Joseph asked eventually. He shook his head. "Who do you think I am in danger from?"

The way he said it, it was evident he was thinking about things like mafia or spies or something equally unlikely. Too much TV. Not enough real-life experience.

"We just want to make sure that you are safe in the home." Letty walked around the living room, looking at the various items on side tables, the books on the bookshelf, the pictures on the mantle.

It wasn't a pigsty, suggesting that there was neglect. Joseph was properly dressed. The living room was not overly clean and neat, which would have been a red flag for her of too-strict discipline, bordering on abuse. Both messiness and extreme tidiness were red flags.

"Of course I'm safe," Joseph said, shaking his head. He looked at his phone, practically pasted to his palm. It seemed like it wouldn't be long before kids would be having them implanted. "Did something happen?"

"How long before your mother gets home?"

"I don't know. She's late sometimes."

"You could text her that she needs to come home to talk to me."

He didn't appear to think this was a good idea. "I don't want her to get in trouble at work."

"Why would she get in trouble for taking care of you?"

"Well, it's not for taking care of me. It's for missing work. For leaving early. She can't just walk out whenever she wants to."

"Has that been a problem for the school?"

Of course, Letty already knew the answer to this question. She knew that the school had asked Mira Demain to pick up her son following the altercation on Friday. And she had not come. She had elected, despite the recommendations of a medical professional concerned with Joseph's health, not to pick him up. Joseph had been having a number of problems lately, maybe as the result of his parents' divorce, and the school had concerns. It was the first time they had made an official report to DCFS, but various concerns had been expressed when the nurse spoke to the call center worker. Not just one incident, but a number of them that had led up to a call being placed when the mother had refused to pick up her son.

"Well…" Joseph tried to formulate an answer. "No, I don't think so. It's just that Mom has had to leave work to pick me up a few times lately, and she couldn't do it last time." He shrugged uncomfortably. "She didn't really *need* to come. I was fine. I went to my classes and I went home at the end of the school day."

"The school was concerned about your well-being, but your mother didn't seem to think that it was an issue. Why is that?"

"Well, it wasn't really that... the nurse just went overboard. She thought I should go home to rest, but I didn't need to. I told her that."

"You told your mother that?"

"I told Nurse Kelly that."

"I'd like you to call or text your mom and tell her she needs to come home. I don't want to wait for hours. And I don't think you want to entertain me for that long."

He gave a little laugh, but he still didn't make the call. "Maybe you could come back at a better time. When she's home."

"That would be rather inconvenient. I'm here now. I don't want to have to come back later this evening. I do have my own family and personal life. Right now, I'm on the clock. In a couple of hours, I need to be home with my own kids, being a mom."

Joseph looked slightly interested in this. A more normal topic, something he could relate to better.

"You have kids? Little kids or big ones?"

"Eleven and thirteen."

"In-betweeners. Who takes care of them when you're not home?"

"They have after-school care. Their father picks them up from there, and they'll have supper together and do homework. Then I'll get home and have a little time to spend with them before bed."

It wasn't very much time. Letty wished she had more. But her life was very busy. Her job took up a lot of time. She and her husband juggled the childcare the best they could. It did make Letty a little sad sometimes. But she tried not to focus on that. She made a big difference in the lives of a lot of children. The kids that she rescued from bad situations; abusive and negligent families, child trafficking, homeless and drug addicted kids on the street. The impact that she had on all of those lives could not be ignored. It didn't outweigh the needs of her own kids, but it had to be balanced against her time as a mother. The work she did was important. It could be of life-or-death importance to those children.

She looked back at Joseph. While he didn't appear to be neglected or abused, looks could be deceiving, and the concerns expressed by the school and Joseph's responses were starting to move the balance.

She didn't like the fact he was so adamant about not calling his mother home. Was it because he had something to hide? Because her work position was so precarious? If he called her, would there be reprisals? A punishment for daring to interrupt her important work?

"Why don't you give me her number, and I'll call her?"

Joseph looked like the suggestion appealed to him. "You'll call her?"

"Yes. If you think that would be better. I just thought you might want to talk to her personally. Moms like to hear from their kids. You could explain what's going on. Prepare her for what will happen when she gets home."

"I'm not sure what's happening," Joseph said, shaking his head. "You'd be better at explaining it than I would be."

"All right. Give me her number."

Joseph did so, and Letty tapped it into her phone. Joseph seemed very anxious, starting to pace around and not sure what to do with himself. The phone rang a few times before Mira Demain answered the call. She was lucky. A lot of people didn't answer calls they didn't recognize. That would force Letty to leave a message or send a text, which wasn't ideal, and then wait for a call back.

"Hello?"

Letty introduced herself briskly and explained that she needed Mira to come home immediately. Mira gave a little gasp.

"What's wrong? Is Joseph okay? Did he have another…. spell?"

"He's all right. He didn't want to be the one to call you because he was worried about your job. He's here with me."

"Did Joseph call you? I don't understand."

"No, we can't give you any of the details about the report that was filed. But it was not made by Joseph."

"No, of course not," she agreed.

"How long will it take you to get here?"

"Is it that urgent?" Mira stalled.

"Yes, we need to get this taken care of."

"It's just that I'm working. I don't want to have to take time away from the job."

"What time are you supposed to be working until?"

"Just until four-thirty," she said, sounding relieved.

"Well, you wouldn't be leaving very early, then. It will take you what, fifteen minutes to get here?"

Mira sounded choked when she answered. She did not appreciate being pressured into leaving work. But she didn't push back any more.

"It will be more like... twenty, twenty-five."

Letty knew Mira was trying to push it as close as she could to four-thirty so that she wasn't leaving early.

"I will see you in twenty minutes, then," Letty told her firmly.

CHAPTER TWENTY

"W" hy don't you show me your room while we wait?" Letty
suggested to Joseph.

He hesitated, looking for a way to turn her down.
But as a teenager, he probably had a pretty good idea that fighting
social services was not a good idea and would not get him anywhere.
If he told her no, she would insist when Mira made it home. Mira
would know it was in her best interest to be as accommodating as
possible if she didn't want to lose her son.

"I didn't get a chance to clean it," Joseph said uncomfortably.

"I've seen messy rooms before. And don't forget, I have two
'tweens' of my own. Children are not exactly tidy creatures, no matter
how hard you try to train them."

He looked amused at the idea that her own children were not
angels. "They don't keep their rooms clean?"

She shook her head. "Nope."

She didn't try to temporize and say that she still tried to keep
them as clean as she could, that they would get grounded if they
refused to do what they were told, or that they were "not too messy"
most of the time. Joseph would relate to her better if he thought that
she was like his mother and that they had the same kind of relationship, whatever it was. She shouldn't say anything to burst that bubble.

"Well…" He shrugged with one shoulder. "This way, then."

He led her down the hall to his bedroom, which she hadn't been able to see through the windows because his blinds were pulled down.

The room was dark and smelled of teen boy sweat. When he flicked on the overhead light, she saw that his duffle bag full of soccer equipment was in the middle of the floor. He obviously hadn't done his laundry yet. Joseph tried to kick it to the side, then picked it up and moved it out of the way, though it was no closer to the laundry hamper than it had been.

"I play soccer," he told her.

"Do you?" Letty looked around the room and saw a number of soccer trophies lining the shelves. "Oh yes, I see that you do. What are all of these?"

Joseph proudly told her about each trophy in turn, often talking about his goals in each game or what other maneuvers he had performed. He had a good memory for his successes and was eager to tell her about each of them.

Letty looked at the dirty dishes on his desk, piled with too much junk—primarily Magic cards and other gaming paraphernalia—to be used as a study desk, socks and underwear on the floor even though there was a laundry hamper just a few feet away, and the wrinkled, unmade bed. All pretty normal for a boy his age. She'd also seen a few neat freaks, or rooms of boys whose mothers insisted on keeping everything in showcase condition, and she had seen poverty and filth that brought tears to the eyes of even the most experienced cops. She knew what was normal and what was not.

Joseph was just finishing telling her about all of his trophies and awards when Mira arrived.

She was not happy, but she didn't rage or snap at either one of them. Letty for showing up unannounced and asking her to come home immediately, or Joseph for letting a stranger into the home and taking her on a tour of the house without her permission.

"I'm Mira Demain," she told Letty, not offering her hand. "I think there's been a misunderstanding. Why don't we go back to the living room to sort it out?"

Letty allowed herself to be led back to the living room. Mira had everyone sit down, directing them to their seats and inquiring brusquely about beverages, which Letty turned down. There were homes where it was not culturally acceptable to turn down a drink or bite to eat, where it caused offense and made the hosts impossible to deal with, but the Demain household was not like that. Mira was only asking to be polite and Letty had no problem turning her down.

"So... explain to me why you're here today?" Mira instructed. "I'm not sure I understand."

"A report was made to DCFS. Concerns were expressed about Joseph's well-being or safety. As I'm sure you can understand, each and every one of these reports needs to be investigated. We cannot ignore reports of children who may be at risk."

"Well, you've had a look around," Mira said, motioning around her with disapproval, "So you can see that Joseph is properly provided for. There's food in the house, he has proper clothes, a bed to sleep in. He attends school regularly and plays on the soccer team. He has everything he needs."

"Maybe you could tell me about what happened on Friday."

Mira looked at Letty blankly. "On Friday?"

"I understand there was an incident at the school?"

Mira turned to look at Joseph, who was sinking into the easy chair and looked as though he wished it would swallow him up. "What happened at school?" Mira demanded.

Joseph cleared his throat and looked away. "Nothing happened," he said flatly. "William was picking a fight. I didn't do anything."

Mira opened her mouth, but Joseph cut her off.

"I did just like you would have said and just sat there, even though he wanted to fight. I just talked to him. And then he flipped the table—the library table I was studying at—and scattered my stuff everywhere. And I *still* didn't do anything. There was no fight. Just him acting like a jerk and trying to call me out."

"Okay," Mira said doubtfully. She turned back to Letty. "I don't see why that would require a visit from you."

"Joseph was apparently having some medical symptoms and was sent to the nurse's office."

"Joseph?" Mira turned back to him again, her tone not a happy one.

"Mom, come on… it wasn't anything. I was just… out of breath from the excitement. My heart pounding. Just like yours would have been."

"And…?"

"And… Nurse Vicky thought that I should go home. And I didn't think so. I thought—I knew I was fine. And that I needed to get to my classes. How am I going to keep my marks up if I miss classes?"

"So… you stayed at school. And that's what this is about?" She turned and looked at Letty again. "Because he stayed at school instead of going home?"

"Joseph called you Friday to pick him up from school at the instruction of the school nurse, and you told him to go to his classes instead."

Mira snorted. "That never happened."

"No?" Letty studied both of them, searching for the truth. They had come up with an innocent-sounding story, but she wasn't sure whether it was the truth or just a well-performed cover story.

"No. I never heard anything about this before today. I did not get a call from the school to come and pick him up and definitely did not tell him to go to his classes in contradiction of the nurse's advice."

"I see."

Mira looked at Joseph, giving him a fierce mom scowl. "You tell her the truth."

Joseph shrugged. "It was all the truth. Just… not everything."

"Spill."

"I knew I didn't need to go home and Nurse Vicky was just over-reacting. There wasn't anything wrong with me. So… I didn't call you. I just *pretended* that I did and that you were going to pick me up. And I went to my classes instead. But then later, she saw that I was still at school and hadn't gone home."

"And you told her that *I* said you had to stay at school."

Joseph nodded, staring down at a hole in the toe of his sock. "I didn't do it to cause you trouble. I didn't want you to get into trouble at work, and I wanted to go to my classes."

"Well, there you have it," Mira told Letty, rolling her eyes. "He's guilty of wanting to go to his classes instead of cutting and lying around at home."

Letty didn't say anything at first, letting the silence draw out.

CHAPTER TWENTY-ONE

I think that if that's all there was to it, I wouldn't be here today," Letty said. "Or I would accept that explanation and go home. But there are other issues."

"What?" Mira demanded.

"Joseph has had some other medical problems lately."

"Well, yes, he has. But I don't see why those would be of any concern to DCFS."

"We do have concerns when we see a child who was previously healthy who, after a family disruption, becomes chronically ill."

Mira's brows drew down at this. Joseph looked blank, as if he had no idea what they were talking about.

"A family disruption?" Mira repeated.

"You and your husband recently divorced?"

"Yes... I suppose it's recent. We first separated about two years ago. The divorce was finalized less than a year ago."

"And that coincides with Joseph's hospitalization for depression?"

"Not exactly. That was a few months later."

"Joseph, how did your parents getting divorced make you feel?" Letty asked, lobbing a softball question back in his direction.

Joseph picked at his nails. "It didn't make me feel good," he said belligerently.

"No, I don't imagine it did. You have probably gone through a lot of different feelings of anger, loss, wishing you could get them back together or that things would go back to normal…"

"Yes."

"And then you became quite depressed after the divorce was finalized."

"The doctor said that's because of the chemicals in my brain."

"Did he know you'd been through a recent family dissolution?"

Joseph looked up from his nails to eye her. "No."

"Because depression can be caused by life circumstances, too. Sometimes it is just genetic or chemical, but sometimes it can be triggered by a particular incident, and I think it is pretty obvious in your case that it was caused by the divorce."

"You're a doctor?" Joseph demanded.

Mira made a sound to quiet him, sending him a look that told him not to make waves. But when was the last time a teenage boy decided not to rebel against an adult he viewed as being unfair?

"No," she answered Joseph, "but I am somewhat experienced in these things. I've seen a lot of families break up and seen the kind of things that have happened afterward. It is not unusual to see one or more family members go through a bout of depression afterward."

"Okay," Mira said, "*so what* if it was caused by the divorce? You can't exactly change that. And it doesn't mean that we did anything to harm him. Just that his depression happened to be triggered by the divorce. So what?"

"If you are not disclosing all of the family circumstances to your health care provider, then they won't know that it is probably a temporary depression that will likely go away on its own rather than something he has to deal with for his entire life."

"Maybe not. That would be good. We would both be happy if it just went away and didn't return. But this wasn't his first experience with depression."

"And that isn't all that has happened. Things have continued to develop. There have been these other episodes. Dizziness, fainting, anxiety attacks…"

Joseph threw a look at his mother, as if she were the one who had disclosed these private medical matters to the social worker. But of course, she had not. The school had been aware of them, and Letty had reviewed Joseph's recent medical records as a preliminary step in her investigation.

"What does that have to do with anything?" Mira asked. "People have medical issues. It isn't like Joseph is being neglected or abused. I don't see what business it is of DCFS."

"Physical abuse and neglect are not the only kinds of abuse. Medical abuse and neglect are things that we need to look at as well. What are a child's medical issues being caused by? Are parents pursuing proper treatment? Are they in denial or refusing needed procedures? There is a wide spectrum of medical issues to be considered."

"Joseph's anxiety attacks are not being caused by anything that is happening at home or any kind of neglect. He has an illness. Anxiety. And we are seeking proper treatment. He's been to the hospital. He's been to the doctor. They've adjusted his meds."

"Mmm-hmm. What do you think, Joseph? Where do you think these anxiety attacks are coming from?"

Joseph scowled and shook his head. "They're not coming from anywhere. They're just… out of the blue. That's what the doctor said: sometimes they can just hit out of the blue, and you have to deal with them. And sometimes, one attack is all you ever have. Most of the time, it's only once. So I can go back to school and don't need to worry about having another one or go home whenever my heart rate is a little fast. There's nothing wrong with me. It was just because I didn't eat anything."

There had been multiple episodes, and Letty wondered whether he was saying that he hadn't had anything to eat before one of them, or all of them. If he hadn't been eating before any of them, then that indicated that he had a problem with food. She would need to follow up on whether he needed to be evaluated for anorexia or another body dysmorphic disorder. It happened with athletes sometimes, even boys.

"Your heart rate was fast on Friday?" Mira asked Joseph.

"Yeah, *a little* she said. That was why she wanted me to go home.

But so what if my heart rate was up a bit? It wasn't up as much as…"
Joseph faltered. He looked at each of their faces and tried to finish the
sentence in a way that didn't sound like there was a real problem. "It
wasn't like it is when I have an anxiety attack. It was just a little
higher than normal because I'd been in an argument and William was
throwin' furniture around. Your heartbeat would have been a little
faster, too."

"What else did Nurse Vicky say? Should I call her to get all the
details, since you don't seem to want to share them?"

Joseph indicated Letty with his eyes, trying to get his mother to
drop the subject when they were talking in front of someone else.

"I told you everything she said," he replied, making a suppressing
motion with his hands. "It wasn't anything bad. I was just fine."

"Did you have a panic attack?"

"On Friday? No."

"Are you sure? Why were you sent to the nurse's office?"

"Just because that's what they have to do with anyone who is in a
fight. It isn't because I had another attack."

"You were just fine."

"Yes."

"And that's why the nurse wanted to send you home. Because
nothing happened and you were just fine."

Joseph rolled his eyes. "Mo-om!"

"I'm going to call her."

"She won't be at the school anymore."

"I know. I'll call her tomorrow when she is."

Joseph put his hand over his face, slumping back in a gesture of
resignation.

———

Letty sat in her car for a few minutes before pulling out, reviewing
what she had seen and making a few notes so that she would have a
permanent record of what had been said and what her findings were
at the Demain home.

She had kept one thing under her hat. More than one thing, of course, since she was legally required to keep certain details confidential.

She had not directly addressed the possibility that Joseph was merely shamming and that he had no medical issues. He could fake a seizure or fainting spell. He could intentionally drive up his heart rate or blood pressure with physical exertion or holding his breath. He could gasp, fake an asthma attack, or hyperventilate to fake breathing problems. There were lots of ways he could fool his mother, teachers, classmates, and even doctors to make them think he was having medical issues when he wasn't.

Munchausen, or factious disorder, as it was now called, was much more common than people thought. People fooled their doctors for years and underwent all kinds of unnecessary surgeries and medical procedures to get the medical attention they desired. Joseph was missing a father figure in his life; maybe he had replaced him with doctors, the principal, and other responsible adults. Other adults who would step in and nurture him in his father's absence.

For that matter, Mira could be making him sick. It might be more than medical neglect, she could be intentionally giving him something that was causing the depression and anxiety symptoms.

The hospitalization after the divorce was suspicious. It sounded like too much of a coincidence not to be related. He had been distressed due to the divorce, and he had acted out and done whatever was necessary to get the attention of his mother and other adults. He wanted to feel safe and protected, and that was what the stay at the psych ward had given him. She could see by the number of trophies he had and how he talked about them that he was the kind of kid who needed a lot of attention. He needed to be the center of attention in his universe and, if he weren't, he would find a way to make it happen.

CHAPTER TWENTY-TWO

T he look on Mira's face after the social worker left was almost enough for Joseph to call her back again. He didn't want to be left alone to face his mother and her questions.

He thought he had gotten away with disobeying Nurse Vicky's direction to have his mother take him home. He had gotten around it and no one would be the wiser. But things had gone badly wrong. And now not only did Mira know about it, but it had somehow triggered this investigation by the social worker, who thought that he had done something wrong by staying in school or that Mira had done something wrong by not going to pick him up when she was called which, of course, was not true because he had never called her in the first place.

"I'm sorry, Mom," he said immediately, heart beating fast in anticipation of her reaction. "I didn't mean to cause you any trouble. I didn't want to interrupt you at work and make you leave early again. I didn't think that there was anything wrong that I needed to go home for and I didn't want you to get in trouble at work."

"Well, you called that one wrong, didn't you?"

He looked down at his well-chewed nails. "Yes. I'm sorry. I didn't know she would call them to report you for not picking me up. I didn't even think I would see Nurse Vicky after leaving her office. She wouldn't know I hadn't gone home, and everyone would be happy."

"You lied to me."

Joseph frowned, thinking about it. "No, I didn't."

"You might not have told me an untruth, but you didn't tell me the truth, either. You lied by omission. You said that everything had gone fine at school. That you felt good and hadn't had any more episodes. You said it had just been a normal day and nothing had happened."

"Well…"

"That wasn't true, was it?"

"No."

"And because you didn't tell Nurse Vicky the truth and didn't tell me the truth, now we have this investigation hanging over us. And it could cause real problems."

"But she said she'd gotten everything she needed and she isn't going to do anything," Joseph pointed out, indicating the door Letty had exited through.

"She said that she wasn't going to do anything *yet*," Mira corrected. "She said that she would need to go over things and that she might have some more questions for us, and a follow-up visit. That isn't *finished* that isn't *closing the file*. She still has an active DCFS investigation into us. Into me."

"It's not just about you…" Joseph protested. But of course it was true. He highly doubted that Letty Miller would question his father. Or the principal. Or anyone else in Joseph's life. Maybe Nurse Vicky. But the nurse wouldn't be in trouble for anything that had happened. Any faults were Joseph's. But they would backfire on Mira. Would they charge her with something? Put her on some kind of probation? Threaten to take Joseph away?

He didn't think that they would put Mira in jail. They didn't do that.

But he thought about Renata, a girl he had met in the psych ward. Not in November, but the time before that, which Letty didn't seem to know about yet. Before his parents had separated. Renata had told him all kinds of wild stories about her mother trying to kill her and being put in prison. Joseph hadn't believed any of them, but now that he recalled them, he worried over them. What if some of them were true?

What if parents really could be put in prison because of some perceived wrongdoing when they hadn't done anything wrong? What if they hadn't done anything to hurt their kids, but DCFS thought they did and had the police arrest them? Renata had insisted that her mother was in prison, and Joseph had thought that part of her story was true.

No one ever came to visit Renata, after all. The rest of the kids who were in Psych always had a parent who came to visit them. Some every day. Some only once a week. But Renata had always been alone. No parent came to visit her.

———

Gabriel had been sitting for too long on the cold pavement. He scooped up the coins that passersby had tossed into his hat, put them into his pocket, and put the hat on his head. He looked around for Renata, but she had not yet returned.

He wasn't too worried about that. Getting around town on buses always took an extended length of time. Even when he thought he could get somewhere in half an hour, a trip could unexpectedly take an hour and a half or two hours. Missing connections, delays because of traffic conditions, passengers suffering medical emergencies or getting into fights, there were all kinds of things that could make it take much longer than expected. Renata wasn't that late yet.

He went to the sandwich shop down the street and paid for a small sandwich. He would keep an eye out for food discarded by other patrons and would end up with enough food for the rest of the day if the pickings were good.

He paused halfway through his meal to take out his phone—the most recent burner—and power it on. It took a few minutes to get to the unlock screen. There were no notifications on the lock screen; he always made sure to turn them all off so that someone turning on his phone would not be able to see anything confidential. They would need his password to access anything. No unlocking biometrics were set up. Someone could not forcibly use his fingerprint or face to unlock it without his permission. He glanced around the small restaurant and tapped in his passcode.

There was a text message. Maybe Renata letting him know that she had been delayed. He tapped the app. What came up on the screen was not a message from Renata, but a photo from someone else.

"What has put that goofy grin on your face?" Renata demanded.

Gabriel startled and looked at her standing next to him. She had drifted in like a ghost and he hadn't even seen her, he'd been so intent on his phone. He needed to keep a better lookout than that.

"Message from Carmel," he told her.

"Oh," Renata rolled her eyes. "I should have guessed that it would be Blondie. What does she want this time?"

Gabriel turned the phone around to show her the picture. Not a selfie of the pretty blond, but the dark face of her half-sister, Kiara, smiling as she showed off her two children, Malachi and baby Ja-Ki, now a few months old, his face filled out, round and happy. Malachi was still a little slip of a thing, but his eyes sparkled with mischief, and the scars from the dog attack were fading. It was lucky that he didn't have any permanent nerve damage. The three of them were all smiling at the camera, including Kiara, who was not much given to sharing her feelings.

Renata's expression softened when she saw the little family, reunited and no longer under the supervision of DCFS. Safe, for now, from any danger of the children being taken from Kiara.

"That's a nice picture. What about Jamal?"

Gabriel shrugged. "He's probably the one who took the picture. Or he's off on a gig with his band."

"They're still together?"

"Yes." Gabriel shook his head. "It's only been a few months since the court case."

"And couples can't split up in a few months."

"Well… yeah, of course they can. But Kiara and Jamal are still together."

"That's good." Renata slid into the seat beside Gabriel, where they could both keep an eye on the restaurant and the parking lot outside.

"How was your research?" He referred to the work she had been doing at the library.

"Nothing significant."

"That's good," he said encouragingly, since she was acting like it was bad news instead of good that they had not found any new medical kidnap cases in the news.

"It doesn't always get reported. I prefer knowing what's going on to being in the dark."

Gabriel shrugged. "I suppose."

"How did *you* do?"

"Not bad." Gabriel didn't take out the money to show her or to count it. Best not to show any cash when other people were out and about. Beating or killing a bum was not an uncommon activity, whether it was to roll him for money or just the thrill. Gabriel wasn't going to do anything that attracted that kind of attention if he could help it.

"Pretty good morning," he told Renata with a nod. "We'll be covered for a little while."

They didn't spend much money. A few dollars here or there for a sandwich. Thrift store clothing. Dollar store sundries, if they needed anything. They rarely splurged on a hotel, not even the ones that could be had for a few dollars, provided Gabriel could convince the desk clerk that he was over eighteen and alone. That was where fake identification came in handy. They had a couple of guys that they used regularly to forge new documents for the families they were reuniting, and Gabriel and Renata regularly turned over their own identities as well. They did everything they could to prevent anyone from being able to track them.

There were too many runaway kids out there for DCFS to care much where they were or spend any resources looking for them. But the fact that they'd facilitated a number of escapes from foster care or institutions elevated their status. It made not only the police more interested in their cases, but also various doctors and other professionals whose pockets they had picked by taking away their test subjects. And Gabriel and Renata had revealed themselves previously when she appeared on a talk show in an effort to expose the medical kidnap and experimentation conspiracies that were going on.

They had thought that they would be able to put an end to it, that the authorities would step in and clean everything up. Unfortunately, the pockets were deeper than they had thought, and there were a lot more people who were involved despite being aware of what was going on than they had realized at the time. It was much more pervasive than they had realized when they had started.

CHAPTER TWENTY-THREE

M r. Kirkwood tapped Joseph's shoulder and bent down to whisper into his ear. He slid a piece of paper across Joseph's desk so that it was centered in front of him.

"They want you down at the office."

Joseph looked at the message slip, but there wasn't anything enlightening written on it. "What for?"

"They didn't tell me."

Joseph stood up. The teacher indicated his stack of books. "You should take all of your stuff with you."

Joseph frowned. He had hoped just to be down to the office and back up again in five minutes, in which case there was no point in carrying all his stuff around the school.

"I can just come back for it…"

"No. You need to take it down to the office."

"Okay…" Joseph drew the word out, waiting to see if Kirkwood would give him any more information than that.

But he didn't. He kept his mouth stubbornly closed.

While Joseph appreciated not having his business blasted all over the school, he wished they would not be so careful of privacy and would tell him what was going on.

He stacked his books and made sure he had all of his pens and other stuff. He patted his phone to make sure it was in place in his pocket. Then he left the classroom, feeling everyone's eyes on him.

Was he in trouble for something? It seemed like everything he had done had been wrong lately. Every time he turned around, he was getting in trouble for something, even though the medical stuff was completely beyond his control.

But maybe it was something good. The principal telling him that they had smoothed everything over with the coach and that he was still on the team and there wouldn't be any other comments made about his abilities or disabilities.

Maybe he had won an award or needed to talk to a scout. That kind of thing happened. He'd had it happen before. Answering questions for an interview or writing a short essay about his game—making sure that he wrote about other team members so that no one could accuse him of being egotistical and hogging the spotlight.

By the time he got to the office, he had almost convinced himself that it would be something good. It was time for something good to happen to balance out the rest of the crap he'd had to go through lately.

No one was obviously waiting for him when he got to the office. He went to the reception desk.

"Uh, I'm Joseph Demain. I was told to come down. I don't know who it is I'm supposed to see."

"You can wait here for a minute for Principal Rogers. He just has someone in with him for a moment."

Joseph nodded. He didn't sit in one of the chairs. He jiggled anxiously and paced a little back and forth. Slowly, so that it looked like he was just walking by, rather than looking like he was anxious about anything. Anyone could look through the big windows that lined one side of the office to see who was inside and what they were doing. He needed to look calm and collected, knowing he was there for something good rather than being in trouble. Again.

Principal Rogers's door opened, but he didn't come out, and neither did anyone else. Joseph looked at the receptionist for a signal, and she motioned him to go in. Maybe he had misunderstood, and the principal had just been on a phone call, not actually meeting with someone. So there wasn't anyone to come out of the office except for the principal, and he expected Joseph to go in to see him.

Joseph took a breath, let it out again, and then stepped into the room.

The principal's office was not empty.

"I think you met Mrs. Miller the other day," Principal Rogers suggested, motioning to her.

Joseph swallowed. Heat flared in his chest. He glanced at the severe-looking woman.

"She introduced herself as Letty. Or something like that."

"Letty is fine," she said. "That's what you may call me."

And not just Letty, but also a couple of uniformed police officers. Joseph shook his head.

"What is this? What's going on?"

"Mrs. Miller would like you to go with her."

"Go with her?" Joseph shook his head, looking at her. "What do you mean?"

"You're a bright boy, Joseph. I don't think you have any problem with understanding what that means. Is this all of your stuff?"

Joseph looked down at the books under his arm. "I've got... just the books for this afternoon's classes."

"You can leave the textbooks here. Is there anything else in your locker that you need?"

Leave his books here?

Joseph shook his head in confusion. "I don't know what you're talking about. Why would I leave my books here? Why wouldn't I need my books?"

"You'll have other books at your new school."

"What are you talking about, my new school?"

Letty stood there looking at him, her arms at her sides, looking like a statue.

"Joseph, you need to come with me. DCFS is taking you into care. We need to see to your medical care and make sure that everything is all right. You won't be able to stay in this school district, so you can leave anything here that belongs to the school. But if there is anything you need to bring with you, we should get it now, because I don't know when the next opportunity will be."

"Taking me into care? How can you do that? You can't do that!" There was a lump in his throat and Joseph had to shout to get the words around it. "Where's my mom? I'm not going with you. I'm not supposed to go with anyone other than her." It sounded stupid and juvenile, like a little kid saying he wasn't allowed to talk to strangers.

"Your mother is being notified. She can't be here right now. We don't want any problems."

"But she has to come here. I can't leave with you. I need to go home."

"Is there anything else in your locker, Joseph?" she persisted.

Joseph didn't know what to say. What was in his locker? He wasn't even sure. It wasn't like he kept anything important in there. A lunch, a jacket, maybe a change of shoes in case he got to school while it was raining and needed something dry.

"Why don't you leave your books here while you go look," Principal Rogers said helpfully. "I'll sort out what belongs to the school. And you can leave your locker unlocked when you are done. We'll clean it out."

"But I'm going to be coming back here," Joseph protested. "I'm not going to be gone forever. Just… a day or two while we convince them that this is… ridiculous."

"Make sure you have your personal stuff. Do you need a box?"

"I don't want a box!" Joseph shouted. "I'm not going with her. I'm coming back here. I'm not going to school somewhere else. This is where I attend school. I'm on the honor list. I'm on the soccer team. I'm not going anywhere. What about playoffs? You need me during playoffs!"

"The team will miss you," Rogers admitted. "I'm very sorry about all of this. We're all sorry to see you go."

"I'm going back to my math class," Joseph decided. "I don't want to miss anything."

He turned to go back to the classroom. One of the cops had moved to block the door. The other was moving toward him.

"Calm down, Mr. Demain," Letty told him. "I realize this is a shock, but you need to listen to the authorities and do what you are told. We want to protect you."

"This isn't protecting me. This is stupid. This is ridiculous. I have a family. I have a mom. I don't need anything else. She takes care of me and I'm… I'm independent, not a little kid. I can do what I want to. You can't take me away from her."

"I don't want this to be a physical confrontation, Mr. Demain. I know you are confused and it seems like we are moving too quickly, but that's what we have to do. Please come with me quietly, and don't escalate this. You're old enough to understand that sometimes we must do things we don't want to. This is one of those times. You'll have the opportunity to express your opinion about it later."

"No." Joseph wasn't going to let this happen. This kind of thing happened to people who were soft and didn't stand up for themselves. This kind of thing happened when social workers were confused and no one set them straight as to the facts of the situation. He could talk himself out of it if he could find the right words. He could walk away, and they wouldn't be able to do anything about it because he was old enough to make his own choices. Wherever they put him, he would just run away and keep running away until they gave up and let him stay with Mira.

CHAPTER TWENTY-FOUR

Joseph took two more quick strides toward the door, expecting the cops to fall back and allow him through. He ran directly into the chest of the burly cop standing in front of the door. It was like running into a brick wall. He was solid and didn't give way.

Joseph had the physique of a soccer player, not a football player. He didn't have the muscle and poundage to actually fight someone with the size and bulk of the cop.

"Hey. Move it," he objected, and tried to shove the cop to the side. "You can't force me to go with you."

"I'm afraid you're wrong there," the cop said flatly.

Joseph expected him to either sound regretful about what he had to do or to be angry and aggressive. But he wasn't either one. He stood there, blocking Joseph but not doing anything else, waiting to see what his choice would be.

"Get out of my way," Joseph gave him another shove to try to shift him out of the way.

He wasn't sure what happened but, in an instant, the cop had Joseph's arm twisted behind his back.

"Ow! Hey! You're hurting me! Let go!"

The cop did not let go. The other one joined him, and together, they handcuffed Joseph's wrists behind his back, then patted down his pockets. One of them pulled out Joseph's phone and passed it to Letty.

"No, that's mine," Joseph protested. "You can't take it away. Get me out of these handcuffs. I haven't done anything. You can't arrest me."

"You're not under arrest. But keep fighting us, and it could become a charge of assaulting a police officer."

"No. I just want to go to my class or home. This is ridiculous."

"Let's go." One of them grabbed him by the elbow and hustled him forward.

"No—" Joseph tried to put the brakes on, but it was no good. The two men were both bigger and stronger than he was and had doubtless wrestled dozens of suspects bigger and stronger than Joseph was. They tightened their grips and continued to haul him out the door, out through the administrative office to the lobby, and from the lobby out the front doors.

There was a police car parked in front of the school. And a dark-colored four-door that Joseph could only assume belonged to Letty.

He stumbled down the concrete stairs, being rushed at an awkward pace that was both too fast and too slow at the same time. But the cops didn't let him fall. Didn't toss him down the stairs to soften him up. Nothing like he had ever seen in action shows on TV. They walked up to the cars and stopped. Joseph stared into the back of the squad car, through the bars set in the window. Were they going to take him in that? Were they really going to put him into a police car like a criminal?

"It's your choice, Joseph," said Letty, who had followed them out. "Do you want to go to the foster home that I have arranged, or would you like to go to the secure facility where we take delinquents who can't follow directions?"

"You can't lock me up for no reason! You can't just send me to juvie for nothing. I have rights."

"As a child, you do not have the same rights as an adult. And one of the rights that you do not have is deciding where you live. That decision is made by your guardian. And as of an hour ago, I am your guardian. And I am the one who will decide whether it is the foster home or the juvenile holding center. Which one do you prefer?"

Joseph swallowed. There were tears on his cheeks now, but he had no idea of when he had started crying. They weren't tears of fear or grief. It was anger. He looked at the two cars, knowing that he had a decision to make and didn't know how to make it.

"You want to go to the foster home," Letty said eventually. "It will be much easier on you. You are not a hardened offender. So, seeing as you want to go to the foster home, you want to get into my car. All you have to do is walk over and sit in the passenger seat."

Joseph tried to swallow the lump in his throat, nodding.

"Okay. The police are going to remove the handcuffs and you are going to get in. Understood? And I expect you to do whatever I tell you to. If I want your opinion about something, I will ask you. The rest of the time, you will listen to what I tell you."

It wasn't fair. It just wasn't fair. Joseph wanted to explode. He wanted to be like the ninja fighters in a TV movie, knocking everyone down like bowling pins and making his escape. Why was this happening? What had he ever done wrong that had led to his being taken away from his mother and his school like this?

"Joseph?" Letty prompted.

He nodded again.

"Okay."

Letty asked them to take off the handcuffs. One of the cops unlocked the bracelets one at a time and freed him. Joseph folded his arms, trying to show that he was doing as he was told and not fighting but, at the same time, that he was not broken. He was not scared. They could not get to him that easily.

What he felt was small and vulnerable. He was smaller than everybody else there. He was too weak to fight them. They had power endowed on them by the government that meant that he had to obey them or suffer the consequences.

He stood there looking at Letty with his arms folded, waiting for her to tell him what to do next. He wanted to go back into the school to look in his locker, though he knew it was too late. What if he had personal stuff in there that would just get thrown into the garbage?

What if there were things of personal importance that he would never see again?

He also still wanted to go back to his class and pretend that it was just a regular day and nothing was happening and nothing would ever change in his life. And he wanted to go home and see that Mira was still there and that none of his possessions had been touched. He would crawl into bed and pull the covers over his head, like when he was little, and used to hide from the monsters that populated his bedroom after the sun went down.

He felt pulled in so many different directions, but they were all directions he couldn't go. He had to listen to Letty Miller and go wherever she told him he had to go.

"Where's my mom?" he asked, hearing a whine in his voice. "Does she know what's going on? I want to talk to her."

"You can't talk to her right now. Please get in the car."

Joseph turned toward it. "This one?"

Was he supposed to get into the front or the back? Would she be offended if he got in the front seat like they were equals? Would she expect him to sit in the back like a child in a car seat, like the little kids she transported? He had so little idea of her expectations; he felt like a leaf fluttering in the wind, shaking all over the place.

Letty gave him a strange look, raising one eyebrow. "Yes, this car," she said, and motioned to the front door. "Climb in. Make yourself comfortable."

Like he would be comfortable sitting beside her or being transported to this new foster family that he'd never even met before. He was the furthest thing from comfortable.

But Joseph opened the door and climbed in. He was doing what he was told. He wasn't ready to fight the two cops and end up in a juvenile home instead of a foster family. At least with a foster family, he would have some freedom of movement and was less likely to get beaten up for looking at someone funny. He wouldn't be incarcerated with a bunch of rejects, most of whom were convicted of something or had behavioral problems. He wouldn't be locked into a cell every night and have to eat slop from a cafeteria line whenever the meal bells rang. All of those other things that he had seen on TV... gangs, shivs, beatdowns in the yard, and worse in the showers.

He swallowed. There was still a big lump in his throat that wasn't going away.

"Seatbelt on," Letty said when she got into the driver's seat. Joseph automatically obeyed, clicking the buckle into place. He always wore a seatbelt when they drove. There wasn't any question of it. How many times had he heard stories of how children had fallen out of cars, been thrown out in an accident, or sustained other terrible injuries because they hadn't followed this simple safety measure?

He wasn't the type to tempt fate.

CHAPTER TWENTY-FIVE

Where are we going?" Joseph asked. He cleared his throat, trying to get rid of the hoarseness. He struggled to breathe, just as he had after the argument with William and the subsequent table-throwing incident. Like he was breathing through a straw, narrow and constricted, laboring with every breath.

"To your foster family."

"I know, but who are they? What are they like?"

"Ah. You are going to the Brewsters. Experienced foster family. They usually have four or five children. They've recently graduated one of their boys, so they have an opening. They'll be a good, stable family for you. Phoenix is a stay-at-home mom. Dad is Quentin. Both are very involved in parenting. I think it will be good for you to be back in a two-parent home."

"This isn't because of my dad leaving," Joseph told her through gritted teeth. He had tried to tell her that before, but she hadn't listened.

"Not directly, maybe," Letty said with a shrug. "But I think teenage boys especially need a stable male influence in the home. We live in a world where there are too few male role models. Or *good* male role models."

"My dad is still a good role model."

She looked away from the street to look at his face for a moment, then focused back on her driving.

"I'm sure he is," she agreed. "But he hasn't been very involved lately, has he?"

Joseph bit his thumbnail, thinking through his answer. He could easily say that his father was involved in his life, but it wasn't really true. He could say he didn't want him to be more involved, but he did. His dad had skipped out on several of his assigned weekends recently and, even if Joseph told himself ahead of time that he was probably not going to show up as scheduled, he still felt both angry and abandoned when his father called with an excuse. Or when Mira called Joe Senior to find out where he was, only to discover that he had forgotten it was his weekend.

How hard was it to mark every second weekend on the calendar?

"He's busy with work. He has an important job," Joseph said finally.

"Uh-huh. Well, you'll see Quentin every day. Not just once or twice a month. I think that will be better for you."

Her assumptions about what was best for Joseph made the lump in his throat grow into a hot ball of fire. Joseph looked out the window, wanting to disengage from the conversation. He didn't want to know anything else about the foster family. He didn't want to know anything else about them or the list of things Letty Miller had decided that Joseph needed in his life. She should have left him at home with Mira, where he belonged. Where he could continue to go to the same school and play soccer.

"I know this is difficult," Letty sympathized. "It would be for anyone, and you've had a hard time the last few months. Your life has been very disrupted, and this is just one more thing to adjust to. I wish there was a way I could solve things for you without causing more disruption, but I can't. So we just have to deal with this transition period, knowing that when you get through it, things will be better for you."

"It's not better to take me away from my mom and my school. That's crazy. She's a good mom. She doesn't do anything to hurt me.

She doesn't neglect me. She works hard to pay all the bills and put food on the table."

"Of course she does. But I think she's trying to do too much, maintaining that home rather than moving to a smaller, more affordable place. She wouldn't have to work so hard if she was willing to make a few changes."

Joseph opened his mouth to argue, then closed it again. When he thought through his arguments, he couldn't follow them through to the conclusions he wanted to make. "She's a good mother," he repeated instead.

"Do you remember talking to a social worker at the hospital?"

"Yeah." Joseph tried to remember the name of the woman who had interviewed him. "Mrs. Kelly?"

"That's right." Letty looked at him again for an instant, and Joseph tried to remember anything he had told Mrs. Kelly that they were now using against him. He couldn't come up with anything. He didn't think he had told her anything that would make her believe he was neglected or abused.

"You told her that you felt like your mother was smothering you and you wanted to be able to do things for yourself and make decisions on your own."

"Well… that didn't mean I wanted to be taken away from her." Joseph shrugged. "Everybody feels like that sometimes. It doesn't mean that she's done anything wrong."

"Of course not, but it tells us a little bit of where your head is. I think you're struggling with coming to terms with your dad leaving and your mom holding you more tightly as a response. And you are old enough that a lot of these decisions should be given to you."

"Then why won't you let me choose where to live?"

"I did. I let you choose between juvenile detention and the Brewsters."

"I mean, I should be able to choose to stay with my mom."

"I think you need some distance from her before making that decision. I think you need to be able to separate from her enough to see how much she is controlling you."

They hit the freeway, which was backed up with rush-hour traffic.

Letty sighed and stopped the car, waiting for the traffic to start moving again. They crept forward only by inches at a time.

"Mrs. Kelly thought that you would benefit from some therapy. Either individual or family therapy with your mom. Maybe even with your dad, to understand all of the issues that are going on and help the family to work them through."

"I told her that we didn't need therapy."

Letty nodded. "Uh-huh."

Joseph looked at her. "If I'd said we would do family therapy, would you have let me stay with my mom? If I knew that, I would have done it. I don't care. It's not going to help, but I would do it if you told me that was the only way to stay with her."

"That isn't the only issue. But everything adds up, and we start to see what an unhealthy relationship it is and how it is damaging you."

"Nothing is damaging me!" Joseph protested hotly. "I'm just fine. Everything was fine before you decided to interfere. Do you know what it is going to be like to try to learn how to live in a new family? How is this going to help me at all?"

"Yes, I probably understand what it will be like for you better than you do. I know it will be difficult, but I think you'll be glad of it in the end."

"I'm not going to be glad about it."

She shrugged. One lane of traffic began to move and like, everyone else, she immediately tried to get into that lane.

"What did your mother and the doctors tell you about these... episodes you have been having?"

Joseph felt on firmer ground here. That was pretty straightforward. Medical diagnoses were something he could talk about with greater confidence.

"They're anxiety attacks. And my doctor adjusted my anxiety meds. The day I collapsed on the field... they thought maybe that was a seizure. And that doctor said that a lot of people only get one, and then they never have another one. So I probably won't get any more of those at all. Why even worry about it, if that's the only one I'm going to have? Nothing showed up in any of the tests, so it isn't like I have a tumor or I'm dying."

"Is that all they told you?"

Joseph thought back to the various doctors who had come and gone and what they had said. He shrugged.

"Yeah, that's about it."

"They believe that the episodes are psychological."

Joseph nodded. "Yeah."

"That they're not being caused by any medical condition in your body, nothing is wrong with your physical health. These episodes are being caused by your brain. By your thoughts and perceptions."

Joseph frowned, not liking the way that she phrased it. "What do you mean?"

"That they are a psychological reaction to your environment."

Wasn't that what an anxiety attack was? An uncontrollable reaction to an outside stimulus?

"Yeah…?"

"I think, and the doctors back me up, that this is the way your subconscious brain is reaching out for help. You need outside help. To be rescued."

How was that any different from what everyone else was saying about his just doing it for attention? Did they all think that he wanted to collapse in the middle of the soccer field? That he wanted to panic when he woke up in the morning or was facing challenges getting along with the other kids at school? Why would anyone want the kind of attention that he'd been getting?

CHAPTER TWENTY-SIX

Eventually, they pulled up in front of a suburban home. It looked like any of the others on the block. Middle class. Maybe thirty years old. A house with a white picket fence and neatly trimmed lawn like any other. He was reassured that there were no broken windows, gang graffiti, or obvious signs of drug use or violence. He wasn't sure what he had been expecting, but it hadn't been this cozy little house that looked no different from its neighbors.

Letty opened her door and nodded to Joseph. "Come and meet your new foster mom."

He opened his door and reluctantly followed. It wasn't that he wanted to stay in the car or was particularly attached to it, but leaving it behind to transition to this new home was daunting. He wanted to stay in the shelter that connected him to his school and everything in his normal life. What from now on would be his old life.

Letty opened the little gate, motioned him through, and closed it behind her. Joseph walked up to the front door with her. They didn't have to knock; Mrs. Brewster was watching for them and opened the door. She smiled at them, pink cheeks glowing on her broad face, and opened her arms wide like she was going to hug them both.

"And this must be Joseph!"

Joseph hung back, using Letty as a shield between him and this ebullient stranger. Letty glanced back at him. "Yes, this is Joseph. He's a bit nervous. He's never been in foster care before."

"Well, don't be worried," Mrs. Brewster told him. "We're not going to eat you! I know how hard it can be to make a change like this. Be open to new things. Ask questions when you have them. We're not afraid of straight talk and open communication. If you're worried or upset about something, let us know. The more open and honest you are with us, the easier it will be to help you and make you comfortable here. Okay?"

Joseph nodded. "Okay," he agreed hoarsely.

"Come on in." She motioned him forward but didn't hug him. Joseph stepped into the house and let out his breath.

"Joseph, you can call me if there are any issues," Letty told him. "Mrs. Brewster has my number."

"Okay." Joseph made a sudden realization. "You have my phone. I need that back."

"I think it is best if you start your life here without a phone distracting you all the time. It's easier to settle in with each other if you don't have that barrier."

"But I have everything on my phone!" Joseph's heart pounded. "My contact numbers, email, messaging, games. I have school notes on there. I need to be able to access those!"

"No. We'll see about working toward earning it back in the future but, for now, you need to focus on actual physical relationships and actions."

"No! That phone is mine! You can't take it away from me."

"I can. And I suspect it is probably actually your mother's. She paid for it, pays the monthly bills?"

"Yes, but it's my phone."

"We'll see about getting you another one when you have been here for a little while, to communicate with your friends at school and take school notes on. We can't expect your mother to keep paying your phone bill when you are not in her house."

"But I'm going back there. I'm not going to be here for that long. I'm going to go back home. Mom hasn't done anything wrong, and you can't just take me away like this."

"I'll leave it with her, and she can suspend her payments on it until you're back there. It will be one less bill for her to pay. You want to ease her burdens, don't you?"

Joseph didn't want to be tricked into saying yes. He knew that was what she wanted him to say, but he wasn't going to do it. He wasn't going to say that yes, she should take his phone away and keep it from him.

"No, I want my phone," he said evenly.

"We'll see about you earning a new one."

Joseph looked around the inside of the house, which now seemed to be much more threatening. He was going to live there, but not to have any access to his social networks, to his friends' numbers, to anything that he had been doing on it. He had no way to reach out past the walls of the home.

The living room was only dimly lit, with the heavy curtains drawn over the windows keeping the sun from entering. The furniture looked old and worn. There were stains and scars in the carpet. The wall, too, though the paint job looked fairly fresh, had odd dents and gouges and places that had obviously been repaired in the past.

"I need my phone. You said that I could call you. How am I supposed to call you without my phone?"

"You can use Mrs. Brewster's phone. Just ask, she'll let you borrow it."

"You can call me Phoenix," Mrs. Brewster said, patting Joseph on the shoulder. "All of the others do."

He pulled away from her.

"Is this something you do?" he demanded of Letty, "Take kids' phones away so that they can't have any contact with the outside world? I have a lot of important stuff on my phone. That's not fair!"

"Much of what you're going through right now is unfair. I know that. You are not being punished. This is not because of anything you did; it's not your fault. You have been through a lot of challenges lately, and it *isn't* fair that you should have this challenge on top of everything else. But that's the only way we will be able to help you move forward. Trust me for a little while. We'll push through this together."

Joseph just sputtered, unable to find the words. What she was saying was all wrong. It didn't make any sense. She was acting sympathetic but, at the same time, was forcing him into an untenable situation. He couldn't live like that in foster care, away from his mother and his school, and not even be allowed a phone. What was he supposed to do in his spare time without a phone or a computer?

Chores, he supposed. They would load him up with various chores to keep him busy and build character. He'd seen those inspirational movies on TV. Usually, it was kids whose parents had died suddenly and unexpectedly but, sometimes, it was kids who were put into foster care or sent to live with an aunt or someone else because they were getting into too much trouble with bad friends and needed to be sent to some horse ranch to rehabilitate the animals or win a ribbon riding them or something equally stupid.

"I'll check in with you later," Letty promised, and she turned and walked down the sidewalk toward her car. Joseph watched her go, feeling helpless. She walked away, severing him from his old life. Taking herself and the car and his phone and everything that connected him to his old life away and marooning him in this new situation that he knew nothing about.

He turned and looked at Mrs. Brewster after Letty drove away. She smiled and patted his arm. "How about a snack? Then I'll show you around. You can see your new room and we can figure out what you need."

"I'm not hungry."

"Come on," she encouraged, motioning for him to join her in the back of the house where the kitchen was.

There was an old stove and fridge, a floor that was worn and cracked in places, and a microwave and modern coffee maker on the counter. There were dirty dishes in the sink, even though a dishwasher hummed beneath the counter.

"Do you like chocolate milk?" Mrs. Brewster asked.

"Yeah."

"And…" she banged through some of the cupboards, looking for something. "How about a sandwich? Do you have any allergies I need to know about?"

"I'm not that hungry."

"Just something small. You'll feel better once you've had a chance to eat here."

Was that some psychological trick she had learned while caring for foster kids? That they would feel better once they ate in your home? Somehow, that would show them that it was a safe place?

Joseph didn't want to be any part of her psychological experiments.

"I don't want to eat," he told her. "No sandwiches."

She eyed him for a moment, then nodded. Joseph didn't like that she was evaluating him, already making judgments based on the fact that he didn't want to eat a sandwich. Did she think that he was stubborn and was going to be a problem? That he was anorexic? He supposed Letty had told her that his explanation for fainting had been that he hadn't eaten. Now she would be watching everything he ate, evaluating whether he had an eating disorder. He'd heard that boys could get them too, but he'd never known anyone with one. Not that he knew of.

Mrs. Brewster still got milk from the fridge and found a squeeze bottle of chocolate syrup in the cupboard. Joseph wrinkled his nose. He had thought she had a carton of chocolate milk for him, not that he had to make his own.

"It's just as good as premade," Mrs. Brewster told him, reading his expression.

"It's not the same."

She put a glass firmly on the table, along with the carton of milk and the chocolate syrup. Joseph looked at her and quickly decided this was not worth fighting over. He sat down at the table and poured half a glass of milk.

"Do I get a spoon?" he asked petulantly. As if she were withholding it. As if she didn't trust him to have a spoon in his hand and she would have to mix it for him.

She silently got out a spoon and laid it on the table.

CHAPTER TWENTY-SEVEN

After Joseph had drunk his milk, managing some small talk with Mrs. Brewster, she offered a tour of the house.

Joseph didn't really want to see the house. All he wanted was to go home. He wasn't going to stay there long enough to need to know where everything was. Mira would call a lawyer or some kind of child advocate. He would get Joseph out and return him home within a few days. He would convince a judge that Joseph didn't belong in foster care. What kind of social worker put a person in foster care just because they'd fainted? It was ridiculous.

But he trailed Mrs. Brewster around anyway, finding out where the bathroom and his bedroom were. And the TV. Those were the only things he cared about. The family computer looked like it was off-limits. He was told that someone had to be in the room when he used it and that internet access was filtered and monitored.

It wasn't like Joseph normally surfed porn sites. But he did watch movies and play first-person shooter games. Things that the Brewsters were more than likely to forbid. Some people were like that. He didn't know why they had to be so strict. It wasn't like Joseph was doing anything wrong or planning to do anything wrong. He just enjoyed some entertainment.

"This is your room," Mrs. Brewster told him, opening the door to a small room with twin beds and a dresser. It wasn't very big, and the mattress had probably been slept on by a hundred different foster kids over the years. It was probably lumpy or had sharp springs poking out of it. It was neatly made, which Joseph supposed he was expected to emulate. At home, his mother was happy if he just pulled the covers up. It didn't have to be military tight.

"Thanks."

"You can put your stuff—" She looked at him, and stopped. "We'll get some things for you. I always have extra toiletries, and we have enough clothes to open up a shop of our own. Do you have any personal items?"

Joseph shook his head, wishing again that he'd at least gone to his locker to get his backpack and any personal stuff he had left there. He felt like a refugee, coming into this strange new country with nothing of his own.

"She came and got me at school. I didn't have a chance to go home and get anything. And she took away my phone."

Mrs. Brewster shook her head. "Okay. That's fine. Sometimes, the kids we get aren't even fully clothed, taken out of their home wrapped in a blanket. We're used to that. It's too bad you weren't allowed to get anything of your own, but we won't have a problem dealing with it."

Joseph looked at the other bed in his bedroom. "How many other kids do you have? I have to share?"

"Yes. Right now, we have four: you and three others. Sometimes, we go up to five, six at the very most. After that, things get a little crazy," she said with a laugh, making a funny face.

Joseph couldn't imagine having that many kids in one house. Even when he slept over with friends, most only had one or two siblings. Things got crazy *after* six?

"You share a room with Axel." Mrs. Brewster looked at her watch. "He'll be home before very long. He's younger than you. And he doesn't snore."

Joseph gave a short laugh. It was a relief that he was not paired with an older boy who might think it was funny to beat him up. A younger boy would be less likely to bother him and he might enjoy being the role model and taking a younger boy under his wing. He could teach him soccer skills or other things. Have a positive influence on his life.

And he didn't snore, so he wouldn't keep Joseph awake at night. Mrs. Brewster seemed to know what to say to make him feel more relaxed.

"I don't have any brothers or sisters," he told her, "So I've never shared a room before. Or had any siblings."

"Well, it might take a little while to get used to the chaos around here if you're used to being alone. But it is fun. Be sure to take a break and have some time to yourself if you get too overwhelmed. Just come in here and shut the door. You can have some alone time."

"Unless Axel is in here first."

"He doesn't like to be alone. I don't think you need to worry about that. He'll be in the playroom or one of the other kids' rooms."

"What are the other two like?"

"We have Tink, a girl just a little younger than you, and Mark, who is seventeen. Just a bit older than you, I think. You're all clustered together, other than Axel."

"Tink?" Joseph repeated, thinking of the fairy Tinkerbell from Peter Pan.

"I wouldn't bug her about her name if I was you. She has known to be quite... irritated with questions about her name in the past."

"Irritated?"

"The kind of irritated that you might need an ice pack for, and results in multiple kids being locked down in their rooms for the evening."

Joseph had a problem reconciling the name Tinkerbell with someone who would actually do him injury. He remembered the little fairy in Peter Pan as being angry and pouty, but she couldn't really do much about it, being so little and weak. She bounced around like a fly off of a window. It was probably a good thing Mrs. Brewster had warned him ahead of time.

CHAPTER TWENTY-EIGHT

A t that point, a door slammed open, and there was the sound of pounding feet and an excited voice.

"Mom! Mom, you gotta see this, you gotta see what I'm doing for after-school clubs!"

"In here," Mrs. Brewster called back.

"Where are you? Oh, here!" The little whirlwind rushed around the corner and nearly ran into Mrs. Brewster. He stopped and stared at Joseph. "Who are you? Are you new?"

Joseph nodded. "Are you Axel, my new roommate?"

"Yeah, we're roommates!" the slim, dark-haired boy exclaimed, running into the room and jumping onto his bed. "That bed is yours and this one is mine. Mine is better because I've been here for longer."

Joseph was startled by Axel calling Mrs. Brewster Mom, when she had said that all of the kids called her Phoenix. Was Axel her own kid? They didn't look alike. But parents and kids didn't always look alike, and it was also possible that they had adopted him but continued to foster other kids as well.

"Okay," he told Axel. "I guess you get whichever one you want."

"Yeah, I do!" Axel jumped a couple of times and did a backflip.

"Axel," Mrs. Brewster warned, "that's enough. No indoor gymnastics."

"Can you do that?" Axel demanded from Joseph. "I can do a-cro-ba-tics." He said the word slowly, enunciating every syllable.

"No. I can't do anything like that," Joseph shook his head. "I play soccer, though. Do you like soccer?"

"I don't know." He looked at Mrs. Brewster. "Do I?"

"You don't play soccer or watch it on TV, but you like bouncing balls off your head."

"Yeah! I like that!" Axel agreed. "Do you like bouncing balls off your head?"

"Yes," Joseph admitted. "Especially bouncing them off my head and into the goal."

"That would be fun!" Axel shouted. "Mom, can I do that?"

"You and Joseph can find a ball in the shed and practice some headshots in the backyard." She looked at Joseph. "If you want to. And you can quit when you want, even if this little munchkin will want you to do it with him for hours."

Joseph shrugged. He had nothing else to do other than wait for the other kids to get home to see if he got along with any of them. "Why don't we see if we can find a ball?"

"Yeah!" Axel yelled. "Yeah, I can't *wait* to bounce balls off my head!" He motored toward the back door. Joseph looked at Mrs. Brewster to see her response to his enthusiasm and saw that she was laughing.

"Enjoy it now," she told him. "In a couple of hours, he is going to crash and, between then and bed, things may not be pleasant."

"Oh." Joseph nodded. "Okay." He followed Axel out to the yard.

Axel rifled through the shed, pulling things out and exclaiming over various toys and equipment as if he had never seen them before, which Joseph thought he must have. If he'd been in the family for long enough to have his pick of which bed was his, and was either Mrs. Brewster's natural son or adopted, then he must have been there for a couple of years already.

Axel's enthusiasm over everything he found meant that he needed to be constantly reminded what they were looking for and that they were going to bounce balls off of their heads, which sent Axel into fits of giggles several times.

Eventually, Axel found a somewhat flat soccer ball, and then they needed to spend a little more time looking for an air pump to pump it up so they could use it. Joseph did a few experimental bounces off his head to test it out.

"Me, me!" Axel shrieked, laughing.

Joseph bumped it with his head so it sailed over to Axel, who caught it instead of bumping it back. He tossed it in the air and tried to get under it, failing the first couple of tries and then getting it square in the face.

"Ow! Ow, ow, ow! Mom!" Axel wailed, and, after scrubbing his eyes with both fists, ran into the house to get consolation from Mrs. Brewster.

Joseph picked up the ball and started doing some drills, bouncing it on his knees, then feet, then off of his head. He bounced it a few times off of the house with his head. Mira hated it when he did that and always came running out of the house to tell him to stay away from the windows. But Mrs. Brewster didn't.

In a few minutes, Axel was back out, carrying two red popsicles. He handed one to Joseph. His mouth and face were already red from the other. One thing about soccer was that the drills left Joseph's hands free, so he could continue playing while he ate the popsicle. He and Axel bounced the ball back and forth and off the house and the side of the shed. Axel got better at bouncing it off his forehead rather than his face, and was soon an expert. The sound of birds chirping in the distance blended with the thud of the soccer ball against the house. Joseph was amazed at how quickly he picked it up. He didn't remember learning the skill that quickly when he was young, and he had been considered a fast learner. Not a phenom, maybe, but he'd always been very good at soccer.

Eventually, they were called into the house for dinner. Joseph was sweaty and pleasantly tired. It felt like the first time in days that he'd been able to exhaust himself with soccer and not have to think about anything else. He was relaxed and loose as he walked back into the house with Axel, who was disappointed at being called away from their games.

"I don't want supper yet," he whined. "I'm not hungry."

"I suppose I shouldn't have given you that popsicle," Mrs. Brewster said thoughtfully. "It has ruined your appetite for dinner. I'll have to remember no popsicles before dinner next time."

Axel's eyes got wide. "I'm just joking!" he protested. "I'm famished. I'm so hungry I could eat a bear!"

"I think that's 'as hungry as a bear' or 'so hungry I could eat a horse,' little man," said a robust-looking man who must be Mr. Brewster.

"Why would you eat a horse?" Axel wanted to know. "You ride a horse. How can you get to the store or your family if you eat your horse?"

Mr. Brewster raised his brows. "Well, that's a good question." He looked at Joseph. "And you must be the new boy. I'm Quentin."

Joseph nodded and extended a tentative hand. "I'm Joseph." He hadn't shaken Mrs. Brewster's hand when they had been introduced. He'd been too wound up to be polite at that point or to let anyone touch him.

Mr. Brewster obliged with a firm handshake, nodding at Joseph as if he approved. "Polite young man. So you and Axel are rooming together. Phoenix thought you would be a good match. Has Axel been wearing you out with his acrobatics?"

Joseph nodded. "Yeah. He's really good."

"Parents were with the circus," Mr. Brewster told him. "Did you know there are still traveling circuses with trapeze acts and the like? I thought that kind of thing went out of style decades ago. But I was wrong!"

"Really?" Joseph shook his head. "I never saw one. I thought it was just something on TV. Or like, from the fifties."

Mr. Brewster spread his hands apart. "Apparently, it is still going on, on a much smaller scale, today."

There were two other teens already at the table. The blond with small features and a pixie cut sitting with her arms folded had to be Tink, and the boy with the dark hair, who was about twice as wide as

Joseph, would be Mark. Joseph looked to Mr. Brewster to see which was his assigned seat, not wanting to disrupt the order of things.

"Why don't you sit down over here," the man suggested, motioning to an empty chair. "Beside your roommate."

Joseph did as he was told, though he felt awkward sitting too far from the other teens to have a private conversation. Were the Brewsters intentionally putting distance between Joseph and the other two? Sleeping with Axel, eating with Axel, being invited to go outside and play with Axel. He wasn't exactly eager to be the full-time companion of a ten-year-old, what he assumed was Axel's age.

"How did school go?" Mr. Brewster asked when everyone was sitting and had started to dish up.

Axel immediately launched into what promised to be a very long and detailed account of his day. Mr. Brewster listened for a minute and asked a question or two, and then he told Axel that it was someone else's turn to share. Axel looked crestfallen, but he had food in front of him and dug in with vigor while the others were each asked about their days.

"Boring," Tink declared. "I'm never going to need any of this stuff. I don't understand it, and I'm never going to need it, so why do I have to keep going to school? I could be making more money working."

"School opens up opportunities," Mrs. Brewster told her. "You never know what you might want to do when you get older, and you don't want to limit yourself by failing to take advantage of getting a good education now. You'll be glad that you did."

Tink wrinkled her nose and shook her head.

"I'm never going to use it. I'm not going to college and I'm not looking for a job that requires a diploma. I can make good money with just these assets." Tink motioned to her body.

There was silence for a moment. Then Mr. Brewster went on to ask Mark how his day had been. Joseph guessed that Tink's declaration probably wasn't as shocking to them as it was to him. He had never heard her say that before, but they probably had. They probably understood that she wanted to be a model or dancer, or whatever she planned to use her body for, much better than Joseph.

"Best part of the day was football practice," Mark declared. "I'd be happy if I didn't have to go to anything else." He rolled his eyes and told Joseph, "If you want to stay on the team, you have to have a good attendance record and maintain your average."

Joseph nodded his understanding. The same had been true for him of soccer. "What position do you play?"

"Halfback. You play?" He eyed Joseph's slim frame and shook his head. "You don't look like a football player, but some guys stay small for a long time before they bulk up. Those guys can be really wiry."

"Soccer," Joseph explained.

"Ah. That makes more sense." He nodded. "You gonna play here?"

Joseph looked at Mrs. Brewster. "I don't know if I can get on the team this late. Do they have one? Is it any good?"

He didn't remember there being a soccer team in the area. Not that his school had played against.

"I think there is a community soccer league," Mrs. Brewster said slowly. "There isn't one at the school, is there Mark?"

"No. Not enough people to form a team."

"It might be too late to join this year," Mrs. Brewster admitted. "We can check and see if they'll allow latecomers, even if it is just to practice. Otherwise, you might be waiting for next year."

"I'm not going to be here for that long."

They just looked at him and didn't bother trying to argue.

"I'm going back to my mom," Joseph explained. "Once they sort this out. It is a mistake. She's a really good mom and hasn't done anything wrong. Once a judge hears that, they'll throw the case out, and I'll go back to her."

They kept their eyes on their plates and continued to eat.

"Me too," Axel said suddenly. "It's a really long time since I saw my mom and dad but, pretty soon, they are going to come and get me. And I'll go back to the circus. I'm really good, you know."

"I'll bet you are," Joseph agreed.

He looked at the others.

"Look," Tink said. "Once you're here, you're here. You're not going back to your mom, especially not as a teenager. When they've got you in the system, this is where you stay."

Joseph shook his head. "They made a mistake. They think I'm sick because of her, or because I made myself sick. But I didn't. They'll see that it's just the flu or something like that. You don't take someone out of their home because they have the flu."

"Maybe if they have it really bad," Axel suggested. "Some people die from it. They would have to go to the hospital."

"I'm going to go home," Joseph told him fiercely, because Axel was the only one who was young enough for him to be so firm with. "I'm not going to stay here."

CHAPTER TWENTY-NINE

Joseph was angry. Probably because he was anxious about starting a new school and adjusting to a new home. Everyone seemed to be telling him things he didn't want to hear, acting like they knew his situation better than he did.

Mrs. Brewster helped him pick out the needed toiletries and clothes. It was like going to a hotel and having the soap, shampoo, and shower cap provided, except it was everything he needed, and full-size. The clothes were not as bad as he had feared, but he still didn't want to wear them, feeling like they must have been worn by a dozen different kids over the years, and he didn't like the idea of their accumulated cooties and how out of date the styles were. Even picking things like a simple black tee, Joseph worried that the other kids at school would be able to tell how old and unfashionable it was. So he snapped at her and knew he was being stubborn and ungrateful when she was just trying to help.

"Mom, I want a snack," Axel whined for about the hundredth time.

"You just barely had supper," Mrs. Brewster told him again. "You can wait."

"I'm hungry!"

"You can have something before bed. Are you ready to go to bed now?"

Axel whined again, "But Mom…"

"You had a good supper. You don't need anything else yet."

"I'm starving! You don't care about me. Why are you being so mean?"

"You get plenty to eat. You know you're not suffering."

Axel started punching the wall. Not hard, but hard enough that it made a noise that grated on Joseph's nerves.

"Why can't you be respectful?" he growled at Axel. "Your mom is really nice. She's not being mean to you."

"Leave me alone! I didn't ask you!"

"You're being rude to her. You shouldn't be."

Axel stopped punching the wall and shoved Joseph instead. "I said leave me alone!"

Mrs. Brewster interfered before Joseph could push Axel away or get into a physical fight with him. "Remember I warned you he was going to crash?" she reminded him. She turned to Axel. "Do you want to spend the rest of the evening in your room with the door shut?"

"No!"

"Then you have to behave. Treat other people the way you would want to be treated."

"I am!"

"You would want to be whined at and shoved around? I don't think so, Axel."

"I wasn't!"

"You were. You have until three to say you are sorry and go find something else to do."

"Mom—"

"One, two—"

"I'm sorry!" Axel snapped. He shoved Joseph again and then took off at a run, protesting again that it wasn't fair he be treated that way.

Joseph shook his head. "What's his problem?"

Mrs. Brewster shrugged. "We all have our own histories and challenges. We try to respect our children's privacy, so I won't share those

151

things with you. But the Axel you're experiencing tonight is the same Axel as you were playing with this afternoon. They're both him. And at both times, he's doing the very best that he can."

Joseph suspected that Axel was on medication during the day that had now worn off. Or else he changed when he started to get tired. He didn't need to know Axel's diagnosis or history. Mrs. Brewster was right; Joseph could show him some compassion, no matter which Axel he was seeing.

He rubbed his temples, aware that he hadn't been his best self the last few hours either. "I guess I'm tired too."

"Well, I won't make you go to bed at eight o'clock, but you make sure you go to bed in good time. You know how much sleep you need to handle the day tomorrow."

Joseph pressed his fingers to his temples. "I don't know how I'm going to get through tomorrow, no matter how many hours of sleep I get. Do I really have to go to school? I can't wait a few days and get settled in?"

"Rip off the bandage. One moment of pain, and then you'll be fine."

———

Joseph didn't get to sleep in good time. He tried to do what Mrs. Brewster advised, going to bed when Mira would have wanted him to on a school night. But he couldn't fall asleep. His brain wouldn't shut off. He couldn't stop thinking and worrying about how things would go the next day.

He had never had to change schools before, other than advancing from one school to another with his grade. He'd never moved and had to get to know a whole new group of kids. And here, he would have no soccer. No one would know him or know how good he was. They wouldn't even care, because the school didn't play. He wasn't going to switch to football instead, even if he could get on to the team partway through the season. And he wasn't going to get into the community team partway through.

He tossed and turned. Axel didn't snore, but he did make some noises in his sleep and moved around restlessly, sometimes calling out for his mom. Did he want his bio mom or Mrs. Brewster? Did his unconscious brain know the difference between them? Did he remember his bio mom? How long had he been with the Brewsters? Had he been with them since he'd gone into foster care, or had he moved around a bit before he had found them?

They kept telling him that he wasn't going back to his mom. There was no way he was going to see her again. Why not? He didn't understand how they could take him away and never return him to her. Wasn't there any oversight to ensure that kids weren't taken away from their families for no reason?

It was nearly dawn before his crazy brain finally let him sleep, restlessly, full of dreams. When Mrs. Brewster told him it was time to get ready for school, he felt rotten.

"I'm not feeling good," he told her. "I don't think I should go today."

"Oh, you're going today. If you skipped today, you would just feel worse tomorrow. So get your clothes on and have some breakfast. I'll drive you today and help you get oriented at the school. Then, after that, it will be up to you to get yourself to classes."

Joseph grumbled. "I don't think I should. I don't want to be sick at school."

"Well, if you are sick at school, the nurse can call me and let me know to pick you up. Otherwise, you'd better be in your classes."

Joseph frowned at her. Her open, pleasant face was not as pleasant as it had been before. She had a firm, forbidding look. Underneath that soft, motherly exterior, there was iron. He should have seen it the night before when she had given Axel to the count of three to shape up. And Axel had done what she said immediately, because he knew she would follow through. Even though he seemed to Joseph to be very much a spoiled mama's boy, he knew when not to cross her.

Joseph decided he'd better follow Axel's lead and do what he was told rather than testing to find out what the consequences of disobedience would be. The Brewsters were used to dealing with teenagers and, if that was the case, they had surely learned how to handle rebellious teen behaviors.

CHAPTER THIRTY

Joseph followed Mrs. Brewster into the school, feeling like a little duckling following its mother everywhere. He didn't know what else to do. He should have been walking beside her, but he found himself lagging. He didn't want to be there and, despite knowing he couldn't simply walk away and postpone the ordeal, that's exactly what he felt like doing.

He was getting a headache, and kept rubbing his forehead and temples while Mrs. Brewster and the principal talked. The principal looked at him several times, smiling and trying to meet his eyes, but Joseph didn't want to connect with him. He didn't want to be friendly with the principal, didn't even want to know him. Or want the principal to know him. That would just result in problems down the line when the principal decided that Joseph had issues and wanted to talk to his parents about them. He had been too close to Principal Rogers. Had known him too well. He had trusted him, and he wouldn't let that happen again.

"Can I get you a Tylenol for your head?" the new principal asked him. "It looks like you're not doing so well there."

Joseph nodded. "Yeah... I should probably go home. I'm not really feeling that well."

"No," Mrs. Brewster told him. "Don't try that again. You can have a Tylenol, as long as it isn't contraindicated by your other medications. But you're not going home. A headache isn't going to keep you in bed."

Joseph opened his mouth to complain further, to tell her just how much it was bothering him. People with migraines were sometimes given a break. A headache could be more than just a headache.

But the look she gave him stopped him in his tracks, and he didn't try to argue with her in front of the principal.

"Yes, ma'am," he said with a sigh.

The principal produced a couple of white pills for Joseph, as well as a glass of water.

"Thanks," Joseph said gratefully. "It was getting really bad." He avoided looking at Mrs. Brewster as he said so. As if he wasn't still trying to get out of going to school that day.

"School can be stressful," the principal said. "If anyone knows that, it is a principal." He gave a little laugh.

Joseph would have laughed as well. The principal was trying. But instead, he just shrugged and looked away. His head hurt too much and he was too anxious to engage with the principal.

There were, he was sure, looks being exchanged between Mrs. Brewster and the principal. He could feel them looking at each other and making comments too low for him to hear. They had probably gone through this scenario a number of times before, as Mrs. Brewster got new foster kids and brought them to the school for the first time. What had the other meetings been like? Did everybody feel the same way about attending a new school as he did? Maybe some of them, like Axel, were excited to make a fresh start and to make new friends. And maybe others like Tink or Mark were so jaded by multiple school and foster family changes that they didn't even care. It was just routine.

"Here is your schedule and a map of the school floor plan so you can find your classes." The principal handed over a sheaf of papers. "Your teachers have been told that you're starting today, but you can show them your schedule, too, so they can ensure you're in the right place."

"Okay."

Joseph wanted to put his head down on the principal's desk and sleep. Except that his heart was pounding so hard that he knew he would never be able to sleep. He felt like he might never be able to sleep again.

"Here is your lock. I'll take you to your locker."

Joseph nodded.

There wasn't anything to put into his locker. And Joseph wasn't sure that he would put anything in it anyway. If he didn't put anything in his locker, he wouldn't have to worry in the future about leaving anything behind. If he had to go to a different family, or if he were allowed to go back to Mira, he wouldn't have to worry that there was another locker filled with personal items that he would never get back again.

He went through his morning classes like a zombie, oblivious to the lessons being taught. The teachers all welcomed him to the class, but Joseph just ducked his head and sat down at whatever desk they pointed him toward. The other students observed him with interested, curious eyes but, by the time he had been introduced to his third class, most had seen him already.

He hesitated about going to the cafeteria at lunch as Mrs. Brewster had advised, giving him enough money to buy himself a hot lunch. At least he didn't have to be part of the free lunch program. But he thought it might be nice to go somewhere else where he wouldn't be the center of attention—or ignored. He didn't want to have to pick a table to sit at, not knowing what anybody else was interested in or what they were doing. What if he chose a loser table? Or a table filled with football jocks who cared nothing about soccer or anyone who played it? What if he sat down and people moved away, gave him dirty looks, or told him that he needed to sit somewhere else?

But he hadn't eaten much for breakfast, and the aromatic smells issuing forth from the cafeteria were too much for him. He didn't want to waste his time searching for somewhere else to eat. So he took a deep, fortifying breath, and proceeded into the cafeteria with the press of students.

When he had his pizza and chocolate milk, he looked around to decide where to sit. This was the defining moment. Loner? Loser? Reject?

"Hey, you're new, right?"

Joseph looked to his right, where a girl was standing and had actually addressed him. He looked her up and down before answering. She didn't look like a geek. She wasn't a cheerleader either. But she was nice enough looking. Normal. He thought about Lora and had to swallow a lump in his throat. Lora had been his best friend, and a pain in the behind, and he would probably never see her again. All those times she had jumped in and stood up for him or done something to make him feel good. All of those times were over and done with.

"Yeah," he said to the girl. "New guy. Mid-year transfer. This is so much fun."

She laughed. "I'll bet it is. So what happened? How come you're moving in the middle of the year? Did your dad get a transfer or something?"

Joseph looked around, hoping that she would pick out a table where he could sit as well. She took the hint and motioned him toward one with a few empty seats left.

"Over here."

"Thanks."

"So?" She asked when they sat down. "What's going on? Why the mid-year transfer?"

"He's with the Brewsters," another boy at the table offered, seeing nothing wrong with butting in on their conversation. "Another foster kid."

"Oh." The girl looked Joseph over again thoughtfully.

"I'm not a loser," Joseph told her. "It's just my mom. She's sick. So I needed somewhere else to stay. I didn't have any relatives I could stay with, so…"

"Your mom is sick? What is it, cancer?"

Joseph nodded. He knew he'd better not make it something that would be protracted and definitely fatal. If he went home, he didn't want everyone to think he had lied about it. At least with some kinds of cancer, she could be better after treatments or go into remission. And then it would make perfect sense that he could return once she was feeling better.

"It's really tough on her," he said. "I wanted to just stay home and take care of her, but DCFS says I can't do that. If she can't take care of me, then I have to go into foster care." He rolled his eyes. "Even though I'm old enough to look after myself."

"Yeah," the girl agreed. She opened her carton of milk. "I'm Brit."

"Hi. Joseph. Though I guess you know that. Everybody got to hear my name. I just have… three thousand names I have to learn."

"You don't have to learn the name of everybody in the school," Brit laughed. "Only the important people."

"Like you."

She smiled. "Aw, how sweet. I don't know that I'm anyone important. But it's nice to have at least one person you can talk to."

"Yeah. I appreciate it. I didn't know where I was going to sit and didn't have anyone to talk to yet."

"Did you have a lot of friends at your old school? I mean, yeah, of course you had friends, but did you know everybody? Or just a few people, or…?"

"Quite a few. I went to school with a lot of them ever since first grade. So even if I wasn't friends with them, I still knew who they all were. Whenever we graduated to another school, like to high school, then I had to get to know all of the new folks from the other schools that funneled into it too, but… at least I still knew a lot of people. So it wasn't like this. Starting out not knowing anyone at all."

"You'll probably run into someone you know. From somewhere else, you know? Church or the mall or Little League or something. Or a second cousin you only ever met at family reunions." She laughed.

Joseph thought about the weird cousins he had met at family reunions and shook his head. "Man, I hope not!"

Brit cackled with laughter. Several people turned around to look at her, then turned back to their lunches when they saw who it was.

Joseph was relieved not to hear any of them mocking her. She must have had a pretty secure place in the social hierarchy.

"So, what do you like to do?" Brit asked. "You got hobbies? What do you do after school?"

CHAPTER THIRTY-ONE

Joseph sighed. "Well, nothing now. I don't have any after-school clubs or teams, no computer. I don't even have a phone. So what I'm going to do after school is probably… practice some soccer skills with my new little brother."

"You like soccer?"

"Yeah. I was MVP on my school team. But now… I'm nothing. I don't have anywhere to go except for home—back to the Brewsters."

She didn't jump in with the suggestion that he could go to her house or join her at the mall or some after-school function that she went to. She was still scoping him out. Making sure that he was safe. A girl couldn't be too careful.

"That sucks," she sympathized. "I don't think we even have a team."

"No. Don't think so."

"Maybe some community soccer. I think I've seen signs. But I've never known anyone who played in it."

Joseph sighed again. He peeled the layer of cheese off of his pizza with his fingers and nibbled it. "It's like my life is over. I know there are other places you can go for soccer, but if you aren't practicing with a team every day, or almost every day, how are you supposed to get good enough to play pro? And where are the scouts going to find you? They're not. There's no way to be discovered."

"Are you that good? That you could play pro?"

"Well… I hope so. I always thought I would at least get offers. Maybe not for Major League, but to at least try out for some team…"

"Wow. You must be really good, then. It sucks that they moved you somewhere without a team."

"It's too late into the season to change teams anyway, I think. Even if you guys had a team, I couldn't get into it."

"Not this year, maybe, but next season."

"I'm not going to still be around here next season."

She raised an eyebrow at him.

"My mom will be through treatments then," he explained. "I'll be able to go back home by then."

"Yeah, maybe. If you're lucky."

She didn't make it sound very likely. Joseph had a flash of memory of Renata in Psych. Dark-haired, frail, she had been full of theories of why the government put kids into foster care and kept them there.

He shook his head to clear the image. "I'll be going back home," he asserted. "Maybe really soon." He remembered his cover story. "As soon as my mom can take me back again."

"Yeah. You hope."

Joseph decided to turn the spotlight around. He didn't like the focus being on him, especially when he had to lie to keep it up. He didn't want her to unravel his story that quickly. "So, how about you? What do you like to do? How do you spend your time when you leave school?"

She slurped a spoonful of her mac and cheese. "Gaming."

"Yeah? What do you play?"

She listed the games that she was most interested in, and Joseph was impressed. They had a number of favorites in common.

"What's your handle?"

"BritBullXP."

Joseph gaped at her. "No way!"

"Yes." She looked at him, eyebrows raised. "And who are you?"

"DemainSlayer."

She laughed, drawing looks again. "Demain," she said. "That's your name."

"Yeah, Joseph Demain."

"I always thought it was a cross between 'demon' and 'the main.' DemainSlayer." She chuckled. "I guess it's not as clever as I thought if it's actually your name."

"Well, you've got Brit in yours."

She nodded, conceding the point. Joseph shook his head, gazing at her. "Cool. I wonder how many games we've played together."

Joseph rolled his eyes. "A lot!"

"Yeah. But I never knew you were into soccer. That's cool. It's good to do something IRL too. Keeps you from becoming one of those guys who just sits in front of the computer drinking gallons of soda every day."

"Yeah." Joseph looked down at his slim physique. He could just imagine what would happen to him if he didn't get any exercise and just ate junk all day. He usually had several hours working out every day. His teenage metabolism and tendency to skip meals helped too.

"You're pretty fit," Brit said. "I thought at first that you were just skinny, but you've got muscles." She nodded to his arm as he reached for his chocolate milk. "But I wouldn't eat too much cafeteria food if I were you!"

———

The afternoon went better. Even if nothing else good happened to him, at least he knew that he had a friend at the school, and they shared a couple of classes together. Brit wasn't just someone who had taken pity on him when she saw him standing alone in the cafeteria. They were already friends, having gone on hundreds of campaigns together. Although it was strange to attach the friendly face to the BritBullXP handle, he got used to it as the day progressed.

It didn't change the fact that they didn't have a soccer team, that he couldn't talk to his mom, or that he was in a new place with an irritating little brother and other people that he didn't even know controlling his life. But it was something he could hang on to.

It was good that he had watched carefully out the window when Mrs. Brewster had taken him to school and that she had pointed out several landmarks that he should pay attention to. He had the address of the Brewster house written down on a piece of paper in his pocket, but the town was not on a grid system and it did not use a system of numbers, letters, or names that progressed in a predictable pattern, so he couldn't find it without a map. And he didn't have a map because he didn't have his phone. Did people even use paper maps anymore?

He made a couple of false moves but, eventually, he found his way to the house and walked up the sidewalk, relieved. He was eager to tell someone about meeting Brit. Even if there was no one he was close to, he still wanted to tell the story. His foster family would have to suffice.

Joseph didn't know if he should knock on the door when he returned. He tried to remember whether Axel had when he had gotten home the day before. Joseph had never knocked on the door of his own home, but now he was living with the Brewsters and had no idea whether the rules were the same.

Joseph decided to knock on the door and enter without waiting for a response. It was unlocked—luckily, since he didn't have a key—so he stepped in as if he belonged there.

"Joseph's home!" he heard the shout from Axel before the younger boy ran into the living room and looked for him. "Joseph!"

He wasn't sure how Axel had known it was him instead of one of the other teens, but he was happy to see a friendly face and be greeted with such enthusiasm anyway.

"Hey, Axel! How are you doing? How was your day at school?"

Axel immediately launched into a lengthy description of everything he had done at school. Joseph tried to listen patiently but, eventually, he had to interrupt.

"It sounds like you had a pretty good day. That's great."

"Yeah. I had a great day," Axel agreed. "Except for social studies. And math. And we had gym in the afternoon, but I don't like gym. Except when we play pirate tag. I like that."

"Why don't you like gym? You're really good at it."

"No," he dismissed. "You have to sit and listen. And play team sports. They won't let us just play and do whatever we want."

"No, I guess not. But team sports are fun."

Axel rolled his eyes. "Not if they just tell you to go away in that corner and not try to catch the ball or do anything. Because you aren't any good."

Joseph tilted his head. "When did they tell you that? I thought you were pretty good! You were great with the ball when we played yesterday. And you're really well-coordinated with all of your acrobatic stuff."

Axel brightened at this. "Can we play ball more today? That was fun!"

"Sure."

"Can we play now?"

"I just want to talk to Mrs. Brewster before we do."

"Phoenix. You're supposed to call her Phoenix."

"*You* don't call her Phoenix," Joseph pointed out.

Axel laughed. "I know!"

"Why do you call her Mom?"

Axel shrugged. "Because she is. I know I'm supposed to call her Phoenix. But she's my mom right now." He stared off, pensive. "I don't know about my real parents. They were in an accident. I don't know if I'll ever go back to them again."

"Oh." Joseph hadn't known anything about what had brought Axel into foster care. "I'm sorry, bud. What happened?"

"It was in a show. They were doing a really hard trick, very dangerous. And they fell."

Joseph blinked. He hoped that Axel hadn't been there to see it happen. That would be very traumatic. He didn't want to know how bad the injuries had been. He could imagine broken backs and other broken bones. Faces, skulls. If Axel didn't know if he would ever be able to be with him again, it must have been horrible. He patted Axel on the shoulder.

The boy brightened. "Let's go play!"

"I just wanted to tell Mrs. Brewster—Phoenix—" Joseph changed his mind. "Never mind, I'll tell her later. Let's go play for a while."

"Yeah!" Axel ran to the door to get his sneakers on, and then was out the door, letting it slam behind him before Joseph could even turn around. "Come on!" he heard Axel call from outside.

Shaking his head, Joseph followed Axel back out the door and around the house to the backyard. This time, they didn't have to dig for the soccer ball. It was still firm enough to play with, so they immediately began to head it back and forth and bounce it off their knees and other parts of their bodies. Joseph tried not to do anything too complicated that would discourage Axel. He wanted the boy to have a good time and see that sports could be fun.

CHAPTER THIRTY-TWO

Gabriel waited for Renata to wake up, staring at the lightening sky. He knew she wouldn't sleep for much longer. They were both used to getting up early in the morning before the cops started rousting the homeless from the parks so that commuters didn't have to see them.

The weather had warmed again, and he was glad to be out of Ray's place. It was hard for them to stay more than a night or two in one place, especially in a confined space like an apartment. Renata had been constantly on edge, even more than usual. She knew her paranoia was increasing, but was having difficulty figuring out whether her thoughts were rational. Sometimes, she could think it through and knew—like the time she saw someone looking in Ray's window—that it couldn't be true. But most of her delusions were not that clear. Sometimes, even Gabriel had trouble telling the difference. They had been through so much and had avoided so many attempts to track or capture them, it was hard to know where their enemies would draw the line.

Gabriel trusted Renata to know when they were walking into danger. And if she went overboard and was afraid of what was only a delusion, it kept them safe. Better to be afraid of too much than ignoring the real dangers.

Renata awoke suddenly. She stiffened, opened her eyes, and looked around. Her hand grasped Gabriel's, and he held it firmly, looking into her face and waiting for consciousness and comprehension to come into her features.

"Morning," he murmured, smiling to reassure her. It was best if she woke up feeling good and safe. Starting the day with anxiety was likely to affect her throughout the day. "How was your night?"

He already knew she had been restless. But they each did this, asking each other how they had slept as if they didn't know. Maintaining the illusion of being separate and normal. Two friends who just happened to sleep a little closer to each other than was usual.

"Fine," Renata said, deciding to act as though it hadn't been a bad night. "Glad it's warmer. Always feel cooped up sleeping inside now."

"Yeah. Ray said to drop by any time. But I'm glad we didn't need to stay another night."

Ray had said a lot more than that. "I don't know how you do it, Gabe! How do you put up with her paranoid delusions? How do you keep her from suspecting *you*? You're with her all the time; you should be the one she sees as a danger, not me."

He was offended at Renata making accusations, expounding on her conspiracy theories. He'd tried to argue with her, telling her she was seeing or imagining things. To reason with her and make her be logical. But Gabriel never did that. There was no point in arguing with a delusion. He and Renata had settled into familiar routines and, if those routines were disrupted by a delusion, Gabriel just waited it out. He didn't push back like Ray did. Ray didn't understand that arguing just escalated Renata's anxiety and paranoia.

But Ray was a good guy, and despite the ridiculous allegations and the trouble Renata put him through, he made it clear that they were welcome to come back anytime. He wouldn't turn them away just because Renata was ill. He had known from the time he met her that she battled mental illness. As difficult as it was for him to understand and put up with, he was still her friend—and wanted to be a little more than a friend.

Gabriel couldn't imagine how the two of them would manage if they ever got married or entered into some other long-term arrangement. He was afraid Renata would kill Ray.

"You think he's okay?" Renata asked. "You don't think that he's…" She trailed off.

"Informing on us?" Gabriel filled in. "No, I don't think he is. If he was, bad things would happen after we saw or talked to him. There would be… people following us all the time. We would be caught and arrested, no matter how careful we were."

He watched her eyes as she started thinking about these things, getting wound up about them. He was feeding her fears, and she immediately looked around for any watchers—anyone who looked suspicious and should not be there.

"But there haven't been," Gabriel finished lightly. "We haven't had any trouble lately. No one following or acting suspiciously. No reunifications that Ray had knowledge of have gone sour. Everything has been quiet. Safe."

"Everything is quiet and safe," Renata repeated. "Quiet and safe. Quiet and safe." She repeated it like a mantra or meditation, listening to the rhythm of it, repeating it to embed it into her brain and drive out all of the bad thoughts.

"That's right," Gabriel agreed. "I don't think anyone is looking for us right now. Everyone who cared… doesn't anymore. We don't know any of the baddies who are knowingly participating in medical kidnap for experimentation. Just doctors and social workers making assumptions and incorrect decisions. The others have gone underground. They're being more careful, and we can't identify them."

"Gone underground. Just like us." Renata gave a sharp laugh.

"Yeah. That's right. Only no one is taking *them* out on the railroad. They can just stay underground. That's the way we like it."

"Dr. De Klerk…"

"Left the state. Maybe the country. Hopefully, he's decided to retire on what he's already made and won't be victimizing any other kids with mito. But if he's still in business… it's far away from here and he isn't looking for us anymore."

"Yeah." She closed her eyes briefly. She breathed in and out a few times. She wasn't saying it out loud, but Gabriel suspected she was repeating it over and over in her mind, trying to make herself believe. She eventually opened her eyes again and stared at him. "Well, we'd better start packing up. What are you sitting around for?"

Gabriel grinned in response. He wriggled out of his sleeping bag and started his usual packing routine. They worked together in silence, accustomed to the process after so much time together.

"Look," Renata said as she worked. "I'm going to have to get a review of my meds. We gotta find somewhere to go where they won't leak my identity to anyone. No reports to social services or putting me on an involuntary hold."

Gabriel continued to work, not responding for a few minutes. "Okay. I've been looking around a bit, trying to figure out who we could see."

"You have?" she demanded, stopping what she was doing and looking immediately suspicious. "Why?"

"You said when we were at Ray's that you were having trouble and might need a review. I wanted to be ready and help you when it was time."

"When it was time? Time for what?"

Gabriel took a breath and didn't answer immediately. He tried to slow everything down. Leave gaps in the conversation for Renata to think and reconsider instead of immediately jumping to the worst possible conclusion.

"Whenever you said it was time to see a doctor. I didn't know when the right time would be. That's up to you."

"Have you been talking to anyone? Talking to these doctors? Who are they?"

Gabriel looked around. They were nearly finished, other than Renata finishing with her pack. Others in the homeless encampment were already gone or were at the same stage as they were, packing up and getting ready to make themselves scarce.

"Cops will be here before long. Finish up, and we'll talk somewhere people won't overhear us."

Renata opened her mouth to argue, but then conceded. She nodded, bent down to finish closing all her straps and zippers, and lifted her backpack onto her shoulders. They drifted away from the encampment slowly, taking care not to make any suspicious movements that would attract attention, keeping their eyes out for any cops or other watchers who should not be there. Gabriel didn't suggest where they should go, leaving it up to Renata. If she was already anxious about him talking to doctors, she wouldn't be open to his making any decisions about where they should go. She wouldn't want to put herself at his mercy and let him turn her over to the new team of doctors who would want to examine her.

Renata made a slight motion with her head to indicate a diner that they frequented sometimes. Gabriel liked it for its fried breakfast sandwich, sort of like breakfast between two pieces of French toast. Renata didn't care what they served, of course, since her only sustenance would be the liquid formula that had kept her alive for most of her life, delivered directly to her stomach via a feeding tube. But she liked the private booths, and the staff had never made any comment or complaint about Renata not ordering food there or using the feeding tube away from prying eyes. They couldn't eat there too often. Couldn't become too familiar or let it become a habit.

Gabriel nodded, already looking forward to the breakfast sandwich. They didn't speak until they were sitting in one of the booths, out of view of anyone but the waitress who occasionally circulated the floor, refreshing coffee cups and seeing that everyone was taken care of.

The smell of freshly brewed coffee wafted through the diner, mingling with the scent of sizzling bacon and eggs. Gabriel's mouth watered. Clinking cutlery and murmured conversations from the other booths created a low hum of background noise.

"Who have you been talking to?" Renata questioned, confirming that she hadn't forgotten the line of questioning that had been interrupted. Gabriel's words and her questions had probably been circulating through her brain the whole time, demanding answers.

"I haven't talked to anyone. I have only done a few internet searches and looked at some printed resources. And not on my phone. Only at the library. And wiped the browser after."

She nodded her approval at these precautions. "You haven't talked to any doctors?"

"No. I wouldn't talk to anyone about you unless you were unconscious. That's for you to decide."

She nodded and didn't talk while she hooked up her line and started her formula flowing. Gabriel eagerly awaited the delivery of his breakfast sandwich.

"So what did you find?" Renata asked finally.

"There's a storefront service offered downtown. Not attached to any shelter. Outpatient only. They only deal with the homeless, and promise privacy and discretion. They write prescriptions and have a dispensary right there."

"I need a compounding pharmacy," Renata reminded him.

"Yeah. I couldn't figure out if they did compounding from the descriptions in the literature. And I didn't want to call and ask anyone."

"Probably not. But you did right not to call." Renata looked around, her eyes sharp as if he might have tipped someone off despite his assertion. "I don't suppose there are a lot of homeless psychotics who have a list of allergies as long as mine. It would be a giveaway."

Gabriel nodded. "I didn't communicate with anyone directly. Just looked at the public stuff."

"Yeah, good." She gave a low chuckle. "If you keep it up, we might have to start medicating you too."

"I don't think paranoia is communicable."

"I'm beginning to wonder."

The waitress delivered Gabriel's sandwich to him and gave him a smile and a raised eyebrow to ask if he needed anything else. Gabriel thanked her and dug in.

Renata watched him. "How is it?"

Gabriel used a paper napkin to wipe his greasy mouth. "It's good we don't come here too often, or I'd get fat. You know I don't like to eat anything too greasy, it messes up my digestion, but with these sandwiches… I would put up with the consequences."

"Yeah?" She laughed. "They smell good."

"But you're probably not enjoying watching me masticate my meal," he teased.

"Disgusting," Renata agreed. "So unsanitary to consume everything by mouth, all of the viruses and bacteria floating around the room landing on it… you really should try some nice sterile formula directly into your stomach. It's the way of the future."

It was not the first time they'd had that conversation. Gabriel enjoyed the banter. He liked flipping the tables, with Renata showing Gabriel the same attitude for eating by mouth as she got from observers who thought that using a feeding tube in a public places was disgusting and unsanitary.

Renata checked her tube. "So, where is this clinic?"

CHAPTER THIRTY-THREE

A
s they walked back into the house after their games outside, Axel's question rang in Joseph's ears.

He didn't know why he hadn't thought of asking it himself.

Why hadn't anyone else considered it?

"If you can't be with your mom, why can't you be with your dad?"

Wasn't DCFS supposed to try to keep families together? To find kinship care for children if their primary caregiver could no longer take care of them? Wasn't the whole point to keep kids with their families or communities as much as possible?

Or was that just something they said in the media, and it wasn't really the way things happened behind the scenes? Joseph recalled the dire warnings from Renata about corruption in the foster care system, especially where medical conditions were concerned. He had dismissed it all as paranoid conspiracy theories. Renata *was* paranoid. She had theories about everything. But what she had said about foster care had stuck. Or it had been buried in the back of his brain and now it came back as he thought about Axel's question and tried to come up with an answer.

Why couldn't Joseph go to his father instead of staying in foster care? His father had a good, steady job, a nice house, and a new partner to look after meals and other household stuff. It wouldn't be hard for Felicity to make sure that Joseph got up in the morning and was off to school. He could take care of himself, of course, but DCFS would want reassurances that someone in the home would be responsible for his care even when his dad was at work. They wanted a two-person home for him? There already was one. He just hadn't thought of it in all of the turmoil of Letty's taking him from the school.

All of their concerns could be addressed by Joseph going to his father. And eventually, when they were no longer so worried that his medical problems were being caused by the trauma of the divorce or his mom working long hours, he could start visitations with her again and eventually transition to being back home with her, at least some of the time. Maybe in a more balanced schedule so that she didn't have to take all of the responsibility upon herself.

It was the perfect situation. And he owed it all to Axel.

Joseph smiled at Axel as he dished up his meat and potatoes. He ate with his head in the clouds, hardly aware of the conversations around him. He was too busy working things out in his head. Thinking about how he would call his father and explain the circumstances and make sure he was ready to take up the case with DCFS. He wouldn't need to take any training courses like foster parents did; he was already Joseph's father and knew how to be a parent.

"Hey, space case," Tink tried to get Joseph's attention.

"Tink," Mrs. Brewster warned.

"Yeah, space case!" Tink repeated, staring at Joseph and waving her hand at him across the table. "Where are you today? Aren't you going to tell us how your first day of school went?"

Something in her voice warned Joseph that she was not asking because she cared about him or wanted to ensure he'd had a good first day of school. There was no need for her to get involved in his life, and it was Mr. or Mrs. Brewster's place to ask him about his day at school and how everything had gone. Not Tink's. What did she care?

He focused on her, trying to pull his mind away from thoughts about his dad.

"What?"

"I hear you were with that weird girl. Brit. That you two are all buddy-buddy now."

Joseph's mind jumped back to school and how excited he had been when he got home to tell Mrs. Brewster—or anyone interested —about Brit and how they had found each other. A smile came to his face unbidden.

"Yeah," he agreed, "Brit is great."

"Sounds like you made friends pretty quickly," said Mrs. Brewster, sounding a little surprised. He didn't know whether to be insulted that she hadn't been as confident about his ability to make friends at the new school as she had suggested before she had dropped him off. She had said that he would make friends, and now she was surprised about it?

"I knew Brit already," he told her.

"Oh!" Her face cleared. "Well, isn't that nice? You already had a friend there and didn't know it!"

"Yeah," Joseph agreed. He started in on a description of how he had met Brit in the cafeteria and then discovered that he knew her from online gaming.

"So you've spent all of that time together online and never met each other in person?" Mr. Brewster asked. "That's kind of funny."

Joseph nodded, grinning and shoveling more of the creamy potatoes into his mouth. "And out of all of the people in the cafeteria, she was the one who came up to me. And she didn't know who I was either. Neither of us knew who the other was."

"She's trouble, you know," Tink warned, trying to throw some cold water on the conversation. "You don't want to get involved with her."

"How is she trouble?" Joseph challenged. "I'm already friends with her."

Tink snorted. "You've played games together online," she sneered, making it sound like something childish. "That doesn't count as knowing someone. I'm telling you, she's trouble. Everybody knows how weird she is. She's always getting in trouble for pranks."

Pranks? Joseph shrugged. What harm were pranks?

"Whatever," he told Tink.

"She's, like, mentally unstable. She's probably on drugs. I'm telling you, she's not a normal person. No one would want her in their inner circle."

"Tink, that's awfully judgmental," Mrs. Brewster chided. "Has she been in any actual trouble? Or are you just calling out someone who is different than you?"

"Hey, if you want him involved with some crazy chick, it's no skin off my nose. What do I care?"

"That's not answering the question. Do you know if she has been in trouble? At school or with the police? Or are you just noticing her because she's a bit different?"

"She's more than a bit different."

"Leave her alone," Joseph snapped, slamming his hand down on the table. "What did she ever do to hurt you? Why do you care if I'm friends with someone who isn't your type? It isn't like *you're* going to hang out with me at school."

He hadn't even seen her there, though it was obvious that she had either seen him or had listened to the gossip about what he had been doing.

"Why would I want to do that?" Tink demanded. "Who would want to hang out with a foster sibling at school? Is there anything that says 'loser' more than that?"

"Maybe sitting around criticizing anyone different than you," he retorted.

Tink started swearing. Mr. Brewster held up his hands. "Okay, okay, that's enough, you two. We don't talk to each other that way. And no arguments at the dinner table, okay? This is a time for us to get together and enjoy each other's company and hear how things went during the day. We are not here to judge or fight or criticize each other. We're glad Joseph had a good first day and made a friend. Or met up with a friend he already had. We can discuss any problems another time. If there are any real problems. I think that maybe Tink is just being a little overprotective of a foster sibling. It's nice to see you guys looking out for each other, and we can talk later about any real issues with this girl, okay?"

Tink stared daggers across the table at Joseph. He didn't know what she was so heated up about. She was the one who had demanded to know how his day had gone. Even though she already knew. She'd obviously wanted a confrontation over Brit. Maybe he'd stepped right into it, but he wasn't afraid to defend his choices. He and Brit were already friends. It was a little late for her to put a stop to that with rumor and innuendo. He knew what kind of a person Brit was. He'd played with her for years and completed dozens, probably even hundreds of campaigns at her side.

He looked down at his plate and continued eating, pretending that he hadn't been pulled into the conversation with Tink in the first place.

CHAPTER THIRTY-FOUR

Can I use your phone?" Joseph asked Mrs. Brewster after the supper dishes had been cleared away and everyone was going in different directions. He had looked around for a landline phone, but didn't find one. That meant he would have to use someone else's cell phone instead. Axel was probably the only one in the family who didn't have a phone of his own.

Or maybe he did, and Joseph just hadn't seen it. He had seen kids in the park as young as six with their own phones, calling their parents to ask permission to go to a friend's house or reporting a bratty brother who was driving them nuts. And, of course, to text each other and whatever else six-year-olds did on their cell phones.

"You're not allowed to call your mother," Mrs. Brewster warned immediately. "She's not allowed direct contact with you without supervision."

"That's stupid. She didn't do anything wrong."

"I know that's your claim. But we have to follow DCFS's rules. We won't be able to keep our kids if we break the rules, and you would not be doing yourself any favors by disobeying them either. There are a lot worse places to be than here."

"I'm not calling my mom," Joseph said in exasperation.

"Are you calling that girl from school? What was her name? Brit?"

"Well, I can't play with her, since I don't have a computer or any gaming device that I could play with her on."

"I know. It must be quite a shock not to have any access to those things right now. Especially if that was how you spent your free time at home."

"I didn't game *all* the time. I did my homework and studied, and I had to spend a lot of time on soccer practice and drills."

He hadn't been the kid who did nothing but game all night. His mom had a rule about shutting the games off at nine o'clock on a school night, so he hadn't stayed up any later than that to game other than on a weekend. And even then, he'd never been one of those who played until four or five in the morning. He knew his body needed sleep, and he would start to yawn and make stupid mistakes in his game if he got too tired.

Mrs. Brewster nodded. "That's good. I'm glad to hear that your time was not spent on the screen. But I already knew that. You have good in-person social skills, and you don't really develop that just typing into a keyboard or yelling into a headset all day."

Joseph nodded, blushing a little at the praise.

"So, can I borrow it for a few minutes?"

"I suppose so," she conceded. She worked her phone out of her pocket and handed it to him. "But please don't be too long. I sometimes get emergency calls that need to be dealt with right away."

Joseph nodded. "Yeah, no problem."

He took the phone from her and turned to go to his bedroom with it.

"Not behind closed doors," Mrs. Brewster warned. "You can talk with her in the living room. That way, we can supervise and make sure that nothing... *untoward* is going on."

Joseph looked at her, shaking his head at first, and then realizing what she was probably talking about.

"We're not sending nudes or something. We're just going to talk."

It was Mrs. Brewster's turn to blush. "Good. Glad to hear it," she said briskly.

Joseph took the phone to the living room. Luckily, no one was there. He couldn't exactly have the privacy he would have liked, but no one was there monitoring every word he said.

Because, of course, it wasn't Brit he was going to call. He hadn't told Mrs. Brewster that he was. That had been her assumption.

Maybe after he'd talked to his dad, he would talk to Brit. He would be nice and relaxed by that time. But he didn't know how long he would be able to use the phone, so he needed to make the more important call first.

He curled up in the corner of the couch and dialed his father's number from memory. Good thing that he actually knew his father's cell phone and hadn't just relied on a favorites list to contact him.

He listened to it ring. Was his father at home? Out at a business dinner or meeting? If he was busy with something else, would he interrupt it to answer a call from his son? Joseph didn't usually call him, so his father would have to know something was wrong. Or at least that it was something important. All he had to do was take a minute to answer the phone and make sure everything was okay, and then to call Joseph back when it was a better time.

"Hello?"

At first, Joseph was surprised that his father didn't know who it was, then realized that since he was calling from Mrs. Brewster's phone, he would have no idea who was calling.

"Dad? It's Joseph."

"Joey! This is a surprise. How are you?"

"Well… I'm okay. But there's been some stuff going on, and I wanted to tell you about it…"

"Uh…" Joe Senior cleared his throat. "Your mother has been keeping me apprised."

He already knew? Maybe, like Joseph, the simple solution had not occurred to him.

"You knew that I got put into foster care?"

"Yes, she told me about that. I'm so sorry about that. How are you doing?"

"It's not the best, but I'm okay. It's just… I wondered about *you*…"

"Oh, we're just fine, Joseph," Joe Senior's tone was warm, misinterpreting Joseph's question. "Felicity and I are getting along well. In fact, well, I do have some news…"

They were getting married, Joseph supposed. They had been together long enough, and the divorce was final, so there was nothing to stop them. Either his father had decided that the only way he was going to hold on to her was to put a ring on her finger, or she had given him an ultimatum. It was hard to believe that Joe Senior was soppily in love like a teenager. It wasn't like that for adults.

"Dad, what if I came to live with you? I'm sure DCFS would say that it's okay. They were only worried about Mom, and about her being too busy and everything. I'm sure they would say it was okay for me to come to live with you. I don't know why they put me into foster care without talking to you…"

"Joey, it's not a good time for us."

"But if you're getting married now, then Felicity will be my step-mom, and DCFS will be happy if I have two parents in the home. They'll forget all of this stuff about me not getting the attention I need."

"It's not that…"

"I won't be any trouble. I look after myself. It's just that family services thinks I can't. But they're wrong. I'm almost an adult. I just need somewhere to live."

"You have somewhere. And I think this foster home you're with is the best possible solution. I know it's not ideal, and I'm sorry, but we can't take on a teenager right now."

"What?" Joseph couldn't believe what he was hearing. He had to have misunderstood. His father wouldn't turn him down. Wouldn't tell him that it was better for him to live with strangers in foster care than with his own family. He'd always gotten along with his dad. They didn't have a lot of shared interests, but they'd always been able to talk to each other, and Joseph didn't feel like his dad was too distant or think that he irritated Joe Senior too much. Sometimes, fathers and sons fought a lot, but Joseph and his father had never been that way. They'd always been cordial and friendly with each other.

"Joey, I need you to listen. Can you do that? Just stop talking for a minute and listen to what I'm trying to tell you."

Joseph swallowed. He cleared his throat. He held the phone lightly to his ear and tried to compose himself.

"Okay. I'm listening."

"Joseph, Felicity is pregnant."

It was a blinding blow, completely unexpected. Yes, he had known that his father and his new partner might decide to start a family of their own, but he was still dumbfounded. He hadn't been expecting it. Hadn't been ready to hear it.

But that wasn't the end of it. He could still go live with them if Felicity was having a baby, couldn't he? It might be a little more awkward, but they could find a way to make it work.

"Well… congratulations!" he croaked.

"Just listen, son."

Was he using the word 'son' now to emphasize that Joseph was still his child, even though he was going to have another one through this woman?

"I'm listening."

"It would be too much for us to take you on and a new baby at the same time. This is a time of transition, and it's very difficult for Felicity. She has not been feeling well with the pregnancy and doesn't have the energy or mental space to be dealing with a teenager as well."

"I could help her with stuff. I wouldn't be more work. I could vacuum and make meals. I'm good at cooking, you know. And I'm not doing soccer anymore. I'm off the team, so I could come home right after school and help with whatever she needed me to help her with. And I can babysit when the baby comes. Change diapers and everything. I'm going to be an awesome big brother. I've been playing with one of the boys here, and even though he's a lot younger, I'm really enjoying it. It's a lot of fun to make him happy."

"You're not listening," Joe Senior said with a huff of frustration.

"I hear you… It's just that…"

"The answer is 'no,' Joseph. I'm sorry about that. I don't like saying no. But I need to look after Felicity and the baby, and think about what's best for them. I'm sure you'll be an awesome big brother, but only for visits. Not for living here, okay? We can't be expected to look after you and your medical needs right now. This is time that we need to spend preparing for the baby and then welcoming him or her."

"I could help," Joseph repeated weakly.

"No. I said the answer is no, Joseph. That's the end of it. I already discussed this with that social worker, and I told her in no uncertain terms that this is simply not something that we can take upon ourselves right now."

Joseph pressed the red End button on the phone.

CHAPTER THIRTY-FIVE

J oseph! Joseph, wake up!"

Joseph became aware of a wailing. He wanted it to stop. It was uncomfortable and he just wanted to retreat into blackness again while he got his bearings. What was going on?

"Mom! Mom, Joseph fell down and he won't get up! Mom!" the wailing and shrieking continued.

Joseph moved his hand to his face, attempting to block out the noise. It hurt his head, which was already throbbing. He moaned, trying to tell the voice to shut up.

"Joseph? Oh, my goodness." There was someone else there. Fingers grasped Joseph's wrist. "Joseph, are you okay? Can you hear me?"

Joseph tried to push her away. He tried to tell her to stop, but couldn't get the words out clearly. He just moaned.

"Is that my phone? Hand me that," Mrs. Brewster demanded.

Joseph felt for the phone that had been in his hand an eternity ago, but couldn't find it. Mrs. Brewster seemed to have it anyway. He could hear her dialing and talking on the phone in a sharp, urgent voice. He couldn't make out everything that was said, but knew who she was talking to.

"Joseph? Can you tell me what happened? Open your eyes."

Joseph didn't. He knew it would make him too vulnerable to the light and the overwhelming chaos of noise and movement. He wanted everything to stay in a soft, warm cocoon inside his body.

There was more noise. More chaos. More reasons to put his arm over his eyes and hide from it all.

But there were stronger hands, louder voices. Insistent pinches and pain in other parts of his body. He tried to fight back against it but, eventually, had to open his eyes and let the rest of the world in.

"He's alive! He's alive!" Axel piped, his voice shrill with relief. "You just fell down, Joseph. I didn't know what to do. Why did you fall down?"

Joseph couldn't even begin to answer him.

"Any idea of medical history?" one of the black-uniformed men asked. "Seizure disorder? Heart? Stroke?"

"No." Mrs. Brewster's voice was worried. "He's had a few episodes lately, but the doctors haven't been able to find anything. They keep saying that everything is normal."

"This is not normal. Got the heart monitor on?" the man asked his identical partner.

The chaos around him was silenced briefly and they could all hear the announcements of the automatic v-fib machine as it booted up and gave his stats.

"Fast," one of the twin paramedics announced, "but a good rhythm."

"What does that do?" Axel demanded. "On TV, they shock them like this!" He mimed rubbing two paddles together and then placing them on a body and making a big thump and jolt.

"It's the same thing," a paramedic told him. "Just not as much fun. But your brother doesn't need a shock."

"Can you do it anyway?" Axel asked excitedly.

"No, bud, we don't do that."

The paramedics talked to each other in doctor-speak, and then turned to Mrs. Brewster to talk to her about the situation.

"We'd like to take him in, see if they have better luck tracking down the problem this time. It could be serious. You shouldn't have a kid this age just dropping for no reason."

"They thought it was psychological. He has… a number of issues. Nothing showed up on any of the tests they did."

"Oh, does he?" Joseph couldn't see the man rolling his eyes, but he could imagine it. "Well, even so, we would like to take him in just in case. See if any tests should be run that they haven't yet."

"Okay. Of course. We want to get him the help that he needs, whether it is physical or mental."

Joseph didn't have the energy to argue about what had happened or to say that it wasn't all in his head.

He was exhausted. Maybe it *was* all in his head. Maybe he was losing his mind. And who would care? His father didn't even want him.

Didn't. Even. Want. Him.

————

Joseph wasn't that aware of what was going on over the next few hours. There were a lot of physical exams, tests, people telling him that they were going to do more tests, and waiting around for the tests and results. He just wanted to sleep and didn't care what was going on around him. They could go ahead and test and test, and they wouldn't find anything.

Maybe it was just all in his head. And who cared anymore?

A soft-spoken doctor came and sat on the side of his bed, talking to him about the results of the tests they had done and asking him if he understood and how he was feeling.

"I just don't want to deal with it. I just want to go to sleep and not wake up."

"Uh-huh. How long have you been feeling this way?"

"I don't know. Everything has been going crazy. I just want to go home, but I can't do that. And I can't go to my dad's. Nobody wants me around. Except I guess the Brewsters, but they aren't my parents and don't know what it's like…"

He knew that Mrs. Brewster was sitting there, somewhere behind the doctor, and could probably hear all of this, but she didn't object. She just let the doctor talk to Joseph.

"You've been hospitalized for depression before."

"Yeah."

"I'd like to have you re-evaluated. See if one of your medications is causing these episodes."

"I don't need to go to the psych ward."

"I think it would be the best thing for you."

"You don't even know me."

"I've read through your medical records. And everything points toward either a psychological cause, or a reaction to your medications. So we would like to address both of those possibilities at the same time. Have you stay here with us for a few days and take the time to sort out what is going on. I'm sure you don't want to continue having these episodes out of the blue and not know what they are being caused by."

"My doctor said they were panic attacks."

"Well, what you had today did not look like a panic attack. You might be having panic attacks as well, and anyone could understand you having anxiety with stuff like this going on, but I think this was something else. And I think we can help, if you give us a few days."

Joseph rubbed his forehead, trying to sort out the doctor's words and to formulate an answer. "Did you give me something? I'm so foggy."

"I suspect you're just tired after dealing with all of this after a full day of school. It's late—or early—and you haven't had a good night's sleep."

"What do you think I should do?"

"I think you should stay here while we sort it out."

"I dunno."

The doctor turned and looked at Mrs. Brewster. "How about you?"

"I don't think we can just continue to let this go on untreated. I'm surprised that it's gone this far. Either his mother or family services should have stepped in early and put her foot down to see that it got taken care of."

The doctor nodded in agreement. "I'm glad to hear that someone is taking it seriously and is committed to getting a proper diagnosis. Let's do that, then. We'll find out what is going on." He patted Joseph on the leg. "We'll get you back into tip-top shape, buddy. Now you go to sleep. You shouldn't have any more interruptions tonight."

CHAPTER THIRTY-SIX

Joseph was so tired the first day that he didn't even care about being in the hospital. He didn't want to be around the foster family, including Axel, and just wanted to wallow in his grief about being abandoned by his father. At least his mother had fought to keep him. It hadn't been her fault that he had been taken away.

He just slept. He suspected the doctor had put something in his IV to make him more compliant. The doctor spoke in a low voice to Mrs. Brewster so that Joseph could not overhear. What did it matter what Joseph did or didn't want? He was a minor. He wasn't allowed to make decisions, even about his medical care.

He thought it was the second day that he started to wake up a bit more. It might have been longer. His brain was restless when he woke up in the morning instead of feeling full of cotton. He could connect thoughts. He could direct where they went instead of just floating along like a piece of driftwood on top of the water, floating wherever the currents took him.

Joseph sat up on his bed and rubbed his eyes. He looked around at the small, white cell. He recognized it as a psych ward room. There was no furniture other than the bed. Even the little drawers he usually saw in hospital rooms or the rolling dinner table were missing. There was nowhere for him to put his personal belongings. But then, he didn't have any personal belongings, so what did it matter? He didn't have anything to put in a drawer or closet. He didn't know where they had put his street clothes. Maybe Mrs. Brewster had taken them home with her.

"Rise and shine, Mr. Demain," a nurse told him cheerfully as she bustled into the room. She offered him a little pill cup. He looked at the pills before taking them. The brightly colored pills were all reassuringly familiar. They weren't trying to dose him with something new without telling him. He had heard of such things being done and didn't want to deal with any of that nonsense while he was there. He should have complete control over his program and what medications he took.

He swallowed the pills with the cup of water that the nurse proffered. He drank the whole cup, rather than just enough to wash the pills down. He was very dry. They had apparently taken out his IV, but Joseph didn't remember it being done.

"How are you feeling this morning?" she asked.

"I'm okay, I guess." He rubbed his eyes. "Not so tired."

"That's good. And how is your anxiety level? Can you rate it for me on a scale of one to ten?"

Joseph thought about it. He hadn't woken up in a panic. Even though he was away from home, he wasn't worrying about it. He didn't have to worry about his reputation at school, because he wouldn't be there for the next few days. He didn't feel anxious about going back to his mom's house or his dad's because he knew he wouldn't be going to either one. All he had to do was sit in a white room. And maybe go to group therapy or talk to a doctor if they told him to.

"I think... maybe three or four."

"Okay." She nodded and noted that down on her clipboard. "And other than that, how are you feeling? Headache? Nausea? Any other symptoms?"

"Headache, maybe." Joseph thought about it. "Yeah, a bit of a headache. Kind of dizzy, but that comes and goes."

"How often does it come and go? How long have you been feeling dizzy?"

"You mean, like, today?"

"When did you start getting dizzy spells?"

"I don't know. Maybe… a week or two."

"And are you dizzy every day? Or only some days?"

"I don't know. I guess… sometimes every day. But it isn't always very bad."

"And today, is it very bad?"

"Not right now."

"What things make it better or worse?"

"When I have a panic attack, it's worse. Or… I don't know. If I work out too hard. Sometimes in the mornings."

"When you work out in the mornings?"

"No. When I work out too hard. Or the mornings. Two different things."

"Oh, got it. Sure."

"But it's just anxiety, right?" he checked. "That's what the doctor said."

"That's one of the things you are here to find out."

"What else could it be? The social worker thinks that I'm faking it. But I'm not."

"We don't know yet what it could be. It could be a drug interaction. It could be something unrelated to your psychological state. It could be…." She shrugged. "Lyme disease. An ear infection. I don't know. You'll work with the doctors for a few days, and they'll figure it out."

"Okay." Joseph shrugged and shook his head. "I hope so. Because I'm not just trying to get attention."

"Honey…" The nurse leaned closer to him and looked over her shoulder before looking back at him and speaking. "I don't believe I know of anyone who has landed in the psych ward just because they wanted attention."

Joseph was happy to hear this reassurance. "So you don't think I'm faking or attention-seeking?"

"Of course not."

He blew out his breath. "Thank you."

She gave him a quick pat on the shoulder. "No one chooses to come here just for the fun of it. We know that when you come here, it is because you are going through a crisis and you need help. That's what we're here for. You tell me if you need anything. We're going to figure this out."

Joseph felt so encouraged by her words that when she had gone on to the next patient's room, he decided to get himself out of bed and join the land of the living. The hospital clothes he wore were, luckily, like scrubs rather than an open-backed hospital johnny, so it was easier to walk out into the ward to see what was going on without holding his robe behind him. He walked out into a brightly lit open area with a nursing station, some chairs and a TV, a bookshelf filled with disintegrating paperbacks and magazines, and a few patients who were engaged in watching the TV, putting together a puzzle, or playing solitaire with a deck of cards.

"Well, hello," one of the other nurses said. It took a minute for Joseph to process her face and put a name to it. Nurse Campbell. She wasn't as bright and cheery as the nurse who had delivered his pills had been, but the serious look that she gave Joseph didn't seem to be forbidding or suspicious. "How are you this morning, Mr. Demain?"

"You can just call me Joseph. I'm… doing okay. I thought I'd see what everyone else is doing. And if I'm supposed to go to anything today."

"Well, that is showing initiative. Good for you. I don't think we have you scheduled for any therapy. The doctor wanted to do a med review before anything else. He'll probably be coming to talk to you in a few hours."

"And do I… have clothes?"

Nurse Campbell frowned at that. "Only whatever is in your room. Don't you have anything?"

"No. I don't know what happened to my other clothes."

"We'll call down to the ER. See if something was left behind there. It will take time. They are never too quick to respond."

It seemed paradoxical that the emergency room should be slow to respond to inquiries. But on the other hand, Joseph supposed that they had a lot of other things to worry about that were more urgent.

He nodded his thanks. "Great. I guess… I'll get them when I get them."

CHAPTER THIRTY-SEVEN

J oseph wandered over to the common area where a few other patients were keeping themselves occupied. They weren't doing anything together, not like in a movie about the psych ward, where the patients were always playing poker for tooth-picks or something like that. They were all engaged in solitary pursuits. Joseph wanted to talk to someone but wasn't sure how to approach any of them. He was almost always the only teen in the ward, and it was hard to know how to approach the adults.

"It's the new guy," said one patient, a man with short, uneven hair that looked like it had been chewed off. He was slightly overweight and wore a t-shirt and jeans with a jacket over top. The kind of jacket that Joseph associated with Oxford or some other British university, several colors worked together and patches at the elbows. Why was something with patches on it considered classy? Shouldn't it be the opposite? "What's your name, Joseph Demain?"

He broke off laughing at his own joke, and wiped the corners of his eyes. Joseph shook his head, unsure what to think of this guy.

"I'm Joseph," he said. "I guess you already know that. What's your name?"

"Milo. Milo Pitch. The eyes and ears of the ward. You want to know anything about what goes on in this place, you ask me." He puffed out his chest in pride. "I know everything."

"Yeah? How long have you been here?"

"I've been here longer than you have."

"Well… yeah. I guess you all have. I assume you all have." Of course, any of them could have come at the same time as Joseph. Or have arrived the day before, when he had arrived two days before. Or what he thought was two days before, if he hadn't lost any more days while he had been sedated. "But I've been here before, and I don't remember seeing you here, so I guess you haven't been here for *that* long."

"You've been here before?" Milo asked and, before Joseph could decide whether this was something he should have revealed about himself, "Who hasn't! We're all just tumbleweeds. Blowing in and out of here. Blowing where the wind blows us."

Joseph nodded. He sat in one of the upholstered chairs in front of the TV, but wasn't really interested in watching the news, which appeared to be some kind of disaster on the east coast. A hurricane or tropical storm, from the looks of things. Now *that* was a wind.

"What are you in for?" he asked Milo.

"Bipolar disorder. And some more interesting stuff recently. Maybe some psychosis. So they are considering schizoaffective disorder." He shrugged. "Or maybe just bipolar with psychosis."

"Uh-huh. I've been in for depression before," Joseph offered. He didn't say what he was there for this time. He wasn't sure how to explain why they thought that his having panic attacks or fainting spells was cause to be admitted to the psych ward. It wasn't one of the disorders he usually heard about there.

"Depression without the mania is just… depressing," Milo offered, and gave a big grin. "You really oughta try the good stuff."

Joseph chuckled. It would be nice if he got to pick and choose his own affliction. But that was certainly not the case. If he got to choose… maybe just a mild depression once a year, that was easily managed with a single prescription. That would be nice. Maybe mild enough that it didn't even need medication. He wondered sometimes what it would be like walking around without all of that buzzing in his head. What if he could just be himself without any depression or anxiety? Or any of the stuff he'd been suffering through lately.

"And now you're in for fainting spells?" Milo asked. "How is that something you get treated for in the psych ward?"

Joseph was floored that Milo would know anything about what he was there for. But he hid his reaction the best he could. No point in giving Milo the satisfaction of knowing that he had surprised Joseph. That seemed to be exactly what he wanted, and Joseph didn't want to give him the satisfaction.

"Well, it's a little more than that," he said coolly.

"Hysterical fainting and anxiety attacks," Milo said. "You've got quite the package there, my young friend."

"It's not that big of a deal," Joseph said. "It's just a med problem or something. They'll figure it out."

"You think so? When was the last time they ever made med changes without causing more problems than they solved?"

"I don't know. They've been pretty good before."

"And that's why you're back here after just a few months?"

"Well… it wasn't my choice. I don't think I need to be here just so they can check my meds. But maybe… they'll run some other tests."

"Sounds like they've already run everything else. X-rayed your head until I'm surprised there's anything left in there. Or maybe there isn't, and they're just hoping to find something."

Joseph sighed and looked at the TV, still broadcasting about the hurricane. He'd be happy if the doctor knew as much about his case as Milo did. What had Milo done, broken into the records room? Hacked the computer? Sat in on a discussion between the medical staff about what exactly the new guy was in for?

"Now I've upset you," Milo observed.

"I'd just like a little privacy."

"In the common room?"

"No, I mean, like, medical privacy. You not knowing everything about my history and what I'm here for."

"I told you, I am the eyes and ears of the ward. I can't help it if I know things."

"You don't need to show it off. Would you like me blabbing everything about your diagnosis to everyone else?"

"Everyone else?" Milo looked around pointedly at the rest of the patients and shrugged. "Sure, go ahead. I already told you why I'm here. It's not a secret."

"Well... it's not the same with me. I'd like to have some privacy."

Milo shrugged. "Have it your way. Don't get your panties in a twist."

Joseph got up and went over to the bookshelf to look for another deck of cards. There were several, so he picked up one box and went to an unoccupied table to lay out a solitaire pattern.

"Now you're going to go pout about it?" Milo accused. "I thought you were interested in socializing."

"Maybe I shouldn't have come out here," Joseph grumbled. "Maybe I'll just take these back to my room."

"You can't take them back to your room," Milo said explosively. "Cards have to stay in the common room!"

"I don't really care. Things are... seems like everything I do gets me in trouble right now. I might as well get in trouble for actually breaking a rule, for once, instead of just for being sick."

"You're not sick," Milo scoffed. He looked around at the other patients to gauge his support. "You're just shamming. Pretending to have some disorder so that the doctors will give you more attention. Factitious disorder. That's what it is called. Wherever you go, that will be attached to your file now. Patient suffers a factitious disorder. And that means that they won't believe anything you say. No matter what you tell them about your symptoms, they will think you're making it up."

Joseph's heart sank. That was one of the things that scared him the most. How would he ever get a doctor's trust? Or a parent's or teacher's trust? If they all thought that he was doing it for attention, they would suspect him with the appearance of any new symptom. They would say that he had Munchausen Syndrome.

"I'm not making anything up. You think I want to faint in the middle of the soccer field? I ended up being pulled from the team, taken away from my mom and the school. I'm living in foster care with people I don't know, no personal possessions, no phone or soccer. And now… I'm here. How do you think any of that is what I want?"

"Well, maybe you do, psychologically speaking. Maybe deep down, that was what you wanted to happen." Milo brightened. "Maybe you feel the need to punish yourself. You feel guilty over something, and this is what you have done to try to atone for it."

"I don't feel guilty for anything." But just saying it made Joseph feel guilty.

Should he feel guilty for something? Had he had the perfect life and blown it? He'd had two parents, been the star of the soccer team, done well in school, had friends, a phone and computer. Maybe he'd had the perfect life and hadn't appreciated it, so it had all been taken away.

"Maybe you *should.*"

"Milo," one of the nurses walking through the common room to the nursing station stopped and looked at him. "Leave the new guy alone. You're not supposed to be harassing the other patients."

"I'm not."

She leveled a glare at him. "You certainly are. Leave Mr. Demain alone."

"Just call me Joseph," he reminded her. "I don't like being called mister all the time. Even just Demain. I go by that too."

"All right, Joseph," she agreed. "If Milo is bugging you, just tell him to shut up. Or come and get one of us. If he is going to harass other patients, he will be sent back to his room."

Joseph eyed Milo. "I'm sure he's finished now."

Milo rolled his eyes toward the ceiling. "All right, all right, point made. I will leave the poor, fragile boy alone."

CHAPTER THIRTY-EIGHT

Joseph wasn't sure whether to stay in the common room and potentially draw more attention from Milo or the other patients. He didn't usually have any trouble in the psych ward, but the incident with Milo put him on alert. Things might have changed. Having lost his status as a middle-class, soccer star teen, had he now been transitioned to loser foster kid, unworthy of any respect? He had always thought how people treated him was based on how he acted and presented himself. He didn't want to believe that people had only treated him well because he was a popular, successful, white boy.

But after Milo was warned to behave himself—and did—the others did not seem inclined to question or bully Joseph. He was allowed to play solitaire without any further harassment. He kept an eye on the TV. The channel was changed occasionally upon request, so sometimes it was the news, and other times it was a soap opera or sitcom. They didn't like to turn up the sound, so he had to be content with reading lips or the captioning if it were turned on. Not that there was anything good on. It was just nice to have the opportunity, when he had felt so isolated without any access to his usual screens.

There was a buzz of excitement when the head doctor for the unit arrived to make his rounds. Nurses were hurrying back and forth to take care of his requests. The patients were on the alert, waiting to be called back to their rooms or Dr. Ratzlaff's office.

Joseph had met Dr. Ratzlaff during his previous stays in psych, so he was not concerned about the doctor's arrival. Mira had always been the one to talk to the doctor, but Joseph was confident he could advocate for his own needs. He was almost an adult. He could certainly tell Dr. Ratzlaff what had been going on. And everything was in his records anyway. Dr. Ratzlaff could read it for himself and then tell Joseph what they had discovered so far and what his plan for treatment was.

Not that he expected anyone to find anything.

They hadn't yet, and nothing had changed to make him think they would.

"Joseph Demain?" The head nurse's eyes scanned the patients in the common room and eventually landed on Joseph. "Hi, Joseph. If you want to come to Dr. Ratzlaff's office, he would like to see you now."

Joseph nodded. She led him partway from the common room down the hallway. "Do you know where it is?"

"Yeah, I've been there before."

"Okay, I'll let you continue on your own. We'll talk after you're done, okay? See if any changes in treatment have been ordered."

Joseph nodded. He always got a motherly feeling from Nurse Campbell. He supposed it was stronger now because he was there on his own. She was not dealing with his mother, but just with Joseph himself. And with whoever they were talking with at DCFS, whether it was Mrs. Brewster or Letty.

She stood and watched him the rest of the way down the hallway, and then, when he was at Dr. Ratzlaff's door, turned and returned to the nurse's station.

Joseph swallowed, took a deep breath, and tapped on the door before opening it. He opened it just enough to put his head in to make sure that the doctor was ready for him and Nurse Campbell had not rushed him in before he was finished with his last patient.

"Come on in, Joseph," Dr. Ratzlaff invited.

Joseph opened the door wider and stepped in. He looked around at the familiar office. Dark, heavy furniture, clean surfaces, and a nice thick carpet that cushioned his feet and was very different from the tile and short pile carpets used everywhere else in Psychiatric.

The doctor, a tidy man with a part to the side of his full brown hair, who always looked neatly pressed despite any negative encounters with his patients, gave Joseph a reserved smile as he sat on the chair at the other side of the desk.

"Hello, Joseph. How are you feeling this afternoon?"

"Okay, I guess. I'd really like to get this taken care of and to go back home... back to my mom, not just to the foster family. They think that my mom has something to do with me having these spells, but that's just stupid. She wants me to be okay as much as I do."

"That's good to hear. I'm sure that we are all eager to have this sorted out. It isn't any fun for you to be sick, is it?" Dr. Ratzlaff's eyes were quick and intelligent, reading Joseph's face. He smiled and nodded reassuringly. "No, of course not."

"I wouldn't choose to have anxiety attacks."

"No. You hadn't mentioned having anxiety attacks in your previous visits here, as far as I remember."

"No. I didn't have them before. They have just started recently."

"Why don't you describe to me what they feel like."

Joseph was sure he'd retold that about ten times and, each time, the details were the same. He didn't understand why they couldn't all just read what was on his file?

"I just... my heart races, and I feel really bad. Like I know that something horrible is going to happen. And sometimes I get dizzy. And... it takes a while before it goes away. It doesn't seem like it matters what I do. I try to relax, do some of those breathing exercises and that kind of thing... but my heart just pounds and I get all sweaty."

"Uh-huh." Ratzlaff made some marks on his file, but didn't seem to be writing anything new. Just making some annotations on what someone else had written. "And how many of these have you had?"

"I don't know. It's just been a couple of weeks, and maybe... four of them. And some other times when my heart was going fast and I thought I was going to have another one, but then it settled down again."

"So maybe there *is* something you can do that helps to stop them."

Joseph thought about it. If he had stopped an anxiety attack from taking place, how had he done it? On those occasions when he had felt panicky but it hadn't developed into a full-blown panic attack, what had been different? Had he done something differently? Or was it just by chance?

"Maybe... when I get distracted by something else. When other things are going on and I forget about what I was starting to worry about. But other times..." Joseph shook his head helplessly. "It just comes out of nowhere. I wasn't worrying about anything, like when I just woke up in the morning, and I hadn't even thought about anything that was going on that day or worrying about anything, and just had my heart going like it was going to burst right out of my chest."

"Yes, I see," Ratzlaff said meditatively, looking down at his notes.

"Do you think... it's just being caused by my meds? That's what the doctor in the ER said. Maybe it's just a side effect of one of the drugs."

"It could be," Ratzlaff agreed.

"My doctor increased my anti-anxiety meds, but that didn't help. So what if it isn't actually anxiety?"

"What do you think it is, then?"

Joseph didn't like having it put back on him. "I *do* think it is an anxiety attack," he said quickly. He didn't want Dr. Ratzlaff to think he was playing games, making out that he was sick when he was not. The attacks were ruining his life. Why would he want that? "I just think... maybe it's caused by something outside instead of inside. I don't think... it isn't my *thoughts* that are causing them. It's... something else."

"Something else."

"Yeah."

"Like...?"

"Like... the meds. Or allergies. Or... I don't know—some kind of virus or bacteria. I've heard of things like that. Some sickness that causes anxiety."

"PANDAS," Dr. Ratzlaff agreed. "But that is usually younger children."

"But it could be, right?"

"Your blood has been worked up a couple of times. No infection."

"But maybe it was gone by then."

"Maybe," Dr. Ratzlaff agreed, giving Joseph a neutral smile. Joseph gathered that Dr. Ratzlaff didn't believe it was a possibility. He was just placating Joseph.

There was a knock on the door. Dr. Ratzlaff tapped his pen on the desk. "Yes?"

The door opened and Nurse Campbell poked her head in. "Sorry for the interruption, but Joseph's case worker is here and wanted to join you...?"

Joseph stood up. "What?"

"It's all right, Joseph," Dr. Ratzlaff told him. "Have a seat. Send Mrs. Miller in."

"I don't want her in here."

"It will be fine." Ratzlaff nodded at the nurse. "Send her in."

Joseph was helpless to do anything to stop her. He was going to get her in his face whether he wanted it or not. The psych ward was supposed to be a safe place, and always had been for him before, but it was beginning to feel like a trap. Like a war zone where snipers were taking well-placed shots at him.

Letty came into the office. She nodded at Joseph and sat in the other chair, where Mira would have sat if she had been with him. Joseph felt the blood rushing to his face. He felt the pounding of his heart and an almost instant headache. Sweat trickled down his back. There was no way he could hide all of the physical symptoms from the two professionals.

"Take a few deep breaths," Ratzlaff advised. "Remember some of the relaxation exercises we have worked on before. Breathe in. Hold it. Breathe out. Hold again. Until your body's responses return to normal."

"What is *she* doing here?" Joseph squeaked. "I don't want her here."

"Mrs. Miller is as concerned about you as we are. And she is your legal guardian, together with your foster parents. We all want to help you. Just take a minute to get yourself under control. You'll feel better once we have had a chance to discuss this fully."

"You both just think that I'm making this up. That there isn't anything wrong with me; I'm just doing it myself."

"I don't think you're intentionally trying to mislead anyone," Dr. Ratzlaff said. "But things do happen. Our thoughts do impact our health. Our needs and wants. Sometimes we don't realize how much control we have over our own health, with the power of positive thinking."

"Positive thinking is going to fix this?" Joseph demanded, gasping for breath. He put his hand over his chest, where his heart was pounding so hard that it hurt. "You're going to kill me and you don't even care!"

"An anxiety attack isn't going to kill you," Ratzlaff assured him. He stood up and walked around the desk to examine Joseph more closely. He held his wrist for a moment to check Joseph's pulse. "Take some deep breaths."

Joseph couldn't even draw in one breath without it hurting. He shook his head. He leaned back in his chair so his back was arched slightly, chest thrust out, trying to get more air into his lungs.

"It will pass," Dr. Ratzlaff assured them both. "This is self-limiting. Once the anxiety reaches a peak level, the brain and the body will automatically return to normal."

Joseph was not reassured. He was the one feeling the symptoms, not Dr. Ratzlaff, and it didn't feel like anything was going to get better. Instead, it was going to get worse. He was going to black out.

Dr. Ratzlaff and Letty watched him, not trying to do anything to help him. If his mother had been there, at least she would have given him a hug and tried to comfort him. Probably she would have insisted he be taken down to the emergency room again. But Letty didn't do anything but sit there, watching him.

CHAPTER THIRTY-NINE

Renata hadn't gone into the storefront clinic immediately. She and Gabriel stood outside for a long time. They watched the doors. They walked around the building slowly, looking for any warning signs. Other people watching the clinic. Surveillance cars. Bugs. Closed circuit TV cameras. People who were just dressed up as homeless people, but weren't really. She was pretty good at being able to tell the difference. She lived the life. She lived with the others in the homeless encampments almost every day. She knew when someone didn't belong, even if they had gone to the trouble of disguising themselves with dirt and BO to make them seem legitimate.

But everyone around the clinic seemed to be who they appeared to be. A few people told Renata that she could go inside and would find the kind of care she needed. People she knew from living in the city in the homeless communities. People she knew she could trust.

Except she couldn't. She couldn't trust anyone. Especially lately. However much she wanted to or told herself that she had every reason to, she just didn't. The demon at the base of her skull, whispering into her ear and sending its tendrils throughout her brain, the paranoia she lived with every day, told her that.

Gabriel had been patient through all of these precautions. He didn't question her, even when she had an inkling she might be going too far on the security. They had avoided capture, so no one could say that the measures they took were not effective. Homeless people frequently had encounters with the police, and those were people who didn't necessarily have warrants out for their arrests. People who hadn't been on TV, their faces shown all over the country fighting a high-level conspiracy with corruption that extended across many layers of government oversight. Exposing them had seemed like a good idea at the time. She had been the one to formulate the plan. But things had not turned out at all the way that they had expected.

Renata and Gabriel had gained support. There were still people finding their way to the Underground Railroad who had seen that news broadcast two years ago and wanted to be involved in the movement.

But Renata knew they could never relax. They always had to be vigilant.

"What do you think?" Gabriel asked when Renata looked at him.

"Seems like a good place," Renata said grudgingly. She wanted to find something wrong with it, because she was afraid of exposing herself. If it weren't for her mito and its attendant mental illness, flying under the radar would be a lot easier. Constantly needing her med and formula prescriptions renewed meant that she had to be in touch with medical professionals. Her name or alias had to be on their records. "But if we go here once, we're not going to be able to come back again any time in the near future."

"Make sure you get enough prescribed for a few months. And then we'll come back to get them renewed on a random day, not when they run out."

If they would prescribe enough. Doctors didn't like to prescribe too much of anything that they thought might be abused or sold, even if it were something like the antipsychotics Renata so obviously needed.

"Tell them you're going on a trip," Gabriel suggested.

"I'm homeless. I'm not jetting off to Hawaii."

"Say you got a seasonal job in Ohio and can't be back until it is done."

Renata grunted. Not a bad suggestion.

They stood there for a while longer before she was finally able to break through her fear and inertia to approach the door.

"You want me to come in?" Gabriel asked.

It would be more comforting to have him there. But they were more obvious as a couple, particularly as a mixed-race couple. People would remember them. They might remember having seen them on TV or on wanted posters, or recall them later when the police were searching for them. She shook her head.

"You keep watch. Make sure…" She shook her head. "You know what to do. Keep a close eye out for anything suspicious. But don't keep walking around the building. You'll get too tired."

Gabriel nodded. "There are plenty of places to sit down and watch from. Who's going to look at me? One homeless guy out of a whole bunch of homeless guys. If I keep my head down, nobody will remember I was ever here."

"Okay. Good. I'll turn my phone on. Text me if you see anything suspicious."

"Will do." He withdrew immediately, not hanging over her, not hovering until she went in the door. An immediate separation, so that he would not be associated with her by the people who saw her inside.

He'd learned well over the years, evolving from the naive, sheltered kid he had been the first time they'd met. He'd had to learn a lot of new skills. And she was proud of him for being so calm and careful.

Renata slipped through the doors and looked around. There were not a lot of people waiting in the common waiting room, eyeing each other and waiting hours for a doctor to see them. Instead, there was a small reception area with a nurse receptionist behind a plastic shield so no one could spit or sneeze on her.

"Hi there," the receptionist greeted. "Have you been here before?"

Renata took another look around, scanning for strangers, microphones, and cameras. "No. Never been here."

"Well then, welcome. We'll need to fill out an intake form. It's pretty short, but we do need legal name and ID for this. You will be interviewed in a private room. Your information is kept strictly confidential. We don't call anyone's social workers or the cops."

They were used to dealing with people who wanted their names kept private. That was good. "Yeah," Renata said hoarsely. "Sounds good."

The nurse pressed a button to open a door next to Renata. Renata entered the tiny room and shut the door behind her with a click.

The nurse entered from a door on the other side of the room. There was barely enough room for them both to fit when they were both sitting down. What did they do if a 300-pound guy came in? There must be another room they could take him to. One of the examination rooms, maybe.

"Okay. Let's get your stats down here," the nurse said, giving her an encouraging smile. "Just the basics. Name, birth, social, preferred gender. Any insurance information, and what meds you are on."

Renata didn't need to get anything out of her backpack to provide any of that information. She had it all memorized. The nurse listened to her describe each of the meds and how she took them, carefully writing each one down and then turning the clipboard around to show to Renata to make sure she had everything right.

Renata didn't like seeing all of her information in one place. But she was glad to see that the nurse had it all right and that she hadn't written down anything besides what Renata had told her.

"Yeah." She nodded. "That's good."

"I'll need to see picture ID to verify your identity."

Renata clenched her jaw and dug her real ID out of her backpack. She handed it over to the nurse to review and, when she was done, hid it back away.

"How long have you been on this supplemental formula?" the woman asked.

"It's not supplemental. It's my whole diet. It's been, like... since I was four."

"This is not something that is meant to be relied upon for long-term nutrition. We should look into some additional supplements that you might be able to tolerate. Make sure you are getting all of the nutrition you need. And have you tried any food allergy desensitization?"

"When I was younger, yeah. But after it nearly killed me enough times, they decided they'd better stop trying."

"There might be some more advanced methods now. And you're older, you might be able to tolerate more since it's been out of your diet for so many years."

"I don't want to do that. I'm not here for my allergies."

"Okay. Fair enough. That's up to you. I just worry about the day when they decide to change something in your formula, and you don't have anything to fall back on."

It was one of Renata's fears. That someday, she would have nothing left to eat. And she would either have to start food challenges or waste away and die of starvation.

"I need a med review. I'm not here about allergies."

"Okay. Have you been experiencing new symptoms? The adolescent years are notorious for meds to stop being effective or start causing unexpected problems."

"My paranoia is worse." Renata looked around. "I've been having hallucinations. Delusions. Worse than usual. I can't tell what is real and what isn't."

"That sounds distressing. You've noticed an increase in the symptoms? Or maybe someone you know has noticed a difference?"

"Both of us. Yeah. I'm seeing things I know are impossible. Someone looking in the window on the fourth floor. People I know are dead or who don't exist. Some of the other things... I can't tell, but my... my friend, he tells me that they don't make sense. If I ask him. He never offers it."

"He sounds like a good friend to have. Well, let's see if we can get that taken care of. I'm going to take you to another waiting room. It shouldn't be too long until the doctor can see you. I'll give him this. You can fill him in on anything else we haven't covered."

"Can I get my formula renewed too?"

The nurse wrote it down. "I'm sure that won't be a problem. Before I take you to the waiting room, I have some questions to ask you. These are questions to investigate whether there are any other services we can help you with, and if you're in a safe situation. We want to give people as much support as we can. If you don't want a service or don't want to answer a question, just tell me."

"I don't want to answer any of them." Renata had been in enough similar situations before. "I'm not in an abusive situation. I don't want help finding a job, or home, or clothes. Food stamps won't do me any good. I don't want any counseling or therapy. Just meds and formula."

"Okay." The woman put the supplemental questions away. "Fair enough. Can I give you my card so that you have my number if anything comes up? If you need a referral to a service, say, or questions about your prescriptions?"

Renata conceded. "Yeah, okay. Just don't expect me to call."

"It's totally up to you."

Renata took the card the nurse offered. It was thin cardstock with just the vital information on it. No QR codes. Renata held it up to the light and could see through it. No embedded chips or wires. She bent it in half in both directions and couldn't feel anything other than paper. She put it into one of the pockets of her backpack.

CHAPTER FORTY

The doctor was a youngish man with dark hair and eyes and silver-rimmed glasses. With a smile, he introduced himself as Dr. Caslan.

Renata looked at her phone when it vibrated, her heart rate rising, immediately going into fight-or-flight mode. She pulled it out and thumbed in the password to access Gabriel's warning.

Everything ok?

Renata swore to herself. He was not supposed to send her anything unless there was a problem.

All clear, she texted back angrily. *You?*

No bogies

She let out a sigh of relief. His code phrase. Confirming that he really was okay, not at the hands of some gunman who was forcing him to tell her that everything was fine when it wasn't.

k cu soon

She pocketed the phone. They were going to have to have a discussion with him about texting her when there was no danger, setting off her alarm bells.

"Everything okay?" Dr. Caslan asked, pushing up his glasses, which had crept down to the end of his nose yet again.

"Yeah."

"Let's get some vitals."

He reached for the blood pressure cuff, and Renata shook her head. "Wait a few minutes."

"Wait?"

"The phone scared me. Everything is going to be elevated for a few minutes."

"Ah. I suppose you're right. Mind if I check your pulse just briefly?"

Renata let him take her wrist. Caslan touched her for only a few seconds. "Yes," he agreed. "It really got your ticker going, didn't it? Let's leave that to settle back down. Tell me about your history with each of these meds."

Renata nodded her agreement and started to go through the list of the drugs she was on, how long she had been taking them, what side effects she had from them, and so on. She remembered every detail.

It was soothing to go through the medication regimen and the history of her treatments over the years. It gave her something else to focus her attention on. Something dry and clinical instead of looking to the future and seeing all of the possible dangers that lurked there. She even shared a couple of funny stories with him about when things had gone wrong with her drugs. Funny to look back on now. They hadn't been funny back then.

Dr. Caslan was good. He asked her about her opinion on each of the drugs, how they were affecting her, and how she thought raising or lowering the dosage might work. He pushed up his glasses again.

"If possible, I would like to avoid trying something new. If we can just adjust dosages, we don't have to worry about the potential of a severe reaction to something that you haven't taken before."

"Yeah, that would be good," Renata agreed. So many of the doctors that she saw were allergy deniers. They said that she couldn't be allergic to everything like she was and that she wouldn't react to a new medication because it was known to be safe.

Just because it was safe for the majority of the population, that did not mean that it was safe for Renata. She was a whole different story.

She and Dr. Caslan put their heads together and made several adjustments to her medication dosages. Because they were in liquid form and Renata measured them out herself, she didn't have to get new bottles of pills. But she did get him to write her new prescriptions for the next few months, mindful of Gabriel's advice to keep them from coming back there too often. The doctor waved away her story about needing them because she was going on a trip.

"You don't need a cover story. The most I can prescribe is three months' worth. Plus, I'll give you a half-month emergency prescription over the phone any time. Three and a half months is the best I can do, then the regulators say I have to see you again."

"Great, thanks."

"Who wants to be coming back here every month to renew meds?" He rolled his eyes. "Besides, if all of our patients come back monthly instead of quarterly, we've got three times the traffic and three times the man-hours to pay for." He pushed up his glasses. "I don't need that," he confided with a smile and a shake of his head.

He pulled out his prescription pad and wrote the prescriptions out in remarkably neat printing. He saw her looking at the printing and laughed. "I know, I'm a disgrace to doctors everywhere. But we don't want the pharmacist misreading my handwriting and giving you the wrong thing, do we? It's even more dangerous for you than for most patients. You be sure to check the label and make sure he got it right, though. Don't trust anything to chance."

"I always do."

"Good. You probably would not have gotten this far if you weren't careful."

He included a prescription for her formula, which Renata needed to have refilled immediately.

Dr. Caslan ushered Renata to the door. He lifted his hand to shake hers, but quickly dropped it again, knowing or suspecting that she wouldn't want to be touched. "Take care. If this doesn't help, then come by again or give me a call. We can discuss possible alternatives. You should notice a change within a day or two. Call if you don't," he repeated firmly, "we'll work on it until we get it right."

"Okay. I will. Thanks."

When she walked through the reception area, it was again empty. No one watching her go other than the nurse receptionist. She didn't give Renata more than a glance before returning to the work she was doing on her computer.

Looking around outside, Renata spotted Gabriel and approached him casually. She pretended she was just waiting for the bus and not talking to him. No one watching her would know that she was there with someone.

"How did it go?" Gabriel asked.

"Great, other than you scaring me to death when you texted me. I was ready to run."

"Dang. Sorry. I just wanted to make sure that everything was going all right. Do you need an extra feeding?"

If she had burned through too much of her cellular energy stores with that hit of adrenaline, she would need an early or extra feeding to restore them before she bonked. Renata considered, reviewing how she had felt after the text and while talking to the doctor. The elevation had only lasted a few minutes, returning quickly to normal as she had reviewed her medication history with the doctor.

"I think I'm okay," she said. "I'll maybe just move up my noon feeding a bit to make sure I don't run out before then."

Gabriel looked at the time on his phone and nodded. "You need to go to the pharmacy?"

"Yeah. Just for the formula. Don't need any new meds."

"He's not giving you anything new?" Gabriel frowned, concerned.

"No, we're trying just readjusting dosages rather than introducing anything new."

"Oh, okay. I guess that makes sense. You want me to wait here while you get it?"

Renata nodded. He probably wanted to get up and move around, but it was best if they weren't seen as a couple until it was time to go. "I won't be long, and then we can go."

"They were pretty good in there? Did we make a good choice?"

"Yeah, it was a good call, Gabe. Good choice. It's almost like they know what they're doing." She laughed.

"Good." He nodded.

Renata moved away. She didn't walk directly to the pharmacy, but wandered around the square for a few minutes, watching everybody else and making sure no one was paying her or Gabriel too much attention. Eventually, she felt sure enough of herself to take the prescription into the pharmacy, where she handed it over at the counter.

"It will be ten minutes," the young technician told her.

Renata raised her brows. "All you have to do is pull out a flat of formula cans and label it."

"I know that. But we have other people here ahead of you and need to process their prescriptions first. We'll get to yours in about ten minutes."

Renata looked around. She didn't like being trapped in the small pharmacy, even for just ten minutes.

"Have a look around," the technician said. "Maybe you need something. Get your shopping done while you wait and, in ten minutes, you should be on your way."

It wasn't that different from spending ten minutes in the grocery store when Gabriel needed to resupply. But Renata couldn't help feeling anxious about it. She nodded and moved away from the counter into the aisles.

Living as they did on the street, they kept their packs as light as possible. They lived a minimalist lifestyle, not buying anything they didn't need daily. So she didn't have any need to stock up on anything. She browsed up and down the aisles anyway.

"Renata?"

Renata jumped like she had been shocked with a cattle prod. She practically changed direction mid-air like a cat and came down facing the owner of the voice, a man she didn't recognize at first. She looked at him, heart pounding, ready to run but unsure who he was or how he had recognized her.

"Hey, it's okay," he said, holding his empty hands up in front of him, showing that he was not armed. "It's me, Ethan."

She worked through her mental contact list. Ethan? Ethan from where?

"Who?"

"Nurse Ethan. Psych ward. It's okay."

Ethan. The recollections came back to Renata as she stared at him. He had always been pretty low-key. She couldn't remember much about him. If she'd had any negative encounters with him, she would remember. So he was safe, at least on that basic level. But that didn't mean he wouldn't mention to anyone that he had seen her there. All of her careful reconnaissance was out the window.

"Uh… Nurse Ethan. Right. Sorry, it's been a while."

"No problem. I'm sorry to bother you; I was just surprised to see you here and… I wanted to see how you were. I'm glad that you're looking so good." His eyes traveled over her, probably trying to read whether she was homeless and what kind of shape she was really in.

But Renata was proud of her appearance. She was careful not to look homeless, unless she was using her homelessness as a cover. If she didn't want people to see her, then looking like she was down on her luck and might ask them for money or drugs was the easiest way to ensure that people didn't make eye contact or look at her closely. They would hurry away and never remember anything specific about her, other than that they had seen some homeless lady. They wouldn't remember her face or any physical details.

"Yeah, I'm good," Renata said. "Are you still there? At the hospital?"

"Yeah. Just like always. But you haven't visited me lately." He faked pouting about it. "We miss you."

Renata shook her head. "Well, I'm doing pretty good. I'm not planning to come back."

"Nothing that makes me happier than that," he assured her, erasing the pout. "I'm really glad. You've had some tough times."

"Yeah. But it's all good right now. Stable, happy…" She felt slightly guilty about lying to him, but not very much. He didn't need to know that she was unstable right now. "Listen… can you not tell anyone you saw me here? It's a privacy thing, you know? I don't need people to know my history, and I don't want people from my old life to know where I am now. I'm in a good place. I don't want people showing up from my past and making a mess of it."

"Ouch." He frowned. "People from your past showing up and

making a mess of things? I'm not going to do that. I just wanted to say hi and tell you I was glad to see that you are doing so well."

"I'm not accusing *you*," Renata clarified. "I just mean that anyone else you tell, if they showed up and wanted to reconnect... it could cause me problems, you know?"

She smiled and fluttered her lashes and did everything she could think of to reassure him that she didn't mean *he* was going to mess up her life by being there, but that she needed a protector from the rest of the big, bad world.

"Oh, of course," Ethan agreed, his expression clearing. "I won't talk to anyone else about it. I don't want to mess up your recovery. You are looking really good. Especially when I think back to how rough things were when you were in psych that last time."

It had been a very tough go and a long haul. Renata didn't like to think of it too much. And she didn't want to go back there for any reason. She needed to stay focused and on target and make sure that no one would come back looking for her.

"Thanks. And I mean *no one*, right? Even if it is someone you think would be safe and wouldn't go blabbing to anyone. Seal the vault."

Ethan mimed zipping his lip. "I won't say a word to anyone. I won't mention your name, won't mention I saw you, won't even say that I ran into someone I knew. Your life will stay completely private."

Renata nodded and touched him on the arm. "Thank you so much."

CHAPTER FORTY-ONE

Joseph lay in his bed for a long time after he woke up. He felt very sleepy and unmotivated to open his eyes or get out of bed. He just floated there, in a timeless void, not thinking about anything.

He didn't think that time was even operating anymore.

Something was wrong, but he didn't care. It didn't matter. Something would always be wrong, but that didn't mean he needed to fix it. He could just... stay there in bed, drifting for as long as he wanted to. There was no need to do anything else.

But eventually, the fuzziness and the feeling of well-being started to wear off and Joseph was forced by his sluggishly working brain to open his eyes to see where he was and to orient himself in time and space. His eyes met a blank white wall. It was another long, indeterminate length of time before he had the energy to roll over and look in the other direction. That was when it became evident that he was in the hospital.

That information stayed in his brain for a long time, simmering, while he tried not to remember why he was there. But eventually, the knowledge came to him as the sense of fogginess continued to wear off.

In the psych ward. He was in the psych ward again. Not for

depression this time, but because he kept having panic attacks and fainting spells. He was gradually losing his mind. That was what was wrong. He was going to get progressively worse and worse, until he had lost everything that remained of his old life. He had lost his family, home, school, and soccer. The only thing left was his mind. And when that was gone, who would he be?

Most of the day had melted away when she came to see him again. Nurses had come and gone, some of them with meals or pills, and some of them just to check on him and give him an encouraging word or two, or to try to get him out of his bed and back on his feet again. They didn't say that was what they were trying to do, but it was obvious.

Letty looked in the door before marching in as if she owned the place and he had no right to refuse her. He didn't know whether he was allowed to do that or not. It used to be his mother who had kept him company, and he had wanted her there as much as possible.

Letty was another story.

But he didn't know what his options were. Lie there and just put up with her presence? That was the easiest. Calling someone or trying to reason with her was beyond his mental capacities.

"Joseph." She entered and sat on the foot of his bed. There was no visitor chair. Not like in a regular hospital room where, even if there wasn't one by your bed, you could drag one over. "Well, you look like a mess today. How has your day been?"

"Been sleeping," Joseph croaked, having difficulty finding his voice.

"All day? You haven't been up at all?"

"No."

Joseph tried to turn away from her so he didn't have to look at her. It would be better if he could get back to sleep and when he woke up again, maybe the nightmare would be over this time. But he found it difficult to move his body. Maybe in a few hours, his body would obey his instructions.

"Dr. Ratzlaff gave you something that he said would lower your anxiety level."

It had lowered Joseph's *everything* level. "Uh-huh."

"Do you want to talk about what happened during your appointment?"

"No. Don't remember."

"We were talking about your problem. These 'fainting spells' or 'anxiety attacks.' And how they are psychologically based. You are so caught up in the pain of losing your father and his influence in your life that you're doing whatever you can to get attention elsewhere."

Joseph grunted.

"I'd like to hear your feedback on that, Joseph. I'd really like to hear your thoughts."

"I don't *like* being sick."

"Nobody does. But apparently, your need for approval and attention overrides any discomfort from being sick. You would rather be sick and get the attention than healthy and not getting that need fulfilled."

Joseph could tell her what he thought of that idea, but doubted she would appreciate that kind of language from him.

"But you're not ready to deal with these issues yet, clearly."

Joseph shrugged. At least, in his mind he did. He wasn't sure that his body followed suit.

For a while, Letty just sat there looking at Joseph. He closed his eyes and pretended she wasn't there. He started to drift off to sleep again a couple of times, but each time he did, she would clear her throat or move slightly, and he was forced back to the real world to deal with his problems.

"Let me explain something to you, Joseph. As long as you refuse to acknowledge your problem, you are not going to get out of here. You will be staying here for a long time."

Joseph wasn't sure whether he stayed awake until Letty left or not. He might have eventually managed to fall asleep while she was there.

Each time he awoke, he was a little clearer, although every time he took a tiny cup full of pills, he hoped that it would put him back into that fuzzy, comfortable place and that he wouldn't have to think anymore. If he couldn't have his life, why not just live in that comfortable, pleasant place? No anxiety. No panic attacks. No seizures or fainting spells. Just floating in a warm place with no unhappy feelings.

But whatever Dr. Ratzlaff had given him after the failed session was apparently not part of Joseph's new regimen. Or if it was, it was in a much smaller dosage.

"Rise and shine," a young, chipper nurse urged him. "I've got your morning pills for you, and today is the day you get back up and face life again."

Joseph sat up, which he found was relatively easy. Surveying things from the upright position, he was more inclined to *do something* than to lie down again and sleep another day away.

"Good," the nurse approved. "Time to get you on your feet again. If you're going to hang around here, you should get into the routine!"

She bustled around him, chattering away and encouraging him to get out to talk to the other patients and staff again.

Letty's voice was still in Joseph's brain, on an endless repeat.

As long as you refuse to acknowledge your problem, you are not going to get out of here.

He didn't doubt that Letty was telling him the truth as she knew it. She wouldn't encourage Dr. Ratzlaff to release Joseph back to his foster home. Would Dr. Ratzlaff do it anyway if he thought that Joseph was ready?

But then, where would he live if he were released before DCFS was ready for him to be? Would he go back to the Brewsters'? Would it be somewhere else? Was there someone else who would take him? Or would it be a group home or juvenile holding facility? Was that the way he wanted to spend his life? If he couldn't be at home with his own family, where did he want to go?

He remembered patients when he had been in psych before who had been there for months. Despite the psych ward's policy to keep people moving through as quickly as possible, to get them back on the street as soon as they could manage it, some people languished there for a very long time until they were stabilized.

He had always felt bad for those people. He knew that even

though his depression was bad, if he stayed there for a little while to get his medications recalibrated and have a few sessions with the doctors, he would feel better and be able to face his life again. Sometimes, it took a week or two, but he would leave feeling better and like he had a path to follow again.

He had wondered what it would be like to have to stay there for months, swinging back and forth, meds being changed every few days or weeks to try to deal with a new symptom or contraindication.

Renata had been one of those people.

It hadn't been back in November, but his hospital stay before that. She had already been there for months when he arrived. He heard the other patients gossiping about her and all of her exploits. How difficult she was for the staff. Almost as if she were being as troublesome as she could.

That was how he had seen her. *Trouble.* Someone who found trouble only because she was always looking for it. Had he misjudged her? Had she been someone who, like Joseph, was not trying to get attention, but just needed someone who tried hard enough to understand and track down the physical causes of her illness instead of attributing it to bad character?

He'd heard the same about kids with Oppositional Defiance Disorder. That even though they looked like they had an attitude and were trying to be as bad as they could, it was really anxiety, not attitude, that drove the behaviors. Just like a hyperactive kid like Axel wasn't trying to drive everyone crazy with his movement and energy. That was just the way his brain worked.

Even though Axel could be annoying, and Joseph *had* thought he was being deliberately irritating at times, he was a sweet kid and was doing his best.

Joseph knew that his own issues were not attention-seeking. He could do without all the attention he'd been getting from the adults in his life lately. They didn't do anything but cause him grief. What was the point of getting negative attention? People who told him nothing was wrong with him and he was just acting out?

He knew that there was a physical reason for everything that had happened. He didn't know what it was, but he knew it was physical and not emotional. Every time they did another test, he expected them to find it, but each time they came back and said that wasn't it, dashing his hopes of finding a solution. He wanted to go back home. Back to his own school. Back to soccer.

But none of that would happen while he was languishing in the psych ward.

Letty had told him what he needed to do if he wanted to get out.

As long as you refuse to acknowledge your problem, you are not going to get out of here.

CHAPTER FORTY-TWO

Joseph had a plan. He started putting it into motion immediately after taking his pills and the nurse leaving his room. He went out to the nurse's station and again asked about clothing.

"If they can't find my clothes, is there any… spare clothing around? Like a lost and found or something? I want to dress like a normal person. I want to start working on getting out. I'll work with Dr. Ratzlaff, do whatever he wants me to do to get out. I don't want to be stuck here forever."

The nurse at the station nodded thoughtfully. "Yes, we could probably find you something. You could ask your social worker to bring more clothes by."

Joseph nodded, sighing to himself. It would have been a good idea if anyone other than his mother had his clothes. He had been forced to wear hand-me-downs at the Brewsters' because he had arrived without anything of his own. What would be great would be if Letty could go to Joseph's house and get some of his clothes from Mira. He didn't see why she couldn't do that. All of those clothes were just sitting there waiting for him. Nobody else was using them.

But he didn't dare suggest to Letty that she should have anything to do with Mira. If he did, she was sure to find something else wrong with her. DCFS would just keep adding deficiencies to Mira's roster, ensuring she couldn't get Joseph back.

He talked to the other patients and tried to show the staff how sociable and normal he was. He ignored any of Milo's needles and just kept acting like everyone there was his greatest friend. He could get along with anyone. He wasn't isolated and in need of special attention from his mother. Or foster mother. Or social worker. He was a strong, confident person with his own mind, capable of directing his own life.

He asked several times after Dr. Ratzlaff and said he wanted to meet with him. While they put him off the first few times he asked, eventually, the nurses tired of his inquiries and told him that they would see to it that he saw Dr. Ratzlaff. So he did get an appointment squeezed in at the end of the day, even though they had initially told him that Dr. Ratzlaff would not be in until the following week. Joseph did not want to wait around for him. He wanted to tackle the problem head-on. Immediately.

Dr. Ratzlaff looked Joseph over when he came into the office. "So, what's going on with you today, Joseph? I hear you've been harassing the nurses."

"Not harassing them," Joseph objected. "I've been very good. I just wanted to see you. I can ask to see my doctor, can't I?"

"Yes, but apparently, you have been quite… insistent."

Joseph nodded. "I know. Maybe I shouldn't be, but… I just really needed to talk to you."

"So what is the problem? Are you having new symptoms?"

"No. It isn't anything like that. I just… Well, Letty—Mrs. Miller —she was telling me that I needed to… admit my problem and work on it if I wanted to get out of here. And I do. I want to get out of here, but I want to work on my problems, too. I want to… get past these issues. I really don't want to be like this. She asked if I want to be sick, and I don't. I want to be like I was before—or better. I want to be stronger. I want to deal with my emotional issues. Not hide from them."

Ratzlaff studied him for a few moments.

"That's what you want, is it?"

Joseph swallowed. He was afraid that Ratzlaff could see through his ruse and knew he didn't want to change. He just wanted to get out of there. But he nodded again. "Yeah. I want to change. I want to get better."

"That's good news. When a patient is ready to take responsibility for his own health, that can change everything. I'm sure you want to go home, but it is good to see that you are ready to work on yourself. When a patient decides it is time to take control of his own life…" Here, Dr. Ratzlaff gave a nod. "It is a most crucial juncture."

Joseph nodded, trying to look as though that was exactly what he wanted. Certainly, it was what he wanted to hear from Dr. Ratzlaff. He wanted to know that his efforts would be taken seriously and be rewarded.

"So what do I need to do to get started?" he asked. "I know today isn't a regular therapy day and I should just wait until we would normally meet, but I want to start now."

"Well…" Ratzlaff frowned, thinking about it. "We need to have a deeper discussion about your beliefs about yourself and your family and how that impacts your health. But maybe for now… some affirmations on how you are a worthwhile person by yourself and don't need a bunch of extra attention from those who are close to you. They will love and care for you no matter what you do. Whether you are the best soccer player on the team, whether you need to take time off because of your depression, or are able to maintain top marks at school. No matter your achievements, they will still love you and do whatever they can for you."

Joseph ran his fingertip down the seam of the jeans that the nurses had been able to find for him. "Do you know… before I came here, my dad had just told me he couldn't take me. I thought that if my mom couldn't have custody of me, then at least he could. That I had another parent who could step in."

Dr. Ratzlaff nodded. "Yes…?"

"And… he told me no. He said that he has a new baby on the way, and he can't take me in. It would be too much for him."

"And how did that make you feel?"

Joseph swallowed. How did Ratzlaff *think* that it made him feel?

"Pretty awful. I thought… if he loved me, it would be okay. He could take me in for a few months until things were sorted out with my mom. I could help around the house. Help with the new baby. I wouldn't be a burden."

"But he wasn't willing to listen to your arguments."

"No. He said I wasn't listening to him. He wouldn't take me in. He figured foster care was the best place for me."

"That was very upsetting, I am sure. Is that when you had your breakdown?"

"Right before coming here… yeah. It wasn't a *breakdown*, though. My chest hurt and I almost passed out and…"

Joseph trailed off, remembering that, as far as Ratzlaff was concerned, his collapse was emotional, not physical. It didn't matter what he had been feeling physically. That was just a reflection of his emotional state.

"I mean… I guess so. I guess that affected me so badly that I just… I didn't know what to do with myself. I didn't know how to handle it. I was so… upset."

"That's perfectly understandable, and I'm glad to know what triggered that episode. As we figure out what things are causing these reactions, we will be better able to combat them. As painful as it might be to deal with these feelings straight on, *that* is the way that we are going to get to the root of your problems. Understand?"

Joseph nodded his agreement. "So…" he swallowed and kept going, "what I need to do is to say that even though my dad can't take me… he still loves me, and I don't need any extra attention from him."

"That would be an excellent start. It was clearly very difficult for you emotionally when your parents divorced. So difficult that even you yourself didn't know it."

"Uh… yeah."

"Well, I must be getting home to my own family this evening, so that's all the time we can spend together right now. But I would like to talk to you again early next week to see how things are going."

"Yeah. Can we do that?"

"Of course. You think about this and work on it until I can

schedule another session for you, and we'll see where you are then. How does that sound?"

Joseph nodded. "Thanks. That would be good. And will you... tell Mrs. Miller that I am working on it? That I'm paying attention to what she said and I'm trying?"

"Of course. I'm glad to see you making this progress, Joseph. I was concerned that you were not willing to look at yourself and your own attachment to these emotional states objectively. We all have certain beliefs about ourselves, and it can be hard to see when we are holding ourselves back."

"I don't want to keep doing that. I want to get over it."

"I'm sure you do, and we are here to help you."

CHAPTER FORTY-THREE

Renata watched as Gabriel finished setting up the tent and then looked around her, eyes sharp, looking for anyone she knew or anything out of place. She liked to be sure of herself. She didn't want to sleep there if there were any potential dangers. They had left the park before due to perceived threats and, at least twice before, she had been proven correct when something had happened in the encampment after she left. Even though they had everything set up and were ready to settle in for the night, if anything didn't seem right, she was prepared to move on.

A woman across the park space from her was watching her thoughtfully, her brow knotted. When Renata met her eyes, she didn't look away, but instead looked as though she would walk over and meet her. Renata stiffened.

Gabriel's head swiveled, and he looked at her. Even though he had not been watching her, he had still sensed her shift and knew something was wrong.

"What is it?"

Renata made a staying motion with one hand, still watching the woman across the park.

She was familiar. Not just because they'd stayed in the same encampment before. A lot of the homeless were familiar to Renata.

They had seen them many times in the last couple of years. She didn't associate closely with anyone other than Gabriel, but they knew a number of people by name or habit.

Gabriel looked across the park and made out who Renata was looking at.

"She's been here before. She's okay."

"She was looking at me."

Gabriel didn't argue that the woman had probably been looking at something else or hadn't intended to stare at Renata or to meet her eyes, or whatever else someone might be inclined to say. Someone other than Gabriel. He knew better than to disagree.

The woman did not walk across to Renata, approaching the tent, but instead twitched her head slightly toward the water fountain that was a focal point for the park.

Renata looked at Gabriel. "Stay with the tent. Be alert. Watch for me to come back."

He nodded his agreement.

Renata walked over to the fountain, her heart pounding and her brain working through all the possibilities. It might be nothing. Just a familiar face, someone who had seen her there a few times and wanted to say hello.

But it could also be someone who planned to turn her in for some kind of monetary compensation or because she thought that what Renata was doing was wrong. Or anything in between.

"Hi." The woman also glanced around, looking just as paranoid as Renata that someone might listen in on their conversation. But the running water of the fountain would help to cover it up. "Renata, right?"

Renata set her jaw. "Do I know you?"

"No, you probably don't remember me. We were together in psych for a while. But I was pretty quiet, kept to myself."

"And I didn't?" Renata challenged.

Anyone who knew her would know that Renata was not a shrinking violet. She spoke her mind, and she had never, as far as she could remember, just kept to herself and not talked to anyone else in psych. She had to talk to people. And even more if she were unstable or on a psychotic break. And she would not necessarily remember anyone she had met while on a break.

The woman snorted. "Have you ever kept to yourself?"

Renata gave a slight smile and shook her head.

"I'm Abby," the woman introduced herself.

"Abby. I've seen you around here before."

"Yeah. I come here sometimes."

Renata nodded and looked at Abby, waiting for her to say what she wanted. She obviously wanted to talk to Renata about something, had taken the time to find Renata, and establish who she was and how they knew each other. It wasn't just a casual nod at each other across the park.

"Do you remember a nurse at psych named Ethan?" Abby asked eventually.

Renata ground her teeth. She had explicitly told Ethan not to mention he had seen her. Not to anyone. And here was someone approaching Renata after obviously having talked to Ethan about her. What did he think she had meant when she said not to mention their chance meeting?

"Yeah, I remember Ethan. What about him?"

"Well, he's trying to reach out to you."

Renata blinked. She studied Abby carefully, trying to reach every part of her expression.

"What do you mean he's trying to reach out to me?"

"He said that he thought you might be homeless. He didn't have any way to find out where you were and didn't have a number for you or anything, but he thought I might have run into you because…" Abby shrugged and motioned to their surroundings. Because she was homeless, and sometimes homeless people ran into each other when they were out and about.

"Okay." Renata thought about that. Her forehead scrunched in concentration. She wanted to find out as much as possible about what was happening without giving away anything about herself. "So why did he want to reach out to me?"

"I don't know. He didn't tell me what it was about. Just that he wanted to get in contact with you if he could."

"So how am I supposed to get in touch with him? I'm not calling him at the hospital."

"He gave me a number." Abby didn't immediately reach for it, looking at Renata for her reaction. Renata nodded impatiently. Abby started patting her pockets and reaching into them, looking for the stray paper. Eventually, she came up with a slip of paper, folded over a couple of times. She handed it to Renata. Renata unfolded it and looked at it.

No names on the paper. Not hers and not Ethan's and, thankfully, not both of them together. Renata didn't want to be tied to anyone else. That would be dangerous. Just the words "call me, private number" and a series of digits.

"Okay," Renata said. "Thanks."

Abby nodded. She smoothed her jacket in case it had gotten rumpled while she was looking for the number. "Are you going to call him?"

"That's not any of your business."

"No, I know that… I just wondered. He's a nice guy. Good nurse. But you're already with somebody," Abby nodded across the park back to where Gabriel stood with the tent, keeping an eye on her.

Renata snorted. She wasn't romantically involved with Gabriel and wasn't about to get entwined with a nurse from the psych ward at the hospital. But she didn't disclaim a relationship with Gabriel. Abby had been around the park before. She knew they were always together and shared a tent. She would just ask more questions if Renata tried to convince her that they were not romantically involved.

"I'm not getting involved with Ethan," Renata told Abby. "I don't know what he wants me to call him about, but it's not *that*."

"Oh, okay. Good. I wasn't sure what it was about."

"I don't know either. I'll find out when I call him. Later. When it's safe."

"Sure. Yeah. When it's safe." Abby looked around, then decided it was time for her to leave. "Well, nice to see you again, Renata. You… take care."

Renata nodded. "You too."

She watched Abby walk back across the park to where she had

been. She waited around for a minute or two, keeping an eye on her, watching to see if she reached for her phone or did anything suspicious. Then Renata walked slowly back over to their tent.

"Everything okay?" Gabriel asked, alert.

"Yeah."

"What was all that about?" He had undoubtedly seen the paper pass hands.

"Someone reaching out to me."

"Her? About what?"

"No. Not her. Someone else. Do you remember the nurse at psych? Ethan?"

"Uh… yeah. I think so."

Renata shrugged. It had been a longer time since Gabriel had been in Psych, and he hadn't been there for as long as Renata. She didn't expect him to remember everybody. It was just an introduction to the topic.

"He told Abby that he was trying to reach me."

"Why would he talk to her?"

"Because he figured she was homeless and hoped she might have some contact with me."

"And how would he know that *you* were?"

"I ran into him at the pharmacy."

Gabriel's brows went up. "You did? You didn't mention it."

"Didn't I?" Renata tried to give the impression that she was surprised. That she thought they had talked about it at the time. "Well, yeah, he was there while I was picking up my formula prescription. I guess he figured that I might be homeless or close to the homeless community because that's where I was getting my prescription filled. But I could have been living over there. Just because I use that pharmacy, that doesn't mean that I'm homeless."

"No. But he figured it out."

"I don't *look* homeless." Renata looked down at herself. She was meticulous about the image she projected. Always very neat and clean. She didn't look homeless unless she wanted to.

"You look fine," Gabriel assured her.

"You say that, but it doesn't make it true. Maybe we're so used to living with these people that we've let our standards fall. Maybe we look homeless and don't even know it."

He considered it for a moment before answering. "I don't think so."

Renata nodded slowly, but wasn't convinced.

"Anyway," Gabriel said, raising his brows again. "You saw Ethan while you were at the pharmacy, and he told her that he wanted to reach out to you after that?"

"Yeah."

"Why would he? Just to make sure that you're okay? Officially following up under some outreach program? What is it about?"

Renata displayed the handwritten note to him.

call me, private number

"Okay…" Gabriel shrugged. "But you don't know what it is about?"

"No."

"You want to call him now?"

"No. Not while someone knows where we are." Renata nodded in the direction of Abby. "I talk to him, and then he calls her to find out where I am, and then we have cops or doctors or something worse showing up here trying to take us into custody." She shook her head. "No, I won't be calling him back while anyone knows where we are."

Gabriel nodded, seeing the wisdom in this course of action. "Do you still want to stay here tonight?" he checked.

Renata looked at the tent. They could pack it back away and move on somewhere else. It wouldn't be as comfortable, but it would be safer.

Abby seemed to have taken precautions to ensure that Renata's privacy was protected. But she could turn around and call Ethan at any moment. But why? Ethan had never been involved in anything bad at the hospital. She'd never had any physical run-ins with him that had gone the wrong direction.

Renata wasn't sure that she had the energy to go somewhere and get set up again. She looked at Gabriel's face. Even though he was offering to go set up somewhere else, he looked as tired and worn out as she felt. Doing too much, forcing him to move when he was already tired, could result in a dangerous situation.

"Yeah, I think we'll stay here," she agreed. "We'll keep an eye out for the next hour or so, but I think we're safe tonight."

Gabriel nodded, careful not to give away his relief, though she knew he must feel it.

"I'll call Ethan tomorrow. Or the next day. After we've been separated from Abby for a while."

CHAPTER FORTY-FOUR

Joseph was feeling pretty good about his progress. He felt like everyone around him had taken note of the fact that he was working on his situation and that he would get out soon. The nurses, doctors, and other patients all knew that he was only going to be there for a short period of time, and then he would be ready for release.

He wished that he had been put on an involuntary hold. That would only have lasted 72 hours, and then he would be back out on the street. Or back with the Brewsters, to be more accurate. But because he was a minor, his guardian was allowed to admit him, not on an involuntary hold, and he was shut up tight. For as long as Dr. Ratzlaff and Letty decided he needed to be.

But he was on top of that. If he agreed with everything they said and put on a good show of doing everything they asked him to, coming to a realization that they were right about everything, then they would have to admit that he was well enough to be released. They couldn't keep him there if he seemed to be stable. No more emotional displays. No more panic attacks or obvious anxiety. Nothing that might look like attention-seeking. Everything had to look normal and healthy. They couldn't keep him after that. Not for long.

Ethan came up beside Joseph. "I need to do a follow-up," Ethan told Joseph. "Come back to your room."

Joseph looked at him for a moment, then nodded. Something in Ethan's eyes said that he had made progress, and it wasn't just to ask him follow-up questions on his medication and whether the latest changes had caused any further symptoms.

They both went back to Joseph's tiny room. Ethan hung around in the hallway for a few seconds longer than Joseph, looking around for anyone who might be paying attention to them or listening in on their conversation.

Then he joined Joseph.

"Okay," he said. "You wanted to reach out to Renata. I have made contact with her."

"You have?" Joseph was floored. He hadn't thought that the nurse would actually be able to reach her. Ethan had already looked up her records and said there wasn't any current address on her file, no phone number that worked. Joseph assumed it was a dead end. Reaching Renata had been a long shot. He hadn't thought that it would work out.

"Yeah. She remembers you from before. She said that if you wanted to contact her, you could."

"You have a phone number now?"

"Yes. It will only work for a few days, so I don't know…" Ethan did not offer Joseph the use of his personal cell phone.

"I don't know if I'll be out of here in that length of time."

Ethan hesitated. "You might be. They seem to be getting close to releasing you. But there's no guarantee."

"Can't I use your phone?"

"If word gets out that I am letting a patient use my phone…"

"You think that would get out? I'm not going to tell anyone!"

"No," Ethan agreed. He looked out into the corridor again. "As long as you don't say anything and no one sees you. But we have to be careful. No one can know that I'm doing this."

"Doing what?" Joseph grinned.

"Let's give it a day to see if they release you or say they are going to release you."

Joseph sighed heavily. Now that he knew that he could get in contact with Renata, he didn't want to wait. He didn't know whether she could do anything to help him, but she was someone who would understand what he was going through, unlike anyone else he knew. He *needed* to talk to her.

Maybe that was exactly what Letty and Dr. Ratzlaff were talking about. How he needed attention. He needed someone else who understood what he was going through. It was a yearning that he couldn't think of any other way to satisfy. He needed someone to believe him. Renata would believe.

"Just another day or two," Ethan said. "It will be better if you aren't here when you contact her. Then, no one can overhear you or trace her. And they won't find any connection to me."

"You haven't done anything wrong. Just helped me to find an old friend from the psych ward. What's wrong with that?"

"You don't know these guys. They can be… very suspicious. They don't need a logical reason to suspect me of anything."

"Paranoid?" Joseph teased.

Ethan rolled his eyes. "No one is paranoid like Renata, I'll tell you that. Even when she's on her meds, that girl is a…" Ethan cut himself off before finishing the thought. He shook his head. "I know you want to reconnect to an old friend, but there are other options that would probably be a safer bet. She's been in some trouble since she was here, you know. And even while she was here. She's… not the kind of person to stay quiet."

Joseph remembered that about her. She had been an interesting person to be around. Life was never boring with Renata Vega around.

"I don't want to wait. If you've got the number now, why can't I call her? She can help me figure out what I need to do to get out of here."

"She's better at getting in than getting out," Ethan disagreed. "You're already close to getting out on your own. Don't do anything to jeopardize that."

Joseph pressed a knuckle into his forehead. "No, fine. I won't. I don't want to get caught 'breaking the rules' and have them give me a longer sentence."

Ethan gave him a sympathetic look, head cocked slightly to the side, and shrugged. He didn't disagree and say that Joseph was exaggerating or embellishing how the psych ward worked there. How could he? Joseph knew that what he was saying was true. If he behaved the way that he was expected to, following the unwritten rules of the ward, then he would be treated better and would be able to be released to the Brewsters much faster than he would be if he fought back with the medical staff, disagreed with his diagnosis, or said that he wanted to get out of there more than he wanted to be cured.

He might not actually get a *sentence* for objectionable behavior. Still, people like Dr. Ratzlaff made decisions over his life, deciding how long he would stay there, what kind of care he would be given, what privileges he would have, and a hundred other choices about his life. They could make him stay as long as they liked and make his life miserable while he was there.

"And you haven't had any other symptoms?" Ethan asked in a crisp tone.

Joseph knew that someone must be in the hall outside his room, behind his back.

"No. Everything is working really well," he assured Ethan.

"All right. That's everything I need from you. You've been doing really well. Keep it up."

"Thanks." Joseph nodded. He turned around and saw one of the other nurses there, pausing to look in on them, though she pretended not to have heard anything. Joseph smiled politely, pretending that he didn't know or care. He was just friendly young Joseph Demain, working on his own stuff, keeping his head down and not causing any trouble.

CHAPTER FORTY-FIVE

Joseph had been waiting for Letty all day. She had said that she would be there at eight in the morning, so he had been ready, dressed in clothes that were not his, waiting for her, since that time. Every half hour or so, he would ask the nurses if they had heard anything. They kept telling him that they hadn't and it wasn't their job to keep the social worker on schedule. Social workers came and went as they pleased. Sometimes, they had to deal with emergency situations. It wasn't all teenage boys who were just fine, sitting on a comfortable chair while he waited for her. Some cases were a lot worse than that.

"I know, I know," Joseph moaned. "It's just that she said she would be here at eight. If she didn't know what time she was coming by, she should have just said that. 'I'll be coming sometime tomorrow,' and it would be just fine. I could relax and do something else while I was waiting. But she said she would be here at eight!"

"We can tell time," the nurse said briskly. "But we can't make her come any faster."

Joseph stood there for another minute. Not because he expected to see Letty walking through the elevator doors into the ward. He just wanted her to be there. She had said she would be there early to take him back to the Brewsters.

It was nearly noon when he finally accepted that she wasn't coming. He took his lunch at one of the tables in the common room rather than retreating to his room so he would still be able to see Letty if she came in while he was eating.

Not that it made any difference.

When lunch was cleared away, she still had not shown up. Joseph sank down in front of the TV, staring up at the screen in an attempt to distract himself from his thoughts.

He wasn't going to get excited or upset. He wouldn't wind himself up or raise his heart rate by being angry. It was what it was.

He had been so excited the night before that he hadn't gotten much sleep, so he ended up falling asleep in front of the TV.

Joseph awoke to Letty shaking him by the shoulder, looking down at him with reserved amusement in her expression.

"I expected you to be pacing around waiting for me to show up," she said dryly.

"I wore out the tile this morning," Joseph admitted. "But I stopped at noon. And then…" He stretched and yawned loudly.

"It would appear you needed a nap."

"Yeah. Didn't sleep much last night."

"Didn't they give you a sleeping pill?"

"No, I didn't want anything."

"Sleep is important to your mental health."

"I know it is, but it was just one night. I'll sleep much better tonight. At home. At the Brewsters," he corrected.

"I'm sure no one would mind you calling it 'home' while you're there."

Joseph hesitated, considering this thought for a minute. "Yeah, I guess you're right. It *is* my home right now. That doesn't mean I'll never see my mom and dad again, but everybody needs a home."

Letty nodded her agreement. "All right, buster. Let's move it out."

Joseph climbed to his feet. He expected her to fill out a bunch of paperwork to get him out of the psych ward. It always seemed to take hours for Mira to get checked out of the hospital, even if the doctor and everybody else had already signed off on it. Even more if you were leaving against medical advice, but Mira had been pretty reluctant ever to do that.

But Letty just gave the nursing station a casual wave and headed for the elevator doors, and they didn't stop her or call her back.

"You don't have to check me out?" Joseph asked.

"We've already taken care of all of that."

Joseph shook his head, but he sure wasn't going to argue and say he wanted to stay there any longer. He wanted to get out of there as quickly as he could. He wanted to hit rewind and have been out of there five hours earlier.

They rode the elevator down to the parking garage, and Letty led the way to her car. Joseph got in and buckled up. He didn't have anything to take with him, since he never had gotten his clothes back from the ER and the Brewsters had not visited and brought anything with them. Even knowing that he didn't have anything, Letty had never brought so much as a pair of socks or stick of deodorant.

Joseph didn't complain. He just got into the car and did up his seatbelt. In a few minutes, he would be back at the Brewsters' and could start on phase two of his plan.

"I've been very impressed with your hard work," Letty told him once they were on their way. "I know it hasn't been easy to change your thinking the way you have and to follow the advice of your therapist. But I know you've been working very hard at it. You are to be commended. I did not imagine that you would be out of there so soon. I foresaw that you would be there for several weeks."

Joseph nodded seriously. He had to admit that even just pretending to follow Dr. Ratzlaff's advice, he'd been forced to dig down deep into his feelings about his parents' divorce and the way they had behaved and had been surprised to find that he did have a number of resentments and fears associated with the dissolution of his family that he had been repressing before. He'd experienced what might be personal growth just in his charade of being a cooperative patient.

"I didn't realize how much stuff affected me. I thought I had just accepted it all and moved on."

"Sometimes we hide or lie to ourselves about things," Letty said.

"We try to avoid confronting those tender feelings. It seems like it would be easier to bury them."

She said it like she knew what she was talking about or had gone through it herself. But Joseph was pretty sure that she hadn't. She had just learned how to talk the talk.

"Yeah, you're right," he agreed. "I guess I would never have seen that if I hadn't been forced to. I know that… you were just looking out for my welfare. But it was hard, you know?"

"Certainly I do," Letty agreed.

They made the rest of the trip back to the house in silence, Joseph pondering seriously on how far he had come since being admitted to the psych ward days before.

When they pulled to a stop in front of the Brewsters' house, Joseph reached for the door handle. Letty reached over and put her hand on Joseph's shoulder to make him wait. Joseph looked at her, a ball of anxiety forming in his stomach. What new demand was she going to make now? Could she really ask so much from him? He was, after all, just a kid. Expecting him to work through all of this stuff like an adult really wasn't fair.

"I wanted to give you something," Letty said. "I think you have earned this."

Joseph's spirits lifted. It didn't matter what she was giving him; it was the fact that she thought he had earned something.

She reached for her large handbag and dug around in it for a minute. Then she pulled out a plastic blister pack containing an electronic device. She turned it around for Joseph to see.

A brand-new cell phone, preloaded with 100 minutes.

CHAPTER FORTY-SIX

Joseph carried his new phone into the house as if it were made of pure gold. Of course, it was just the cheapest thing on the market. The kind of thing that he could have picked up for a few bucks at any corner store. But after having nothing, not even clothes, and no way to contact anyone, he didn't care about any of the bells and whistles that had made a difference to him when he had put so much time and research into his last phone purchase. He didn't care about apps or memory or whether he could stream video. All he cared about was that he would be able to call Renata, Britt, and Lora.

Letty had made it clear that he was not allowed to call his parents. Joseph suspected she would have let a call to Joseph's father slide, since he had already said he didn't want Joseph. But she did not want him calling Mira, telling her all his woes, and trying to get back to her. If she discovered that he had made contact with his mother through anything other than a supervised visit, he would be in big trouble, and he could say goodbye to the phone and any replacement. As long as he followed the rules, she would refill the minutes as she saw fit so that he could keep in touch with the people he needed to. Of course he needed to be able to reach his foster mother, his doctor, and schoolmates who could give him his school assignments or help him to complete them. And his case worker.

"I absolutely trust Mr. and Mrs. Brewster and do not expect you to have anything to worry about with them," Letty told him, "but if you did have any concerns, either with the way they were treating you or with one of the other foster children then, of course, I would expect you to call me. I would also like to know if you have any more medical episodes."

Joseph nodded obediently. "Yeah. Sure. Of course."

"You can call me if you have any questions or concerns, whether it is about home or school or your health. I wouldn't have given this to you a week ago. But you've been very responsible and done a complete about-face in your attitude. I believe you will work with me and help me to find the best solution for you."

"I will. I want things to work out. I want to get better."

What he wanted was to go back to his mother, but he knew not to ever open his mouth about that again. He had learned to play the game.

"I know you do." She looked at him fondly, as if he were a favorite pet. He thought that she would reach over and tousle his hair like a little kid.

"Joseph!"

Joseph tried to avoid a collision with the bullet that was Axel as he came racing into the room, but that was out of the question. He gripped the phone tightly and reached out his arms to guide Axel into a bear hug rather than trying to push him away. He squeezed the boy, laughing.

"How can you like me that much?" He asked Axel. "I've only known you for a few days!"

"But you play soccer with me," Axel declared. "Other people don't play soccer with me."

"No, and have we been hearing about it while you have been gone," Mrs. Brewster told Joseph with a laugh. "You would think that he'd lost his best friend."

"He *is* my best friend!" Axel declared, giving Joseph a rib-crushing hug.

Joseph felt a little guilty about Axel's dramatic affect. He wished that he felt the same way about the younger boy. Their feelings seemed so unbalanced, it was embarrassing, and he didn't know what to do about it. He hadn't spent any of the time that he was away in psych thinking about Axel and how he was managing while Joseph was away. He'd only thought of himself.

Mrs. Brewster gave Joseph a wink that he thought was meant to convey that he wasn't to take Axel's declarations of devotion too seriously.

But it was one thing to tell him not to make a big deal of it and another to deal with Axel in a way that wouldn't break his little heart.

"I haven't played any soccer while I've been in the hospital," Joseph told Axel. "So I might be a little rusty today. Were you practicing while I was gone?"

Axel nodded vigorously. "That's how you get better," he told Joseph earnestly. "You have to practice every day."

"He's not kidding about that," Mrs. Brewster confirmed. "He has been doing it every day. You'd better watch out, or he'll be better than you."

"Uh-oh. You're not going to be better than me, are you?"

Axel grinned and nodded, his round face earnest and cherubic. "Let's go! Can we go play now?"

"Yeah, I guess. Let's go."

Axel whooped and raced outside. Joseph slid the new little phone into his pocket and double-checked to make sure it was secure. He would have to find a time and place where he had some privacy to call Renata. He couldn't call from his bedroom, with Axel either there or pounding on the door to be let in.

By the time he got to the backyard, Axel had the ball out and was bouncing it off of the house with his head. It ricocheted off a window and Joseph hurried to stop him.

"I don't know if Mrs. Brewster will like that. You could break a window. Let's pass it back and forth."

"She *doesn't* like it," Axel said with a giggle.

"I didn't think so! You need to be careful not to break anything."

"She wouldn't do anything," Axel assured him.

"Well, she might ground you. Or not let you play outside. Or make you pay for the damage when you break a window. I don't think you would like that."

"She wouldn't do anything," Axel repeated. He shook his head. "Mom isn't like that. She's really nice."

"But she still has to do something to stop you from breaking her windows."

"She just says to stop."

"Well… that's pretty nice," Joseph agreed. He wondered whether it was true, though. He was sure Mrs. Brewster would impose an appropriate "consequence" if Axel didn't listen to her.

"I talked to her on the phone," Axel said, chattering away about something while Joseph had been thinking his own thoughts.

"Mrs. Brewster?" he asked.

"No, not her, my bio mom. I talked to her on the phone last week."

"Oh, did you? How is she doing?"

Axel shrugged, bouncing the ball on his knees before passing it over to Joseph.

"She says maybe I can come see her sometime."

"So…" Joseph tried to reconcile this with what he already knew about Axel's parents. "She must be doing better if she can use a phone and thinks you might be able to visit her."

"Doing better?" Axel echoed.

"Well… since their accident. She must be recovering."

Axel made a brushing-off movement with his hand. "Oh. Yeah. She's getting better after the accident. Feeling lots better."

"Good. Maybe you'll be able to go back there sooner than they thought."

Axel bit his lip, watching Joseph bouncing the ball. "Yeah, maybe," he agreed uncertainly.

Joseph realized he shouldn't be speculating about it. A kid like Axel might take everything he said to be gospel, and that could cause major problems with DCFS, who had all of their own ideas and plans for reunification. Or not doing reunification. He didn't really know anything about Axel's family.

He passed the ball back to Axel, who bounced it around his body as if it were attached by a string, impressing Joseph.

"Wow, you have been practicing, haven't you? You see? You told me you couldn't even catch a ball. Now look at what you can do."

"If you want to learn something, you have to practice it every day," Axel repeated.

CHAPTER FORTY-SEVEN

I t was hard to get through dinner without being distracted with thoughts of his phone and the chance to call Renata. He was eager to get to it as soon as he could. He had played with Axel, and shortly after supper Axel would hit his daily crash and would take the Brewsters' attention. If Joseph could be alone during that time, he could talk to Renata.

Tink and Mark seemed unimpressed by Joseph's return, mostly ignoring him, other than making the occasional discouraging comment when they thought he needed to be put in his place. Tink wanted to know how soon he was going to go back to school and if he was going to be hanging around with that loser Brit again. Mark put down any mention of soccer skills and boasted about football being a much better game, much more important in America than soccer. Accompanied by many eye rolls.

Mrs. Brewster met his eyes one time after one of these jabs and gave him a sympathetic smile. He hoped she was impressed with how easygoing and unconcerned he was acting in the face of all of the attempted provocation from Mark and Tink. She was lucky he was trying so hard and didn't give in to any impulse to retaliate. He might not be able to beat Mark in a physical fight, but he could at least make a ruckus and get in one or two blows before they were broken up. It would be over quickly, so he didn't need to be good. Just to show that he wasn't afraid of Mark and his stupid comments about football.

Finally, supper was over, and they were all supposed to be working on their homework in separate rooms. Some families did homework around the dining room table, but it was easy to see why the Brewsters would insist that the kids be in separate rooms during homework time. Maybe the kind of cooperation and working close together only happened on TV.

Joseph went to his bedroom and shut the door. Mrs. Brewster needed to supervise Axel's homework closely, so he was the one who got to sit at the dining room table, where he would mostly shout and complain about the work he had to do.

Almost as soon as he shut the door, there was a knock on it. Joseph slid his phone under the pillow before answering it. He was relieved to see that it was Mr. Brewster rather than Mark on the other side of the door. He opened the door the rest of the way. He supposed Mr. Brewster would want to say something about how Joseph had done at the hospital and what the rules were now that he was back again.

Mr. Brewster shut the door again behind him and stood there against it rather than advancing farther into the room and looking for somewhere to sit down. It was a small room and the only two options were the beds.

"I just wanted to have a private word with you about Axel and his situation," he said in a quiet tone.

"Oh, sure." Joseph was surprised. He didn't think that they wanted him to know anything about each other's "situations."

"It's just because you need to be careful what you believe," Mr. Brewster said, "and don't get too caught up in whatever stories he might come up with."

"Oh. He told me about them being in an accident."

Mr. Brewster grimaced. "Yeah. He likes to make things up about them."

"They weren't in an accident?" Joseph thought about the dreadful fall he had pictured, the devastation, the shattered bones. He'd been horrified to think of what they had been through, and about how it had affected Axel. Had he seen? Had he been taken away from the hospital into foster care wondering if he would ever see them again?

But it had all been fake. There had been no accident. He could tell from Mr. Brewster's face that this was not the first time it had happened, and he was sorry to have to tell Joseph the truth of the incident.

"So there was no accident."

"No, there wasn't."

"Well… that's a good thing, right? I'm glad that they didn't get hurt and Axel didn't have to go through that, wondering if he would ever see them alive again. That would be really tough on him."

"But maybe easier for him than dealing with the truth. A lot of times… foster kids make up stories to cover the pain of what really happened. They don't want to have to deal with reality, so they make something up that would be less traumatic. Axel's stories can get quite long and involved and descriptive. He's a good little storyteller. But you need to take them for what they are. A way to avoid the reality of what really happened."

"You said that they were circus people. So that part is true."

"That part is true," Mr. Brewster agreed.

"That must have been a really interesting environment to grow up in. And what do you threaten to do when you're not happy? Threaten to run away and become an accountant?" Joseph laughed at his own cleverness.

Mr. Brewster didn't crack a smile. "The environment that Axel grew up in was not fun or exciting. It was dangerous and abusive. He needed to be removed for his own protection. His parents were not in an accident, or eaten by tigers, or kidnapped by pirates. They were predators who were more interested in exploiting their child than nurturing him."

Joseph lost the grin pretty quickly. He pressed his lips together and felt his face reddening in embarrassment. He hadn't meant to make light of something that was so serious. He was glad that he hadn't said something like that in front of Axel and discounted his pain.

"Oh. Sorry." He gave a little shrug, ducking his head down like a turtle pulling into its shell. "I didn't know that. I didn't mean to be a jerk."

Mr. Brewster forced a smile. "Of course not. That's why I'm talking to you privately. So you have a better understanding of what Axel is dealing with and don't step into the trap of romanticizing the circus or feeling sorry for his parents."

Joseph nodded. "Okay. Yeah. Thanks."

The man nodded. He patted Joseph on the shoulder and turned to open the door again. "That's all. No big lecture or problem. Just a heads-up."

"Thanks."

Mr. Brewster left, shutting the door after himself. Time for Joseph to do his homework.

Except that he didn't have any homework because he hadn't been to school. But he did have a project to work on.

He pulled out the phone and the number that Ethan had given him. With his heart pounding much harder and faster than he would have liked, he punched in the number and waited for Renata to pick up.

But she didn't. The line just rang and rang until a computer voice eventually told him that the subscriber could not be reached and to try again later. Not even a voicemail prompt.

Joseph sat there staring at the phone, trying to figure out what to do. How was he supposed to get ahold of Renata when he didn't know when she would be available and she didn't have voicemail?

He tried the number again, in case he had misdialed. Again, it rang until the robotic voice told him she could not be reached and disconnected the call.

Eventually, he decided to send her a text. He didn't expect to see any response immediately. Maybe she was somewhere she had to have her phone turned off. A visit to the hospital. But when she turned it back on, he wanted her to know he was trying to reach her.

CHAPTER FORTY-EIGHT

Gabriel settled in with a cup of coffee for breakfast, and Renata hooked up her feeding tube and started her formula flowing. She felt like she was a little more stable. Maybe the reformulation of her meds was working, reducing the paranoia that was a symptom of her mito. She felt a little less anxious and a little more confident that she knew what was going on in the real world and could tell the difference between a real threat and one that her brain had just concocted. She could never be one hundred percent sure, of course, but she was feeling better about it and hoped that she wasn't overreacting to as many things.

She turned on her phone while they sat in the quiet of the morning. She didn't like to have it on, too worried about the possibility of being tracked or eavesdropped on. It was too bad more of the prepaid cell phones didn't have removable batteries, or she would have taken the battery out as well. No power to the SIM card or any of the other electronics, no possibility that the government or another entity could turn it back on remotely or track her with the residual electricity that flowed to the inner workings even while it was powered down.

It took a few minutes for the splash screen to appear and the phone to run through its initial start-up procedures. Renata watched it carefully for any new screens she hadn't seen before, any lengthening in the time it took to complete each step. Any slight deviations, and she would ditch the phone and open a new one.

The text messages had come up on the screen and, after Renata was sure that everything had loaded, she tapped on the icon to see who had sent her a text.

She looked at the brief text message for a moment, considering it.

"Got something?" Gabriel asked, looking at her face.

"Maybe," Renata said.

She thought about Joseph. Tried to remember everything she could about him. She had not known him for a long time. They had spent a little time together in the psych ward, but he had only been there for a short time while he got his meds balanced out again, and she had been there for a significant length of time as they tried to stabilize her.

"Who is it?"

"Joseph. This guy I met in psych. A while back. Over a year ago... after you and me met, when I had to go back."

Gabriel nodded, waiting for the story.

"I don't remember a lot about him. I wasn't in a real good place while he was there. He probably had to listen to me spouting off every day while they tried to get my brain under control. But... something made him reach out."

"Is this the guy that Nurse Ethan was in contact with?"

"Yeah. He is in psych now. Or he was when I talked to Ethan."

"I don't remember you ever mentioning him before."

"No, I doubt it. He wasn't anyone that I really connected with. We weren't great friends. He was just... another kid in psych. It can be tough when it's just adults there, and there isn't anyone to talk to."

Gabriel nodded. "Yeah. I remember."

She'd been happy when Gabriel had been admitted. She'd had Skyler, but he was a lot younger, not someone Renata could share much with.

"So tell me about him," Gabriel suggested.

"Not a whole lot to tell. He had depression. He didn't spend a lot of time there, but he was suicidal on the meds they had him on and they needed to get him straightened out again."

Gabriel nodded. "Okay. Sounds straightforward."

"Yeah. He wasn't there for long. A few days or a week. I'm sure it wasn't more than two weeks."

"And… I guess he's there again now. Probably the same thing again?"

"Maybe. He doesn't say. Just that he wants to get in touch. Ethan didn't tell me much, either. Just that Joseph was stuck in psych and wanted to contact me."

Gabriel's eyes flashed. "*Stuck* in psych?"

Renata thought back, trying to remember Ethan's words. Had he really said that, or was that her own spin? Just because she had felt stuck in psych in the past, that didn't mean that was how everyone felt about it. If he just needed a med rebalancing, he might not feel stuck. He might feel like it was where he was supposed to be until everything got straightened out.

But then, why had he reached out to Renata? If everything was fine, why would he try to get ahold of her? Just because he was thinking about her when he was returned to that environment? Just for old-time's sake?

She didn't think he would call her just for old time's sake.

"I think Ethan said stuck. But I'm not sure," she confessed to Gabriel.

"Well, if he's calling you for help, I guess he is stuck."

"Yeah, must be."

"So what did he say in his message?" Gabriel nodded toward the phone.

"Just his name and that he wanted to talk." She nodded and grudgingly admitted, "He was pretty discreet."

"You think it's something we can help out with?"

"Won't know that until we meet."

Gabriel nodded. He didn't prod for information on where and when they would meet or what arrangements she would want to make.

Renata took a breath and let it out. She looked around the diner to see if there were anyone nearby who was likely to overhear their discussion. There were only a few early-morning customers, and they were paying attention to their phones and newspapers, several tables separated from Gabriel and Renata.

She tapped the phone number of the text message and then hit the phone icon. There was a pause as the phone considered her request, and then decided to connect the call.

It rang a few times. Renata didn't like it taking so long to connect. Still, sometimes, with cell phones, it would be ringing on the caller's end for thirty seconds before it actually started ringing on the recipient's phone, so she waited patiently, hoping that Joseph would be able to pick it up.

If he was in psych, he might not have immediate access to his phone. The administrators liked to lock them up "for security" and not allow patients to use them while they were there. Some people managed to keep contraband phones hidden from the administration. But in either case, Joseph might not have access to his phone at all times. Or it might take a while for him to recover it from wherever it was hidden.

"Hello?" Joseph's voice was soft, confidential. The voice he would use if he were trying to keep from being overheard.

"Joseph? You know who this is."

"Yeah." He didn't say her name, which was another point in his favor. So far, he had been good about keeping her privacy. Other than the problems with reaching out through Ethan, leaving more than one opportunity for someone to track her. "How are you?"

"The question is, how are you?" Renata asked. "And where are you?"

"I'm... doing okay. And I'm out now. In a foster home."

Renata considered the various implications of this information. He was out of psych, so he didn't need her help with that aspect. Which was good, because she couldn't give him much advice on breaking out of psych. She and Gabriel had both done it themselves, but it was easier if they were actually released from psych. Foster care was much easier to escape from than psych, and often only required walking away at the appropriate time and having a place to go.

Reunification with the family was another story. Or another page in the story. It was more difficult, but that was what they did.

"I don't want to discuss details over the air," Renata told him. "Can we meet?"

"Yeah, I guess so. Where and when?"

"Are you able to get away from there any time? Only during school hours? What's the best way?"

"Well," Joseph's voice was hesitant, "tomorrow is Saturday. So, no school. Nobody has *said* that I can't go out anywhere. I just got out of the hospital, so it would make sense that I want to go for a walk or to get some fresh air, right? Or to visit with my friends from school. Hang out at the mall?"

"Makes sense to me," Renata agreed. "Can you sell it? And what if they say no?"

"I'll just go," Joseph said. "What are they going to do to stop me? If I leave early enough, when things are busy around here, probably no one will even notice until later. I have a phone now, so they can call me if they're worried. I'll just stall about getting back. It will take me a while to get there. It does, when you have to walk and take transit."

"It sure does," Renata agreed. The number of bus seats that she and Gabriel had worn out over the past couple of years! It seemed like they spent days at a time on the bus. Not just getting from point A to point B in a straight line—when did buses go in a straight line, anyway?—but also doing various transfers and doubling back to ensure no one could follow them. "Okay. So let's go with a mall so that you're in a place that makes sense if they call or track you. And malls are good because there are a lot of people, so no one stands out. Good camouflage. Do you know the city?"

"Pretty well, yeah."

Renata gave him directions as to where to go and what procedure to follow. Joseph would have to jump through several hoops before he actually saw Renata. She was good at what she did, or she would have been captured a long time ago.

Eventually, she terminated the call and shut down her phone. She nodded at Gabriel. "We have a date."

CHAPTER FORTY-NINE

Joseph had doubled back and looked over his shoulder several times to make sure that no one would be able to follow him.

Not that he thought anyone was.

He had gotten away from the Brewsters' house cleanly, without anyone appearing to notice his departure. Even though it was a Saturday, Axel was up early and demanded attention. Both Mr. and Mrs. Brewster were involved in trying to get him satisfied and settled down so that they could relax. Tink and Mark were both still in bed, so he didn't need to worry about them.

Joseph tried to appear casual as he left. It was important not to look suspicious, he had discovered over the years. As long as he looked like he wasn't doing anything wrong, he wouldn't likely get caught. He was sure that the same principle applied for master criminals, but he had never gone beyond walking away from where he was supposed to be or slipping in somewhere he was not supposed to be. He wasn't actually shoplifting or committing heists or any other kind of fraud. All kids did things like that. He wasn't alone in it.

What exactly did he think he was doing? Why did he even need to talk to Renata? At first, he had wanted her help in escaping from the psych ward. She had talked about having done it before, so he figured she could help him figure out how to do it too. Now that he was out of the hospital, he wasn't sure why he was still following through on his plan to see her.

He wanted to hear what she had to say about his being placed in foster care after the episodes. She had talked a lot when they had been in psych about how doctors and social workers were taking kids away from their parents for no reason. For bogus, made-up reasons. For medical mistakes and misdiagnoses. She had gone on and on about it, and he had just listened and held his tongue and let her talk. She was one of the only people who would talk to him or have anything to do with him there, so he would take whatever topic of conversation she was interested in.

But of course, he had not believed in it. He knew that she was paranoid and unstable and that all of the conspiracy theories were completely imagined. It was sad. But it was also entertaining to listen to her and hear all the accusations and theories. He could laugh at them behind her back, as long as he showed polite interest to her face. And then his days were not so lonely.

Only now, it was happening to him. All of the things she had said could happen, the things he had blown off, were actually happening. He had been taken away from his mother. He had been diagnosed with some mental illness to account for the physical ailments he was experiencing. Instead of trying harder to diagnose what was happening to him, they had decided that it was all in his head. And they had decided that Mira could not take care of him anymore. So now he was living with a family he didn't even know, pretending to be friendly with him while they collected the paychecks from DCFS for allowing him to sleep under their roof.

Joseph followed the directions that Renata had given him, stopping at the big clock in the mall and looking around for anyone who looked suspicious. He'd seen enough TV dramas to know that the FBI could be disguised as sanitation workers, mothers with baby strollers, and homeless guys picking through trash for bottles or anything else of value. And the mall was swarming with possibly suspicious individuals.

He discounted anyone who was younger than twenty. No one that young could be a cop or a doctor. But that still left a lot of possibilities. Joseph watched people coming and going carefully. No one seemed to be paying him too much attention or to be watching or staring at him.

He checked the time and moved on to the second checkpoint, waiting in line at the pizza place in the food court. When he got up to the counter, he broke off from the line, since he didn't have any money to buy a slice, no matter how delicious it smelled.

Joseph looked around for Renata, wondering whether he would be able to spot her watching him as he went through the process of making sure he was not being followed or working with someone. She had to have eyes on him at some point but, so far, he hadn't seen any sign that she was nearby. She was good at what she did. Paranoia paid off when you were trying to avoid an actual conspiracy plot.

He sighed and reviewed the rest of the process he was supposed to follow in his mind. The next stop was almost all the way across the mall at a shoe repair place in a back hallway. Joseph figured that was because no one else would be hanging out there. It would be too isolated and unpopular for there to be any concerns about spooks watching him.

His feet were getting sore. He'd had to walk and bus all the way over there, and now he was walking up and down the length of the mall, which was several blocks long, just to prove that no one was following him. It was ridiculous.

He was going to need his shoes fixed by the time he got to the shoe store. He was going to wear right through the soles.

Eventually, he reached the other end of the mall, checking his phone again in anxiety because he had not been able to make it in the allotted time. Renata had failed to anticipate how long it would take for him to cover that distance with sore feet.

"Hey. This way." Someone tapped Joseph lightly on the shoulder and then moved away from him. Joseph whirled around to look at him—a skinny Black teen. Not moving quickly, but not looking back to see whether he was following. Joseph looked in the direction Renata had told him to go, and then at the other teen. Was it a test to see whether he stuck to the plan or was flexible enough to follow someone else? Whether he recognized when there was a danger or a change in the plans or just ignored it? If it was a test, then which thing was he was supposed to do?

He followed the other boy, quickly catching up to him.

"Hey! Do you want to stop for a minute to tell me who you are and what's going on here?"

The boy shook his head and kept moving. "No, not out in the open. Pretend we're together."

Unable to decide what else to do, Joseph chose to follow and do what he was told.

CHAPTER FIFTY

J oseph didn't have any trouble keeping pace with the other boy. Once he had caught up and walked beside him for a moment, he realized that the boy's gait was stiff, slow, and awkward. He continued to move through the crowd at a steady pace, but it seemed like there was something wonky with his legs. They walked through a couple of crowded areas, and then the crowds petered out again and they were once more in a sparsely populated area. The boy went through an *Authorized Personnel Only* door and, with only a split-second's hesitation, Joseph followed.

The boy had turned around to face Joseph. He put his finger to his lips and made a *stay there* motion with his hands. Then he walked to the end of the corridor and looked around the corner. He gave a nod, and he motioned for Joseph to follow. Joseph did, and caught up in a moment. They traveled several more corridors and entered a storage room with only dim lighting. Lots of dust on the surfaces of the box that testified to the fact that it was not used often. There, Renata was waiting. She handed the boy a pair of crutches, and he settled onto them with a sigh of relief, then found himself a box to sit on. Renata turned to Joseph. "You made it," she observed.

"Yeah. But I didn't finish the whole cloak and dagger routine before your friend got me."

"That's okay," she said. "We only needed you to follow it long enough to demonstrate that you were alone. After that, we get you out of sight again."

Joseph looked around. He wasn't sure what he had been expecting, but it wasn't to end up in this little storage room having a tete-a-tete with Renata and her boyfriend. He looked at her again. He had been expecting a hug of greeting after not seeing each other for so long, but apparently, Renata was not a hugger. She didn't step any closer to him, nor did she offer to shake hands. She probably had OCD and was a germaphobe, too. Joseph found a box of his own to sit on.

"We're meeting here, then?"

Renata nodded. Without a word, she stepped back out of the storage room into the hallway. She looked up and down it, then returned, letting the door shut slowly on its pneumatic closer and snick into place again.

She seemed hesitant to sit down but, after pacing back and forth several times, she eventually chose a box near Gabriel's and sat.

"This is Gabriel." She nodded to the Black boy.

"Hi," Joseph greeted, and Gabriel gave him a nod of acknowledgment.

"So, tell me what's been going on," Renata instructed.

"Well…" Joseph blew out his breath uncertainly, "I'm not sure where to start."

"Start with the social worker."

"Which one?"

"Which one came first?"

"Uh… okay. The first one, Miss Kelly, I saw her at the hospital."

"In psych?"

"No. Before that. A few weeks ago."

"What were you in the hospital for?"

"I've been having these… episodes: blackouts or panic attacks. I was at the hospital because… I fainted at a game. A soccer game. I was supposed to be playing. I was playing. And then… blacked out right there on the field." Joseph thought that blacking out sounded more manly than fainting.

"Were you too hot?"

"No. It was at the beginning of the game, and it wasn't a hot day."

"And it was a blackout? What kind of blackout?"

He looked at her. "Are there different kinds?"

"Well, yeah. There's 'I'm feeling a bit lightheaded and can't go on,' and there is 'face plant in the middle of the field,' for one."

"Well, I guess this would be the face plant in the middle of the field kind."

"Yeah? And had you had it happen before? Or was that the first time?"

"I don't know. Not like that, I guess. But once or twice since. The other times... it wasn't like I was lightheaded, exactly. But one time I was really dizzy, could hardly stand. And a couple of times, it was an anxiety attack. Like, really panicky feeling, and heart racing, and unable to do anything."

"All kind of different."

He nodded. "But sort of the same, too. And it all started around the same time, a few weeks ago. But they decided that it was all just psychological. Like it's all in my head, not physical. They think I want it to happen. Maybe just subconsciously, but it is because I'm doing it to myself. I am all traumatized by my parents' divorce and want the extra attention and love."

Renata snorted. "And is that your analysis of the situation?"

"No," Joseph couldn't help smiling at her derision. "That's what the doctor has come up with. Him and my social worker, I guess. They seemed to be together on everything."

"Did they bother to test for *anything*?"

"Yeah," Joseph admitted. "They did a bunch of tests. Blood tests, urine, biopsies, all that kind of thing. But everything was normal."

"Does anybody have a record of all of it? Your mom?"

"She was there for the earliest stuff. But I don't know if she wrote down all of the results or anything. And then after DCFS took me away from here, they did a bunch more tests. I guess DCFS would have copies of those, if they asked for them. Otherwise, just the doctors, and there was more than one doctor; I guess they would all have their own records."

"Did you have a case manager or anything like that? Someone coordinating it all and making sure they have all of the results and that they are cross-checked?"

Joseph was already shaking his head, and her words petered out.

"No case manager," Renata said.

"No case manager."

"Do you think that your foster mom could order copies of everything? How cooperative is she?"

"Cooperative?"

"Like, if you do something that might be against what your social worker says, and she knows that, would she let you get away with it?"

"Uh... I have no idea."

"Didn't anybody ever tell you that teens are supposed to test your limits?"

"No. I've just been trying to be cooperative... I figured that the only way to get out of psych was if I pretended to agree with them and to do everything that they said to do. So... I haven't been testing any limits until I came here today. I've been careful to do everything that I was told."

"Yeah. That's a good plan. We all have to do that sometimes. But there are other times you need to stretch... refuse to do something. See what happens."

Joseph shook his head. "Not with this social worker."

"What's her name?"

"Letty. I don't remember the last name... something pretty common."

"Miller?"

"Yeah. Letty Miller. I forgot for a minute there. Because she said just to call her Letty."

Renata nodded. "Yeah. We know her. She's pretty strict."

"You know her?"

"We've dealt with a lot of the social workers. Not directly, necessarily, but we know them through the other kids that we've dealt with."

"What other kids?"

Renata looked at him for a minute, not answering. She leaned forward.

"Why did you call me?"

"Well…" Joseph cleared his throat uncomfortably, not liking the direct question. "It's just that before, when we were in psych together, you talked about… about kids who were being taken away from their families because of medical conditions they had. That they were misdiagnosed, or their parents weren't treating them the way that the doctors thought that they should, things like that."

Renata nodded her agreement. That was, at least, the first step. He had been half afraid that she would brush that away as the ravings of a paranoid person, that she didn't believe it anymore, now that she was stabilized. But she waited for him to go on.

"I don't remember what you called it."

"Medical kidnap."

"Yeah. You said that DCFS was accusing parents of abuse because of the kids' medical conditions. That there were other things wrong with them, but the doctors couldn't find it and the social workers didn't believe it, so they got taken away from their families. The social workers said it was Munchausen by proxy or that they were being abused or neglected in other ways, so they just took the kids away, even though the parents weren't doing anything wrong. And they put them into medical programs or foster families and wouldn't give them back."

Renata nodded again. "You've got a good memory. I'm not sure how coherent I was when I was there. I could have told you all kinds of things!" She gave him a smile.

Joseph put out his hands, palms up, to signal that was all he knew.

"I guess… I was hoping that since you knew so much about it, hopefully, you would tell me what to do. How to get out of it again and… maybe go back to my mom, if I can."

Renata looked at the other teen, and they communicated something to each other without words.

Renata looked back at Joseph. She indicated the boy with a tilt of her head. "Gabriel and I both have mitochondrial disease. They took

Gabriel away from his mom because she wouldn't treat his mito the way that the doctors wanted her too. They stuck him in an experimental program that nearly killed him. I'd been away from my mom for a long time because of everything she tried to do to me. But I have a lot of allergies and other issues, you remember from when I was there. And they nearly killed me a few times. I broke out a few times before I managed to get away and make it stick. We did a big exposé on TV about medical kidnap and, because of that, they tried to murder us outright."

Joseph tried to mask his skepticism, but was obviously unsuccessful. She could see it a mile away.

"They killed Nick, one of our group. Another one of them went underground and we thought they'd gotten him too. One of the doctors came after me and tried to inject me with one of my allergens to kill me."

"Why would they do that?"

"Because they make good money for running experiments on kids in foster care. And we were threatening that with what we were doing. They didn't want us to put an end to the good thing they had going. We're talking hundreds of thousands of dollars here. Maybe millions, I don't know. The stakes were high."

"And you got away and survived… so I guess you have some experience in what I'm trying to do."

"We have more than that. The whole time since we escaped, we've been helping to get other teens away from their foster families and to reunite them with their bio families."

"What?" Joseph wasn't quite sure he believed it.

"You didn't just contact an old friend from psych who knows a thing or two about medical kidnap. You contacted the head of the Underground Railroad that gets kids back to their parents."

CHAPTER FIFTY-ONE

Joseph stared at Renata, waiting for her to grin and say she was stringing him a line. But she didn't. She sat there on the box and waited for his reaction.

"The Underground Railroad," Joseph repeated. "Like the slaves who escaped from their masters?"

Renata nodded. "Yeah. Like that. I can't say that history will look at us the same way. Or that history will even remember us at all. This is just a small movement, way underground, in a small section of the country. Probably no one will remember what we did here."

"I can think of a few people who will," Gabriel countered.

"A few," Renata allowed.

"So... how can you help me? Can you get me a seat on this Underground Railroad of yours and get me back to my mom?"

"Well, it isn't as easy as you might think. And we don't work with everyone. We can't help in every case. And some cases that come to us aren't medical kidnap cases. Sometimes, it really *is* an abusive parent who is trying to hide behind the guise of medical kidnap. If the kid or the parent isn't willing to work with us, or if there is too much risk for us to get involved..." She shrugged. "We can't always do anything. We also don't work with little kids or babies, only teens."

Joseph thought about Axel and wished that he could do something to help him. But Mr. Brewster had said that the environment that Axel had come from was really bad. Not something that Joseph would have wanted to return Axel to.

"Yeah, I guess I can understand that," he said. "But you must be willing to work with me, or you wouldn't have gotten in touch with me. You would have just ignored it when Ethan reached out or when I texted you."

"I wanted to hear what happened, why you called me. I didn't know at that point whether you had a case that we could intervene in or not."

That part didn't matter. "What matters is what you think now."

"I still don't know. We have to gather a lot more information. Your full medical history. We need to talk to your parents. Your mom and your dad. We'll want to look into the foster parents, social workers, and doctors. See what's really going on."

"I told you what's going on."

"You only told me a minuscule piece of what's going on. There's plenty more to find out."

———

"So, what do you think of Joseph?" Renata asked after a while.

Gabriel had been waiting for her to bring it up. He didn't want to be too eager and push it before she was ready. She needed time to think it through and to see what kind of history she could find for him on the internet and any other sources she had. While she could judge a person or a case very quickly, she tried to be fair and give everyone the benefit of the doubt if they had the time to do so. It wasn't easy for her to do, given her paranoia. But she did the best she could to be fair and impartial with each of their cases.

"He seemed like a nice enough guy," Gabriel said carefully. "His is the kind of case we like to take on, if it is all as it appears on the surface."

"Uh-huh." Renata pushed herself back from the library table. She looked around. "We should move on."

They couldn't stay in one place for too long and attract the attention of the library staff and security. They were there often enough that their faces were known, but they tried not to do anything that would get them classified as unusual, rule breakers, or trouble. They were just a couple of teens that came in to use the computers now and then. They were quiet, kept to themselves, and didn't cause anyone any hassle.

They both made sure that their stations were clear, that they weren't leaving anything personal or any notes behind. Renata would already have cleared the browser cache on her computer, and Gabriel did the same with a few keystrokes. They walked away from the desk. They would go for a short walk. Maybe go to one of the other computer banks on another floor of the library if they still needed to do more research.

"He's kind of a jock," Renata said.

Gabriel glanced at her, startled, then realized she was still talking about Joseph. He had to think about it. Joseph had been cooperative enough with them, though he had pushed back on their having to dig so much into his life. Who wouldn't be annoyed at the intrusion? Renata's characterization of him as a jock didn't just mean that she thought he was good at sports. The term was far more loaded for her.

Both of them had grown up being about as far from athletically gifted as a person could be. Lots of disabilities and challenges due to their mito. And the kids who were good at sports and phys ed were typically not particularly tolerant of people who weren't. They had their own little circle of friends, and anyone who was challenged in that department was looked down on, made fun of, teased, and bullied.

Jock was the equivalent of "jerk," and several other loaded words. Jocks were the bane of their existence.

And Joseph? Was that the kind of person he was?

CHAPTER FIFTY-TWO

ell... I guess he is," Gabriel admitted after a little consideration. "He's really focused on soccer. It's obviously the center of his life. And up until now, he's been able to do very well. He's the star of the team—"

"To hear him tell of it," Renata interjected.

"Well, yes. I assume that it's true to at least some extent. That he's good. He scores goals. That he has earned trophies and awards over the years."

Renata snorted. But she didn't disagree.

"So it must be tough for him to suddenly be facing this... weakness," Gabriel suggested. "Suddenly, he starts blacking out on the field. He's moved to another home and another school where he can't even play his favorite sport. That's pretty hard on him."

"Yeah. He's had everything taken away from him," Renata agreed, though she didn't sound sympathetic. "His family, his home, his school and sports, everything. And now he has to figure out how to carry on."

"This thing... you don't think it's just psychological, do you? I mean... you know how they make assumptions. Decide that we're only sick because we want to be, and if we just had a positive attitude, everything would be fine?"

"I don't think that someone whose whole life is centered on a sport would suddenly throw it all away because he wanted attention from Daddy. He's gotten attention for playing sports before, why would he want negative attention now?"

"It's not negative attention," Gabriel disagreed.

Renata looked at him, cocked her head, and waited for his argument.

"The kind of attention that a normally healthy person gets when they are suddenly faced with severe illness or injury… it tends to be very positive. The doctors like kids who are normally healthy and vigorous who suddenly have a broken arm or something that can be fixed relatively easily. Pat him on the head, put the arm in a cast, and done. Parents lavish them with attention, telling them that it will all be okay and that it will heal quickly. Friends send cards and flowers and come to visit. Coaches and teachers and the professionals are concerned and encouraging. All very positive."

"Not the same as someone who is chronically ill," Renata stated.

"No. Someone who is chronically ill is seen as a whiner. Doctors can't fix them; they can only give them occasional relief with medication changes or surgery. Parents have to deal with constant pressure and kids who always need something more. It exhausts them. They don't go to school regularly and don't develop the same relationships."

Gabriel didn't need to go into any more detail. They had both dealt with it their whole lives. While there were a few bright spots—doctors who were cheerful and encouraging, a teacher at school who gave them special attention, maybe one friend who thought it worthwhile to see them even though it was the hundredth time they had been in the hospital—people with chronic illnesses faced a lot of negative attention.

"When Joseph first got sick, he got some positive attention. Lots of people were worried about him. Who thought that he would get better soon. He might have thought it would just continue, that the sicker he got, the more attention he would get. He hadn't anticipated the negative consequences."

Renata nodded, conceding the point. "Okay, so he got positive attention, to begin with, so he was conditioned to think that sickness equals good attention. But if he was shamming, he would have stopped by now, because he would figure out that he was getting a lot of negative attention that he didn't want."

"It all happened pretty fast. It might have been too late to stop. And if it was a subconscious drive for attention rather than conscious, then he couldn't just stop. He couldn't decide that it was bringing him negative consequences and that he needed to stop."

"So you think it could be psychological," Renata said.

"I can see that side of things. I can see why someone would think that. But I don't think that's what's going on. I think… that he did get sick. This was a major change."

She nodded. "We've seen it before. Someone gets sick. The doctor can't find what it is. So, he decides that it's psychological. If they can't find a physical cause, it is all in his head."

Gabriel had not only seen it happen, he'd had it happen to him— more than once. Doctors always assumed that anything they couldn't see wasn't actually there.

"So why didn't they find it in their testing? It sounds like they at least looked for something."

"They looked for the wrong thing. Or they looked at the wrong time."

"Something like blacking out on the field should be easy to find a cause for."

"You would think," Renata said darkly.

"Well, yeah, you would."

"But if it is something wrong with his brain, then it's back to 'I can't see it, so it must not be there,'" Renata pointed out. "Seizure, stroke, tumor, who knows. People deal with these things for months or years without doctors figuring out what's happening. How many times do kids with mitochondrial disease go undiagnosed for years? They're just lazy, whiny, whatever."

They had told Gabriel that he didn't need braces and crutches. He needed to stop lying around feeling sorry for himself and put some effort into things. He'd been told that he was just lazy, even by professionals who knew that he had mitochondrial disease.

"He said that they had done an EEG and imaging. Wouldn't that have shown that he had seizures, a clot or bleed, or a tumor?"

"It wouldn't show that he was having seizures if he didn't have a seizure while they were testing. And the imaging isn't perfect. You might just see a shadow. Or what you want to see might be obscured. Or the tech reads it wrong and says everything is clear when it isn't."

"So you think it is something in his brain?"

"Or a sleep study," Renata suggested.

"You think he's falling asleep?"

"Narcolepsy can happen anywhere."

"Running across a field?" Gabriel challenges.

"I don't know. I'm going to say yes, unless you can disprove it."

"Did you find anything in your research that we didn't already know?"

"Most of the stuff online is just about his soccer skills. But there is some stuff about his academic leadership. School awards and scholarships. And his mom is on social media, posting stuff about herself and about her family. I don't know if she realizes everything she posts is public."

"Personal stuff?"

"More personal than I would share about myself."

Gabriel rolled his eyes. "You wouldn't share anything about yourself."

"You asked."

"Did she say that he was sick? Or that she didn't think he was sick? Anything about the apprehension that was useful?"

"She's been pretty quiet since the apprehension. Maybe she didn't want her family and friends to learn about it."

"Because it was embarrassing?"

"People know they are going to be judged. Even if she posts that Joseph was taken away from her for no reason at all and how upset she is about it, there are still going to be people who judge her and say it's because she's a bad mother. People who think that DCFS is always right and she must have been doing something wrong."

Gabriel nodded.

"She posted a little before that about how he'd been sick at school and, you know, pray for us or something like that because she was worried about Joseph. How upset she was about it…" Renata made a motion alternating raising her hands as if weighing it. "I dunno. Seems more like she was downplaying it than trying to get attention for it."

"Well, that's good, though. Right? Because it argues against Munchausen by proxy. If she doesn't troll for the attention, then she probably isn't the one making him sick."

Renata nodded slowly. "Yeah, parents with MBP are usually over-involved in their children's lives. Overly interested, oversharing, and asking people for help and advice. She doesn't share any details about Joseph's episodes, and someone with Munchausen will usually give you every last gory detail. They delight in telling it over and over. Getting sympathy every time they recite it."

"Do you think DCFS has a case for Munchausen? Or that we're facing something else here? Just regular old abuse or neglect."

"From what Joseph said, neglect. She didn't figure out what he had, didn't put enough time and effort into it. Didn't pick him up from school when he was sick, but told him to stay there and tough it out anyway. After the nurse said that he needed to go home. That's classic neglect."

"And it's just Joseph's word against his mother's?"

"Yeah." Renata grimaced. "Even though he changed his tune and said that it had been his fault and he had told her not to come, they don't have to believe him. They can believe that she coerced him into changing his story. He feared punishment, so he did what his mother told him to do and recanted. It happens all the time."

Gabriel had witnessed that himself. Children's relationships with their abusive parents were tangled and treacherous. Even when they dared to admit what was going on, the parent could hurt and threaten them until they complied and told the investigator that it wasn't true; it had all been a lie. Seasoned social workers learned to watch for the false cover-up after the fact just as much as the denial and obfuscation before an admission.

"So it will be pretty hard to convince anyone that Joseph lied to his mother. They're just not going to believe it. She will have to work around them believing that she neglected Joseph on at least that one occasion. What about others?"

"We need to see her before deciding anything about the case. See how she comes across, if she's believable, if we think there was abuse or neglect going on. Getting a good diagnosis would go a long way to making DCFS seem... less competent."

Gabriel grinned. "Yeah, I'm sure you're right."

CHAPTER FIFTY-THREE

Gabriel and Renata had told Joseph to obey his social worker's instructions and not to contact his mother to tell her they were on their way. And certainly not to contact her under any circumstances on the phone that Letty had given him. She would undoubtedly have recorded the IMEI number of the phone before giving it to him and would be able to track it or get the call history if she believed that a law had been broken. The phone belonged to her or DCFS, not Joseph, and she would use that to her advantage.

So Mira had no way of knowing that Gabriel and Renata would pay her a visit. No way of knowing that they were legitimate or about the work that they had done with other families. They would be going in completely cold.

But it wasn't the first time they had faced this challenge.

They surveilled the house for a while before approaching. Joseph had told them her usual schedule so they wouldn't have to stand around for hours waiting for her.

There wasn't any unusual activity around the house. No vehicles with unexpected antennae. No one sitting in their car on the street, watching, for hours. They wouldn't have any reason to surveil Mira, thinking that Joseph would return to her when he was living safely with the Brewsters. They had no way of knowing that Joseph had any contact with Gabriel and Renata or that they would show up at the house. DCFS was too overtaxed to put extra manpower into ensuring that Mira Demain didn't break any of the conditions they had undoubtedly imposed on her. And the police couldn't afford to put surveillance on random houses they had no reason to believe were places criminals might consort.

They circled the block to make sure that there was no one hanging around the back, and then they returned to the front door and rang the doorbell.

Mira didn't answer immediately. Maybe she was looking through the peephole at them and wondering who they were and what they wanted from her. Selling Girl Guide cookies? They kept standing there and ringing, even though Renata knew that it attracted too much attention to them, but it was a quiet Sunday afternoon and hopefully, there were not too many people outside watching them.

Eventually, Mira opened the door, too curious to leave them standing on her front porch, ringing the doorbell until eternity. If it were someone she didn't want to talk to, she could at least send them away. And call the police. She didn't have to put up with harassment.

She frowned at the two teens on the doorstep.

"Can we come in?" Renata asked, stepping forward and putting her hand on the door as if she were going to march right in, with permission or without.

Mira stepped back, confused, which allowed Renata to do just that. Gabriel trailed in behind her and shut the door.

"Uh—who are you?" Mira demanded. "I think you must have the wrong house."

"Not the wrong house," Renata told her. "We're from Joseph."

Her jaw dropped and she stared at them. "What?"

"Joseph sent us. So we're not here to hurt you or steal anything. You don't have to worry about that. We're here to help."

"Help what?" She stood there looking thoroughly bewildered.

"Help you to get him back, if possible," Renata said crisply.

Normally, she would not have dangled that hope in front of the mother without knowing a lot more about the situation. But they needed a way to convince her of who they were and that she needed to cooperate with them, which wasn't easy going in cold. They knew it could take a few weeks to warm up a parent and get the situation under control, but Renata was antsy about getting in there quickly. Maybe because she knew Joseph from psych and wanted to get him the help he needed as quickly as possible. The fact that he had effectively sneaked out of psych by lying about himself and his symptoms meant that he might be in a pretty unstable state, and they might have only days to deal with him before he was hospitalized again. And it was a lot harder to get a kid out of the secure psychiatric ward than it was to get him out of the foster home.

"Help me get him back?" Mira shook her head, her limp blond hair falling around her tired face. She pushed too-long bangs out of her eyes and to the side. "How can you help me to get him back?"

"It's what we do," Renata told her. "Are you going to invite us in to sit down, or do we have to stand the whole time we're here?" Renata motioned to Gabriel on his crutches to demonstrate that they could not stand the whole time.

"Yes… do, come sit down."

CHAPTER FIFTY-FOUR

S he ushered them into the living room and picked up a few things. A stack of flyers and an open newspaper. A blanket that she had probably thrown over her lap and feet in the late night or early morning hours when she had the thermostat turned down to conserve energy and save money, but it was still cold at night. A couple of cups with the dregs of tea in the bottoms, which she took into the kitchen. She returned to the living room absently, looking a little lost about what she was supposed to do next. Renata and Gabriel took seats, and Renata gestured towards Mira's easy chair, silently suggesting she should join them.

"*Who* are you?" Mira asked.

"I'm Renata and this is Gabriel," Renata introduced. "I know Joseph from when we were both in the hospital at the same time."

Gabriel noticed that she didn't use the term "psych" as she usually did. She liked to let it all hang out and be completely open about where she had been and her mental health challenges. But she didn't want to set off Mira, making her think that her home was being invaded or she was being taken hostage by a couple of psychotic patients.

"Oh." Mira nodded eagerly. "You know Joseph. How is he? I haven't heard from him."

"I wasn't with him this time," Renata clarified. "I was with him once before. But he remembered me and called me to talk about... the situation. That's why we're here."

"The situation."

"About him being apprehended. He doesn't want to be in foster care. He wants to get out of there, to get back to you."

And his life. His soccer. But neither of them mentioned that. Because chances were, if they were able to help Joseph and Mira to reunite, he would not be going back to his old school and his old soccer team. They would be moving out of state in order to avoid detection. Sometimes, they could get a judge to rule the way that they wanted to and a child could go back to his parents and his old life as if none of it had ever happened. But more than likely, They would not be able to get a judge to rule that Joseph be returned. He would have to run away and leave the state. And his mother would have to do the same.

"How could you do that?"

"There are different ways to approach it, and we'll try several different prongs at the same time. One of them is to convince DCFS or a judge that you are not a negligent parent and that Joseph should be returned to you. That they made a mistake in removing him. Or that you have complied with their demands and it is a safe home and he should be reunited with you. Because DCFS is always supposed to be working toward reunification and, if there isn't any danger in him being here, they need to return him. And the other way..." Renata looked around, double-checking there was no one else in the house. Or a tape recorder or cell phone video camera capturing everything she said. "The other thing that could happen is that you might decide to move out of the state. And Joseph might decide to run away from his foster family. And somehow, the two of you might happen to meet up."

Mira's eyes got wide at this. "Move out of the state? I couldn't do that."

"You couldn't?" Renata challenged. "Even if it was the only way to get Joseph back?"

Mira just stared at her, dumbfounded.

"I need to know," Renata said. "If you seriously would never consider leaving the state, I need to know that. If you're going to take one of our options off the table at the get-go…"

"No, I didn't say that," Mira said, holding up her hands. "I'm just… I don't know what to say. This is all so sudden, and I don't understand exactly what is going on. You can't be for real…"

"We're as real as you are," Renata said. "And if Joseph was here, he could vouch for us, but he can't, because he isn't allowed to have any contact with you, and I told him to follow those rules to the letter."

"You know him? Tell me again how you know him."

It wasn't like it was difficult to understand, but it was hard for her to believe. And to trust people who had just shown up on her doorstep and thrust themselves into her life as they had. Trust took time to establish, and Renata wasn't doing them any favors by trying to shortcut the process.

"He was in the hospital a couple of years ago," Renata said. "For depression. Getting his meds stabilized. Some of these drugs can make teens suicidal instead of helping their depression. So he was in there for a few days, maybe a week or ten days, and I was there at the same time. Two teens… we gravitated toward each other because old people aren't that much fun to hang around with. No offense."

Mira didn't even crack a smile at that. She was still trying to catch up to Renata, not sure what to believe.

"So when Joseph was in the hospital again this time—"

"Which time?" Mira interrupted, holding her hand up to stop Renata.

"Last week."

"He was in the hospital last week?"

Renata didn't roll her eyes or say Mira should have known that. She shook her head.

"Oh, they didn't bother to tell you, huh? Yeah. He had another one of his 'episodes' at the foster family's house, and they decided he needed to be admitted to Psychiatric to get him straightened out."

"They think that his meds are off?"

"They think that it's all in his head. That these fainting spells, or whatever they are, are attention-seeking behaviors."

"Attention-seeking?"

"Yeah." Renata leaned forward, perched on the edge of her seat. Gabriel was half afraid she was going to topple off. "They said that because of the divorce, he feels like he isn't getting enough attention, and that is why these anxiety attacks and fainting episodes have suddenly appeared out of nowhere. It's all a reaction to the changes in the family structure and him needing more attention."

Mira leaned back against the chair, looking exhausted and defeated. "That's ridiculous. I can't believe they would come up with something like that."

"You think I'm making it up?" Renata looked at Gabriel to back her up on this.

"I think... that DCFS is insane," Mira clarified. "There's no way that this is because of the divorce. Nobody is thinking or talking about the divorce anymore. We have moved on. Joseph knows that his father and I couldn't keep living together and that we're not going to get back together again. How many of his friends have two parents at home? None of them. Everyone's parents are divorced these days. Or they are single parents and never were married in the first place. Why would he care about the divorce now? If this had happened when we first separated, then *maybe* I could understand where they are coming from. But now? Just out of the blue? When everything has settled down?"

"You don't think that he's upset about the divorce?"

"Not anymore. Maybe he is disappointed, but that is as far as it goes."

"And when did he find out that his dad and Felicity were going to get married?"

"Get married?" Mira shook her head. "I haven't heard anything about him and the bimb—new girlfriend getting married. I know they're living together, and I'm sure they both deserve each other, but I hadn't heard they had made the decision to marry."

Renata looked at Gabriel and then back at Mira. "They're having a baby. They're not going to get married?"

She swallowed. "I don't want to sound like an echo here, but— they're having a baby?"

"Yeah. He didn't tell you that?"

"Who, Joseph? No. He never said anything to me about it."

"And his father? He didn't say anything about it?"

"We don't speak to each other. So, no. He didn't tell me."

"Do you think *that* could have set off Joseph's issues?"

Gabriel opened his mouth to point out that Joseph hadn't learned about his father's impending arrival until after that, but Renata motioned for him to be quiet. She understood the timeline. She was checking a hypothetical. And maybe also checking to see whether Joseph had told the truth. Just because he said he'd only just discovered Felicity's pregnancy didn't mean it was the truth. He might have learned some time ago and only felt like revealing it now.

"I don't believe that any of this is psychological," Mira insisted. "It's physical. Just because they can't figure out what it is, that doesn't mean that it's all made up or subconscious or anything like that. Joseph... he has problems. Sure. Any kid does. You know that he suffers from depression. I'm not saying that he doesn't have any psychological problems. But this... I'm convinced this is not."

CHAPTER FIFTY-FIVE

Renata nodded. "Okay. Can you tell me all of the testing that Joseph has had done? Did you track it all?"

She opened her mouth, then shook her head. "No. I just... I just kept a running list in my head of what they had done. And all of it was negative, so there wasn't any need to keep track of results. Because it wasn't anything that they tested for."

"He's had brain scans? Looking for any physical abnormalities?"

"Yes. I was scared to death that they were going to find something, but everything came back fine. No brain bleeds, no tumors. Everything looked perfectly normal."

"And EEG? They looked for abnormal brain waves? Seizure activity?"

"They initially thought that maybe it was a kind of a seizure. But nothing showed up when they did the testing."

"Did they try to provoke one?"

"One what?"

"Did they try to provoke a seizure? Get him to hyperventilate, flash the lights, that kind of thing?"

"I... don't know. I guess so. He had to be tired. They said he was more likely to have a seizure if he was sleep deprived."

"But nothing at all."

"No."

"Blood tests? Urine tests?"

"They checked for everything, I swear. Every time, a doctor would come in and say that they had an idea of what might be causing it, and they are going to check with this new test... and then nothing. Not an infection. Not a seizure. Not a clot."

"They checked his heart? His breathing?"

"Yes. Everything."

"Allergies?"

"Allergies?" Mira echoed. "Allergies can cause fainting?"

"They can cause a lot of things. Did they test for allergies?"

"I don't think so."

"How about low blood pressure?"

"He's had his blood pressure taken a hundred times. Sometimes, it is a little low, but nothing that the doctors have been concerned about. They say that is normal for athletes like him."

"How about a tilt table? Did they try that?"

"No, I don't think so."

"What other heart tests did they do?"

"I don't know." Mira shook her head. "They didn't think that there was anything wrong with his heart. He's an athlete. They did imaging and said that he didn't have any blockages or narrowing of the arteries. They ran EKGs. Lots of them. All of the doctors who looked at them said that they were perfectly normal. That he had a strong heart and that wasn't the problem."

"So what do you think it is?"

"I don't know what it is. But I don't think that it is all in his head."

"I want you to go back to the doctors and hospital and get all of the records you can. We will need to look through them to see what had been checked and what might still have been missed."

"Why do you need to know any of this? If you're going to... either talk DCFS into letting him come back home, or encouraging him to... *leave*, then what does it matter?"

"Because if it is physical, do you really want him to return home just to have another incident he doesn't wake up from?"

Gabriel's hand shot out to stop Renata from saying it, but he was too late. Mira's already pale face drained of color. She stared at Renata. Renata looked at Gabriel, his hand up to stop her too late.

"You think I should sugarcoat it?"

"No. Not sugarcoat it. Just... being a bit more sensitive. Don't just drop it on her like that."

"Okay. Sorry." Renata shrugged. "I got a big mouth sometimes. I get impatient. It's best... if you get a proper diagnosis before moving him somewhere else, where you might have to start over or have a hard time getting the previous records that you need. Or if you are living under another name, getting medical procedures done is much harder. They want to see all of the medical records. So whether you stay here or not, you really should have hard copies of all of the records you can get your hands on."

"Okay. What do I tell them? What if they know that Joseph isn't in my custody anymore? What if they talk to the social worker about it?"

"You don't ask for permission. You don't tell anyone anything about him not being in your custody. They get a hundred requests a day for records. You write a form letter saying you want them and send it out. They're not going to check to see whether you have physical custody or not. You're listed as his parent on their records. If not, they check the birth certificate, and you're listed there. Just ask like you don't expect there to be any problem."

"And what if his social worker wants to know why I'm doing that?"

"Because you're being a diligent parent and trying to figure out what is wrong with him, even though he isn't in your custody anymore. You want him to be healthy whether he is there with you or not. You don't want anything to happen to him."

Mira nodded. "Okay."

"You're a good mom, right?"

Mira's face twisted into a scowl. "Why would you ask that?"

"You're the best mom to him that you can be, right? You've been looking after him and trying to help him succeed his whole life. You've given him all of the things he needs. You've taken him to the doctor. You make sure he has plenty to eat and that it isn't just junk. You taught him to take care of his body, and you never let anyone abuse him."

Mira perked up visibly at the list of things she had done. Her successes. The things that showed she was a good, diligent mother who had done the best that she could to look after her son.

"Yes. I've done all of that."

"This is just something that a good mom does. Makes sure that she has all of her kid's records and that they are all organized and accessible for when you need them. Maybe, when you have them all together, you'll find something they missed. An anomaly that was never followed up on. A test that was ordered but never performed, or that the results are missing. You think that all of the doctors get everything right? People are killed every day by physician mistakes."

"Well, sometimes I did feel like Dr. Shapiro wasn't listening to me. That he had his own ideas of what was going on and he was just following those instead of any concerns that we raised with him."

"Then you should follow up on that. Make sure that nothing got missed. No one else is going to check to make sure that he didn't miss anything. You are Joseph's only hope."

"And you think... Do you think that I'll be able to get Joseph back again? He's so old that I'm afraid that he is going to end up in one of those dreadful detention centers instead of a foster home. Or that they'll put him in a group home where he's basically on his own. Then you know that once he turns eighteen, they just turn him out on the street."

"Once he's eighteen, he can decide to come back here. And they can't stop him."

Mira brightened at that. "Well... that would be good, at least. But all of the time between now and then, when we can't see each other... and something could happen to him."

Renata nodded. "Yeah. Being on your own isn't the worst thing in the world, but a lot of abuses happen inside foster care."

"I don't understand why they just jumped in and took him. He was never in any danger, and I don't see how they could have thought that he was."

"I think it all boils down to you not picking him up when the nurse said to. She said he wasn't well and needed to go home, and you told him just to go back to classes."

"I never did that!"

Renata shook her head. "As far as they are concerned, you did."

CHAPTER FIFTY-SIX

Gabriel looked in on Renata, who had been sitting in front of the computer for too long. She had been completely wrapped up in reviewing Joseph's records, going over and over the medical tests, hoping to find the one thing that would help them to get him closer to a diagnosis, which could change his life and get him back onto a better track. Something other than foster care.

Renata had commandeered Joseph's computer, unused since his apprehension. She had been going over the records that Mira had provided, printing out bits of articles and studies, sticking them up on the wall or laying them out on the bed and floor. Gabriel kept expecting to enter Joseph's bedroom and find red strings leading from one note to another, forming a spiderweb all over the room, like in some TV drama about an obsessed serial killer, a cop trying to solve his mother's murder thirty years later, or a paranoid schizophrenic. Renata's paranoia seemed to have eased a bit since she'd gotten her prescription changed, but Gabriel worried that it would be back in full force with the way she was working on the computer. She seemed to be down the rabbit hole. Or a whole warren of rabbit holes.

"Renata."

She didn't look away from the computer. "Uh-huh?"

"You're late for your lunch."

She grunted back at him. Gabriel knew she expected him to just move on, let her work, and come back later when she wasn't so busy. He didn't move from the doorway.

"Renata."

"What?" Her voice was louder this time, more irritated, letting him know that he was crossing the line.

"You need to take a break."

"I will."

"Now."

"I'm busy."

"I know. But you need to take care of yourself. You're not helping anyone if you crash."

"I'm not crashing. Just let me work this all out."

"No. Renata." Gabriel entered the bedroom. He hadn't wanted to intrude on her, but she wasn't listening and he didn't want her to end up in the hospital. Or to watch her through a crisis, wondering whether she would get through it and at what point he should call for help.

He went to her backpack, which he never touched, and unzipped it.

"Hey!" Renata tore her eyes away from the screen. "What the hell? Get out of my bag!"

He pulled out one of the packets of formula she had already mixed, combining the powdered formula, distilled water, and meds she needed at each feeding.

"Get out of there," Renata kicked at him. "And give me that." She snatched the formula from his hand. "You're not in charge of me."

"Who is going to help you if you crash? Who is going to be responsible then?"

"I'm not going to crash." Her fingers worked automatically to unfasten a couple of buttons on her shirt in order to access the feeding tube. "You don't get to decide what I need."

"Are you paying attention to me now?" Gabriel demanded. "Did you look at the time?"

Renata's eyes went to the system time on Joseph's computer, her face twisted into a scowl. She leaned closer to look at it as if her eyes were not working properly.

"This isn't right. What time is it?"

"Almost two o'clock."

She normally took her lunchtime feeding at noon. If she neglected to eat at regular intervals, it could spell disaster. By the time she realized her cellular energy was depleted, she no longer had the ability to hook herself up and, if no one like Gabriel or a medical professional were there to provide for her needs, she could quickly fall into a coma and die.

Renata looked down at the formula bag in her hand and attached it without a word. She swallowed and looked at him.

"I didn't know it was that late. You should have told me sooner."

"I did," he pointed out. "This is not the first time I have come in here and told you to eat. You keep putting me off."

"Well, don't let me do that," she told him wryly.

Gabriel grinned and shook his head. "Am I forgiven for touching your bag?"

"Of course."

They sat for a few minutes in silence. Gabriel wanted to make sure that the formula was flowing and that Renata was going to be okay before he pursued any conversation.

"How is it going?" he asked eventually. "I don't like to ask, because you'll tell me when you're ready, but it seems like you've been very busy…" He looked around the room at the various papers. "Have you managed to track anything down?"

Renata nodded. "Maybe," she agreed. She pointed to a paper in front of her on the wall. "Check out that one."

Gabriel walked over to it and read the headline. It was a story about a hockey player who had died on the ice at a game. Gabriel leaned in to read the smaller type. While there was no diagnosis mentioned in the article, it did mention several other cases where similar deaths had occurred, and the need to screen athletes properly for congenital heart conditions.

"Okay," he said. "So you think maybe it is heart-related? But

Joseph has been tested already. He's had several EKGs and even an ultrasound of his heart and the blood flow."

"But he hasn't had the right test at the right time."

"Okay. What did they miss?"

"Stress test. They need to run an EKG while he's exerting himself. And look for a long QT interval. And if that doesn't work, wear a monitor twenty-four hours a day and look for changes in his rhythm. But some people don't show the classic signs. It can be very sneaky. And he has not been given the genetic tests for Long QT."

Mira appeared in the doorway. "You think it's his heart?"

"Do you know if anyone else in your family has ever had this? Fainting during exercise? Sudden death at a young age?"

"I don't know. I don't think so. If Joseph has it, then why didn't it show up during his EKGs?"

"Because it can change throughout the day. They need to seriously look for it to find it. Just looking at his EKG when he is lying in bed isn't enough."

"He said that he fainted because he hadn't eaten."

Renata checked the flow of her formula and leaned back in the chair, stretching. "Well, I hate to tell you this, but…" she trailed off.

"What?" Mira demanded.

"Kids lie. Not just kids, everyone lies. And some guy who is embarrassed at fainting in the middle of the field in front of everyone and wants to protect his reputation makes up whatever he can to avoid looking weak."

"He wouldn't do that."

"Sure he would. He didn't want to go through a bunch of medical testing. He didn't want to have a disease or disorder that made him look weak or prevented him from being able to play. So he just said that he hadn't eaten."

"Is that what he told you?"

Renata shrugged. Her eyes closed to slits. "No. He tried that line on me, too. But I can read him. He was covering up."

"There are a lot of things he could be covering up," Gabriel pointed out. "Things like drug use, not taking his prescriptions, using some supplement that was supposed to improve his performance. Or another panic attack."

"They checked his blood for drugs and his med levels. They aren't panic attacks." Renata pointed to a short stack of papers on the bed. "Take a look at those. Elevated heart rate, sweating, feeling of doom. Sounds like a panic attack, right? But it's not. It's long QT syndrome. Palpitations or tachycardia."

Mira looked at the papers, frowning, but didn't enter the room or pick them up.

"Dizziness?" Renata offered, pointing to another study. "Fainting or seizures when working out? All of his symptoms are here. And he did not get the proper stress test needed to diagnose it. Even then, some people just don't show what you would expect on the EKG. Sometimes, they only know because they find it in the genetic testing. It *can* be familial, but not always. Or we don't know all the genes that can cause it yet."

"If it matches all of his symptoms, then why didn't they test for it?"

Renata rolled her eyes. "Are you really going to ask me that? Do you think that doctors diagnose everything that everyone walks in the doors with? No way. People take months or years to get diagnosed sometimes. And with a lot of people with Long QT Syndrome..." Renata pointed to one of the news articles on the wall. "Sometimes, the first time you know anything is wrong is when the person drops dead in the middle of the field."

Mira went pale looking at it. "This is something that could kill him? It isn't just... fainting spells."

"Of course it could kill him," Renata said irritably. "What do you think I'm telling you here? He has a heart problem. That's *serious*. They need to run the proper tests to get him diagnosed. He should be on beta blockers. He should get an internal defibrillator."

"But we can't make DCFS get him diagnosed with this problem," Gabriel pointed out. "They have already run all of the tests that they're going to. They've decided that it's psychological. They're not going to keep running tests because they think that is what he wants.

That he gets a kick out of all of the medical attention, so that's why he is having symptoms in the first place."

Renata covered her eyes with both palms as if she were warming them. Too much time staring at computer screens. Not enough time blinking.

"We'll brainstorm," Gabriel suggested. "Maybe you tell them that he has a second cousin who was just diagnosed with this Long QT Syndrome and that the symptoms sound *exactly* like what Joseph had. Put them onto the right track that way."

"They're not going to believe me," Mira said. "They think that I'm either negligent or that I'm poisoning him to cause these symptoms. The backup diagnosis if they are not psychological symptoms is that I am the one making him sick. Either he's imagining it, or it's me."

"Well then, the foster family. They say that they recognize the symptoms. That they read an article. Something like that."

"How are you going to get the foster family to cooperate? I can't get in touch with them, and you certainly can't contact them."

"Have Joseph leave articles about it around the house," Gabriel suggested, which he knew was probably stupid. The foster parents wouldn't guess that they were being played? They wouldn't know where these articles came from? That Joseph was trying to tip them off to his diagnosis? He might as well come out and ask them about it. They weren't stupid.

"Heather," Renata suggested.

Gabriel looked at her.

"Who is Heather?" Mira asked.

"She was my foster mom for a little while," Gabriel explained. "She takes lots of kids with medical issues. So she's really good at that stuff. But..." he addressed Renata, "How is she going to get involved in the case? She doesn't have anything to do with them. She can't say that she just happened to think that this other kid might have Long QT Syndrome when she has nothing to do with him. They'll want to know where it came from. Who has been in touch with them. It would look too suspicious."

Renata was nodding, her brow furrowed as she thought about it. "They have these email groups, foster parents with medical kids who talk to each other about problems, symptoms, things like that. Help each other out with stuff that they have experience with. If Joseph's foster parents are part of that group… even if they aren't, they could still copy them on an email they send out to a bunch of the local foster parents. They say they have a kid with Long QT, and has anyone else dealt with it? She lists the symptoms that this fictional kid has…"

"And Joseph's foster parents recognize it as the symptoms that Joseph has."

"Yeah." Renata looked satisfied with herself. "How about that?"

"What about when they don't have a kid with those symptoms? Aren't the other parents going to ask whatever happened with that kid with Long QT that you had? Or what if a social worker sees it and knows they don't have a new kid?"

Renata grunted. "Then… she says that she has a friend in another city who has a kid with these symptoms, and it has just been diagnosed as Long QT Syndrome, and she is looking for other people who have dealt with this before and know about the surgical and medication options. What if the kid wants to be involved in sports? Prognosis. That kind of thing."

Gabriel rolled it around in his mind. "Yeah. That could work. We'll explore it. I think the first thing to find out is if they are in any of the same email networks. If they're not, it will look a little strange to be copying someone they have never dealt with before."

"They just say that they wanted to broaden the reach to everyone who might have experience. Or they were looking at a list of foster parents in the area and meant to put someone else on the list and included them by mistake. Serendipity. 'Wasn't it lucky that we accidentally included you.'"

"And what if they don't read their emails?" Mira asked, making a face. "I know plenty of adults who never read their email."

"It's a good first shot," Gabriel told her. "If it doesn't work out, then we go on to plan B."

CHAPTER FIFTY-SEVEN

J oseph sat in the doctor's office as Dr. Russell reviewed the latest test results. He certainly hadn't expected anything definitive to be discovered in the latest round of tests. He'd been disappointed too many times to get his hopes up. He had fully expected it to be a dead end, despite Renata being sure that it was the answer to the mystery that had baffled all of the doctors. How did an untrained teen girl come up with the diagnosis that had eluded them all? She was bright—Joseph would readily admit that—but she wasn't a doctor. Not any kind of professional.

But Dr. Russell acted as though he had been the one to come up with the suggestion. He showed them the EKG strip that showed Joseph's heartbeat during the stress test, pointed to the various peaks to indicate which wave was which, and showed the milliseconds that separated the Q wave from the T wave.

"It can be very hard to pin down," he explained to Phoenix. "That's why it did not show up previously. And you really have to be looking for it on the EKG. It's very rare, and gets overlooked a lot. But this incident with Joseph passing out on the field, that's what tipped us off."

He said it as if it had been the doctors who had come up with the idea, rather than having to have it put in front of them with the demand that they look into it.

"The gene test will take a few months to come back." Russell sighed and shrugged, acknowledging his lack of control over the DNA lab's processing time. "We'll see whether it is a genetic form that we know of or not. But in the meantime, we can proceed based on the results of the stress test."

"Proceed to do what?" Phoenix asked. "Someone said that it can be controlled with medication."

"We will want to put him on beta blockers immediately. And to consider any other drugs that he's taking. Some medications like SSRIs can actually make Long QT Syndrome worse. It's possible that it was the medications that exacerbated Joseph's Long QT symptoms in the first place."

"But the beta blockers will help that?"

"Yes. It might be a bit of a balancing act, because the beta blockers can contribute to depression." He shrugged. "Interestingly, one study shows that the QT interval can predict clinical depression and anxiety and their severity. Treating both can be a challenge. Like always, we might need to experiment to find the right dose for Joseph. It's not fun, but we'll find the right level to keep him well and happy." Dr. Russell looked at Joseph momentarily and threw a reassuring smile in his direction. Joseph wasn't exactly a participant in the conversation but, every now and then, the doctor remembered he was sitting there.

"Joseph will also have to make some lifestyle adjustments. Avoiding caffeine or other stimulants. We recommend not waking up to an alarm. Avoiding whatever shocks he can."

"What about surgery?" Joseph asked. "I was reading an article that talked about a pacemaker thing."

"An internal defibrillator," Dr. Russell said slowly. "Yes, that is something to be considered. We find that beta blockers manage the symptoms in most cases. But there are situations in which the defibrillator is recommended."

"I want to play soccer again."

"Well, a little exercise doesn't hurt…"

"Competitively," Joseph told him. "I was the star of my school team. I was going to go to university on a scholarship." That might be stretching it a little, but he wanted the defibrillator. He wanted to know that if his heart got into a dangerous rhythm, that if he passed out or got close to it, the defibrillator would ensure his survival. He knew that DCFS might not want to put that much money into surgery for a foster kid, but he didn't want to die. He knew what it felt like to hit the turf and not know if he would get back up again.

He wanted to be able to get up again.

"Well…" Dr. Russell pursed his lips and considered this. "As a competitive soccer player, you probably don't want just to be relying upon just beta blockers. New recommendations are being considered for allowing players diagnosed with Long QT to continue to play. Right now, there are a lot of restrictions, but players with internal defibrillators are being allowed to continue playing even if they don't meet the qualifications."

Joseph looked at Mrs. Brewster and held her gaze. "You have to make sure DCFS approves it. It's the only way I can keep playing."

"It won't be up to me… but I'll recommend it as strongly as possible."

"Please. They have to do it. I did everything they told me to when they thought it was all in my head. I knew it wasn't, but I still did everything they said. They owe me."

Mrs. Brewster raised her brows. "I'm not sure about that. But as I said, I will recommend it. I'll tell them that you need it. But I can't promise that they'll approve it. If they decide that the beta blockers are sufficient, I can't do anything about that."

———

She must have done a good job about it, because the powers-that-be in DCFS approved his surgery despite the expense. Joseph figured they must be worried about being sued if they didn't. He certainly would have raised a stink if they had denied it. And his dad would have helped convey the seriousness of the threat. He might not want to look after Joseph, but that wouldn't stop him from writing a threatening letter and making a few well-placed phone calls if he felt that they were putting his son's health at risk.

But they approved it, and it wasn't long before he was admitted to the hospital for the surgical implant. Joseph was eager and anxious at the same time. It was a good thing he was already on the beta blockers, which prevented his heart from speeding too much. He could worry about the surgery without worrying that the anxiety was going to kill him.

Tink and Mark were not interested in seeing Joseph at the hospital, of course, but Axel demanded that Mrs. Brewster bring him along so that he could see for himself that Joseph was okay before Joseph went into surgery. He stood by Joseph's bed, looking him over worriedly.

"Does it hurt?" he asked Joseph.

"The surgery? I don't think it will be too bad. There will be stitches, but it will be... just a cut. They don't take anything out. They just put a little box in here," he tapped his chest, "and it makes sure that my heart keeps beating the right way."

"Like that thing on TV," Axel observed.

"What thing?"

Axel mimed rubbing cardiac panels together and then putting them on Joseph's chest. "Clear!" he announced, before pretending to shock Joseph.

"Like that."

Joseph and Mrs. Brewster both grinned and nodded at him. "Yes, like that," Joseph agreed. "Except it will do it inside, and you won't even be able to tell."

"Oh," Axel looked disappointed that he wouldn't be able to see Joseph receive a dramatic, body-arching shock. "Will you? Can you feel it?"

"I guess so. I don't know exactly what it feels like. I guess I'll find out."

CHAPTER FIFTY-EIGHT

Gabriel tried to remain calm as Mira paced around the house, dusting and looking for something to do with herself. Although there was no more dusting, she continued to go over the same surfaces, pretending there was work to be done. The house smelled strongly of bleach and other cleaners.

Gabriel's phone vibrated. He looked down at it to read Renata's message. He looked at Mira and smiled.

"He's out of surgery. Looks like everything went fine."

"I can't believe DCFS won't even tell me anything," Mira said, shaking her head. "You would think that they would at least have to tell me that he was having this surgery and then let me know how it went. But they close me out completely. If something happened to him, if he died, they would call me then, wouldn't they?"

"Well... you would hope," Gabriel said uncomfortably. "I have heard of cases where the parents are not told until months later. But that's not the way it's *supposed* to work."

"Oh, well, that's reassuring," Mira growled.

Gabriel shrugged. He knew it was bad, that the system needed reforms, but there was nothing he could do about it. He was already doing what he could, working outside the system, helping those he could. He had to leave the rest in someone else's hands.

It had been a relief to hear that Joseph had been approved for the implant, and now to know that it had gone well. He couldn't help thinking about the way he had been treated when he had been in foster care and placed in Dr. De Clerk's experimental mito program. If he hadn't run away and escaped that program, he was sure it would have killed him. And he'd heard lately there had been a couple of deaths of children in that program. Nothing that was ever actually attributed to the mito protocol, of course. No, those children had only died of their mitochondrial disease or related complications. But Gabriel knew. He had been lucky to escape with his life.

"Now that his problem has been diagnosed and he has been given the defibrillator, we can start working on reunification, can't we?" Mira suggested. "I was worried about being able to pay for the surgery, so I'm happy they did it. But now... they took him out because he was having these health problems, and they thought I wasn't taking care of him properly or was causing them. Now that they know what it was and he is healthy again, I'll get him back, right?"

Gabriel sighed. "I hope so. Now that he's been properly treated... it's time to ask them to review the case and start on reunification."

———

Gabriel knew. He had hoped that he would be wrong, but he had known when Mira asked whether DCFS would start the process of returning Joseph to her now that their concerns had been addressed and they knew what had really been causing Joseph's episodes. He knew that DCFS would not initiate those proceedings right away. Even if Mira filed a request for the case to be reviewed by the court, they would be lucky to get an order in her favor.

Rather than making a formal request, Mira asked Letty whether it would be possible. She didn't refer to Long QT Syndrome or the surgery Joseph had just had, since, as far as they were concerned, she hadn't been informed of them. She just asked what it would take for them to be reunited and what she would have to do.

As Mira had described it to Gabriel in an outraged tone over the phone, Mrs. Miller had removed her glasses, flipped through a few pages in Joseph's file, and shook her head sadly.

"I think we still have a ways to go on this, Mrs. Demain. As a single mother, you don't have a lot of time to spend with the boy and, as a medically fragile person, he really needs to be supervised. I understand that society thinks it is completely acceptable for a child of his age to be home alone between getting out of school and you arriving home, but imagine how you would feel if something happened to him during that time. If he had one of his episodes and by the time you got home, it was too late to do anything about it."

Mira had to bite her tongue, knowing that Joseph wasn't going to have any more episodes since he was on beta blockers and had an internal defibrillator.

"What if I arrange for after-school care?" It was ridiculous, with Joseph being so old. After-school care was for little kids. But she wanted to show that she was willing to do anything. To break down all the barriers and find out exactly what would be required to get him back.

"How are you going to afford that? I understand your husband is not paying child support. You're paying the mortgage and other bills yourself, and you can't take on childcare expenses as well. You want to find a way to reduce your hours, not to have to increase them."

"What if I could pay for after-school care and cut back my hours?"

Letty shook her head. "How are you going to do that? Do you have something lined up?"

"No, but if I could get something, would that work? Then you would consider giving him to me?"

"It's not just the money that I'm concerned about. There are also your emotional resources. You deal with depression yourself, don't you?"

Renata had warned Mira this would be a problem at some point. Mira had never told Letty or anyone at DCFS that she dealt with mental illness as well. But she had posted about certain parts of her struggle online. Viewable to anyone in the public, including Letty.

"My mental health is stable," she told Letty. "I take antidepressants and have not had any issues with them. I've been able to take care of Joseph up until now. I don't see it being a problem in the future."

"Hmm." Letty's tone was not encouraging. "Even before I was called to be Joseph's case worker, after the fiasco at the school, there had been some concerns reported."

Fiasco was an unfair characterization of Joseph's deciding not to call her to be picked up and staying at school. Joseph had believed that he was fine and could safely remain at school and complete his day, which had turned out to be true. He had been safe and well. It wasn't a fiasco. Just a teen deciding that the nurse was wrong about what he could handle and how well he was.

"What other concerns?" she demanded. "I'm not aware of anything else. No one ever talked to me any other time about concerns for Joseph's health or safety."

"Those reports are confidential. But suffice to say… I am not yet comfortable with considering Joseph's reunification at this time. Maybe some parenting classes, you addressing the areas of concern mentioned, and an improvement in his health. Perhaps then, we can discuss it."

That was when Mira knew that there was no way DCFS would consider returning Joseph to her. They would keep stalling and saying that Mira needed to do more, until Joseph aged out of the system and could come home on his own. At that point, DCFS couldn't do anything about it and would stop getting government monies for his care. At that point, they would cease to be concerned.

Even though Mira had been initially resistant to having to leave the state if she were to have any chance of a successful reunion on the other side of the law, that was no longer a problem.

"They aren't going to let us reunite while I am still working this job and living in this house," she sighed. "So either way, in order to get him back, I have to start a new life somewhere else."

"And you can do that?" Gabriel asked.

"I can do that," Mira promised.

CHAPTER FIFTY-NINE

J oseph!"

Joseph awoke to a high-pitched scream and something landing hard on top of him.

His eyes flew open, his body convulsed, and he sat up in shock, his heart beating a million miles a minute. His heart gave several hard palpitations and then settled down again. Joseph looked at Axel, sitting on top of him, his eyes wide and a big grin on his face. Joseph had arrived home while Axel was asleep, so it was his first chance to welcome him home.

"Axel!" he croaked. "You scared the heck out of me!"

Mrs. Brewster hurried into the room. "Axel!" she shouted. "What did we talk about? What was the first thing I said? We talked about scaring Joseph or waking him up!"

Axel looked at her, the smile dropping from his face. "I forgot."

"You could give him a heart attack. I don't mean just that you could scare him, but that you could really give him a heart attack. You could send him right back to the hospital."

Or kill him outright, but Mrs. Brewster was too kind to tell him that. Mrs. Brewster grabbed for her phone as it started to whoop, a loud klaxon, not the vibration or quiet ring that she normally had set. She looked at the alert on the screen, and then at Joseph.

"Your defibrillator fired," she told him.

"Uh—yeah. It did," Joseph agreed. They both looked at Axel, he looked back with a stricken expression on his face.

"I didn't mean to," he protested.

"Well, I guess it worked," Joseph said with a little nod.

"It worked!" Axel repeated. "It worked! It worked!" he chanted, excited again.

"Yeah, it worked."

Joseph's phone started ringing. He looked at the caller ID and picked it up.

"Hello?"

"Is this Joseph?" an official voice demanded crisply.

"Yeah, this is Joseph."

"We got an alert that your defib fired."

"It did."

"What happened?"

"Uh… my alarm clock. I forgot to turn it off when I got home last night, like I was supposed to. It woke me up this morning and got my heart going."

"Turn it off now."

"I did. It won't happen again."

"Your rhythm and rate look okay now. But we might want to increase your beta blockers a bit. Can you come in for a checkup today?"

Joseph looked at Mrs. Brewster. "Doctor wants to see me today."

She rolled her eyes and massaged the back of her neck tiredly. "Yes, of course. See what time you can get in and I'll arrange it."

———

Before leaving the cardiologist's office, Joseph informed them that he needed to change the phone numbers that his defibrillator would alert, and the nurse receptionist showed him how to log in through his phone app to change the settings.

He wouldn't want Mrs. Brewster to get any future alerts. And his own phone number would be changing, as well as the number of cardiologist that monitored his progress. A lot of changes were in store.

CHAPTER SIXTY

Gabriel and Renata had not been onboard with Axel assisting with Joseph's escape. But Joseph knew Axel could do it, and he refused to abandon Axel without saying goodbye or explaining where he was going. Axel might talk to either of the Brewsters about Joseph's plan. Still, he didn't know where Joseph was going, the timeline, or the other participants in the plan, so he couldn't do anything more than admit that he had been a part of the plot. Joseph warned him not to but, if he did, the only person who would suffer for it was Axel, and all they could do was tell him he shouldn't have helped Joseph.

Joseph needed a distraction. To give himself plenty of time, he needed to slip away without Mr. or Mrs. Brewster realizing it. They would think he was still in his room, sleeping or doing homework. He didn't have any appointments or commitments so, with any luck, they wouldn't discover that he was missing until several hours later. Enough to give him a good head start.

He heard Axel crying for help outside and almost went out to see what was going on himself before he remembered that it was an act. He heard Mrs. Brewster's footsteps as she hurried down the hall and out the front door, looking for Axel and calling out to see what was happening.

Her voice outside was less distinct than Axel's, until she turned around and called back into the house for Mr. Brewster to come outside to help. Joseph stood there listening for a minute to Axel's shrieks that he had climbed too high in the big oak tree in the front yard and didn't know how to get back down. Both parents calmly tried to talk him down, but it wasn't working.

Joseph picked up his backpack and headed out. He closed the bedroom door and cut through the house to the kitchen and the back door. When he stepped out of the house, he was startled to find himself face-to-face with Tink on the back porch.

He froze and stared at her, heart speeding up. Not enough to trigger his defib or an alert on the phones. The beta blockers were keeping it at a good level, though he found they did make him a bit tired.

"Uh… hi."

Tink looked at him, her eyes taking everything in. She raised her brows. "Where do you think you're going?"

Joseph shrugged. "Out. Going to do some homework with a friend from school." He lifted one shoulder to indicate his backpack.

"A friend from school? The only friend you've got at school is that weirdo Brit."

"I'm getting some help with my homework. For the stuff that I missed while I was in the hospital."

"And Axel screaming in the tree out front, that's just a coincidence?"

"Sounds like he got stuck or something."

"Axel? If you'd lived here long enough, you would know there's no way he'd ever get stuck in that tree. He's like a monkey."

"Well… maybe he caught his shoe in a branch."

She chuckled. "You think you're going to escape that easily? Just walk out of here? And go wherever you're going? Are you running away with Brit?"

"No."

They stood staring at each other for what seemed like a long time. Joseph knew better than to ask her not to talk. That was all it would take to convince her to tell the Brewsters that he had run away. Tink would always do the opposite of what she was asked.

"Well… see you around," Tink said with a shrug. "I don't know if they'll bring you back here or toss you in the clink. Have fun, wher-ever they put you. Hope it's worth it."

She turned away from him, pulling out a cigarette and cupping her hand around it while she lit it, pretending he wasn't there.

Joseph looked at her for another moment, wondering whether she was truly going to let him go without raising the alarm. She ignored him. Joseph took it as his cue to leave and not ask any questions he might not like the answers to. He settled his backpack on his shoul-ders, running his thumbs under the straps to ensure they were lying flat. Then he continued with the plan, leaving the yard and crossing the back lane to the crescent behind the Brewster house, working his way through the neighborhood until he reached a main street with a bus stop.

Waiting for the bus was excruciating. He had done his best to time it so that he would be there within a minute or two of the bus's arrival but, of course, that didn't work. When did buses ever run on time? He didn't like standing there at the stop, in full view of anyone who happened to drive by.

But he was just another kid at the bus stop. Nothing of any interest to anyone. He had a backpack, just like any of the other kids. Nothing to set him apart. It was a full fifteen minutes until the bus finally got there. An accomplishment when that route was supposed to run every ten minutes. No one looked at him as he got on the bus. They were all too busy driving, staring out the window, or using their phones. No one cared about one more kid getting on the bus.

He followed Renata's instructions and switched routes a couple of times, watching for any followers. But of course, there were none. That was just Renata's paranoia. But it had kept her alive and out of trouble while she had been on the run, so he would do what she said.

He arrived at the mall. As expected, it was full of teens and preteens shopping and visiting. Hanging out and enjoying time away from parents and school and all of the other pressures that teens were subject to.

He was supposed to take some time to make sure, again, that no one had followed him or looked suspicious. He pulled out his phone to check the time and didn't remember until he looked at its blank face that he had powered it down before setting out, as he had been instructed. And now it was time to ditch the phone. But not into the garbage. Gabriel had started to give him instructions on how to take out the SIM card and destroy it before tossing the phone itself, but Renata disagreed.

"Let's give them something to follow," she told them. "Toss the phone into someone else's bag. If you can't get close enough to another teenager, put it in a baby stroller. They're always full of bags and junk. No one will notice the difference. They won't find it until they pack their stuff to go home. If you're lucky, they won't find it until they've driven all over town and left a false trail."

"But not if it's turned off, right?" Joseph asked. "I should turn it on before I do that?"

"Easier to track if it's turned on. But they can still do some fancy stuff even if it is turned off," Renata told him. Joseph wondered whether the authorities could or if it were just one of Renata's conspiracy theories.

There weren't as many moms with strollers around as there were teenagers, but there were enough that Joseph found a good target. There was a diaper bag in the bottom cargo area of a big double-stroller, and the mom was sitting down on the other side of the stroller, talking on her phone, distracted. Joseph knelt on one knee to tie his shoe and slipped his phone into the diaper bag.

CHAPTER SIXTY-ONE

J oseph took out the second phone, the one that Renata had given him, and powered it up. In another fifteen minutes, he received a text giving him new directions. He wasn't supposed to answer the text or call the sender unless it were an emergency. He found his way to the big fountain, expecting to be given another instruction once he got there but, instead, Renata and Gabriel were waiting there for him, chatting casually like any other teens. Gabriel leaned on his crutches, a cup of coffee in one hand.

"Hey," he greeted Joseph, looking as cool as if they were just a couple of friends meeting up at the fountain. He took a sip of his coffee. "How did it go?"

Joseph swallowed and nodded. "Pretty good." He told them about Axel's masterful performance, attracting both foster parents to the front of the house while Joseph slipped out the back. They both grinned.

He didn't tell them about running into Tink in the backyard.

Renata left Gabriel and Joseph chatting by the fountain while she took a walk around, making sure that everything looked kosher. Gabriel asked Joseph about his phone and a few other questions to ensure he had followed their instructions.

Renata returned. Her expression was blank. Gabriel studied her. "What's wrong?"

She glanced around. "Nothing. Everything looks good."

Gabriel's brows drew down. He looked around as well, taking his time to study their surroundings. "You see something?"

"No." Renata shook her head. "Just a bad feeling. It's probably nothing."

Joseph shrugged, brushing it off as Renata's paranoia. Gabriel, however, still seemed concerned. He looked around for some previously unseen danger. Joseph was irritated.

"She said it's nothing. Let's move on. We don't want to hang around here all day."

"Better to hang around here for a while and identify the danger than to go on oblivious," Gabriel said. "We haven't gotten this far by ignoring gut instincts."

Joseph clamped his mouth shut to prevent himself from saying the obvious. This was just part of Renata's paranoia. She herself had recognized this and said it wasn't anything. Good for her. So why was Gabriel holding them up?

"Let's just walk for a minute," Gabriel suggested. He turned slowly, looking in each direction before making a decision. He nodded his head, and the three of them walked in the direction Gabriel had indicated for a few steps. Then Renata was peeling away from them again to check out their surroundings.

Joseph kept walking with Gabriel. "Do we really need to do this? I mean... she said it was fine. I don't see anything, you don't see anything. None of us have actually *seen* anything, so why can't we just go?"

Gabriel shrugged as he walked. He watched the faces of people around him. Joseph rolled his eyes and looked away. He knew he was acting like a little kid. They knew what they were doing after that long, and he should listen to their instincts. But he couldn't help thinking that they had just been on the outside for too long. They were no longer operating on the same basis as the rest of society. They had become accustomed to a higher level of vigilance and were locked into it, not realizing how illogical they were being.

He stopped and stared at the TV screen in an electronics store they were walking by. Gabriel turned and followed his gaze.

"Uh-oh."

Joseph's face was on the screen. The crawler along the bottom of the screen gave his name and said that he was missing and that he might be in the company of someone who intended him harm. Joseph had no idea who they might think he was with that would cause him harm. Or maybe they didn't think any such thing; it was just intended to break through people's inertia and tendency not to report anything, convincing them that they needed to be alert and respond for Joseph's own safety. The crawler gave his description and said that he had physical disabilities and needed special medication and that, if anyone knew where he was, they should contact the number shown on the screen or 9-1-1 immediately.

Renata circled back around to join Joseph and Gabriel and looked at the screen. She swore under her breath.

"Okay. We need to get you out of here," she concluded. "This is the last thing we needed. How did they figure out you were missing so fast? I thought your little act with Axel was supposed to keep them from finding out that you were gone so quickly."

"It was," Joseph insisted. "I don't know what happened! He was in the tree and they were out front. No one saw me leave—" He stopped.

Renata looked at Joseph's face, scowling. "No one saw you leave?" she repeated.

"One of the other foster kids. I didn't think she was going to say anything."

"Well, I guess you were wrong. Maybe she was caught doing something she wasn't supposed to, so she threw you under the bus to distract them."

Joseph thought of her lighting a cigarette as he left. Renata was probably dead on. He swore under his breath. She shook her head.

"You've screwed up the operation now. We'll do what we can to recover. But this is going to make it hard for us to get anywhere. Public transit is out. You aren't anonymous anymore. They will be looking for you at all of the traffic hubs, street cams, all of that. You ditched the phone?"

"Yeah. Here, like you said to. In a diaper bag in a stroller."

"Hopefully, that's the first thing they'll latch on to. Follow it around for a while. But they'll eventually figure out that she picked it up at this mall, and they'll look at the surveillance video to find you." She growled in frustration. "And to see who you were with. 'Might be with someone who intends him harm'? That's going to hurt us. Why would they say that?"

"I don't know. Maybe… they think that my mom picked me up. That's the only thing I can think of."

She nodded. "First thing to do is get out of view of the cameras and figure out what we're going to do. We can't leave here together. They'll know that you met us, but we have to make sure they see us going in different directions."

"What am I supposed to do?" Joseph demanded. "I don't have a car. How am I supposed to get anywhere without a car or public transit? You expect me to *walk* out of the state?"

"Well, that's a possibility," Renata said with a scowl. "Or you might have to go underground and wait for things to cool off before you go anywhere. In a week or two, they won't be watching transit anymore."

"A week or two?" Joseph was dismayed. It had already been so long since he had seen Mira. He'd been looking forward to getting to see her again. He kept thinking about it, getting excited about finally being able to be with her again. He'd never appreciated his mother so much. The idea of having to wait for even longer was intolerable. Where would he stay during that time? How would he eat? Where would he sleep?

"Come on." Renata tugged at Joseph's shirt to get his attention and encourage him to go with her. "I told you, we have to get out of the range of the cameras?"

"Where?"

"We know a few places," she assured him. They moved at a brisk, but not attention-getting pace. It felt both too fast and too slow at the same time. Joseph was sure someone would recognize him from the TV and any alerts that had gone out over other channels like police radios and internet broadcasts. He felt like there was a big, bright spotlight on him that everyone would see.

CHAPTER SIXTY-TWO

Gabriel and Renata took Joseph to a back hallway, which led to another Authorized Personnel Only area and a storage room with no surveillance cameras or microphones.

"Okay." Renata sat down and motioned for Gabriel and Joseph to do so as well. "Time for a new plan. What are your ideas?"

"Who do you know with a car?" Gabriel asked Joseph. "Who can you trust?"

"I don't know. I can't really go back to anyone at my old school." He thought for a minute of Lora. She would help him, of course. If she could. But he didn't think she had access to a car. Most of the kids he knew from school who had cars were jocks, on the soccer team— more affluent kids. The same kids had turned against him when they thought that he was trying to get all of the attention for himself.

If they thought he had been attention-seeking before, what would they think when they saw his picture on the TV as a runaway or missing person?

"And at the new school…" Joseph thought about Brit. Was she a safe person to contact? They had known each other much longer than he had been at the school. He had a more solid relationship with her than anyone else he had only been in contact with since he had been in care. "I have… one friend. That's all."

317

"Okay. Who's he?"

"Uh, she. Brit. She's... an old gaming buddy. I met her face-to-face at the new school. Before that, we had only ever met online before. But she was the one person who was nice to me and reached out to me at the new school, and then it turned out it was someone I've known for years online."

Renata considered this, her brow furrowed. "Good indicators," she mused. "You think you can trust her to keep a secret?"

"For sure. She's a friend from way back. She wouldn't turn me in."

"And you think she has access to a car? Could drive you out of the state? That's a pretty big ask. Especially when it could get her arrested."

"Arrested for what?" Joseph demanded. He wouldn't ask Brit to do anything illegal. He didn't want her to end up in prison on his behalf.

"Nothing that would stick. But they'd arrest her if they could and sort it out later. Kidnapping. Impeding a police investigation. Aiding a runaway."

"I don't want her getting in trouble."

"That's good. Maybe you'll be more careful for this part of the operation."

Joseph opened his mouth to object that he'd done everything she told him to and it hadn't been his fault that Tink had raised the alarm. But he knew she would argue it. He should have called off the escape and waited until another day. He should have told Renata about Tink as soon as he had seen her. But he'd been too invested in getting out immediately.

So he closed his mouth instead and waited to see what else Renata had to say. She looked at him for a moment before nodding.

"Like I said, they won't be able to make it stick. But most girls I know wouldn't risk it."

"She would," Joseph said with certainty. Brit was loyal. She was a good friend. She would help him. She would do whatever it took to help a friend.

"Do you know her phone number? Have you been calling each

other since you've gone to that school? The cops will look at your call history and try to identify everyone you've been in contact with."

Joseph shook his head. "No—we haven't been calling or texting each other. I've been going through the gaming app we use. You can message or live chat with each other. No one will know that unless they get into my chat history on the server. And none of it is permanent. It self-destructs after a few minutes. It's not for permanent records."

"Nice," Renata nodded, approving of this. "That's excellent. But what about when they get into your phone? Will they be able to see who your friends in this game are?"

"I deleted it. Wiped everything I could off the phone. I know they can still get deleted stuff off of electronics. But I downloaded a bunch of bloated apps I never used too, so maybe it would overwrite some of the deleted bits. Hopefully, they won't even be able to tell that I used that app."

Renata smiled. "Well, maybe there's some hope for you after all. Okay, tell me about this friend of yours."

He shrugged. "I don't know. What else do you want to know about her? Like I said, she's someone I've been gaming with for years. Then we met at school, like it was meant to be. It's been fun getting to know her in person but, most of the time I was in foster care, I wasn't actually going to school. I was in psych, or getting my surgery and recovering. I haven't gone to school that much since I was moved."

"Anyone know that the two of you are friends?"

"No. Just her and me."

And Tink and Mark. And Tink had already betrayed Joseph once.

"And...?" Gabriel read Joseph's expression.

"And... Tink. My foster sister. The one who probably told them that I'd left."

"If they asked who you were friends with at school, she would be able to tell them her name?"

Joseph nodded miserably. "Yeah. She made comments to me more than once on being friends with a 'weirdo.'"

"What would your friend do if the police went to her to ask her if you'd been in contact with her?"

Joseph chewed on his lip. "She could tell them we'd been in contact through the gaming platform. But we never made any plans to run away together. Even if the server keeps a record of our conversations… it's going to all be gaming stuff. Campaigns that we joined together."

"She might still be workable then," Renata said slowly. "If we wait until after they've had a chance to talk to her and decide she wasn't involved in anything, then you could contact her privately. Feel her out, see if she could get access to a car and be interested in helping you escape the state."

"The police could still be watching for him to contact her through the game," Gabriel pointed out. "If they know she was his only friend at school, they'll watch for a few days, at least."

"You can create a new profile on this server?" Renata suggested to Joseph. "New name, picture, all that kind of thing?"

"Yeah."

"Can you make it so that she recognizes it as you without tipping off anyone else?"

Joseph rubbed the center of his forehead, thinking about it. They had talked about their names. They had known each other for years and served on hundreds of campaigns together. Even without any special clues, she would probably know after two minutes of text chatting with him who it was.

"Yeah. That's easy."

"And could you tell her what was going on and what you needed her to do without actually telling her?"

That might be more of a challenge. Joseph thought it through.

"Uh… yeah. I could cloak it in game talk. If she's seen the alerts on TV or online and been contacted by the cops, I don't have to explain what happened. Just what I need."

Renata nodded her agreement. "It's workable. Next steps: we all need to get out of here. Not together. We'll separate, spend the day apart, and then get back together to finalize arrangements. Gabe and I will contact your mom and let her know that things are on hold, but we're still working on it. You can set up your game platform on that phone?" She motioned to the burner she had given him. "I know it's just cheap and has no memory…"

Joseph had already noted the platform and memory limitations when it had booted up. It was, of course, as cheap as possible. Old version of the operating system. There was enough memory for just a few songs, photos, podcasts, and personal details. Not permanent storage or big gaming platforms.

But he didn't even need to be able to run the games. All he needed was to be able to message Brit within the app. "I think so. I'll… maybe I should make sure it runs before we separate."

Gabriel and Renata nodded in agreement. Joseph would have been more confident if it wasn't such an old version of the operating system. And who knew if they had sandboxed it, making it so that nothing but the natively installed apps could be installed? He could always switch to text messaging with Brit, but that would give away his phone number and maybe his location.

Joseph pulled out the phone and went to work. He had to set up the app, and also had to set up a new email address that he could use for the new profile. He got a number of errors within the app that it would not run until he updated the operating system, but it still let him create a new profile and verify it.

"So far, so good," he told Gabriel and Renata, wiping his face. They were both waiting, but trying not to look like they were hovering over him or monitoring every second that passed to determine his level of success.

Joseph took a deep breath in and let it out again. He was feeling anxious, but his heart rate didn't get out of control.

He sent a test message to Brit asking to connect.

> SLAYEROFDEMONS wants to connect with BritBullXP

He didn't expect an immediate response. Brit might be away from her computer or phone. She might be talking to the police. She might be shopping. Sleeping. On another campaign.

BRITBULLXP accepted connection request

"It's working," Joseph told them. "She already accepted my connection request. We can message now."

Renata nodded. Her eyes were intent. "We don't want to start the conversation yet. You don't want to tell her anything before she talks to the police. She can't have any knowledge that came from you. Let her know you'll message her in a few hours. Something that will keep her from calling you or worrying that something is wrong. You haven't been kidnapped. You just need to stay under cover until you're ready to reach out."

Joseph nodded. He looked down at his phone.

AFK fr now. Covert op. Later

Renata was looking at him curiously. Joseph turned the phone around to show her the message before hitting send. She read it in a glance and nodded.

"Good."

Joseph sent the message.

K 10-4

He smiled and turned off the phone. He let out a sigh. "Now what?"

CHAPTER SIXTY-THREE

They went their separate ways. Joseph was anxious entering the public areas of the mall again, knowing that he was visible on cameras and that the police could go over all of the footage when they discovered that his phone had been at the mall. The mother with the stroller might take the police on a wild goose chase around the city but, eventually, they would figure out that she had picked up the phone at the mall and, therefore, Joseph had been at the mall, and they could pull all of the footage they wanted to and watch him.

It was like trying to walk normally when he knew someone was trying to analyze his gait. He suddenly didn't know where to put his feet or how to walk normally anymore. He tripped over his own feet and generally looked like someone who had just learned to walk. He'd be better off using crutches like Gabriel.

After he got out of the mall, he would have to disappear for a few hours. Make sure that he wasn't seen by anyone who might know him or recognize him from the news alerts. They would all go in different directions. Then he would meet up with Gabriel or Renata again, or both of them to take the next step, reaching out to Brit.

He rechecked the mall map, disoriented. He usually had a pretty good sense of direction, but going into the rabbit's warren of corridors away from the stores had turned him around. He tried to match the landmarks against the map and then to figure out which way he wanted to go. How would he occupy himself for the next few hours without attracting any attention?

"Joseph?"

Joseph jolted at the woman's voice. He whirled around to find the owner. He looked at the woman for a moment without recognizing her.

He was used to seeing her neatly dressed in her school "uniform." Now she was in jeans and a t-shirt that was a little too tight, looking like someone's mom on the weekend instead of like one of the school officials.

"Oh... uh... hi, Nurse Vicky."

She looked him over, her eyes wide and concerned. "Joseph. I wasn't expecting to see you here."

"No," Joseph agreed. He looked around for some avenue of escape. He needed to tell her what he was doing there, where he was going, and give her some explanation for his actions in case she found out that he wasn't supposed to be there. Something normal and routine, boring even. But it would have to totally explain why he was there when he was supposed to be home with his foster family and they thought that he had run away or been kidnapped. "I was just... seeing someone."

"Seeing someone," she repeated. "I saw on the news... there was an alert..."

"Oh, that." Joseph tried to laugh and keep his voice calm and measured. "That was a mistake. Just a mix-up over schedules." He shook his head and laughed again. "I can't believe that it got so blown out of proportion. It will probably be hours before they stop showing it on the TV." Hopefully, that would cover any concerns when she saw that it was still on TV after they separated. "I just had an appointment."

"What kind of an appointment?"

Joseph widened his eyes, looking at her. "That's private."

"Well... yes, of course. I wouldn't ask you for anything confidential. I just meant... your parents would know your schedule. They wouldn't send you to a doctor's appointment alone."

Joseph blinked at her. "Why not?"

"Because... parents go with their children. They are in charge of keeping track of the medical information, giving instructions, and following up on previous orders or getting prescriptions. They wouldn't expect you to go to an appointment on your own."

"I'm almost an adult," Joseph pointed out.

"Well, it's just... I can't see it. Someone needs to make sure that you follow the doctor's orders and remember everything that he said..."

Joseph had to remember that Nurse Vicky was the one who had reported his mother for not coming to pick him up when she had thought that Joseph was too sick to stay at school. She was the one who had taken it upon herself to call DCFS and accuse Mira of being a negligent parent because she hadn't followed Nurse Vicky's orders. She was overly protective and didn't trust kids to be able to look after themselves. She was used to dealing with kids like Nestor Smith, who couldn't even keep a full inhaler with him.

"Usually, one of them does come with me," he told her politely. "But Mr. and Mrs. Brewster were both busy with other things today, so they said that this once, I could go on my own, and they would get a report from the doctor on the phone. It was just a routine check of my defibrillator. So..." he shrugged, "neither of them put it on their calendars because they weren't coming. And then they forgot that was where I was."

Nurse Vicky looked at Joseph doubtfully, not quite believing him. He laughed and shook his head.

"You can call them and tell them that you saw me here. But they already know that this is where I am and are pretty embarrassed about the whole thing. After the fuss that they stirred up, they had to call it all off, explain that they had just gotten confused about schedules and I am just fine. After all that stuff about 'Might be in the company of someone who wants to do him harm.' Mrs. Brewster says she wants to crawl under a rock after doing something so silly in public. It's not just like when you trip and fall walking across a stage. People have been working all morning on getting the word out, and now they have to undo it all."

Nurse Vicky herself looked a little pink and embarrassed. "That would be embarrassing," she admitted.

"Yeah. Here you are, an expert. A foster parent. Someone used to handling medically frail children and getting them to all of their appointments, and making sure they do everything they're supposed to. And they forget about mine."

"I find it a little bit hard to believe."

"Yep," Joseph agreed comfortably. "It was pretty crazy, all right. But like I said, it was just a maintenance checkup. Make sure that the defib is communicating all of the telemetry right and is calibrated correctly for my heart rhythm." Joseph threw out as many medical terms as he could. Nurse Vicky wasn't a cardiologist and probably knew little about internal defibrillators. "They have to adjust it to the right number of milliseconds between the Q wave and T wave so that it doesn't shock me when it doesn't need to, but still shocks me in time that I don't pass out."

"What's it like?" the nurse asked curiously. "I suppose you haven't gotten a shock from it. I don't think they would want it to shock you too often. They wouldn't want it to be too sensitive."

"Actually, yeah, I have. And it's like… I dunno. Like a really big heart palpitation. Like being kicked in the chest by a horse. But from the inside instead of the outside."

"Does it hurt?"

"Kind of. But mostly, it is just… I dunno. A surprise."

"A shock," she contributed.

"Yeah," Joseph chuckled. "Literally."

Nurse Vicky wasn't moving on. He looked for some way to get her on her way. He straightened and grabbed his pocket, feeling for his phone. He pulled it out, tapped the screen, and raised it to his ear.

"Hello? Mrs. Brewster?" He feigned listening to her part of the conversation. "Yeah, I'm out already. Everything is fine; he didn't have any concerns. But he said he would email you anyway to confirm." He nodded his head, staring off into the distance. "Mmm-hmm. I'm going to grab a burger, and then I'll be on my way. Hey, you'll never guess who I ran into at the mall."

Nurse Vicky shook her head slightly as if afraid that Joseph would put her on the phone.

"It's the school nurse from my old school! She saw all of the coverage on the TV, and she was ready to call the cops when she saw me."

He chuckled, listening to the phone.

"Do you want to tell her that…?"

Nurse Vicky again raised her hands in a "no" gesture, indicating that she didn't want to talk. She took a step back, away from him. Joseph pulled the phone away from his ear and turned it slightly toward the nurse, hoping she wouldn't notice that the screen was dark and there wasn't actually a live call.

"No," Nurse Vicky said. "No, it's all right. I don't want to make things worse. They're already dealing with the fallout of this… misunderstanding."

"Oh, okay." Joseph put the phone back to his ear. "No, she's in the middle of shopping. She says she understands. Mistakes happen. Everyone makes them. Okay. See you soon. Yeah, right after I get a burger."

Joseph pulled the phone away from his ear, tapped the screen, and put it back in his pocket.

"She says thank you for being so understanding. She's pretty embarrassed about the whole thing."

"So…" Nurse Vicky looked at Joseph, meeting his eyes. "You're okay. I really don't have anything to worry about. You're just heading back home."

Joseph pointed to the Burger Shack just a few stores down from where they stood. "Burger first. Then I'm heading home."

"Okay. Well, that's good. I'm glad you're all right. I was worried when I saw the coverage this morning."

Joseph nodded. He headed over to the food counter.

He could still feel her eyes on him. Even when he was standing there ordering his burger, he could still feel her eyes. He didn't want to keep turning to look back at her. He didn't want to look nervous or paranoid. He was completely relaxed. Just a kid getting a burger and then going home. Not a kid on the run. Not a kid afraid of being spotted, followed, or reported.

He bought a meal deal. It was a good thing that he had obeyed Renata's suggestion and grabbed some emergency cash from the house. He had to keep up the charade of actually buying food to eat. And he did need something to eat since he wouldn't be meeting up with Gabriel and Renata again for several hours. He had felt guilty taking any money from the Brewsters. But they wouldn't have wanted him to go hungry.

He strolled out of the mall. Watching for Nurse Vicky's reflection in the store windows all the way and occasionally catching a glimpse of her. Did she think she was going to follow him all the way home?

When he got out of the mall, he made his way to the nearest bus stop and sat down to eat his lunch while he waited for the bus. She wouldn't have any idea what part of the city he lived in, would she? That wasn't something that had been mentioned in the news reports.

She would have her car at the mall. She wouldn't have arrived there by bus or on foot herself. And even if she had, the chances that she would actually be heading back in the same direction as he chose was remote. If she got on his bus, he would transfer. Renata had drilled him on a few strategies to lose people on the bus, making sure that he knew what to do if he did discover that he had a tail.

Had she noticed that his phone had not been on? Had he done something else that had tipped her off that he was telling her a story? Screwed up on one of the words he had used to describe the fictional medical appointment?

The bus pulled up in about five minutes. Joseph put the remainder of his burger in the bag and got on the bus. He paid his fare and watched out the window to make sure she didn't follow him. She could be dialing the phone to report to the police which bus he had gotten on and which direction it was heading. He waited until the bus had passed two stops and had left her behind, out of sight, and then hopped off and crossed the road to catch a bus on a different route, going the opposite direction.

Even if she had called the police, there was no way they would figure out where he had gone. They could call the Brewsters to verify his story and find out it had all been a sham, but they would not know where he was going.

CHAPTER SIXTY-FOUR

SLAYEROFDEMONS is online

Welcome SlayerofDemons

Hi BritBullXP

How U?

Good. Interested in new campaign?

Always

You see enforcers?

Here and gone

All OK?

No casualties

What about elders?

Concerned but clueless

Upcoming campaign will need armored transport

You are carrying a key

Is there fuel in tank?

How much

May need to drive off map

You have a full tank

When u have time to play?

Need 2 get rations. An hour?

ok. Game on server mainand8

You need rations? Any other supplies?

Am ready 2 play

J oseph had no idea what kind of car Brit drove. She didn't usually drive to school. He didn't think that she had her own vehicle. But she could drive, and that was the critical part. She had said she could get transportation, so he would rely on her to be at the roundezvous point after she finished having dinner with her parents. He wasn't sure exactly what time it would be, whether she would leave her home in an hour or be at the meeting place in an hour. It didn't matter. He would be there, and she would get there when she got there.

Eventually, an old-model green sedan pulled up to the convenience store at the intersection of Main Street and 8th Avenue. Joseph watched Brit get out, look around for a moment, and then go into the convenience store. Joseph kept an eye out for any suspicious vehicles entering the parking lot or stopping on the street nearby. No other cars stopped. If the cops were tailing her, they were forced to drive by and circle back around.

Joseph watched and waited for a few minutes, then crossed the street and approached the car. He could go into the convenience store to talk to Brit, where he might be on the store's indoor surveillance camera, or he could wait until after she got out and be seen by the cops or anyone else who might be around or picked up by one of the outdoor surveillance cameras on the store or its neighbors. He didn't particularly like either option.

Instead, he made an impulse decision. When he reached the car, he quickly opened the back door, which he was pleased to find unlocked. He slid into the back seat, closed the door, and lay down.

In a couple of minutes, Brit was out of the store. She sat down in the driver's seat and started the engine. Joseph didn't know what to say to alert her to the fact that he was there. He didn't want her to keep waiting for him and didn't want to scare the pants off of her by speaking up when she thought she was in an empty car.

Brit put a coffee cup into one of the driver's seat cup holders. She reached behind the center console and lodged a second one into the backseat cup holder.

Joseph snickered. So much for her thinking she was alone in the car. He wasn't quite as covert as he had thought.

Brit buckled her seatbelt and pulled out of the parking space. She got back onto Main and was quiet for a few minutes.

"Hey, Slayer," she said eventually.

Joseph started to sit up. "Brit—"

"No, stay down for a bit. Gotta make sure we don't have any bogies."

Joseph laughed. None of it felt real. He had been anxious and tense since he had left the Brewsters' house that morning, especially after they had discovered him missing so quickly. But pairing up with Brit made him feel like he was in the middle of a game instead of real life.

"This is fun," Brit said, echoing his thoughts.

"Renata said to drive at random for half an hour to figure out whether you have anyone following you."

"Okay. Who is Renata?"

"A girl I knew in—in the hospital. She's helping me to get away. They have this whole organization to help kids get away from foster homes and back to their parents."

"Isn't that kind of risky for them?"

"They only help older kids. Teens that know what they want. They're not taking little children back to abusers."

"As long as they don't make any mistakes."

"Someone my age knows when he wants to go back to his parents. I don't think you can make a mistake with that."

Brit picked up her coffee cup and sipped it. "This is awesome. I always wanted to go on a real adventure. Cooler than online campaigns."

"Yeah." Joseph's heart was pounding, but not too fast. It was exciting. And he was going to see his mom again. He hadn't anticipated how much he would miss her. He knew he would be old enough to leave home soon. Kids his age went away to college, some of them choosing programs halfway around the world. He had thought that living without Mira would be like that. An inconvenience. A growing experience. She always tried to do too much for him, and it would be good to get away from her and rely on himself a bit more.

But it hadn't felt that way at all. He'd been totally isolated from her, unable to even talk to her. He felt homesick. He worried about her. He wanted her to teach him how to do things that he suddenly realized he didn't know how to do on his own. He was excited about seeing her again after their separation of weeks.

"Where are we supposed to go? After we're finished driving around to make sure that we are not being followed, I mean."

"I have directions. It's out of state," he warned.

"I figured. You don't know where it is?"

"No, it's sort of like a treasure map. Distances and landmarks with turn-by-turn instructions." He shrugged. "They're the experts. They divide stuff up a lot… make it so that people only know half of the mission so that they have to work together. And if someone gets caught or is a mole, they don't know the whole mission."

"Cool. I love spy stuff."

Joseph readjusted his position and propped himself on his elbow to take a drink from his cup, being sure not to sit up above the level of the back seat so no one could see that there were two people inside the car.

CHAPTER SIXTY-FIVE

Crossing the state border was anticlimactic. Joseph had been half-expecting to cross it with the police on his tail, with them having to screech to a stop when they reached the state line, marking the end of their jurisdiction. But everything was quiet; traffic looked just as it always did. It was dark and there were few cars on the highway. No one who appeared to have followed them or who knew who they were.

Joseph sipped his coffee, now cold, looking out into the night. He turned on his phone and looked at the rest of the instructions Renata had given him.

"Turn right in two miles," he told Brit.

"Okay."

It was only a few more miles. Just a few more, and he could see his mother again.

It was a restaurant. Open 24 hours a day and catering to the trucking crowd. Joseph hadn't known whether Mira would be inside or out. But there was quite a nip in the air when he opened the car door and he decided it was too cold for her to be waiting outside.

Brit rolled down her window. "Do you want me to wait out here?"

"No… come in with me."

A grin blossomed on Brit's face. "Awesome!" She rolled up her window and jumped out of the car.

Joseph was glad not to be going in alone. He and Brit walked into the restaurant and looked around. Would Mira be there waiting for him or had he gotten there first?

He looked into the booths along the side of the restaurant and saw a familiar figure. He barreled past the hostess offering to seat them, practically sprinting over to Mira.

Renata had advised him not to make a big scene of it.

That plan was out the window.

"Mom!"

Mira's head turned toward him, and then she was out of her seat. The two of them met in the middle of the aisle and Joseph grabbed her up, squeezing her tight and whirling her around. Mira was crying and Joseph's face was wet too, even though he was grinning so wide he thought his face would split.

Eventually, he managed to put her down and settle down enough to join her at her table. Brit stood to the side, smiling. Joseph introduced her.

"This is Brit, a friend from school—and a gamer I've been playing with for years. She drove me."

Brit reached her hand out to shake, but Mira pulled her in. "Thank you, Brit!" Mira pressed her cheek to Brit's. She wasn't normally a hugger, but Joseph could see that Brit wasn't going to get away without having the life squeezed out of her first. None of them could get enough of it, emotions overflowing.

After a while, they all sat down and a grinning waitress came over to the table and took their orders. Joseph was ravenous.

"How are you feeling?" Mira asked after the waitress left again. She looked Joseph over with shining eyes. "You look good."

"I am. Feeling really good." Joseph sniffled. "I'm so sorry, Mom. I caused all of these problems. They were my fault. I should have told you what was going on, and instead, I kept covering it up. I was embarrassed. I felt weak for having panic attacks and... these other spells. I felt like everything was out of control and if I could just explain it away..."

"You would take back your power?" Mira suggested.

"I guess. It didn't make sense, I know, but..."

"Feelings don't have to make sense," Brit contributed.

"But it's better now?" Mira asked. "Your pacemaker? Everything is working?"

"It's not exactly a pacemaker. But yeah, it's working. Fires when it is supposed to. Keeps me from passing out. Stops my heart from going all weird."

"They should have figured it out! I told them you weren't just making it up or acting out."

"I lied to you... said I hadn't eaten when I had. Told the nurse I had called you when I hadn't. I just didn't want to bother you at work again. I didn't want you to lose your job. I had no idea she would call DCFS and they would take me away."

"Of course not. It's okay. It's all right now. We're together. We'll... find somewhere you can play soccer. Get you enrolled."

Joseph shook his head. "I don't care about the soccer. It will make it too easy to find us. I just care about being back together again. Being back with my own family."

"Were they that bad? Your foster family? Did they hurt you?"

"No. They were nice... good people... But it wasn't the same as being home, and they thought I was just making it up. Or making myself sick because I wasn't getting enough attention. There wasn't anything wrong with them. But they weren't you. They weren't my real family."

He wiped at his eyes, which still seemed to be leaking, and told her all about Axel and his exploits, making her and Brit both laugh.

The waitress brought over their orders. Joseph dug into his pancakes. "I thought... maybe instead of soccer, I would go into medicine," he said, and touched his chest where the defibrillator was. It had changed his heart in more ways than one. "Where I can make a real difference in people's lives."

Mira reached across the table and touched his arm. "Whatever you want to do. We'll find a way to make it work."

"You're not paying for it all. I'll figure out how to make it work with scholarships and loans. You need to cut back. Stop working so many hours." He gazed at her. "You look exhausted all the time."

Mira rubbed at her eyes self-consciously. "I know. I look awful. But it's not that bad."

"One job. One full-time job. That's all I want you to do. We can get a little place where the rent is low. I can work part-time to help out."

"You need to take care of yourself too."

"I will. With this thing, nothing is going to hold me back."

EPILOGUE

Renata actively discouraged people from calling her and changed burner phones frequently so that it would be harder to track her. Mostly, if people wanted to reach her, they had to do it through someone else in the Underground Railroad network who she or Gabriel would be in contact with. It sounded inefficient, but actually worked pretty well.

She was going to ditch her current burner, but saw as she booted it up one last time that a message was waiting for her. She didn't have voicemail enabled, but there wasn't much she could do to prevent text messages from reaching her. Not when she would occasionally need that functionality.

She considered the message for a moment before deciding to call the sender. Gabriel raised his brows at her, wondering who she was contacting. She didn't like using phones and usually left it up to him to relay comments and questions.

"Hello?"

Renata's caller ID was blocked, so there was no way for the receiver to know who it was. "It's Renata."

"Oh, Renata. I'm glad I got you. I just wanted to see how you are and how our mutual friend made out."

Ethan. She knew his voice now. "He reached the end of the line," Renata confirmed. "A successful transfer."

"That's good to hear. I'm glad that he was able to be successfully reunited."

"Don't try me at this number again. I won't be here next time."

"Well, thank you for letting me know. And how are you? Is everything... okay with you?"

"Yeah." Renata thought about how she had been feeling in the weeks since the doctor at the clinic had rebalanced her meds. "Actually, yeah, I'm doing pretty good."

Gabriel looked up from his newspaper again, searching her face, then nodded and returned to reading. Renata was pretty happy with where she was. Not too many false alerts; her paranoia seemed to have settled back to the level where she could handle it and wasn't facing a lot of threats that she knew logically were impossible. She wasn't getting a lot of looks from Gabriel that told her she was going over the edge and he was concerned about her.

She was in a good place.

SLAYEROFDEMONS

SlayerofDemons is online

BRITBULLXP

Welcome SlayerofDemons

Hi BritBullXP

How's life?

Good. All quiet. No enforcers.

And the matriarch?

Settling into her new functions

I have message from TripleAxel

:-) How is he?

Made it into U10 soccer camp. Really excited

Tell him "way to go"

TripleAxel talking other day. Said you were drafted
into pros and that why you gone

LOL. Sweet. Fist bump from me if you see him IRL

I will

can't chat long tonight got to study

me too. Glad u safe

Thx to you. Talk again later

Did you enjoy this book? Reviews and recommendations are vital to making a book successful.

Please leave a review at your favorite book store or review site and share it with your friends.Don't miss the following bonus material:
Sign up for mailing list to get a free ebook
Read a sneak preview chapter
Other books by P.D. Workman
Learn more about the author

DON'T MISS A THING! GET THE LATEST NEWS AND A FREE EBOOK

Your First Taste

PDWORKMAN.COM/SIGNUP

I don't have another Medical Kidnap File for you yet!

If you have not read the rest of the series, be sure to pick it up! You can get books 1-6 in one collection.

And check out these other YA series:
Between the Cracks
Breaking the Pattern
Tamara's Teardrops

Following is a preview of Tattooed Teardrops, **Winner of Top Fiction Award, In the Margins Committee, 2016,** the first book in the Tamara's Teardrops series.

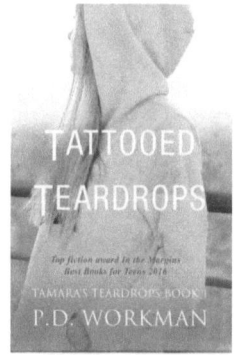

CHAPTER ONE

(i)

TAMARA FRENCH HAS BEEN *a model inmate throughout her incarceration.*

Great reference. You could go far on that one. Tamara sat on an uncomfortable bench in the brightly-lit lobby waiting for her ride. It was strange being on the other side of the guard booth. She stared at the too-white sneakers that stuck out below her dark pant cuffs, wondering what kind of life she had to look forward to with that ringing endorsement. She jiggled her legs up and down, trying to resist picking her nails. Eventually, a tall, middle-aged woman with a bun came in and stood before her. Tamara stared at her boxy black shoes for a moment before reluctantly looking up at her.

"Tamara?" the woman said.

"Yeah."

"Ready to get out of here?"

"I guess."

"I expected a bit more enthusiasm," the social worker said with a hint of a smile in the corners of her lipsticked mouth.

"I'm sorta nervous," Tamara said.

"I guess that's understandable. Come on, let's go."

Tamara sat there for another moment, then finally stood and followed the woman out of the juvenile facility. She got in the car and buckled up, holding her bag tightly on her lap.

The social worker introduced herself, but Tamara paid no attention, completely forgetting her name the next minute. The woman attempted small talk a few times, but Tamara turned on the radio and stared out the window, freezing the social worker out. Eventually the woman got the message, and stopped trying to engage her.

(ii)

They pulled up in front of a brick house that was at least a hundred years old and needed some work. There had been an attempt made at landscaping, with some flowers and bushes bunched around the concrete steps leading up to the porch and the front door. There was peeling paint on the fence and mailbox post.

"Here we are," the social worker announced. "Let's go in."

Tamara unbuckled and got out slowly. The social worker took her in, knocking on the front door and entering without waiting for an answer.

"Hello, Marion, come on in," a woman's voice called from up above. "I'll be right down."

Tamara stood beside the social worker, waiting. She held her paper bag awkwardly at her side, wishing that she didn't have anything to hold onto. She made a show of examining the front hall and living room of the house, but in all honesty, she didn't care what it looked like. It wasn't prison. Her concern was not with the house, but what the foster parents were going to be like. The front room was fairly neat and presentable. No children's toys scattered about. A load of laundry neatly folded in the basket sitting on the couch. The TV shut behind the doors of an entertainment center so it would not be the central focus of the room. The furnishings were nice, not thrift store or destroyed. There were footsteps on the stairs, and Tamara looked up for her first glimpse of her foster mother.

Mrs. Henson had a pleasant, round face. Blond hair that had

been lightly styled in an attempt to hide that it was starting to thin. She didn't look more than forty. She was overweight, but not grossly. She just looked soft and comfortable. She was wearing a sweater and pants, and inconsequential gold jewelry. She didn't look anything like Mrs. Baker, but that was no guarantee.

"Hello!" her voice rang out cheerfully.

"Gerry, this is Tamara," Marion introduced as Mrs. Henson reached the bottom of the stairs. "Tamara, Mrs. Henson."

"Hey," Tamara muttered, without meeting her eyes. "Where do you want me?"

"Your bedroom is at the top of the stairs. First door on the right," Mrs. Henson offered. Tamara made the trek up the stairs. There was a dark wooden bannister, ornately carved. Not too scarred for being in a foster home. Tamara turned at the top of the stairs and opened the door to her right.

There was a bed and a crib, and Tamara stood there, her heart speeding up, wondering if she'd been sent to the wrong room. Surely they wouldn't have given her a room with a crib in it? She could almost see Julie's still form lying on the high mattress... Mrs. Henson was there a moment later, having said a quick good-bye to Marion. She breathed a little heavily after her trip back up the stairs.

"Go on in," Mrs. Henson encouraged. "We sometimes take teen moms, to help teach them how to take care of their babies. We don't have any right now, so you get this room. That way you don't have to share."

Tamara walked into the room. The walls were a light green, freshly painted, with a white board wainscoting all the way around it. There was a pull-down blind with gauzy green curtains around the window. Tamara tossed her bag onto the bed, where it sat looking pitiful and inadequate.

"The others will be getting home soon," Mrs. Henson offered. "I'll introduce you then."

"Yes, ma'am."

"I'm happy to have you join us, Tamara. I was very impressed with your file."

Sure. It was certain to be the last place she went that anyone was impressed with her prison record. She'd wowed them all at her parole hearing. There had been tears, and not all of them hers. So many of the inmates protested their innocence and refused to take responsibility or express remorse at their parole hearings. Tamara had been working on her performance for three years, and it was good. The board's vote was unanimous. Now she was free. But to what kind of life?

Mrs. Henson stirred, making Tamara jump, startled. They both looked at each other, not knowing what to say. Mrs. Henson smiled and nodded.

"Make yourself at home," she encouraged, motioning around the room.

Tamara nodded. Mrs. Henson backed off, and left her alone. Tamara stretched out on the freshly-made bed to wait. If there was one thing she was used to doing, it was waiting.

(iii)

There were no bells that rang to mark the passage of time and the transition from one activity to another. Instead, disconcertingly, it flowed along with small shifts and gradual transitions. Tamara heard the front door open and close several times, with voices reaching her ears even through the closed bedroom door. Mrs. Henson did most of the talking and others answered her questions or made comments during the pauses. Tamara couldn't tell what any of them were saying, just the tone of voice. They all seemed to be casual and relaxed.

There was a knock on Tamara's bedroom door, and before she could get up to answer it, Mrs. Henson poked her head in.

"We're going to get dinner going," she said. "Why don't you come down and help? Then you can meet everyone."

Tamara studied her for a moment, assessing her options. Was it a choice? Was there a consequence for not complying? She was so unused to making her own decisions that she wasn't sure what to do when faced with one.

"Come on," Mrs. Henson encouraged, motioning for Tamara to come.

Tamara got up slowly and followed her foster mother down the stairs and to the kitchen. She was suddenly confronted with a whole pack of new people to meet. All bigger and older than her. Tamara made an effort to unclench her fists and not look confrontational. This wasn't juvie. She didn't have to prove herself physically here.

It hadn't occurred to Tamara when she had met Mrs. Henson that the foster children would not all be white like her. But of course, she already knew the statistics. There were more non-white children in foster care, and very few non-white parents. So they couldn't pair black children with black parents. Tamara was intimidated by all of the dark faces looking back at her. She wasn't prejudiced, but juvie had taught her to be acutely aware of race relations, and how her white-faced, blond-haired presence could be aggravating to others. They would immediately judge her as stuck-up, privileged, and ignorant.

Tamara was fifteen, and not tall. There were only four other children, Tamara realized, not the mob that she had originally perceived them as. They were all bigger than her. Most of them taller than Mrs. Henson. Studying their faces, Tamara figured that they were seventeen or eighteen. One boy seemed even too old to be eighteen.

"Everyone," Mrs. Henson said, "this is Tamara, our new foster child. I know you'll all make her feel comfortable and help her get settled in."

They all nodded, smiled, and waved. Tamara nodded back.

"Hey."

Her voice was hoarse, the greeting barely audible. Tamara wasn't sure any of them had heard her. She nodded again and didn't repeat the greeting.

"Okay, are you ready?" Mrs. Henson asked with a wide smile. "This is Nita," a Hispanic girl with long hair and perfectly plucked eyebrows, "Deshawn," the darkest face, a girl with cornrows and a brilliant white smile, "Jason," black skin, close cropped black hair, probably eighteen, "and Harry." Harry seemed a particularly non-ethnic name for a boy who appeared to be some mixture of black, Hispanic, and native. He smiled nicely for her, but his resting face was serious, contemplative. He was the one that Tamara was sure must be older than eighteen. He should have already aged out of the system.

Tamara nodded again and swallowed. Now what? Was she supposed to repeat them back? Greet each one separately? Shake hands? Tamara just stood there, lost, then looked at Mrs. Henson for direction.

"Okay, let's get started on dinner," Mrs. Henson suggested. "Nita, why don't you show Tamara where the dishes are, and she can help you set the table…" She went on, but Tamara didn't hear the rest of the instructions she gave to the remaining kids. She had her instructions. Go with Nita and set the table. She made her way across the room to Nita, and Nita smiled at her.

"Welcome," she said in a low voice that was almost a whisper. "I hope you like it here."

Tamara nodded. "Yeah. Thanks."

"Well, come on. The dishes are in this cupboard here, and the glasses, and the cutlery." Nita indicated each location.

"How many…?" Tamara asked. She cleared her throat. "Is there a Mr. Henson? Or anyone else?"

"Yeah, Jesse will be home for dinner. That's Mr. Henson. So seven altogether."

Tamara counted out the plates and trucked them over to the table, where she put them down carefully. Her hands shook slightly as she set them down, and it was an effort not to let them clatter. There was a baby's high chair, pushed against the wall. Tamara looked away from it and continued with her work, breathing shallowly. Setting the table only took a couple of minutes, and then Mrs. Henson gave them various other small tasks until everything started coming together for the dinner. She looked at her watch.

"Thanks guys. Take a break for about twenty minutes. Then everything should be done cooking, Jesse will be home, and we'll eat."

The kids dispersed. Tamara headed back up to her bedroom. Deshawn stopped ahead of Tamara, blocking her way into her bedroom.

"Do you need anything?" she asked Tamara.

Tamara shook her head.

"Sometimes… people don't come here with very much," Deshawn said. "Missus buys up extra toothbrushes and all, and we all share clothes…" She glanced over Tamara's figure. "My pants won't do you much good, but if you want a shirt, some accessories…"

Tamara stood there and contemplated the idea. For three years, she had worn nothing but an orange prison jumpsuit. Social Services had provided her with two very basic changes of clothing for her release. T-shirt, pants, socks, underthings. One pair of white tennis shoes. It was more fashion than Tamara had access to in all her time in juvie, but she was aware that it was sorely inadequate for a teenager on the outside.

Deshawn made an encouraging motion.

"Come on. Let's see if there's anything you want to borrow," she said.

Tamara followed her to one of the other bedrooms.

"Nita and I share the room," Deshawn commented. Nita was not there; maybe she had gone to watch TV or something. The room was painted sky blue. There was a utilitarian set of bunk beds, a couple of dressers cluttered with scarves, jewelry, and books, and a closet that was jammed full. The knobs on either side of the open closet door had been pressed into use to hold more hangers full of clothes. "It's mostly thrift store," Deshawn said, "but you can find some pretty good stuff if you look hard enough. Sorry, it's sort of a mess. Come on. See what you like."

Tamara went to the closet and looked over the hangers full of brightly-colored clothing. It didn't appear that either Deshawn or Nita went for anything understated.

"If you want t-shirts, they're in the dresser," Deshawn pointed, "and just grab whatever you see that you like. Just bring it back or throw it in the laundry when you're done with it."

Tamara saw herself in the mirror mounted on the back of the closet door. There hadn't been any full-length mirrors at juvie. And the only mirrors that had been there were polished metal or plastic, and you could never really see your reflection very well. Tamara had grown up a lot in juvie. She wasn't the soft, shy little farm girl she had been when she went to the Bakers. They had changed her. And juvie had changed her. The years had not been particularly kind ones. But she had developed a figure now, and was going to have to learn how to dress it up, instead of simply shrouding it in a jumpsuit. She had tattoos and piercings that she hadn't had before her incarceration. Her hair was dull and lank, like everybody else's in juvie. Tamara wound one lock around her finger, staring at the stranger reflected in the mirror.

"Why don't we do something with your hair?" Deshawn suggested. "There's not much time, but if we blow-dry, we could be done before supper."

Tamara raked her fingers through her limp blonde hair, disgusted with it.

"Yeah. Could we?"

"Mmm-hmm," Deshawn agreed with emphasis. "We'll shampoo it in the bathroom, and use leave-in conditioner..." she led the way out into the hallway, still chattering away to herself what they would do. Tamara just followed.

Tamara knelt by the tub while Deshawn used the hand-held shower attachment to quickly wet her hair down. The warm water felt so good on Tamara's scalp, she wished she could get in for a full shower, and just luxuriate in it for hours. Three years of quick, cold showers. But Deshawn turned off the water way too soon, and applied a fruity shampoo with strong, capable fingers; working it in and then rinsing it back out. She handed Tamara a towel and while Tamara rubbed her hair, Deshawn rifled through the myriad toiletries lining the back of the counter, the medicine cabinet, and a couple of deep wicker baskets under the sink.

(iv)

"Girls! Dinner!" the impatient call came again from downstairs.

Deshawn poked her head out the door.

"Just one more minute," she called back. "We'll be right down!"

She returned her attention to Tamara.

"Okay, just sit still for one more minute, girl," she instructed.

Tamara sat frozen, while Deshawn wound sections of her hair

around the fat curling iron, holding it and then releasing. There was no way that she was going to be done the whole thing in another minute. But Deshawn worked quickly, sure of herself.

"That will do it for now," she announced.

She laid the curling iron down on the counter and unplugged it from the wall. Standing Tamara up, Deshawn shuffled her over and turned her to face the mirror.

"Ta-da!"

Tamara looked with astonishment at the face in the mirror. She was amazed at what a big difference a hairstyle could make. She still didn't have on any make-up, hadn't changed her clothes or accessories, all she had done was let Deshawn clean and style her hair. Her image in the mirror was no longer so harsh and plain.

"You're gorgeous," Deshawn gushed. "You've got really good color and proportions. We can have a lot of fun glamming you up. For now, this will do."

Standing behind Tamara, Deshawn used her fingers to wind and readjust a couple of curls. She lowered her head so that it was on the same level as Tamara's, and gave her a smile.

"What do you think?"

"It's… it's really pretty. Thanks," Tamara said. She cleared her throat, realizing that she was whispering. She had learned in juvie to use a strong, confident voice, not to be soft or timid. The Henson's home was so different in atmosphere, she felt like she was in a library or something. That she needed to be quiet to avoid upsetting the peace of the place.

"Come on, we've got to get down to dinner, or Missus will not be happy!"

Tamara followed Deshawn back downstairs and to the dining room table that she and Nita had set. It was now covered with serving dishes, and everyone was seated, waiting for them. All eyes turned to Tamara as she looked at the three empty chairs, trying to decide which one she should take.

"Tamara, doesn't that look lovely," Mrs. Henson complimented. "Here, sit down. These boys will eat everything before we even get a bite, if they have to wait much longer."

She gestured toward the empty chair nearest to her, and Tamara went over and sat down. Deshawn took what appeared to be her usual seat, beside Nita, which left one empty chair at the table of eight. Tamara looked for the first time at Mr. Henson. Slim, on the tall side. Handsome boyish face. Short-cropped curly red hair. He smiled at Tamara.

"Welcome, Tamara. I'm Jesse."

Tamara nodded, looking down at her empty plate. Her stomach tightened and it was suddenly hard to breathe. The only men that she had been around for three years had been guards, doctors, and administrators. The last man she had lived with before that... her foster father, Mr. Baker... that had been a bad scene. A very bad scene. Tamara swallowed. She tried to slow her breathing, but it just made her breath louder in her own ears. She was sure everyone would be hear how loudly and quickly she was breathing.

"Dig in," Mrs. Henson said, and Harry and Jason acted like two Rottweilers just told to attack, diving into the serving dishes immediately. Conversation started up around the table, and rather than trying to follow any of it, Tamara just let it wash over her like white noise. She served up small portions of each of the dishes that passed her, and dutifully passed them on.

"So tell us about your last home, Tamara," Nita said. "Where did you come here from?"

Tamara looked at Mrs. Henson. The woman just smiled and gave her a small nod, and didn't jump in to help her out. If Tamara didn't want to answer questions, she was going to have to be assertive and speak up. The conversations around the table quieted as the others paused to listen for her answer. Tamara swallowed a very dry mouthful of potatoes. They stuck right in the middle of her chest.

"I wasn't at a home," she said finally, careful to keep her voice up, not to duck her head down. She was not vulnerable and had nothing to be ashamed of. She was strong and knew how to take care of herself. She had just as much right to be here as any of them. "I was in juvie."

There was an initial silence, and then conversations started back up again without further comment on Tamara's answer.

"Sorry," Nita said. "I didn't know."

"It's okay," Tamara said, shaking her head. "It's not a secret. That's where I was."

Nita nodded.

"Most of us have been in trouble at one time or another."

Tamara glanced around at their faces. None of them looked particularly troubled. They seemed happy and relaxed. At peace with themselves. Maybe they had been in trouble before, and maybe they hadn't. You couldn't always tell by looking at someone.

"Harry's probably spent the most time in juvie," Deshawn contributed, nodding to her brother. "How much time, Harry?"

"All together?" Harry questioned, laughing. "I don't know. Longest stint was two years. But I had plenty of shorter stays before that."

Tamara studied him more closely. He met her eyes and nodded.

"Harry's twenty," Mrs. Henson said without being asked. "So he's not officially a foster child anymore. But we told him he could stay on here while he does some more schooling and gets on his feet."

Tamara nodded, looking back down at her plate.

"That's really nice of you."

"It's to our benefit too. Harry contributes a lot to the family, and since he's working part-time, he's also paying a bit of rent to help keep us afloat. So it works both ways."

Tamara bit into some sort of casserole.

"I guess you'll learn about everyone's backgrounds gradually," Mrs. Henson said. "We try to be open with each other. Everybody's been through some pretty tough stuff. We don't judge. We just try to help."

"That's cool," Tamara said, pushing her dinner around on her plate. She wasn't hungry.

She watched everyone else chow down, and conversations flowed back away from her again. Tamara watched for the appropriate time to leave the table. There was no end-of-dinner bell anymore. She had to relearn all the social graces. How to judge the end of a conversation. When one could politely leave the dinner table. How long she could look at someone before they decided she was being too aggressive. It was like living in a foreign country. A dangerous foreign country.

"Not very hungry?" Mrs. Henson observed, as dinner conversation started to peter out.

Tamara looked down at her plate, still nearly full.

"No. I'm sorry… it's good… I just feel kind of… my stomach hurts."

"It's all right. It takes time to adjust. You can scrape it into the garbage. Nita can show you where. Everyone rinses their own plates and puts them in the dishwasher."

"Sure," Tamara agreed. She stood up, grabbing her plate, and Nita got up and led the way back into the kitchen, where they took care of their dishes. Tamara looked back at the dining table. "Do you want help with clean-up?" she asked Mrs. Henson. "Or would I be in the way?"

"Of course you can help. Usually, I'd probably tell you to go do your homework while I cleared, but you don't have any today, so why don't you and I clean up together?"

Tamara nodded, and she and Mrs. Henson bussed the serving dishes back to the kitchen, found lids for things, and put them into the fridge. Mrs. Henson turned the dishwasher on and wiped down the dining room table.

"You can watch some TV or take some 'down' time. In bed at nine, and lights out at ten."

"Okay," Tamara agreed.

She wandered around the house a bit, but wasn't comfortable sitting down with anybody else, and so she made her way back to her bedroom. As she approached, the door to the other girls' bedroom opened. Nita peeked out.

"Hey," she said. "You need anything? Do you have pajamas?"

Tamara shook her head.

"No," she admitted. "If I could borrow a t-shirt or something…"

"You bet. Come in."

Nita opened the door the rest of the way for her, and Tamara went in. Tamara looked down at Nita's feet, nails freshly painted and toes spread apart while they dried. Nita giggled and hobbled on her heels over to the dresser.

"You want to do yours?" she asked. She pulled out a handful of shirts and tossed them at Tamara.

"No. Thanks," Tamara said, fumbling with the shirts to see what her options were. "I'm going to hit the sack."

She found herself strangely unable to choose one of the shirts. There were three of them. They were all cute. Any one of them would work. All she had to do was decide which of the three she liked best. Nita was watching her, head cocked slightly.

"The blue one is a really good color for you," she suggested.

Not the blue one. Tamara looked at the other two. She didn't know which she wanted, but she had to decide before Nita made another suggestion. She had to make her own choice. Tamara tossed the blue one back to Nita, and with a knot in her stomach, tossed Nita the pink one too. Tamara looked down at the purple and blue patterned shirt in her hands.

"This one is good," she said.

She felt a little sick. Worried that she had made the wrong choice. How silly was that, to be worried that she had picked the wrong t-shirt to wear in the privacy of her own bedroom? But she was. She had an overwhelming feeling of dread.

"Have a good sleep," Nita said with a smile.

"Thanks."

Tamara went back to her room. She changed into the t-shirt, long enough to reach her mid-thighs. She lay down on the bed and stared at the ceiling. There would be no bell ringing to tell her when to go to sleep. Would her body know when it was time, without the bell? Would she be able to adjust to a new schedule? Not feeling the least bit tired, Tamara lay staring at the ceiling, twitching her foot and waiting for sleep.

CHAPTER TWO

(i)

TAMARA AWOKE. SHE WAS confused at first, disoriented by the sight of a bedroom around her instead of her familiar cell. Turning her head to look at the clock beside the bed, Tamara saw that it was five forty-five on the dot. The usual time for the reveille bell. Groaning, she rolled over and slid out of bed.

She didn't know what time the others usually arose, but she imagined there would probably be a bottleneck waiting for the shower. Moving as quietly as possible, Tamara tiptoed across the room and opened her door. She listened for any sounds of movement. There was a light on down the stairs, but it wasn't bright. It could just be a streetlight through a window, or a nightlight. The shower was not running, so Tamara darted into the bathroom, shut the door, and turned on the light. She started the shower running and stripped down. For the first time in three years, she stepped into a warm shower. The tantalizing sample of the night before when Deshawn had helped her wash her hair didn't even come close to the luxury of a hot, whole-body shower. Tamara took a deep breath. She could get used to this.

More out of habit than anything, Tamara very quickly soaped up and rinsed off. She forced herself to shut off the water again immediately. Even though she would have loved to have stayed in the shower for an hour, until the hot water ran out and people started banging on the door to tell her to get out, she knew she had to be considerate and leave some hot water for the others. With a family of seven, you couldn't be selfish and use it all yourself. Shivering, Tamara grabbed the closest towel and dried herself off. She realized with dismay that she hadn't brought in any clothes to change into. She only had the makeshift nightshirt she had just taken off. Tamara swallowed and steeled herself. She wrapped the worn towel around her body. It didn't cover much, and wasn't long enough to tuck it back into itself. So holding the towel with one hand, Tamara tucked her shirt under her elbow, and used the other hand to open the door.

Her room was conveniently right across the hall from the bathroom, so she only had to take three steps, and she was safe in her own room again. She heard the click of another door down the hall, and a minute later, the bathroom door closed and the water turned back on. Had whoever was in the shower now seen her in her dash from the bathroom? She hadn't dared to look for anyone. Tamara pulled on her sad little Social-Services-provided outfit and looked for a comb. She found one in the top drawer of the dresser, along with a few other necessities. As she carelessly pulled the comb through her hair to get it in order before it finished drying, Tamara's eyes sought out her reflection in the mirror over the dresser. Did she want a prison hairdo for the first day of school, or something nice, like Deshawn had done for her last night? But the curling iron was in the currently-occupied bathroom.

Trying to breathe calmly through her anxiety, Tamara crossed the hall to the bathroom door. The shower was still running. She knocked on the door and opened it up a couple of inches.

"Can I just get the curling iron?" she asked.

She didn't look toward the shower or the foggy mirror. She just kept her eyes down, waiting for a response.

"Sure, go ahead," a male voice answered. The voice was deep, probably Harry, but Tamara wasn't sure.

She opened the door far enough to rifle through the contents of the vanity and the baskets underneath, and found the curling iron, a brush, and some hairspray. Tamara retreated from the warm, misty bathroom and hurried back to her own room.

(ii)

Breakfast at juvie was served promptly at six and was over at six thirty, so by the time Tamara was finished styling her hair, she was starving. She went down to the kitchen to see what she could find to eat. Mr. Henson—Jesse—was eating a bowl of cereal on the kitchen island, reading through a newspaper. Tamara stopped short. He must have heard her footsteps on the stairs, though, because he looked up at her and smiled.

"Come on in, don't be shy," he invited.

Tamara approached cautiously, not getting too close. She knew foster dads. She'd dealt with a foster dad. But she'd learned how to protect herself in juvie. How to be careful and not leave herself open.

"You're an early riser," Jesse observed, dropping his eyes back down to his newspaper and taking another bite of cereal.

Tamara watched him for any change in attitude, any extra watchfulness. He glanced up again, then back down at his paper.

"There's juice in the fridge. Cereal and bread in the cupboard," he pointed. "Coffee's fresh."

"Thanks," Tamara said.

She kept an eye on him while she opened a couple of cupboards to locate the mugs, and poured herself a cup of coffee. Tamara inhaled the soothing aroma while she waited for it to cool down a bit. Perhaps Jesse could feel her gaze, because he looked up at her expectantly, eyebrows up. Tamara looked away.

"Sorry," she said. "I'm a bit dopey. Still getting the engine started."

He chuckled.

"Did you sleep well?"

"Well… okay, I guess. The bed is really comfy and everything. It's just…"

"Somewhere new," Jesse finished for her, nodding. "That's

perfectly understandable. It will take a while before it feels natural. Like home."

"Yeah."

Tamara wondered if she would ever feel like this was home. She had been warned that parole wouldn't be easy. She knew inmates who had been back within a week of being released. Some had intended to follow the rules, and slipped. Some had never intended to follow any rules. She remembered when Mitchell had come back. Tamara had thought that she would make it. Mitchell was tough, one of the few who had managed to survive juvie without getting in with one of the gangs. She was strong-willed, and made it known that once she got out, she wasn't going to be back. She would do whatever it took to stay on the right side of the law and make a life for herself. A straight, honest life.

On her return, Mitchell's dark eyes were underscored by shadows. She looked almost haunted.

"I just couldn't do it," she told Tamara, as they both stood at the sinks in the restroom. "I felt so… exposed. I didn't belong out there."

She had held up a convenience store at knife point. With no mask. In full view of the security cameras. Not because she needed money, but because she wanted to go back. Back where she belonged.

Tamara sipped her coffee. She considered what else she might want for breakfast. Her stomach was still growling. She wasn't going to be able to make it to lunch on a cup of coffee. She was used to a full breakfast at juvie.

With another careful look at Jesse, she went over to the cupboard that he had pointed out, and got herself Cheerios and a slice of bread, which she threw into the bright red toaster on the counter. She prepared the cereal and started to eat, leaning against the counter and waiting for the toast to pop.

"You can eat at the table," Jesse said. "You don't have to eat standing up just because I am."

Tamara didn't move. He didn't pursue it. She and Jesse continued to eat in silence. Mrs. Henson joined them as Tamara moved on to her toast, searching the fridge for some jam.

"You're up early," Mrs. Henson observed. "Couldn't sleep?"

Tamara nodded. She moved to the dining table as Mrs. Henson entered the kitchen, feeling crowded, anxious at both foster parents being in such close proximity. Mrs. Henson gave her a smile and got herself a cup of coffee. Tamara took a few quick bites of her toast and then laid the remainder down.

"Sorry, I took too much," she said. She dumped the toast in the garbage and slotted the plate away in the dishwasher. Then she retreated to her room.

As Tamara got upstairs, Deshawn was knocking on the bathroom door.

"Come on, Jason! Time's up! There's a line-up out here."

She smiled widely at Tamara as she waited for a response.

"Hey, girl," she greeted. "Go on in." She gestured toward her own bedroom. "Help yourself to whatever you need. Nita's awake, she's just playing possum."

Tamara hesitated.

"Go ahead," Deshawn pressed. "You going to go to school without putting your face on?"

Tamara had no experience with makeup, but she knew most of the other girls at school would probably be wearing it, and she didn't want to look any more different than she had to. So she nodded and went into the bedroom, tapping lightly on the door before she went in.

Nita didn't play possum, but propped herself up on her elbow, yawning.

"Mornin' sunshine."

"Hey. Deshawn said…"

"Yeah, of course. Help yourself to whatever you see. Except that orange scarf over there," Nita nodded at it. "That one's calling to me this morning."

"I'm kind of sick of wearing orange," Tamara said.

Nita snorted. "You don't say," she said with a giggle.

Tamara looked over the clutter of accessories on top of the dresser. She tried on a couple of necklaces before settling on one with a large, brassy sun-and-moon medal on it. She put in chunky earrings. She looked at the makeup and didn't know what to do with any of it.

"You want some help?" Nita offered.

Tamara hesitated, not wanting to owe Nita anything. She felt vulnerable letting anyone help her. Nita sat up and swung her feet over the side of the bed. She stretched and stood up.

"Why don't you sit?" she suggested, motioning to the chair in front of the small mirror and pile of makeup.

Tamara sat down. Nita started pawing through the makeup, sorting out what she wanted to use. Without further discussion, she started by applying some moisturizing cream. Then she brushed on some blush.

"Is everyone always so nice and perfect around here?" Tamara asked, watching Nita's actions in the mirror.

Nita laughed.

"We're far from perfect. We still have our fights and rough spots. But…" She paused while she moved onto selecting a shade of eye shadow. "We've all been there. Moving into a new home. Starting over again. Trying to figure out your place. First day of school. It works better if you're nice to newcomers rather than getting all territorial. A lot less grief."

"Oh."

As if to underscore her words about not being perfect, Deshawn pounded on the bathroom door, yelling at Jason again to quit being inconsiderate and get his bony butt out of the bathroom. Tamara and Nita laughed.

"And luckily, Deshawn and I both love having sisters to share with. Neither of us grew up with much family."

Tamara was going to nod, but thought better of moving while Nita worked on her.

"Me neither," she agreed.

"Yeah? Well, there you go. Now you've got two sisters who are going to love dressing you up and showing you how to do your makeup."

Tamara studied Nita's face in the mirror. Nita was beautiful. The lines of her face were almost perfect. Her smile was bright and even and could have been an advertisement for a dentist. There was the tiniest shift to the lines of her nose that made Tamara wonder if it had been broken at some point. Without thinking, Tamara touched the bump in her own nose. Nita stopped for a moment and pushed Tamara's hand away.

"Don't you worry about that," she said. "It's not obvious unless you're looking for it."

Tamara put her hand back down again. Nita handed her a tube of lipstick.

"I think you can do this part," she said.

Tamara screwed the lipstick out, and applied it to her lips. She looked at her face, at the overall effect of the makeup. It still looked like her. There was nothing too obvious or stark about the makeup. But her face was softened, more feminine. Framed by the silky blond waves, she could almost be pretty.

Nita was over at the closet, pushing clothes around. She was wearing a long Minnie Mouse nightshirt that reached her calves. She pulled out a couple of button-up shirts.

"Now how about one of these layered over your t-shirt?" she suggested. "I think that would be really cute."

Tamara took one of the shirts from her and pulled it on, then shook her head and took it back off.

"Not really my style," she said.

Nita shrugged.

"You want anything else? Don't be shy, just try on whatever you like."

Tamara joined Nita at the closet, and looked through the offerings. She pulled out a black jacket with silver hardware, and tried it on. Nita looked her over and nodded.

"You like it?" she asked.

"I think so."

"It's yours."

Tamara smoothed it with both hands and nodded, smiling shyly. "Thanks."

(iii)

Neither of the other two girls went to the school that Tamara would be attending, so she was on her own. Mrs. Henson offered to make the proper introductions at the school, but Tamara shook her head.

"Just drop me off," she said. "I can find the office and they'll give me what I need."

She didn't need to look like a little girl who couldn't manage to go to school on her own. She was strong. Mrs. Henson agreed. She drove slowly, pointing out landmarks that would help Tamara to find her way around the neighborhood in the future. Tamara stared out the window, not commenting, her stomach in a tight, sick knot. She was not looking forward to school. Of course she'd gone to all of her classes in juvie—not like she had been given a choice—but public school was not something she was looking forward to.

She checked in at the office, was given a locker, schedule, map, textbooks, and a number of covert looks. She was told who her guidance counselor was and invited to set up an appointment with him any time.

Tamara went to her morning classes, and at lunch went looking for the students' illicit smoking hangout. She had a few cigarettes left over from juvie, but getting her hands on more might be difficult. It didn't take long to find a small knot of students wreathed in smoke. Tamara nodded briefly and cupped her hand around a cigarette to light it. She drew the smoke into her lungs, the tension in her stomach subsiding slightly.

"Sucks being new," one girl offered.

Tamara nodded.

"Especially halfway through the year," she agreed.

"I'm Sybil." She had dyed black hair, a post through her lip and a piercing in her nose. Her makeup was stark, but not goth.

Some of the others offered their names.

"Hi. Tamara."

"You're staying with the Hensons?"

"Yeah." Tamara shifted her feet. "You know 'em?"

"They go through a lot of kids there. Some of them go to school. Some don't."

"Uh-huh."

Since Tamara was not yet sixteen, she didn't have a choice about school attendance yet. It was mandatory. Especially if she wanted to stay out of juvie. One of the boys, slim and pale and wearing a black leather jacket, looked her over curiously.

"So being with the Hensons, does that mean you've been in trouble?" he inquired.

Sybil rolled her eyes.

"Smooth, Jason," she objected. But that didn't stop her from listening with obvious interest for the answer.

Tamara blew out smoke in a thin, white stream. It was a question bound to be on everyone's mind.

"Yeah, I've been in trouble."

"What kind of trouble?"

"I just got out of juvie. Three years. Made parole." Word would get out one way or another. It might as well come from her and at least be accurate to start with. The more she tried to hide her past, the more the rumors would fly.

Jason whistled through his teeth.

"Wow. What for?"

"Murder," Tamara said flatly. No emotion in her voice or expression. Nothing that would show weakness or vulnerability.

"You're pulling my leg. Seriously?" he demanded.

Tamara shrugged. He could interpret the gesture as he liked.

"Who'd you kill?"

"None of your business."

"Some guy who asked too many questions," Sybil teased, and cracked up.

Tamara grinned at Sybil. Jason opened his mouth to ask another question.

"Shut up, Jason," Sybil snapped.

He closed his mouth and rolled his eyes. They continued to smoke. After a few minutes, Jason stepped on his cigarette butt and left. Sybil looked at Tamara.

"You want to walk?"

"Sure."

They walked in silence for a while. Tamara tried to make her cigarette last, not knowing how hard it would be for her to get another pack. In juvie, it was surprisingly easy. Here, she was going to have to get someone who was old enough to buy them for her, once she could get her hands on some money.

"News travels fast," Tamara observed.

"The grapevine is humming away," Sybil agreed. "Some of Henson's kids have made things… interesting around here, so when word gets out that they got someone new—well, the news travels."

"Great."

"Sorry. It'll die down again. Unless you're planning on making a splash."

"I'm not looking for attention."

Sybil nodded. They continued to walk and make small talk.

"So what was it like?" Sybil asked, and at Tamara's questioning look, elaborated. "In juvie."

"Not somewhere you'd like to be."

Sybil waited for more information, but Tamara shook her head and didn't enlighten her.

(iv)

The teacher walked up to Tamara while she was doing her class-work, and put a slip of yellow paper on her desk. Tamara looked down at it, and looked up at the teacher questioningly.

"You're wanted down at the office. That's your hall pass."

Tamara looked at it for a minute, and then closed her books and stacked them up. She picked up the yellow paper and headed out of the room and down the stairs. She got turned around a couple of times, but eventually found her way to the administrative office where she had started her day. She presented her yellow slip to the gray-haired woman at the reception desk.

"Yes. Tamara," the woman said, looking at the paper as if there was something wrong with it. "You are in conference room B."

Tamara looked around, and the receptionist pointed to a closed door behind her.

"Right there. Go on in."

Tamara wasn't sure what was going on. Was she in trouble for something already? Maybe someone had reported her for smoking. Or maybe it was something they always did at the end of the day when a student transferred mid-term. Checking up to make sure that everything had gone all right. That they had found all of their classes, hadn't had any trouble...

She put her hand on the doorknob. The receptionist had said to go right in, but she didn't feel right about it. Tamara knocked lightly on the door, and opened it, poking her head in. It was a small meeting room, four chairs around a small table. A tall black man sat in one with his long legs stretched out in front of him. He was dressed in a suit. His head was bald, maybe shaved. He smiled, but didn't show any teeth. The smile didn't reach his eyes. His face immediately fell back into a tired, grim look.

"Tamara," he greeted. "Come on in. Shut the door and have a seat."

Tamara obeyed, trying to analyze him. Not the principal. Maybe a counselor, if he'd been a cop in a previous life. He had the air of one of the guards in juvie. Not one of the day-to-day guards, but one of the supervisors or something. Higher up the food chain. More reserved, not as quick to pull out his baton or taser. Tamara sat down in the chair across from the man and waited.

"My name is Chad Collins," he introduced himself. "I'll be your parole officer."

"Oh." Tamara blew out her breath. Now it made sense. She wasn't in trouble. Not yet. This was her new shadow. The man who would be watching for her to fail. "Hi."

"I've read your file, and I think that you can make this transition successfully, if you put your mind to it."

Tamara nodded.

"It will be hard," he went on, "but you can choose to be a different person than you were before you went to juvie. Or while you were at juvie. It's a pivotal time for you. This is your chance to turn things around."

He rubbed his chin, looking down at the slim file in front of him.

"Okay," Tamara said.

"You don't want to be sent back for something stupid. It's important that you understand the terms of your parole."

Tamara nodded again.

"So what…" she started. She cleared her throat and tried to strengthen her wavering voice. "What are the rules?"

He pulled a single sheet out of the file and placed it in front of Tamara.

"Okay, let's go over it." Pointing to the top line, he started out. "I will tell you when and where our meetings are, and you'll be there. On time. Every time. You're living with the Hensons, and you're not allowed to move anywhere else without my say so. You have a nine o'clock curfew. No matter what, you're home by nine o'clock every night. Right?"

"Yes, sir," Tamara agreed.

"No weapons, no alcohol, no drugs. Not on your person, not in your room, not anywhere near you. You don't associate with anyone carrying weapons, alcohol, or drugs. You'll submit to random drug testing. Whenever I say. On the spot. You are not allowed to be around anyone who has been convicted of a felony."

"What if…"

"No one. No 'what ifs'. It doesn't matter if you knew them in juvie, before juvie, or met them since. No criminal associations."

"Okay." Tamara nodded.

"You're not allowed to be around young children. No one under six. And you'll attend mandatory counseling at least weekly."

"Yes, sir," Tamara said. "What kind of counseling?"

"Something to help to ease the transition, give you the skills that you need to stay clean outside of juvie. Anger and stress management. Addictions counseling, if you need it. Anything that I or your therapist decide that you need."

Tamara nodded and swallowed.

"Okay."

"Do you have any questions?"

"No, sir."

"What are you going to do if you think of questions? If you're not sure about something?"

She continued to stare at the paper in front of her.

"I guess I call you," she said.

"That's right." He pointed to his contact details at the bottom of the page. "Do you have a cell phone yet?"

"No."

"When you get one, you put me on your number one speed dial. I'm the person you call if you have any questions."

"Yes, sir."

"What if you slip up and break a rule, what do you do?" he demanded.

Tamara picked at the skin around her nails, hiding them under the table.

"Fix it," she suggested. "Don't do it again."

"The first thing you do is call me. You report yourself. 'Mr. Collins, someone offered me a beer and I was stupid enough to drink it.' 'Mr. Collins, I was ten minutes late for curfew.' 'Mr. Collins, a friend from juvie called me up, but I hung up on her.' Any violation, no matter how big or small. You call me. Got it?"

"Yes, sir."

"Things will be much worse if I hear it from someone else, or it shows up in a drug test or something. Tell me, and you might not get sent back to juvie."

"Okay."

Tamara had an overwhelming desire to bite her nails, and it was only with a huge exercise of will that she was able to keep her hands in her lap, hidden, away from her face, still picking at the cuticles.

"What if you have some other kind of problem?" he questioned.

Tamara looked up at his face, the slight flare of his nostrils and curl of his lip.

"Call you?" she suggested.

He nodded.

"Now you're getting it," he agreed.

Tamara mirrored his nod. Neither one of them said anything for a while, and Tamara eventually looked back up at Collins again, wondering what else she was in for.

"How was your first day?" he asked.

Tamara relaxed a little in her seat, letting out a pent-up breath.

"Okay. Not bad. The Hensons all seem really nice."

"They're a good family," Collins agreed. "They've dealt with a lot of tough cases. Everything is pretty calm there now, and I'm hoping that you won't make things too difficult for them. Give them a bit of a rest."

"I don't plan on getting in any trouble."

"Good. But it can be harder than you would think. These things are rarely planned. But temptations show up, catch you at a weak moment. You feel loyal to a friend or family member and think nobody will know, nobody will get hurt."

"I don't do drugs," Tamara said. "Or drink. I never even had a cigarette before juvie."

He studied her, eyes narrowed slightly. Tamara felt the need to defend herself further. She might not care what the kids at school or the Hensons thought, but she thought her parole officer ought to know what kind of a person she was.

"I'm not a troublemaker," she said. "You look at my juvie file. Or my school records before... before it happened. I never got in any kind of trouble. Ever."

Collins rubbed his chin, his dark eyes boring into her.

"You have admitted to the murders more than once. In court and to the parole board."

"Yes."

"What does *that* say about you?"

Tamara stared back down at the paper again. She picked at her cuticles under the table.

"It was a bad situation," she said. "I was trapped, and hurt, and the hormones... made me so foggy and emotional. I didn't know what to do. I know it doesn't make sense when you say it like that, but I was so... confused."

There was silence from Collins at first.

"This time," he said finally, "you have someone to talk to. You're not alone."

Tamara looked at him again. His voice was low, almost gentle.

"Call me," he said, tapping the piece of paper with the eraser end of his pencil. "For any reason."

"Okay. Thanks."

Tamara nodded. She felt very teary and emotional all of a sudden, and she didn't like it. She couldn't let her guard down. Couldn't make herself vulnerable. Collins' lips pressed together in a thin line for a moment, then the look vanished. Collins unfolded himself from the chair, towering over her. Tamara scrambled to get to her feet. He offered his hand, and Tamara shook it, feeling a bit awkward.

"Call me tomorrow before curfew," he instructed.

Tamara nodded.

He was still holding her hand, and looked down at it. Tamara saw that her fingers were bleeding around the nails, and pulled her hand out of his grasp, hiding it behind her back.

"I'm not the enemy, Tamara," Collins said. He sighed. "I'll get you in to see the therapist as soon as possible. Transition and stress management. You'll go."

"Yes, sir."

"Talk to you tomorrow, then."

Tamara nodded, and he left the room. The door swung shut behind him, clicking softly into place. Tamara put her hands over her face and tried to calm and compose herself. She was tough. She could manage it. She'd show Chad Collins that she wasn't like any of his other parolees. He didn't know her. She could make it.

———

Tattooed Teardrops is the first book in the Tamara's Teardrops series
by P.D. Workman
can be purchased at shop.pdworkman.com

———

ABOUT THE AUTHOR

P.D. Workman is a USA Today Bestselling author, winner of several awards from Library Services for Youth in Custody and the InD'tale Magazine's Crowned Heart award, and has published over 100 mystery/suspense/thriller and young adult books, including stand alones and these series: Auntie Clem's Bakery cozy mysteries, Reg Rawlins Psychic Investigator paranormal mysteries, Zachary Goldman Mysteries (PI), Kenzie Kirsch Medical Thrillers, Parks Pat Mysteries (police procedural), and YA series: Tamara's Teardrops, Between the Cracks, and Breaking the Pattern.

Workman loves writing about the underdog, who the reader may love or hate. She has been praised for her realistic details, deep characterization, and sensitive handling of the serious social issues that appear in all of her stories, from light cozy mysteries through to darker, grittier young adult and mystery/suspense books.

> P. D. Workman, does not shy from probing the deep psychological scars of childhood trauma, mental illness, and addiction. Also characteristic of this author, these extremely sensitive issues are explored with extensive empathy, described with incredible clarity, and portrayed with profound insight.
>
> — —KIM, GOODREADS REVIEWER

Some of Workman's titles have been translated into Spanish, French, Portuguese, German, and Italian.

Workman began writing at an early age and is a prolific reader as well as writer. She is also passionate about teaching and learning, expresses her creativity through art and cooking, and loves exploring the Calgary parks and green spaces where the Parks Pat Mysteries are set. She was a legal assistant for many years and has done extensive charitable work.

Workman was born and raised in Alberta, Canada, and is married with one adult son.

———

Please visit P.D. Workman at pdworkman.com to see what else she is working on, to join her mailing list, and to link to her social networks.

———

If you enjoyed this book, please take the time to recommend it to other purchasers with a review or star rating and share it with your friends!

tiktok.com/@pdworkmanauthor

facebook.com/pdworkmanauthor

x.com/pdworkmanauthor

instagram.com/pdworkmanauthor

amazon.com/author/pdworkman

bookbub.com/authors/p-d-workman

goodreads.com/pdworkman

linkedin.com/in/pdworkman

pinterest.com/pdworkmanauthor

youtube.com/pdworkman

patreon.com/pdworkmanauthor

reamstories.com/pdworkmanauthor

Find P.D. Workman's books at

PDWORKMAN.COM

Scan the QR code below